THE CHOSEN CHRONICLES

CHOSEN
THE
REDEMPTION

K.A. PARKINSON

Books in The Chosen Chronicles
(in reading order)

For Dad, my hero,
United States Marine Corps Vietnam Veteran.

And for all the men and women
in our military who fight for our freedom,

THANK YOU FOR
YOUR SERVICE AND SACRIFICE.

Do not go gentle
into that good night.

Rage,
rage,
against the dying
of the light.

—Dylan Thomas

THE PRISONER

To an outsider, his guards looked the part for a place like this. Dirty brown pants, grungy long-sleeved shirts, bandanas around their necks for protection from the sandstorms that plagued the country and black-market AK-47's hanging carelessly over their broad shoulders.

But this was no ordinary prison, and the guards weren't blocking their faces from the wind. They feared the light of the sun. Light that would reveal the truth of what they really were.

Darkened. Humans who had turned to darkness and become demons in the flesh.

The Darkened could have tried to hide the truth, remained far enough away for the prisoner not to look into their soulless eyes…but the smell gave it away.

It wasn't the odor of human waste, sweat, and rot—the smell you would expect from a godforsaken place such as this. It was the quieter sweet tang of death mixed with sulfur and earth. And something else, a smell that tickled his senses and triggered his fight-or-flight reflex.

Not all evil had a stench, just pure evil—the kind of stinking malignancy that meant the Dark lurked here in force.

Not every human being could smell it. But he could.

The humans in the cells on either side of his still believed themselves to be in some third-world prison as prisoners of war. Night after night they screamed when the invisible Tormentors came to torture their minds. Their pleas echoed like fierce wind through the stone halls, haunting the prisoner's dreams, but he did not try to fight the nightmares. Focusing on the horrible pain of his fellow inmates kept him from feeling his own, kept his mind occupied. Grisly and selfish, yes, but necessary.

He could try to tell the other men the truth—if they were allowed to speak to one another—that they *were* prisoners of war, but not a war of men, a war between Light and Dark, good and evil. A war that had been going on, hidden from the sight of humans, for centuries. But they would not believe him. Despite what they'd experienced, they would hold to their false beliefs of reality and continue to endure the torture, clinging to the illusion that one day rescuers would come.

They would not.

Once the Dark got what it wanted, the prisoners would be eliminated. He could not see the mass gravesite proving this fact from his cell. The one tiny window was set too high, almost to the ceiling, and only let in the barest amount of light—but the smell that wafted in when the dusty wind blew from the east told of its existence.

He did not hope for rescue. But he did hold to a different hope. Likely just as futile, but still a hope.

For ten years they had sought his secrets, and he'd told them some, just enough for them to keep him alive as they continued trying to break him. But mostly he listened. He listened to the careless guards who spoke in coarse whispers over cards and drink. Neither they nor the Tormentors realized how much sound carried through the stone walls, how much a person who *understood* would learn.

He had scratched their secrets into the loose wood planks beneath his bed in a code few knew. If they searched his cell they would only see scratches, the nonsensical actions of a man losing his mind. These secrets he hoped would one day make it into the hands of fighters for Light. He could not fathom how, but still he listened. Still he scratched. Still he hoped.

Only in the last few days had his focus faltered, and his Darkened guards had noticed.

The face of his daughter had interrupted his usual nightmares and he'd woken shaking and screaming—something not a single Tormentor had been able to make him do in ten long years.

Sensing a breakthrough they had become more forceful in their torture and he had to fight twice as hard to keep thoughts of her at bay. Despite the drain on his body and mind he held on, knowing if the Dark were to discover who he really was, who his daughter really was, they would stop at nothing to get his secrets. For it was his secrets that could change the tide of the war, his secrets that could give the Dark the ultimate weapon.

One of the Darkened pacing outside the cell bars paused. Meeting the prisoner's eyes, he bared his rotting teeth and hissed.

The prisoner's time was getting short—either he would break or they would kill him.

Death was the only option.

CHAPTER 1

LEAVING

THE MORNING SUN fought against the ankle high mist covering the tiny island on Lake Michigan, but it wasn't just the mist that created the chill shivering through Macy's bones. Not one cloud, not one single trace of the previous night's monstrous storm marred the deep blue sky. Birds chirped, leaves swayed gently, reverently, as if evil had never touched this place, as if no one had died here last night.

"Are you ready?" Tolen pushed her messy blonde ponytail over her shoulder. His gentle eyes—one brightest blue, the other deepest brown—held a mixture of love, grief, and guilt. Despite everything everyone had told him, he still blamed himself for Darsapean's escape.

Guilt and pain. Tolen wasn't the only one who felt it.

Macy tried to murmur her assent but her voice had become trapped in her throat, her feet rooted to the dirt beneath her feet, her gaze locked on his, pleading. For what she wasn't sure. Reassurance they were doing the right thing? He knew her thoughts, as the Ninth Chosen he could read them, but he said nothing. After a moment of seeing her own torment reflected in his eyes, she realized it wasn't that he wouldn't, but that he *couldn't* answer. He may be able to see pieces of the future, but even he didn't know everything that lay ahead in their journey. Only one thing was certain. Their path forward would test them both.

There were a million reasons for Macy and Tolen to hurry, no reason to wait, no reason to stay, other than the pull of her heart. She drew in a shaky breath and pushed her voice past the lump in her throat. "Let's go."

Her fingers sought the Radia shard resting against her throat, seeking both comfort and courage. A tremor of warmth and concern touched her life force and she pulled her gaze from Tolen, letting it fall upon the rows of people who had fought beside them through the night. People who believed in them, people who had already spoken their goodbyes and now gathered behind to see them off. Tolen's friends: big brave Mahto, fierce Sienn, sweet young Blaze, wise Quasar, and the rescued Lafar elves. A painful jab hit her chest when she looked at the rebels who had become her family: Toke, Brina, Rune, and Keelyn—with an empty space beside her that should have held her twin brother Connell.

They were some of the best defenders of humans and the cause of Light that she had ever met in her ten years as a Chosen.

And now none of them would ever be the same.

There was no joy in their success with Connell gone. She should be glad they'd only lost one fighter for Light, that only one of their own had perished while they had defeated at least a thousand followers of Darkness. But gladness remained out of reach. Connell should be standing there with them, as ready as the rest to move forward with their next missions for the Light.

Tolen raised his hand to begin the rite that would open a gateway to their next destination. In a moment she would once again see the forest that encircled her birth town, Whisper, West Virginia.

"Wait." Rune dropped a hand on Tolen's arm and they spun around.

Keelyn stood tucked beneath Rune's shoulder, her red hair stark against her pale skin, her tiny frame cradled against his broad chest. Keelyn's wounds had been healed by Tolen, but Rune still bore the remnants of battle. His blonde hair was tied back in its usual ponytail revealing a mishmash of new cuts and bruises that joined the long, jagged scar on his left cheek. The pain from the loss of Connell hung heavily over them both.

A bubble of excitement pushed past the grief and Macy's mouth popped open ready to scream, *yes!* But Tolen's simple question directed at Keelyn had her mouth shutting with a snap.

"Are you sure you want to come?"

"I am." Keelyn's voice remained steady despite the turmoil in her hazel eyes.

"When the Seraph gave us all our assignments, she said we," Rune motioned between him and Keelyn, "had to release the past." He stood with his feet planted, leaning slightly forward, fingers trembling, his blue eyes urgent, almost frenzied with need. "The best way to do that is to make sure this world has a future."

Tolen nodded, but Macy could feel concern and doubt emanating from his life force. "Well, we definitely welcome your help." A kind smile brightened his face as Rune stepped forward to shake his hand.

Rune then shouldered both his and Keelyn's large packs that hid his sword and Keelyn's bow from sight. Toke and Brina wrapped them in a final fierce embrace with whispered well wishes and watery eyes. Tolen spoke a string of Hidden language and a gateway shimmered in front of them. With a final wave behind, the foursome walked through the gate into the large and familiar Monongahela forest.

Macy moved closer to Tolen as they stared at the rows of thick pines in front of them. A tremor in the Balance brought prickles to her skin and shimmers of heat to her palms. "Do you feel that?"

Tolen nodded, wrapped his arm over her shoulders and pulled her tight against his side. "The light's different too."

"Grayer. Less yellow. Less warm." Keelyn shivered beside Macy. "The island didn't feel like this."

Rune, copying Tolen's move, put his arm back over Keelyn's thin shoulders. "Probably the Seraph's visit. Her light overshadowed the darkness."

Tolen gazed up into the nearest tree. His eyes closed for a moment and Macy wondered if he was connecting to its life force. But when he spoke, the words were almost monotone, as if not his own. He was accessing his *Second Sight*. His chin dipped as he watched things only he could see. "As Darsapean's strength grows in the Shadow Realm, darkness deepens here, shadowing the light. What happens in one realm is mirrored in the other. Darsapean's escape belongs to every person on this planet. Every time a Being chose darkness over light they made it easier for evil to thrive and weakened the barrier that kept the ruler of the Dark from escaping his prison."

Tolen's hand twitched where it rested on Macy's shoulder. "For now there is enough light and goodness on the earth to bind him to the Shadow Realm, but every day darkness grows in the hearts of man, allowing more and more demons of the Dark to enter the earth. Before long the Balance may shift too far to darkness and Darsapean and all his armies will lay siege upon the unsuspecting human race."

The muscles in her shoulders tightened as Tolen spoke. If the human race, *her* race, was to stand any chance in the war to come, she had to do as the Seraph had directed. Despite her doubts, her fears, and the vastness of the unknown, she must sever the Pact that hid creatures of darkness from human eyes. They had to know what they were up against. They had to band together if there was any hope of defeating the Dark.

Macy gauged the reaction of Keelyn and Rune as they watched Tolen. They didn't know him the way she did. To them he was a person spoken of in legends only, a myth, an oddity, something to be feared. She felt her defenses rise as their expressions shifted back and forth from awe to unease.

Tolen's voice returned to his own timber, but his eyes remained closed. "Darsapean's captains are massing. I saw a meeting between several of them. Our pal Daemon has been charged to release something called *Legion*."

"Legion?" Deep wrinkles creased between Rune's brows. "Like *Legion* in the human bible? As in thousands of demons contained in the body of one man?"

Keelyn's eyebrows jumped to her hairline, but Rune shrugged it off. Him reading the bible wasn't near as crazy, or scary, as the idea that he could be right.

"Did you see it?" Macy squeezed Tolen's arm. "Is that what Legion is?"

"I didn't see the creature. But whatever it is, it's something they're very excited about. They are planning to release creatures in bursts throughout the earth realm to increase the darkness affecting the Balance. If they can tip it far enough, Darsapean will have the power to set Legion free. They also talked about something called the *Fallen* and creating more Darkened."

Macy's hand flew to her mouth, Rune's face paled, and Keelyn's knees wobbled.

A familiar frustrated crease appeared between Tolen's eyebrows. "Apparently *Fallen* is another Hidden term I need to know about and am not going to like."

Macy shrugged a shoulder with forced nonchalance. "What else is new?"

Tolen's cheek lifted the tiniest bit at her attempt at humor, but the frustration didn't completely leave his eyes. "Right."

"The Fallen are Watchers who've turned their talents to the Dark. My dad had some notes on them..." Macy started to tug her back pack around but Rune loudly cleared his throat.

"Let's finish discussing the bad stuff once we're under cover." He held a hand up to shield his eyes from the rising sun, taking in the familiar forest, the July heat already rippling down in waves. "We're closer to the town than Toke's place, so I'm guessing your plan involves going back to Whisper?"

Macy shifted her feet. "Yeah." Tolen seemed to sense her sudden nerves and grabbed her hand.

"And why exactly?" Rune's tone sounded simply curious, but she knew they were expecting some grand reason for why she'd brought them back to the place where they'd had to rescue her from a small army of Daklafar elves just days ago.

She felt everyone's eyes on her but kept her gaze forward, not really looking at the trees. She hadn't had time even to tell Tolen exactly why she wanted to come back here, he'd just trusted her feelings and followed her lead, as always.

"Um, well..." When she actually thought of speaking the words aloud, doubt crept in. Her reason sounded more idiotic the longer she thought about it, but they were all looking at her, waiting. "You know how sometimes you get this feeling and you just act on it because it feels right, but then you start thinking about it and it sounds really dumb?"

Rune's eyebrow lifted. "I already think you're an idiot, so just say it."

Keelyn smacked Rune's chest with her tiny hand. "Macy's not an idiot."

Macy glanced at Tolen, but he was glaring at Rune. She sighed. Having them here would be harder than she thought. Rune's personality took some getting used to. Then again, Tolen eventually got used to her sometimes crass behavior. Maybe there was hope the two could be friends.

"Takes forever to answer a question though." Rune tapped his foot impatiently.

Then again, maybe not.

"The Seraph said my plan to sever the Pact has been accepted by the Light." She cast them all a quick glance. "But to do that I have to find the Relics, the nine Descendants of the original Pact makers, and awaken them one at a time."

Keelyn raised her head. "So is there another Relic here, besides the Claver you found before?"

Macy sighed. "No, I don't think so."

"A descendant then?" Rune asked.

"Um, no. I don't think so."

"O…kay?" His brows came together.

Sensing another obnoxious comment, and sure Tolen only had so much patience, she quickly pulled Bastian's keys from her pocket and held them up. "When I met you guys I was following a path set by my dad, a path I'd never known about until Bastian—you know, my Watcher—until he finally gave me my father's notes."

"The ones you showed us before that lead to the Relics." Keelyn nodded her understanding.

"Right. Well, I think there's something else here, in Whisper, I was supposed to find, something besides the notes and the Claver. But the fight with the Daklafar kinda made me forget all about the key. But when Tolen wondered where to go next I just knew."

"Key?" Interest replaced some of the sarcasm in Rune's voice.

Macy showed them the key with *Whisper* carved into it. "None of the other keys are engraved."

"And you're sure it wasn't just to lead you to the Claver Relic?" Keelyn's tone, though kinder than Rune's, held a similar note of skepticism.

"No, I'm not. But I can't get it out of my head. I think this key leads to something that will help us in our search for the Relics and the Descendants." She watched their faces, warmth creeping up her neck.

Rune scratched his chin, his eyes thoughtful. "Well, since severing the Pact is such a *great* idea," he shook his head and Tolen tensed beside Macy. She tightened her fingers around his. Rune had been the ring leader of his little band, hot headed, but not stupid. *Wait,* she thought, hoping Tolen was listening. A second later she felt him relax, *slightly.*

"And you're the only one with the lineage to do it." Rune flicked a piece of her hair. "We'd be the idiots not to trust your instincts."

A slow smile lifted Macy's lips. "Okay, on to Whisper then." She waved to the ferny path among the trees and the four of them began the long trek toward town, her mind spinning in circles as they walked. A million questions and fears rolled back and forth. "So, did you see anything specific that Darsapean is up to?" she asked Tolen.

"Boiling babies," Rune quipped before Tolen could answer. "Dancing naked under the full moon."

"Seriously." Macy rolled her eyes.

"Seriously?" Rune tugged his pack higher on his shoulder. "Based on Tolen's little vision back there," he pointed a thumb over his shoulder, "you can bet your skinny little butt he's plotting against the Chosen, the only army he truly fears. He knows the Ninth issued the Call to gather. He's going to do everything he can to keep us from uniting." He glanced down at Keelyn.

"He's going to use the Fallen to hunt us down one by one. And if this *Legion* is as formidable as it sounds, I'll bet you a million bucks its sole purpose is to aid them in the hunt."

Tolen shuddered in her peripheral vision and Macy wished she had picked a different subject. She squeezed his hand and he squeezed her fingers back but his eyes stayed fixed on the forest and neither confirmed nor denied Rune's statement.

But the worry coming from his life force was confirmation enough.

CHAPTER 2

BASTIAN'S SECRET

TWELVE HOURS LATER they were all physically, mentally, and emotionally exhausted. One night of rest hadn't been enough. The battle on Eamun's Island had taken more than their energy, it had taken its toll on their gifts as well. Macy shouldn't have dragged her friends all over this tiny town in search of who-knows-what. They should have gone to Toke's home, hidden conveniently in the middle of the forest. It would have been a great place to hole-up for a few days, rest, and come up with a *good* plan. What was she thinking?

They'd grabbed a map of Whisper at the first gas station they found, borrowed a tattered copy of a phone directory, and created a grid of every storage company in the town with plans to hit other possible locations as they went. Whisper wasn't large by any means, but it still took time to try every lock in every storage shed company door, abandoned building, or old barn that felt even the tiniest bit familiar—all while trying to avoid suspicion. They'd even walked the perimeter of her old house just in case something sparked a memory.

Nothing.

They'd paused for lunch at McDonald's and taken a few bathroom breaks but other than that they'd searched relentlessly and not a single lock fit the key Bastian had engraved. And Tolen's patience with Rune's snarky humor had gotten less and less as the day went on. Fatigue bore down on them.

They couldn't keep this up much longer, but the key had to mean something. She knew it, she'd felt it! Her Watcher had been known to be cryptic, but this was almost too obvious.

Their current location, *Ted's Storage Sheds*, was the sixth shed company they'd stopped to search and the second to the last one in town—they had less than a quarter of Whisper left. *Ted's* was quite a ways off the main road, down an unpaved side street and in the middle of an old farm field. Rusty tractors and the skeletons of ancient vehicles, covered with a thick layer of West Virginia silt, cast long shadows over the hard packed gravel surrounding the rectangular building.

If you could call it a building.

A cacophony of rusty metal sheets in various colors and states of decay formed the outer walls, punctuated by six doors on each of the longer east and west sides. Sticks, leaves, and other filth completely hid the material of the barely slanted roof. Each swing-out shed door was made of different types of material "Ted" must have had lying around his farm—wood planks, uneven squares of metal or tin, warped plywood sheets—all on rusty hinges.

"Anyone crazy enough to store here doesn't value the crap they put inside." Macy paused by the first door. "We're not going to find anything in this dump."

Sweat plastered Tolen's brown hair to his neck. Rune leaned against the building, straggles of his blond hair had escaped his ponytail and stuck to his face. Both boys had dark shadows beneath their eyes. And she didn't even want to think how gross she looked. But if their disheveled appearances were disturbing it was nothing next to Keelyn tucked beneath one of Rune's thickly muscled arms.

Her breathing seemed labored, her freckles more prominent than usual against her pale skin, her warm hazel eyes locked on the ground. Macy's chest tightened. "I'm so sorry guys. This was stupid. Let's find a place to stay for the night. We can come back tomorrow. And if we don't find anything…" She pushed her sweaty hair off her forehead. "Then we'll go back to Toke's place and figure out what we should do next."

Macy lowered her voice so only Tolen standing closest would hear. "I'm such a schmuck. I didn't think this through. Why do I always rush into things?" Her fingers curled around the lock but she made no move to try the key.

She'd ignored the fact that her friends were grieving. Unintentionally maybe, but as she thought of Rune and Keelyn, she suddenly remembered with painful clarity, how it had felt when her parents were murdered by the Shadow Wraiths. The loss, the fear, the *pain*.

"Let's go." Macy ignored the tremor of impatience coming from the Radia Shard hanging around her neck and focused on the need of her heart, not the source of her gifts. No matter how demanding it was, her friends came first.

Keelyn shook her head. "No. I—I don't want to go back to Toke's. Besides, we've almost covered the whole town. Let's do this thing." She mimicked Rune's deep voice and gave a tiny smile, but her eyes were pleading. She *was* in pain, she *was* exhausted, but she needed the distraction from the *real* pain of losing her brother. Pain that would only intensify if they went back to Toke's and she was surrounded by memories. Macy knew from experience how physical exhaustion often seemed like a blessing. Once you finally were able to stop, you were too tired to think. She also knew that avoiding grief would only bring more pain for her friend in the end, but only time would teach Keelyn that. Right now all Macy *could* do was offer the distraction.

Macy took a slow breath, pushed aside the guilt and nodded. She lifted the rusty padlock hooked to a door made from a metal panel and plywood attached to the back side by rough planks. *Ugh, seriously Ted?*

"Stop doubting yourself." Tolen whispered.

For a moment she became distracted by his eyes. The pupil in his blue eye dilating big to small. *Watching.* She forced a grin. *Is it my shaking hands that gave it away or are my thoughts that loud?*

"Both." His lips lifted in his characteristic crooked grin. "Trust your feelings."

"Okay, Jedi Master."

Tolen chuckled and placed his hand over hers. She could feel his power, the power of the Ninth Chosen, gifted defender and last hope for both mankind and Hidden, stronger than ever—his body literally pulsed with it. He'd grown so much in their time apart. She'd always found him attractive, distractingly so, and her Kuna had always reacted to his touch. But this new, confident Tolen, did much scarier things to her gift of fire.

The heat wasn't painful in her palms like the first time he kissed her and she'd accidentally set him on fire. This was different. Deeper flame had ignited and continued to grow the longer they were together. A soul fire that both excited and frightened her. She licked her lips, fighting the urge to bridge the distance between them.

"Bastian said there is purpose in everything." Tolen moved a piece of hair away from her face, making her cheek tingle where his fingers brushed against her skin. "Trust your Watcher. But more importantly trust yourself. You felt like coming back to Whisper was the right thing to do."

"I did."

Tolen's grin was back. "Then prove the big sarcastic guy wrong," he pointed his chin toward Rune.

She chuckled and he pulled her close to kiss the end of her nose.

"And you're not heartless just because you're focused, Macy. You love her. She knows that. The bond between you is powerful." A little crease formed between his eyes. "Keelyn's here because she loves you too. It was more her idea than Rune's to come along."

Macy's shard zinged, sparking her Kuna, and she knew Tolen spoke the truth as he'd seen it in Keelyn's mind. She swallowed the lump in her throat but didn't comment. Tolen always felt compassion first. It was just the way he worked. He couldn't possibly know how hard it was for her to change the way her heart and head worked, or didn't work, together.

Tolen lifted an eyebrow and she shrugged. Then again he probably knew exactly how she felt. Either way she vowed to be more attentive to her friends' needs in the future.

The lock was a no go. So were the next five. Stars winked in the pale light of dusk. The dumpy facility remained empty aside from them, and not a single car had passed since they'd arrived. They weren't doing anything illegal, but it wasn't the cops she was afraid of meeting once the darkness settled in. Last time she'd faced the Dark in this town she'd only survived the encounter because of Rune and his band of rebels.

Tolen squeezed Macy's hand drawing her attention but he only tipped his chin toward Keelyn and glanced pointedly at his watch.

Hurry?

Tolen barely nodded.

When there were only three of the funky doors left she could feel Rune's concern like a weight on her shoulders. He held Keelyn against him as they walked, her feet dragging. He'd even stopped the comments, his worry too vast to cover up with snark.

But it was Tolen's worried glances that scared her the most. Tolen had completely healed the physical injuries Keelyn had suffered in battle, but he had said her injured heart may never fully heal.

Can you like, give her energy or something?

Tolen gave an almost imperceptible shake of his head, his eyes pools of concern. His abilities as the Ninth Chosen allowed him to sense the needs of those around him and heal almost any physical injury. If Tolen couldn't do anything to help her, Keelyn was in trouble. Real trouble.

Distracted, Macy placed the key in the second to the last padlock, the rustiest one yet, with the worst looking door so far—a piece of tin hammered haphazardly with rusty nails to yet another warped sheet of plywood. It was a moment before she realized why her heart had increased its rhythm. The door was heavier than it should be for tin and plywood, the hinges holding it up were bigger than any of the other sheds'. And the lock—covered in rust, but sturdy...too sturdy—had a symbol etched beside the keyhole, one she could just make out under the sickly yellow glow of Ted's ancient floodlights. A sun, half-black, half-white. The Movan symbol.

"Guys?" Macy's voice trembled. "This is it."

CHAPTER 3

NITROUS OXIDE

THE LOCK FELL with a thunk to the dust at Macy's feet.

Tolen grabbed the handle. The door, belying the rusty hinges, hardly creaked as he pulled it open.

"*To'inreedo.*" Macy whispered, and instantly the dark interior brightened to her vision and she was able to see in perfect detail the contents of the shed. She heard the others copy her action behind her.

A three-inch layer of silt covered the floor, the makeshift shelves hanging on the walls, and the cover over the single item in the shed.

Seriously, Bastian? Her shoulders slumped as she turned to the others. "I'm sorry guys. It's just another one of Bastian's cars."

"No, it isn't." Keelyn whispered walking slowly forward, Rune right beside her, arms slightly outstretched as if to catch her if she stumbled. "Can't you feel that?"

Macy pushed aside the disappointment and focused her life force on the Balance, searching for what Keelyn was talking about. It was subtle, but there. A gentle sway of Light energy. Her shard connected to it and she felt eager, almost anxious. She hurried forward and Tolen helped her toss the car cover off.

Her stomach leapt into her throat.

"Wow. I've never seen one of these fully restored." Rune walked around the car with wide eyes, his fingers around Keelyn's wrist as she followed close behind.

Keelyn touched the glossy hood, "What kind of car is it?"

Macy, trailing her fingers across one of the flawless yellow fenders, answered before Rune. "It's a 1972 Plymouth, Barracuda. 340 engine, six-pack of Holley carburetors, twin rear shocks to reduce squat on take-off, and an extra 40 gallon gas tank in the trunk to compensate for the seven miles per gallon it gets running three deuces."

Keelyn paused with her mouth open her gaze shifting to Rune. "And I thought you were the gear-head."

Rune's forehead creased. "No one can tell that just by looking at it. She *knows* this car."

"It was her father's car." Tolen spoke gently, speaking the truth from her thoughts.

He put his arm around her shoulders and she had to swallow twice before she could get any words out. "I—I helped him rebuild it," she closed her eyes as the memories flooded her thoughts. "I was only five…" She chuckled past the pain. "So mostly I just watched and handed him tools."

"And you remember all those details?" Keelyn whispered with a tiny shake of her head.

"Yeah. I guess I had it stored away with all my other memories of him." She tugged Tolen with her to the driver's side door and lifted the handle. It opened silently, perfectly oiled and balanced. She pulled off her backpack and handed it over before sliding into the stiff vinyl seat. He leaned across the open door and an image flashed in her mind, her tiny hands resting over her father's on the steering wheel. Her stomach swooped, an echo of the excitement she'd experienced the first time she'd heard the rumbling engine start, the way it moved so smoothly down the road, as if they were flying.

"This'll be yours one day baby-girl." Her dad's gentle timber seemed to carry over the years.

"Is it fast?" Keelyn's soft voice snapped Macy back to the present.

"Very." She didn't need to ask why as the shift in the Balance shoved her body into fight mode. "Get in!"

Macy's memories had her digging under the rubber floor mat to find a shiny set of keys as Tolen rushed to the other door and popped the handle to move the seat forward. They tossed their bags in, then Rune helped Keelyn into the back seat and dove in beside her. With no time to do a trip check on fuel integrity, or cracked hoses, she cranked the engine as Tolen's door closed.

The motor turned over on the first try. Not pausing to wonder over this anomaly she shoved the shifter to low, slammed the gas—pelting the back wall of the shed with two clouds of rock and dust—cranked the wheel the moment the car cleared the doorway, weaved around the rusty tractors and junk in the field, and plowed back onto the road.

"What's coming?" Macy asked, her thoughts more on driving than the specific Dark creature vibes affecting the Balance.

"Raksasha." Tolen glanced back at the dirt billowing behind them as they swerved onto the dusty road.

Blood trackers. *Great.* An image of the black skeletal creatures with glowing yellow eyes and long poisonous fingernails filled her mind. Raksasha were fast, but this car was faster. They hit main street and she pushed the pedal further toward the floor. The Barracuda responded like a caged animal set free.

"Not fast enough!" Rune shouted.

"Raksasha aren't this fast!" She yelled back.

"It's not the Raksasha gaining, it's something else," came Tolen's calculating tone.

Macy risked a quick sideways glance. Tolen's eyes were narrowed, he met her eyes briefly, long enough for her to see the blue eye dilating and constricting focusing on things only he could see. "Tolen?"

"The leader is running on all fours, his face keeps shifting, a *Gungruin.*" He closed his eyes and dipped his chin. "Wait, he's not *the* leader, just leading the Raksasha. The creature driving them, controlling them, is in a car not far behind…image is hidden in shadow, almost like vapor, but not…In thirty seconds the Gungruin will get close enough for us to see." Tolen leaned forward and pressed his fingers to his temples. "Whoever is driving the car is blocking my *Sight.*"

Seconds later their hunter appeared, running through a gap between two buildings, and Keelyn gasped. Macy caught a flash of red hair from her peripheral.

The Gungruin was mimicking Connell! That meant it had to have been one they had fought on the island. *How?*

Rune cursed. Keelyn's gasps turned to sobs. The fury in Rune's voice could have melted metal. "What the hell? The Fallen have found us!"

"*Heck*, Rune." Macy shifted into low as she skidded around a corner. *Thank goodness the traffic's not bad*, she thought as she blew past an old white Chevy Malibu earning a rude gesture from the driver.

"*What?*"

"Say, heck please." She moved quickly up to second, third, and then back to drive, thrilled at the old engine's power, but praying there was enough gas to wear out their pursuers.

"You're seriously going to lecture me on cussing when we're being chased by a frickin' Fallen?"

Macy tested the Balance to feel for any humans or creatures ahead as she blew through three stop lights and squealed onto the freeway ramp, barely missing a green Jetta. "Yep. And how the *heck* do you know it's a Fallen?"

His voice came back a low growl. "I know *that* car."

Macy glanced in her rear-view to see a shiny black car catching up. It vaguely resembled a '69 Camaro. But it was too short, the nose pitched down too far, and it glided far too easily between the other vehicles on the freeway to be any sort of normal. The Gungruin/Connell ran up to its passenger side and seemed to melt through the door. She could no longer see any Raksasha.

The closer the car got the more intense the darkness became around it, turning early evening into sunset, swallowing the bits of light from the just popping on street-lamps, distant businesses, even the first blinks of the stars. Her fellow drivers turned on their headlights, but they couldn't dispel the gloom. Definitely a Movan creation, technological geniuses they could infuse manmade items with either Light or Dark energy. The downward tug on her life force said this creation was most definitely not infused with Light.

Her shard suddenly became heavy, like a weight around her neck.

You cannot escape. A raspy female voice spoke into her mind and the look on the other's faces said they heard it as well.

"Oh yeah? Watch us." Macy pressed the pedal to the floor and the needle climbed over one-hundred and kept climbing. Sirens wailed, but even the red and blue lights could hardly pierce the gloomy darkness. She kept her eyes on the road, weaving and swerving, focused only on putting as much distance between them and their pursuers as possible. *Come on car!* Her eyes fell on a tiny red button beside the radio. She pushed it without questioning and a burst of speed propelled them forward. *Right-on dad!*

"Yes! NOS!"

Macy glanced in the rear-view to see Rune's furious expression lighten the tiniest bit.

A grin pulled Macy's cheeks up despite their predicament as she explained Rune's excitement to Tolen. "Nitrous Oxide. Big power boost."

"How long will it last?" Tolen asked.

"Depends on how much is in the tank and how much heat the motor can take." A tan minivan pulled out in front of her while trying to pass another car. She swerved into the left emergency lane to avoid clipping its fender. "We've gotta lose them."

Tolen stuck his hands out the window and began twisting his fingers. Macy peeked in the mirror to see the gale he aimed directly at the strange vehicle engulf it in choking dust and shove it off the road. Focusing on their speed, that was slowing slightly as the NOS tank emptied, she didn't risk another look until Rune laughed. Tolen had caused a huge maple tree growing alongside the freeway to reach out and snatch the car, its mangled body was being slowly passed from tree to tree deeper into the surrounding forest.

The stars reappeared, the street-lamps and headlights brightened, and the Dark vibes affecting the Balance fell farther and farther behind them.

CHAPTER 4

CONVERSATIONS IN THE DARK

RUNE LAUGHED AGAIN, but anger marred its authenticity. "Man, she's going to be pissed!"

"Rune!" Keelyn chided, her voice still thick with emotion.

"Sorry."

Macy kept the pedal floored, moving between cars until the last of the NOS ran out. The temperature gauge still read only half so she felt safe to keep their speed in the nineties, her eyes on the road, her ears tuned to the conversation. The creatures would have a hard time catching back up to them, but she could still feel the Dark's vibes filling the night, always hunting, always seeking.

"Rune, you knew the driver of the car?" Tolen rolled up the window.

Rune grunted. "I thought she was dead."

"How do you know one of the Fallen?" Macy asked at the same time Tolen said, "What exactly can the Fallen do?"

Rune didn't seem keen on answering Macy's question, so Macy tried to answer Tolen's. "I don't know a ton about them. Bastian didn't talk about them much. I know that instead of using their Second Sight to watch over and train the Chosen, they use their connection with other Watchers to spy on those who serve the Light. I didn't know they could talk in our heads like that."

Tolen gazed out the window at the darkening night and Macy noticed goosebumps on his arms to match her own.

She pushed against the eerie cold running across her shoulders. "My dad's notes said they are the inventors of *Fear*, the Dark's ultimate weapon, and they can control the Shadow Wraiths. He said some of them had children with human women and their mutated offspring are revered by the Dark because they are the only creatures who can hide their evil from affecting the Balance. They are responsible for the humans who become Darkened."

Macy's hands convulsively tightened on the wheel and she had to focus to ease her grip. "He also believed that the Fallen could be connected to the Guardian's failing Second Sight." She bit her bottom lip. "Bastian worried that because now I wear a Watcher's shard they will try to use it to spy on, or even tempt me, now that it isn't in his care to tame. That could be how they are tracking us." She laid her hand over her heart where her Radia Shard hung beneath her shirt, warm against her skin.

"But your shard merged with his." Tolen's concern flowed over her, heightened by the connection between their shards. "It's as much yours now as it was Bastian's."

She tilted her head, acquiescing, "True. . ." but the feeling of unease didn't leave. "I feel stronger and more in tune with my abilities with them as one. I can feel its allegiance to me. I don't think it would purposely let the Fallen in, but if Bastian was concerned—"

"It's not your shard that led them to us." Rune's fingers gripped the back of Tolen's seat.

"Rune, you don't know that." Keelyn's hand appeared over Rune's.

He pulled her hand free and a check in the rearview showed him lowering Keelyn back to her seat. "Yes, I do. You heard her voice. It was her." He took a deep breath and a wave of pain seemed to swirl through the car.

Macy swallowed. "Was she your Watcher?"

"Sorsha. Her name is Sorsha."

Something heavy settled over Macy's heart. Toke had told her Rune's tale was more tragic than her own. Despite Rune's brash personality she had learned to care for him, like she imagined she would care for a big brother, but she did not know his story. The pain she felt from him now, she wasn't sure she wanted to.

His eyes found Macy's in the mirror, icy blue pools of sorrow. "You knew when we met that I didn't use my Kuna, but I never told you why and you were respectful enough not to ask. When I was with *her*, with Sorsha," his lips curled in disgust, "I used my Kuna to fulfill her twisted ideals. I ran away from her with the belief that if I stopped using my Kuna, denied my birthright and the reason she was set to watch over me, she would no longer be able find me. It wasn't until some years later, when she found me again…" His voice dropped and Macy tilted her head closer to the back seats to better hear. "That I learned the flaw in this idea as well as the real way to hide from her. If I used my Kuna only for good then she, who only follows darkness, would not be able to recognize my signature."

He paused and when Macy looked in the mirror he was staring out the window, Keelyn's hand on his arm. "This same person who told me the real way to hide from her also told me I would meet someone who could teach me how to use my Kuna the right way." His voice softened and his eyes met hers in the mirror again. "*You*. I thought I could do it. Change my signature—use my Kuna for only good. And I believed it was safe enough to try. I'd thought—hoped—Sorsha was dead. But on that island, when those creatures killed Connell, when they shot Keelyn…" He buried his face in his hands, Keelyn's hand still on his arm, tears trailing once again down her cheeks. "I allowed hate to fuel my Kuna again, and it led her right to me."

"Maybe." Macy swallowed against the growing lump in her throat. "But, maybe not." She tapped the steering wheel. "It could have been this car. The moment I touched it, it recognized me. It's loaded with Movan tech. If that woman had some sort of tracker—"

"It's all speculation, and speculation won't solve the issue we face right now," Tolen added gently. "The only way to know for sure would be to ask the person driving that car, and I for one don't have any intention of letting her near enough to ask." He took a slow breath and his eyes searched the darkening sky. "Let's just worry about getting somewhere safe for the night. Tomorrow we can look more into the car and our questions."

Macy glanced down at the gas gauge. "We've probably got about fifty miles left on this tank before I'll have to switch to the auxiliary one in the trunk. As long as that one's full, and not so old it's nothing but water, we should be able to go about 300 more miles before we'll have to stop for gas."

Rune's head popped up. A tiny spark in his anguished eyes. "We can trade off driving."

In her time spent with the rebels they'd been running from one stressful situation to another, she hadn't discovered that a love of cars was something Rune and her would have in common, aside from sharing the same Kunamin gift. The brotherly affection increased and she found herself suddenly hating this Sorsha, and unlike Tolen, wanted to get near enough to not just meet, but kill the source of Rune's pain. The intensity of the emotion surprised her and she jumped when Tolen spoke.

"Sounds good." Tolen's posture relaxed. "I'll drive next. You guys go ahead and try to get some sleep."

Rune settled back against the seat and pretended to close his eyes to get Keelyn to follow his lead and relax, but while she did rest her head on his shoulder, her wide eyes stayed open staring at nothing. The hollow emptiness in them caused a tremor of dread to rock through Macy's core. A foreboding feeling she couldn't explain and was afraid to think about.

Keelyn's tears hadn't yet dried. The tactic used by the Gungruin mimicker and Rune's cruel Watcher had done its job. The earlier determination and bravado Keelyn had displayed had gone, a mask removed, revealing her inner pain. Macy forced her focus on the road, trying not to look too often at the occupants of the back seat, but she couldn't stop the roll of her thoughts.

Prickles rose on the back of her neck. Tolen's earlier vision, and Rune's speculations had been correct. The Fallen were not only here but hunting them. Which also meant some scary demon-thing called Legion could appear at any moment.

An hour later her eyes were too heavy and her brain too distracted to keep driving. She pulled off the highway to switch with Tolen. They paused at the trunk and he wrapped her in a quick hug, understanding lighting his eyes, always aware of her inner turmoil. He held her hand and opened the passenger side door, waited for her to slide in and closed the door. She buckled the seat belt, noticing Keelyn had finally succumbed to sleep, her head resting on Rune's chest. Rune sat with his head at an awkward angle so he could peek at her beneath his lashes. The love between them was so powerful—if only they would admit it to one another. Keelyn's cheeks were still wet. Macy shifted her gaze to Tolen as he buckled in and put the car in reverse.

He touched her cheek and reentered the freeway. Once the pavement resumed flying beneath them he reached over and put his hand over hers where it rested on her knee. She flipped her hand over and threaded her fingers through his.

Are they okay for us to travel all night?

Only she could have heard his soft sigh that said he heard her unspoken question. "Why don't we drive another hour and find a place to crash. We could all use a shower." Tolen sniffed under his arm. "Especially me."

Macy appreciated Tolen's gentle humor. But another hour would only get them about a hundred more miles from the threat, and whether because of her, the car, or Rune, they could be leading creatures to them everywhere they went.

"*Treasta!*" Macy spun around. "Rune—" but he was already digging through her pack, being careful not to wake Keelyn.

"Treasta?" Tolen gave her a sideways look.

"Bastian gave it to me." She watched Rune tap the palm-sized silver Treasta. "It's a Movan device he had made for me as a child when I hadn't yet developed the skill of hiding my life force from affecting the Balance. It sends a signal out that messes with the vibes. Like camo from the Dark." She turned back to face the front. "I have no idea how the weird thing works. But if we're going to stop for the night—"

"Yours and Rune's suspicions seem too accurate." Tolen nodded.

"Right, but—"

"There's more." He interrupted. "If that really was one of the Fallen—"

"It was." Rune grumbled.

Tolen flipped the lights to high-beam as they entered a stretch with no traffic. "Then they've probably been tracking us since we left the Light Realm."

Macy raised her eyebrows, he glanced over and a hint of pink touched his cheeks. "When you're really focused on something your thoughts are especially loud."

"Isn't it like that with everyone you hear?"

Tolen glanced over his shoulder to change lanes. "Not exactly. With you it's clearer, more forceful. If I didn't know better I'd think it was more like you were putting your thoughts in my mind. Not me reaching to hear them."

"So it's my fault you try to speak for me?" Macy bit her lip to hold back a smile. He looked so guilty it was cute.

"Sorry."

She lifted his hand to kiss his knuckles. The pink in his cheeks deepened, and a real smile played across his face. Once the intrusion on her thoughts bugged her, but now, it didn't bother her at all. She loved sharing everything with him.

A funny swoop ran through her stomach and her nerves slowed, almost like her Watcher was here with them, protecting them. She didn't need Rune's confirmation to know Bastian had rescued them again. How much she missed that wrinkly old man!

I'm always with you, though not as wrinkly. Bastian's voice whispered in her thoughts, her shard pulsed with love, and Macy couldn't hold back another smile. Yes, Bastian would be with them, in power, if not in body.

Rune settled back in his seat and closed his eyes. Macy pulled two purple suckers from her pocket. She unwrapped one and held it out to Tolen. "This brings back memories doesn't it?"

Tolen chuckled and put the sucker in his mouth.

"Except last time I thought you were the end of my world." She leaned over and kissed his cheek, causing heat to flood her palms and surge through her body. He smiled as he sensed the awakening of her Kuna. She unwrapped her own sucker and popped it in her mouth.

Tolen rolled the sucker to the inside of his cheek. "That night was the first time I ever touched your hand. You hated me and I knew it, but when I touched you, I felt your Kuna. Fire and ice, love and fear, fury and peace. Intriguing, frustratingly attractive." He flashed her his crooked grin and her heart kicked against her ribs. "It never gets old."

Rune cleared his throat loudly and Macy jumped, her cheeks warm. She shimmied lower in the seat and pulled her knees up to her chest, letting the conversation end, and the car fall silent aside from the steady thrum of the motor and Keelyn's soft breathing.

CHAPTER 5

PAIN

Tʜᴇ ʜᴇᴀᴠʏ ᴡᴏᴏᴅᴇɴ door of the motel lobby closed behind Tolen with a snap, rattling the tiny window in its center. He walked across the grungy linoleum, an awful puke green marked with rips and years of ground in dirt, past a lopsided metal table surrounded by faded orange and yellow plastic chairs, to the single olive colored counter cutting across the room. A dim yellow lamp, wrapped in funky brown macramé, hung from the ceiling. Its weak light fell on a sign telling customers to ring the doorbell for check-ins after 7:00 PM. Tolen checked his watch, 11:56 PM. This should be fun.

Fifteen minutes later—after a big tip from Bastian's cash supply stopped a long-winded lecture from the matron—Tolen walked back to the car with a room key in hand. Macy had moved to the backseat with Keelyn and Rune, Keelyn's head now rested on Macy's shoulder.

Tolen's footsteps dragged the rest of the way. He had to tell her. Macy had to know what was happening to her friends. "Everything okay out here?" He asked as he approached.

"So far so good." Rune answered through the rear window, his voice forced casual. "Treasta seems to be doing its job." Tolen knew Rune had somehow sensed what was happening to Keelyn, but was in denial to the seriousness. Rune's mind was guarded, only snippets of his thoughts occasionally slipping into Tolen's consciousness. But it had been enough for Tolen to see the strength of his feelings for Keelyn.

Secrets lay behind the seventeen-year-old's handsome face and gruff attitude. Much like Macy when Tolen first met her, Rune had a past that had altered him, and if the flashes Tolen kept getting about him came to pass, his future could do far worse—it could destroy him.

"Any trouble inside?" Rune's question pulled Tolen from his thoughts.

"Nah. The lady who owns the place was a little upset when I woke her up, but she settled down when I waved the cash." Tolen opened the door to help Macy out. "Let's get inside, clean up, and order some food. I saw an ad for an all-night pizza place in the lobby."

Tolen's foot tapped an annoying rhythm on the shag carpet as he waited for them all to take turns in the tiny shower. Macy kept throwing him concerned looks where she sat next to him on the single tiny couch, and he tried to stop tapping, but his mind wouldn't quit buzzing with everything he'd seen. He wanted to tell her, but he had to do it right. Seeing the future was a huge responsibility. If he'd learned anything from Bastian it was that some things should be shared, and some things should not—until the time was right. And sometimes *that* time would never come.

Rune was the last and the quickest to clean up, obviously not wanting to leave Keelyn's side any longer than necessary. The pizza arrived just as he stepped out of the bathroom, towel-drying his long hair. Macy gave the sleepy-eyed young man a nice tip and they ate mostly in silence, each too tired or caught up in their own thoughts to bother with conversation.

Every once in a while, Rune would look at Tolen with suspicion, but he never spoke up.

A flicker of Rune's future passed through Tolen's mind again and the bite of pizza he'd just taken turned sour in his mouth. He swallowed hard and stood up.

"I think I'll take this box to the trash and do a quick perimeter check. Macy, you wanna come?"

"Yep." Macy wiped her hands on a napkin, jumped off the couch, and took his outstretched hand.

Keelyn didn't look up from the slice of pizza she was picking at, but Rune spoke up. "Sounds good. We'll see what's on TV." His voice still held a relaxed tone but Tolen felt his eyes follow them all the way out the door.

Once the door clicked behind them Macy spoke. "What's up? You were nervous as a rabbit in there."

Tolen winced and the pizza turned in his stomach. "Come on." He tugged her hand and led her into the dimly lit parking lot pausing beside the car.

Macy leaned against the fender and wrapped her arms around her chest. "Tell me."

Tolen opened his mouth, closed it, paced the length of the car twice, stopped and put his hands on Macy's shoulders. "I'm so sorry Macy. I don't know a good way to put this." He squeezed gently, the pain building in her eyes making him wish he didn't have to tell her, but if his visions were correct, she'd figure it out all too soon. "Keelyn's condition, it's—it's so much more than grief." *Why did this have to happen now?* She'd only just begun to let people in, and her connection to these two, it went beyond friendship. They had become her family.

"Tell me." She bit her lip but not before Tolen saw the slight tremble.

He kept his hands on her shoulders and took a deep breath. "Keelyn's light is fading."

Her eyes narrowed and he felt her Kuna spark. "What does that mean?"

"Keelyn's *Lóklana*, it's fading." He put his hand on her cheek. "Her gift is leaving her, and if she continues down this path, she…" he forced the words past the lump in his throat. "She will die."

"No." Macy shook her head, the denial in her thoughts an unspoken scream that cut deep into his own heart. "Humans don't die when their gifts leave them."

"*They* don't." He sighed, weighing the consequences of sharing the knowledge he was gaining with his Sight.

A tiny flare of heat warmed his chest and he let the words free. "Keelyn isn't completely human. I saw into her past, and pieces of her future. Her and Connell were raised in an orphanage in Ireland. They," he couldn't hold back a wince and moved past the images of beaten and starving children, "had a rough experience there. Their Radia Shards arrived, but Watchers never showed up. Keelyn somehow knew what to do—she had them put their shards on, they instantly connected to their gifts and were able to run away." He closed his eyes following the flashes of past. "Their shards guided them to an old woman, Hidden-kind. She taught them what she could. They fought the Dark, alone, until the woman knew she had little time left. When they were thirteen she helped them secure passage to America. Toke and Rune found them in New York."

He opened his eyes and met Macy's anguished gaze. "She does not know her true lineage. Her and Connell are direct Descendants of the Lóklana, but Keelyn has the higher concentration in her DNA. Lóklana are literally creatures formed from light. It is a part of their genetic makeup, if she lets her light fade, she will fade."

Macy slid down the fender to the grungy pavement, and put her hands over her head. "I guess not all Chosen are human then—besides you."

As the Ninth, he experienced her pain, mingled with his own, but hers was so much more acute—stronger, fiercer than could be comprehended. Overwhelming.

He swallowed hard, dropped to her side, put his arms around her, and whispered in her ear. "I'm so sorry Macy."

"Can we save her?" She asked, her voice muffled by her arms.

Tolen ran his fingers through her ponytail. "I don't know. My gift of healing seems only to work on her physical body. I have the Lóklana gift but I'm not one of them. I tried to connect to it and push it toward her, but it's almost like there's a wall blocking it. If we could get her to a true Lóklana maybe they could do something more." He sighed, "There was a guy in Hunsí's village that mentioned some lived not far from there, but…"

"But we can't risk everything on a maybe." Her voice trembled. Tolen squeezed her shoulders.

"Her future is choppy, uncertain. Rune seems to be the only thing that is keeping her holding on. It won't be us that saves her. It will be him."

Macy's despair hovered over them like a dark cloud. Her thoughts relayed what she'd learned from her time with them, that Rune loved Keelyn, but his fear of losing her had kept him from telling her. "We have to tell him." She whispered.

Tolen pulled her tighter to his side wishing it were that easy. He considered revealing what he'd seen of Rune's future, but it didn't feel like the right time. She was dealing with enough at the moment. "Just because I can see the future doesn't always mean I can meddle with it. Agency is important. If Rune is to tell her he loves her it has to be because he wants to and he's ready, it can't be out of fear. Fear isn't binding, it's confusing and misleading."

Macy lifted her head and gave him a steely eyed glare through her tears. "You know, this new Jonas-y knowledgeable you is sexy and all, but do you *have* to be right all the time?"

He kissed her cheek, sending some of his light into her, hoping it would offer additional comfort. "I'm sorry. We'll do everything we can to help her see she won't be alone, that she will be with Connell again someday, that she is needed here, but we have to leave the rest to Rune."

He took a deep breath and tugged on her arm. "Come on, I bet there's donuts in the gas station on the corner, maybe dessert will cheer her up."

o o o

Back in the room Tolen assured everyone that although the Dark was out there, it wasn't focused on them…for now. The Treasta should allow them a few hours rest, before they figured out the car. Then, donuts left untouched, they settled in for sleep.

Tolen sprawled in his sleeping bag on the floor beside Macy's bed, but she dangled her fingers over the side to clutch his hand, and fell into a fitful sleep. The sounds of Keelyn's muffled sobs from the bed next, and Rune's attempts at soothing, flowed into her dreams.

Tolen stayed awake long after her dreams faded from his thoughts and worried over Macy, her friends, and where the Light would lead them next.

C HAPTER 6

VISIONS

Tolen's eyes snapped open as the voice repeated in his mind.
Dembashi. . .

Conchla Mindra. . .

Watcher. . .

Ninth Chosen. . .

Tolen rubbed the sleep from his eyes. *Sashan?*

Dembashi…

Yes, that was definitely Sashan's voice. The room was still dark, the
slit between the curtains revealed the sky outside had barely lightened.
His watch said 4:57 AM. Steady breathing drifted from both beds and
he shut his eyes again.

Sashan, what do you want me to see? He pushed his thoughts into the
void, concentrating on the young boy—leader of the Watchers—that
he'd been taught by in Hunsí's village. He had no idea if it would work.
Sashan hadn't spoken to Tolen's mind outside their lessons and Tolen
had never tried to make the connection go the other way.

But instead of Sashan's voice answering, a flood of images flew
across Tolen's mind. A dank cell that smelled of human waste and rotting food. A humanoid creature with lifeless eyes and blackened teeth
paced outside—a Darkened? Or one of the mutant spawn of the Fallen?
And a peaceful village, infused with light, made up of small wooden huts
in various shapes and sizes, nestled among tall palm trees and sandy

streets. Contradictory, but there was a connection…the images faded and he knew without searching that Sashan's influence had fled.

Macy snorted in her sleep and a smile pushed at his lips despite the worry plaguing his mind. She had a way of doing that to him. She was his greatest strength and his greatest weakness all in one. The trigger for his gifts, his motivation to fight for Light, and—according to Kichaya, Honitahai tribal elder—if he wasn't careful, his downfall. The pull Macy had on his heart had him often making decisions based on his love for her and fear for her safety rather than what was right or best for the moment. He'd grown a lot in his time with Hunsí and the Honitahai, but it still took concentrated effort to keep his priorities in the right place.

Heart and mind as one. He took a slow breath in and out, pushed his palms together and focused. His Second Sight flashed with colors and images. It took a moment to focus and only pull the brightest most vivid images forward.

There were two that demanded attention. The first was of Macy, but it was an image of her from the past. Her eyes glowing fiery gold, the light emanating from her body pure and powerful—the moment when her destiny as Light's Aid had shown itself. He watched again as the fire shot from her hands and destroyed the gate Daemon had been building, stopping him from releasing hordes of Dark creatures into the earth realm.

With the image came a surge of protectiveness that went beyond anything he'd ever felt. He'd always wanted to protect her, above nearly every responsibility he'd ever had, in fact it was this desire that had almost been the end of his role as the Ninth. When the Light gave him the choice to remain the Ninth or renounce his destiny in order to live a human lifespan with Macy, he'd been sorely tempted and almost given in. It had been the hardest decision of his life, but this was different. This desire to protect Macy was not only his own. It was bigger. *Much* bigger. Where before he'd needed to set aside his concern for Macy and focus on his task as the Ninth, something had changed. Something that would change the way he saw everything.

His heart hammered as the image faded and the second image moved to the front of his mind, an image that flipped to different people. Blaze—the child Lafar he had saved who now was the Keeper of the powerful Last Shard; Quasar—the Lafar elf who had saved Tolen's life and become his closest friend; Brina and Toke—Macy's friends; Sienn and Mahto—Tolen's adopted family. The Seraph of Light had given all of them different missions, different tasks to complete, yet they were all connected. What was it about their situations that he needed to see? He separated each image, focusing.

Blaze. Tiny, black-haired, healthy, determined, being taught by Sashan, protected by Quasar, and surrounded by his people. *Quasar.* Patient, loyal. *Waiting.* But for exactly what Tolen did not know. Quasar's thoughts were on his son, Spark. Tolen had forgotten he'd had a son, had never even known his name. Quasar had shielded his thoughts well. Sorrow for his friend pierced Tolen's life force as images of Spark flashed across his vision. The child's first steps, his first hunt, Quasar and Nebula holding his little hands as he walked happily between them. Spark as an adult dying in Quasar's arms. Soon Tolen would need Blaze and Quasar's help, but his *sight* did not show him why.

Brina and Toke. The kind girl who had befriended Macy and the gentle leader who had watched over her. They were searching for the "father" as the Seraph had directed, but their path had taken an unexpected turn. They'd found new clues leading to what had really happened to Brina's father, but they'd found something else. Something that had them heading in an entirely new direction. He saw the flash of an owl leading them. Tolen had a fleeting feeling they would be needing something from him soon, but the image lost its clarity and he could see no further.

Sienn and Mahto. The image of them hazy, their current paths changing—Sashan had told them to head east. He felt a wave of concern, but then the image flipped.

Keelyn. Her light fading, her body turning to gray ash, Rune's face, distorted with pain and laced with fury, changing, darkening, his blue eyes deepening to flat, soulless black.

Kichaya and Sashan. The tribal elder and the Watcher child, deep in conversation. Sashan's head turned, his sapphire eyes met Tolen's, a flash of red-gold, the image of a *Fallen* one—a leader, powerful, brilliant. A creature swathed in shadow, its features too blurred to make out what it could be…Legion?

A feeling of deepest despair.

Be prepared, Sashan's voice whispered and the vision ended. Tolen's breath came in short bursts, sweat covered his face and plastered his hair to his scalp. The despair crushed against his ribs and he had to use an image of Macy, whole and happy to get it to leave.

He thought through the images trying to sort them, give them meaning. The vision consisted of Macy along with the "Eight" set apart by the Seraph. Each person had a part in the prophecy with roles only the Light fully understood. As the Ninth Chosen, Tolen was meant to *watch* for the whole world. His visions only ever had something to do with that destiny. This vision indicated something coming. Something big. But what? What was he supposed to have learned?

Sashan?

No answer. The void was just a void once again, no light or knowledge offered in its depths of past and future.

He ran a hand through his sweaty hair and noticed Rune watching him curiously.

Tolen swiped the bottom of his shirt over his face. The image of Rune turning into a Darkened flashed again across his vision, his stomach turned and he squeezed his eyes shut. One of the most difficult parts of Second Sight wasn't seeing the future or reading people's thoughts, it was feeling what they felt. The pain in Rune's heart was equal to what Tolen had felt when he thought Macy was about to die. *Too much.*

He swallowed and glanced up at Macy. Her hand lay cupped under her cheek, her wavy hair spilling around her head like a pillow of hay. Her snores were quieting, she would wake soon. He'd have to sort out the vision later. *If* he could.

He met Rune's gaze and whispered. "Today isn't going to be easy. What we escaped back there, that's not going be the worst we face going forward."

Rune gently moved a strand of red hair off Keelyn's forehead. "I know." He let out a slow breath. "So, are you gonna tell me what else is going on?"

Tolen raised his eyebrows feigning innocence, but heat filled his cheeks.

"Dude, your poker face sucks." A forced grin, more like a grimace, lifted the scar on Rune's cheek. "You told Macy something, something you didn't want me to know. You guys came back in the room and neither of you would look me in the eye the rest of the night."

Tolen leaned forward and dropped his elbows to his knees. "Are you sure you're ready to hear it aloud?"

"You say that like I already know." Rune's eyes narrowed, but Tolen felt his emotions tense.

Tolen lowered his eyes. "You do. At least to a degree. I've sensed the fear in your thoughts."

"I've been blocking you." Rune's glare could have melted a glacier.

"You can't block your thoughts about her," Tolen sighed. "The emotions behind them are too strong."

"Then she's better off if I leave. Safer." Rune's teeth ground together.

"You can't leave." Tolen held Rune's glare. "You are the only reason she has to come back."

Rune's shoulders trembled and he glanced at Macy.

"Yes, Keelyn loves Macy and the rest of your family, but it's not enough. She needs you." Tolen waited for Rune to meet his eye again. "And you need her." The truth echoed back in Rune's blue eyes—he knew it, but he hated it.

The strength of Rune's connection to Keelyn sent ripples through the Balance and Tolen saw again the sliver of the young man's possible future.

If Keelyn died, the Rune before them would cease to exist. Tolen barely repressed a shudder. Despite the challenges ahead, and the extreme need to get this mission moving, something had to be done to help these two—and not just because it would break Macy's heart to lose her friends. It went even deeper than that, to a place even he couldn't explain. "It's only going to get harder from here—and I'm not talking about battling Dark creatures."

"I know."

Tolen took a slow breath, seeking to soften his next words as much as possible, but knowing they would wound all the same. "I'll do all I can to help her, to help you, but you have to know, there are some things that are out of my hands. Even out of the hands of the Light. If she doesn't *choose* to live, there's nothing any of us can do."

Rune's eyes hardened for a split second, before his shoulders sagged. He tilted his head and for a quick a moment it seemed he would press his lips to Keelyn's hair, but then his trajectory shifted and he laid his cheek on the pillow propped up behind him, his eyes focused on the ceiling.

Tolen stood up, joints popping, and pushed Rune's emotions as far from his own heart as he could. His eyes drifted to Macy and warmth flooded his body, shifting him from the role of the Ninth, to the young man in love with the sleeping girl on the bed. The last of the despair fled.

How quickly everything fell into place when he focused on her. Kichaya had told him she was not his trigger, not the key to his gifts, but he knew the truth. The fire that came alive in his veins every time he looked at her, the purpose that flowed through his life force. Opposites in so many ways, yet she made the world make sense. His life make sense. His whole world lay there in one tiny, beautiful, little package. She was everything.

The more time they were together the more this awareness grew and molded into him. For so long he'd been motivated by fear. Fear of losing her to their dangerous destiny, fear of their differences—she being human, he Hidden kind—and outliving her by possibly thousands of years. Funny how the events of the last few weeks hadn't changed those fears so much as made them almost silly.

As he'd transcended and held her in the world of the "between" he'd realized for the first time just how powerful and transcendent love is. No matter what happened from here on out, their love would transcend every earthly and hidden care. If their mortal time was a few months or decades, he would live every possible minute to its fullest by her side.

A pang of envy from Rune drifted through the Balance as he moved to sit on the edge of Macy's bed. "Morning beautiful." He whispered next to her ear.

She slowly opened her eyes and covered a yawn. "Morning." She smiled, her tiny dimple appeared, and he kissed her quickly, aware of Rune's gaze.

Macy's eyes flicked to Rune laying on top of the covers, Keelyn sleeping against his chest, her face anguished even in sleep.

Tolen could feel her concern for her friends—concern and understanding. Rune hurt not just because he loved Connell too, but because he loved Keelyn and her pain was his pain. *So painful, so powerful.* Macy's thoughts pushed into his mind. *I guess love just works like that.* He ignored the ache at the truth of that statement.

"How'd she do?" Macy whispered.

Tolen glanced at the clock on the nightstand, 6:23 AM. The light between the curtains now cast a slight bluish glow into the room. His vision had lasted nearly an hour and a half. "She did pretty well until about three o'clock, when she woke up crying."

Macy sat up. "I didn't hear anything—"

"That's because she went right back to sleep once Tolen started singing," Rune whispered, his eyes flicked to Tolen and something changed between them. A piece of Rune's guard had broken away. In time they may even be friends—*if* Keelyn survived.

"You sang?" Macy eyed him with something that looked like pride.

He shrugged and picked at the bottom of his shirt, warmth rising in his cheeks. "The words just sort of came to me. It seemed like the Light wanted her to hear it."

"It was Hidden language." Rune brushed another of Keelyn's red curls off her cheek.

"What did it say?" Macy touched Tolen's hand where it rested on the bed.

He continued to stare out at the sliver of morning peeking through. "It spoke of peace, understanding, hope, and comfort. Love everlasting."

"I wish I would have been awake to hear it."

Tolen shrugged again, uncomfortable with the eyes on him. "We have a lot to do today. I know Keelyn needs to rest, but it isn't safe for us to stay here much longer. We've got to decide where to go next."

"We probably need to figure out what's up with that car before we go anywhere else in it." Macy tossed her legs off the side of the bed and reached for her boots.

Rune pointed out the window. "The Treasta needs to be recharged by sunlight every eight hours, we don't have much time left before it runs out of juice. I'll stay here with Keelyn while you guys search the car." He tapped his Radia Shard. "Signal me when you want me to wake her up. I'll get our stuff, check out, and we'll meet you in the parking lot. Once you're sure it's safe, we'll figure out where to go next."

"Sounds good." Tolen stood up and waited for Macy to slip on her boots and grab the Treasta from the nightstand. Rune was a natural-born leader and Tolen was content to let him lead for the time being. His own thoughts needed to be focused elsewhere.

CHAPTER 7

MAX'S' PLAN

MACY TWISTED HER hair back into its ponytail and led the way across the brightening parking lot. Tolen took her hand when she finished threading her fingers through the tangles. She loved the feel of Tolen's hand in hers, despite the pitch and roll of emotions rocking in her chest. It seemed to be the only sure thing in her life right now—his love for her and hers for him. She couldn't decipher between what she was worried about the most: the mission, or Keelyn's predicament. She was pretty certain she was supposed to be more concerned with the mission, but then she'd think of her friend and her heart hurt so bad it felt like the Kuna living inside her had burned a hole through it.

Tolen walked beside her, leaving her to her thoughts, the only sound coming from their feet crunching over the loose gravel on the cracked asphalt. He was generally pretty good at letting her think without interruption when she needed it. And today she needed it. She glanced up. A cloudless morning, the sky lightening to brightest blue. Beautiful…and unnerving.

The Shadow Wraiths had been occupying the worst of thunderstorms, unnaturally sustaining them, using them to hunt up and down the country for weeks. From the moment they found Tolen in Utah, the Dark had been moving in silent waves, increasing in numbers. The battle on the island was only a taste of what was to come. A tremor moved across her shoulders like the icy fingers of a Kinchomen demon lizard. The Dark was biding its time.

"You can signal each other through the Radia Shards?" Tolen asked as they neared the car.

She shook the chill from her body and pushed the fear aside. "It's not something Bastian ever taught me to do, but then again I never trained with any other Chosen. The few times I ever met any Bastian was always in a hurry." A fact that she'd never thought much about, but she had to wonder why her Watcher hadn't taught her to do something that now seemed pretty important.

Tolen nudged her shoulder. "I'm sure he had his reasons."

She twisted a strand of hair around her pinky finger. "As always." She sat the Treasta on the trunk, the tiny screen lit up, pulling in the light from the sun. Macy ran her hand over the fender. The yellow Barracuda would have stood out in a row of cars, but being one of three in the whole lot, it stuck out like yellow caution tape around a crime scene.

"Think we should paint it?" she asked without conviction.

"Let's take a look first." Tolen tapped the window. "If we can't take it with us there's no sense in changing anything."

"You think we'll need to leave it behind?" Heaviness settled in her chest.

Tolen shrugged.

"Why would Bastian want me to find it then?" She stuck her hands in her pockets.

Tolen leaned against the fender. "And how did he know about it in the first place?"

She shook her head. "Since when has anything Bastian said or done ever made sense right away?"

"Good point."

Macy pulled the keys from her pocket. "It's just so weird."

"What exactly?" Tolen's brows pulled together.

"The worst thing you can do to a vehicle is let it sit. Remember that old Jeep?"

"Yeah, you could barely keep it going down the road." Tolen chuckled at the memory and Macy couldn't help but smile as well. It had been the first time they'd really talked as they drove that rusty Jeep toward the California coast, right toward the Shadows, in the hopes that the Doogar dwarves could help protect and train Tolen. Funny such a scary memory could also be a good one.

She moved the Treasta to the top of the car and separated a key from the set, but paused before inserting it in the lock. "Octane evaporates over time making the fuel mostly water. Grease thickens in the bearings and gears. Oil isn't moving through the engine so things rust and freeze up. Hoses harden and crack, brake pads deteriorate. Dust and dirt collect inside and out. Yeah, it had a cover over it, but this thing is pristine. It's been in that shed for ten years. It shouldn't have started on the first try and it had way too much power." Tolen seemed to be fighting back a grin. "What?"

Tolen bit his lip but his eyes twinkled. "Nothing." Her eyebrows pulled together and he touched the line between them with his finger. "It's just incredibly attractive listening to you talk car." He sucked in a breath and dropped his hand. "So, is that like some Movan thing maybe?"

Her heart gave a single hard beat, her palms tingled, and trickles of pleasurable warmth ran from her chest down to her toes. She forced herself to look away and tried to remember what he'd asked. "Could be I guess. Or someone has been taking care of it."

"You said Toke was living outside the town waiting for you to come back. Could it have been him?"

Macy shook her head, "I don't think so, or he would've mentioned it. At least I hope he would've." She stuck the key in the trunk lock and twisted. Nothing happened. She wiggled the key but it still it wouldn't unlock.

"Take the key out and touch it with your finger." Tolen held out his hand for the keys. The pupil in his blue eye was shifting, big to small, *watching*.

Macy dropped the keys onto his palm and touched the lock with her finger. It glowed blue for a fraction of a second, then clicked and the hatch popped open an inch. "What do you see?" She asked as she lifted the lid.

"The past." He'd closed his eyes. His chin tilted down. "This car it—it *does* know you. I see Bastian and you. You're six, it's only been a few hours since you've been chosen. You're sleeping in a hotel. Bastian is staring out the window *watching*. I can see his vision. He sees this car and your father is—he's programming the car, he's rushing, anxious, worried. Bastian sees your father placing a box filled with notes beneath the floorboards of that shed at the very back of your yard close to the river."

Tolen paused, Macy put her hand on his arm, and after a beat that felt like an eternity as her heart pounded in anticipation, he continued. "The vision of Max ends there. Now I see Bastian setting up protection about the room and over you—something that will keep you asleep—and he goes back to your house. Firemen, police, and neighbors mill about, but the shed is hidden deep in the trees. In the chaos he sneaks into the shed, the car is parked inside. He finds the box. It contains a thick letter addressed to you. The car suddenly starts, it senses your connection to Bastian. There's a secret road through the trees. He drives to the storage shed facility. Keeps the box. He goes back to you, takes you away from Whisper." His eyes opened and his Watcher's eye settled back to normal vivid blue.

Macy didn't realize she'd been holding her breath until colors started to dance before her eyes. "Breathe." Tolen touched her cheek and she took a quick breath.

"You…you saw him? My dad?"

Tolen nodded and tucked a strand of hair behind her ear. "His hair was darker than yours, more brown than blonde, but you have his eyes."

A lump lodged in her throat. "I miss him so much. Both of them."

Tolen reached up and brushed the moisture from her eyes before it could fall. "You're so incredibly like him Macy. He's very much a part of you, they both are."

She shook her head. There wasn't time to spend down memory lane, and she really didn't want to sit here and bawl. She tossed her ponytail over her shoulder and lifted the hatch.

Circuit boards covered half the floor of the trunk, wires crisscrossing between each one. Some wires glowed blue, others soft white. Three backpacks were wedged in the space between the auxiliary gas tank and the trunk wall. She reached out to grab the first pack and the wires glowed brighter. A tingle started in her fingers the closer she got to the auxiliary gas tank. When the tingle became almost painful a lid in the floor popped open. A small leather-bound notebook rested inside.

She licked her lips, pulled it out, and flipped it open to see a folded note with her name on the back. With trembling fingers she unfolded the letter.

Tolen stepped closer to read over her shoulder. It was written by her father, three days before her sixth birthday. Three days before he and her mother were killed and Macy was chosen.

October 20, 2003

Allison,

If you're reading this then I'm betting you no longer think I'm crazy with all my talk of Dark and Light and monsters. Now maybe you'll understand why the events surrounding your sister and my recent injury have brought me such great concern.

It also means our plan to flee has failed and I am no longer with you. I am so very sorry. I thought I could keep you both safe. Protect us all. I can feel the Balance shifting around us, and I know Macy will be Chosen. I think I've known from the moment she was born that they would pick her. She's so special, our little McLacy, so incredibly important.

Tolen placed his arm around Macy's trembling shoulders. She leaned into him as she continued, her heart in her throat, her fingers tingling.

I wanted to leave three months ago when I first felt the shift. There's so much to do, the Dark is growing stronger, and I am certain they are looking for me, but I understand why you insisted we let Macy have a normal birthday here, at home. You have made such grand plans for her future. As dangerous and risky as it is, I didn't want to take this last birthday away from you, despite the feeling that it might be a mistake.

If it was, then everything has changed. Sweetheart, I don't know how to tell you this, and I know I should have before now, but once Macy is Chosen she will be placed in the care of a Watcher, those people I told you about, and you will be on your own. Your religious beliefs have helped you sense the Dark in the past, and will help you stay safe as you go forward, as will this car, until the day Macy comes back for it. And she must. One way or another you must convince her Watcher to let her return to it, to you, before she Transcends, so that she can discover what she must do. What she must finish.

I've taught Macy the stories. She should understand what they mean one day. When she comes, tell her I've collected everything needed to complete the Awakening.

Macy paused to look up at Tolen. "What the *what?* The Awakening?"

Tolen shrugged and she went back to reading, biting down on her lip so hard she could taste blood.

It took a few years and much help from Toke to figure out the Movan tech, but I think I've got the car just right. If I did, you and Macy will be the only ones able to access its special features. I had you both help me build it for a reason. I needed Macy to remember it. And I needed you both close so that each part of the car would be able to recognize your bioelectricity when the time came for you to access its special abilities. It knows you. It will care for itself, cycling through the systems, circulating lubricants, oil, fuel—adding octane as needed if it is stored over long periods of time.

Keep the contents in the hidden compartment where you discovered this note. Don't take them out, don't show them to anyone. Only Macy can know about them. I hope I have provided enough clues for her to move forward and complete my self-appointed quest. I must assume that once she is Chosen, and I am gone, the task would fall to her anyway. I wish I could explain things more clearly Alli, but should this car fall into the wrong hands I can't risk it.

I wish I would have succeeded and made the world safe for you, sweetheart. Safe for Macy.

Be strong.

I love you both. Forever.

Max

Tolen pulled her to his chest, letting his shirt catch the tears that wouldn't stop, as she folded the note and looked at the first page of the notebook.

It was a schematic of the car. It seemed her dad had gone a little overboard, but much of the car's features would come in handy. It had an onboard Treasta that would disguise its power and alert the driver if the Dark nearby was focused on them. It had stealth mode that would quiet the engine, and even a color change feature.

Tolen leaned forward. "What's that?" He reached toward the compartment that had held the notebook, but six inches away a bolt of electricity jumped from the car to his fingers. "Ow!" He pulled his hand away and stepped back.

Macy dropped the notebook. "Are you okay?"

"I don't think I'm allowed in there." She caught Tolen's crooked smile as she leaned in to see what he was reaching for.

Tucked into the compartment was a small black drawstring bag. She reached for it and heat filled her chest.

"Careful."

She nodded as her Kuna rushed to her hands, and smoke started to curl from her fingertips. She pulled back the power, tugged the bag free, and pulled the strings open to look inside. "Holy crap!"

"What is it?"

Macy opened the bag wider for Tolen to look inside.

"That's not—? Is it?"

"I think it is."

"The Relics?"

"Every last one of them."

CHAPTER 8

WHAT?!?

MACY BALANCED THE bag in her palm, pulling back the sudden flare of her Kuna.

"You better make sure that onboard Treasta works." Tolen whispered.

Macy dropped the bag back in the compartment, snapped the lid shut, slammed the trunk closed and hurried to the driver's side door. "Right. And we're going to have to make sure we keep the other one charged and on us any time we're away from the car until we figure out how they're tracking us."

Tolen grabbed the Treasta off the roof, waited for her to slide into the seat before handing it in through the window, and kissed her forehead. "Maybe see about that color change option while you're at it."

Macy sat the Treasta on the dash where it could keep soaking up sunlight and started flipping through the notebook.

"I'll go get the others. I think it might be a good idea to go somewhere else to plan our next move."

Tolen rushed back across the parking lot while she continued flipping pages. They'd have to get Rune to show them how to do that Radia Shard signal thing.

According to the pictures, a keypad was concealed behind the radio and she just needed to enter a certain sequence using the station buttons to get it to open. She ran her palm across the shiny black dash and a slight vibration tickled her fingers, like a purring kitten. "Seems like you missed me." The purring increased. She bit back a smile, and patted the dash once before pushing the station buttons 1, 3, 2, 5.

The front of the radio popped down revealing the keypad and a tiny computer screen. It didn't take long to access the Treasta program and get it functioning. The screen even showed little bright blue dots indicating the closest Dark creatures. The instructions stated that if the Dark creatures were aware of the car and its occupants and moving with intent, the dots would turn red.

Macy's attention turned to her Radia Shard. It had been pulsing slightly ever since they'd first got the car, as if it wanted her to connect with it, as if it had something to show her. She bit her lip—despite having connected to it back on Eamun's Island, the shard's power still made her wary. It was so much stronger now. Besides, was it really a good idea to connect to it with the Fallen out there watching? She squeezed the warm shard in her fingers. Maybe she'd just connect for a few seconds and pull back. She let her Kuna zing just to her fingertips, matching the warmth of the shard, her eyes on the blue dots on the screen. A surge of joyous heat flared in her chest as life force and shard connected. Suddenly she could see them, the creatures represented by the dots, in her mind. She could see them and their surroundings. It was at least a dozen Kinchomen, their scaly lizard-like bodies crawling around, their long nails scrounging through the bones at their feet, their orange eyes searching for more meat. *Gross.*

She wasn't afraid of Kinchomen, but they were still nasty little creatures. The forest surrounding the creatures was darker, the sun had yet to send them into hiding until the night—so at least a mile or so away? Nothing else seemed to be moving. She pulled back the connection, secretly a little thrilled by what she'd been able to do with a full shard.

She tapped a few keys and brought up the color change program. She really hated the idea of changing the beautiful car, but yellow was too memorable. She clicked through the options and selected a faded stock green, the color of baby poop. It even had rust around the fenders, bumper, and a few dents. The car made a few popping noises, and when she glanced out the windshield she'd swear she was in a totally different car. She probably should have waited until they were somewhere less conspicuous, but the parking lot was still, the morning light barely illuminating their space.

She was scanning through the other various perks and self-defense capabilities of the car when the others returned.

Tolen tossed their bags in the back and waited for Rune and Keelyn to climb in before taking the seat next to Macy. Her heart and the emotions emanating from her shard both leapt the moment he sat down.

"So, this looks different." Tolen fingered the now cracked pleather seat beneath him and unfolded an area map he must have picked up when he checked out.

"My dad's nothing if not thorough, I guess." It was like getting to know a side of her father she never knew existed.

"Guess we know where you get your weirdness from." Rune winked.

"Shut up." Macy rolled her eyes. "Where to?"

"Let's stop at that grocery store we passed coming in and stock up." Tolen scanned the map. "Looks like there's a park just off the highway about 10 miles from here. I say we stop there, eat, and discuss what we found in the trunk."

"What exactly *did* you find in the trunk?" Rune leaned forward with his hands on the sides of Tolen's seat.

"You're not going to believe it…" The car backfired once, all in character with its new look, as she pulled out of the lot. "But my dad found all the Relics and he hid them in the trunk."

"Bull—"

"Rune!" Keelyn covered his mouth with her hand.

○ ○ ○

Macy turned the car into the crumbling lot and grinned, not just from how much fun it had been to watch Rune stewing in the back seat. She'd been skeptical when Tolen had first said "park", imagining parents with their children chasing little dogs everywhere, all wondering at the group of teenagers crammed in an old car without any adults. But she needn't have worried.

Most likely the only human beings to set foot in this park for the last fifty years were kids looking for drinking spots or vagrants. Only the skeletons of rusty playground equipment remained, creaking morosely in the slight breeze. Silt covered the cracked and broken asphalt. Bits of sunlight sparkled off chunks of glass that littered the ground next to makeshift fire-pits. In the distance a few solitary chimneys or cement foundations peeked up from the tall grass and seedling trees—it wouldn't be long before the forest completely reclaimed its territory.

Perfect.

Tolen noticed her observation and elaborated. "The dam a few miles north broke in 1955 and wiped out the tiny town. The devastation was enough that the people never returned to rebuild."

"How do you know that?" Keelyn gazed past the park into the surrounding forest.

Tolen sighed and Macy noticed his eyes shifting. "You saw it?"

He didn't respond—it must have been bad. She let it drop and led everyone to what was left of a metal picnic table.

They covered the table-top with an old blanket Rune had discovered under the front seat and set the Treasta up at the center before dropping their packs on the ground beside them. Tolen spread out a make-shift breakfast with the perishables they'd purchased at the grocery store.

Rune made sure Keelyn was eating an orange before he was back to business. "So your crazy dad left the Relics in the car?"

"He's not crazy!" Macy threw a chip at his face, the breeze caught it before it hit, and it fluttered uselessly to the table.

"Right, and you're not blonde either." Rune laughed but it didn't touch his eyes.

Keelyn pinched his arm. "Knock it off you two. Let's see them."

Macy held out the bag. Rune took it and peeked inside. His eyebrows pulled together and then another smirk touched his lips. He pushed the Treasta to the side and tipped the bag upside down, unceremoniously dumping the bag's contents over on the table.

"Dude!" Macy leaned back. "What the heck?"

Rune moved the items around until they were all separated by a few inches. "They're fakes."

"What?" Macy and Tolen said together.

"They're not the Relics." Rune held up a small white crystalized rock and twisted it in the light. "This is nothing like the one you showed us back home. Even though it only reacted for Keelyn, we all felt something from it. Something *other*. I don't feel anything."

Macy snatched the rock from his hand and frowned. Nothing. With the Claver—the Watcher Relic—now hidden safely in her pack, she'd felt something from it the moment it touched her fingers—even now it was as if it called to her, an annoying voice in the back of her head. But this? It was just a rock, nothing more.

"What made you think they were Relics?" Keelyn picked up another item, a tiny block of wood covered in scratch marks.

Macy handed Keelyn the letter. "Because of what my dad said in this."

Rune leaned his head toward Keelyn to read at the same time.

While they read, Macy pawed through the useless stuff on the table. Besides the white crystal rock, and the block of wood, there was a keychain from some dive in Colorado, a pocket knife that likely came from a tourist shop, a pair of tiny purple dice, a piece of faded denim with a series of numbers written in permanent ink on the back, a smiley face button, and a chunk of Fools Gold. Macy absently reached out and touched the golden rock with her finger, seeking for some sort of sign, feeling, anything.

And then she felt it. A yearning, a need, a call, but not the same feeling as she had from the Relic in her pack, but as if from somewhere else. She closed her eyes. *Dad, what are you trying to tell me? What does all this stuff mean?*

Tolen took her hand and his blue eye went crazy, black to blue alarmingly fast. He sucked in a quick breath. She leaned forward to look in his eyes, but it was like he was looking through her not at her.

"Nine Relics…" Tolen whispered as his eye slowed and she squeezed his hand.

"Would one of you like to tell us what the heck is going on?" Rune's impatient voice broke Tolen's focus and he looked up.

"It's—" He picked over the fake Relics. "They're clues. Clues to the actual Relics. Macy's dad did more than just make a map to the Relics. He actually found them…all of them."

Rune whistled between his teeth. "Well, well, well. Maybe Max wasn't so crazy after all."

"Yes, but it means finding them is going to be more dangerous than before." Tolen rubbed a thumb against his temple.

"What's this?" Rune was pulling something else from the bag, a faded piece of leather painted with images and strange lines set in rows like some form of writing.

Macy snatched it out of his hands. "I know this!" She twisted it around, her mind flashing back to the time as a small child she was fishing through her grandmother's chest. Her father had tried to get her to pay attention to the leather, but she was too focused on the baubles and shiny stuff. "My dad tried to teach me about it but I was distracted."

"So you have no idea what it is?" Tolen asked.

She shook her head. "Can you read it?" She held it out to him.

Tolen flipped it around looking at it from all angles. "No. It's not Hidden language—at least not the kind I know."

"Wait, look!" Keelyn held out the block of wood, the scratches weren't actually scratches, but similar to the strange writing on the leather.

Macy took the leather back from Tolen and compared it to the block of wood.

"Well, it doesn't do us any good if we can't figure out how to read it." Rune popped a chip in his mouth. "Your dad obviously moved the Relics from where they were originally hidden by the Guardians, which was smart—if the Dark ever did get their hands on one of those maps Toke talked about, they're going to be very let down when they don't find a single Relic. But the fact that they were looking for you the first time you were in Whisper, and knew you had the Claver Relic, chances are they were on to your dad. Which means we need to get figuring out these clues as quick as we can."

Tolen was running his fingers over each of the fakes, his blue eye shifting black to blue and back again. "Tolen?" Macy put her hand over his.

He held up a finger, "There's more…" and closed his eyes. Five minutes passed. They felt like five hours with Rune shifting and huffing impatiently. Tolen finally opened his eyes, the blue eye still and bright.

"What did you see?" She rubbed the back of his hand with her thumb.

"I can't quite…Get that map your dad made—the one Toke thought led to the Relics—his copy of the prophecy, grab a pen and that notebook from the car. Rune grab the map from the glovebox. I'm going to need all your help to figure out what I just saw."

CHAPTER 9

NOT SO NORMAL

Tolen pushed aside the remains of their makeshift meal and laid Max's map over the table, his body tingling in anticipation.

He took each of the fake Relics, set them in a row, and put the map and notebook to the side. "I think…well, I'm pretty sure I just saw the eight remaining Descendants. Max found them all, and each one has their Relics in their possession." He squeezed his eyes shut once. "And Max is going to lead us to them."

"What?" Macy, Rune, and Keelyn all asked at once.

"Max hid them really well. There's a haze over their locations, I only get feelings, no specific scenery or images to connect to." A flicker of the Descendants passed through his mind again. All of them were pure hearted and very gentle in nature. Protected through the generations by the Light. Three of them had been diagnosed by humans as Autistic, but they didn't understand. It was purity not disability.

"Okay slow down." Rune laid his palms on the table. "You're saying there are eight humans out there with Relics, right now? And this map is going to lead us to them?"

"Yes to the first question. Sort of, to the second." Tolen's eyes narrowed as he sifted through the images, trying to piece together what he'd seen.

"Are they *awake*? Can they see the Dark?" Tolen noticed Keelyn's Irish accent became more pronounced when she was nervous.

He met her gaze. "Yes."

Macy shook her head and squeezed his arm. "Tolen, you've got to start at the beginning. Just give us the pieces and we'll help you with the puzzle." She said as she kissed his cheek and the warmth surged through him again.

His heart kicked up a notch, heat flooded his body, and he was sure his cheeks reflected the fact.

Tolen picked up a fake relic and twisted it in his fingers before dropping it back to the table, trying to pretend he hadn't lost his focus. "Max, Macy's dad, he was a total genius. He no longer had a Radia shard to give him the ability to see the Dark, strengthen his physical body, or connect to his gifts, but he was sensitive enough to the Balance and how the Dark worked that he knew what to watch for and how to stay beneath their radar. The Fallen want the Relics as bad as we do. Finding them has become their main decree from the Dark. , butseeing Max fight and knowing he was doing it all by instinct was amazing—fighting beings that weren't even visible to him!"

Tolen shook his head at the memory. "Since the Relics give the Descendants the ability to see the Dark, once he found the Claver he could see again—but the only gift he had was the one the Claver wielded—the Watcher ability. He figured out how to connect to it and was able to use it to track down the other Relics."

He picked up one of the purple dice and twisted it between his thumb and first finger. "Each time he found a Relic he used Movan tech, and sheer genius, to hide it, then used the Claver to track down the human linked to that Relic. He united them, awakened them to the Dark, and hid them together. He found the last Descendant just a few days before Macy's sixth birthday—about the time he wrote the note. He hid the Claver in the tree, knowing she would need it. He didn't put it in the letter to his wife, but he knew, the Claver had shown him that he—he wouldn't be the one to complete the Awakening."

Macy leaned back and wrapped her arms around her middle. "Each Relic is meant for a specific descendant?"

Tolen dropped the dice back to the table. "Yes."

"But then," Macy rocked forward. "If the Claver was my dad's Relic—which means it's now mine—why did it work for Keelyn, but not me?"

Rune shifted closer to Keelyn's side. "Toke thought they might work for any human, and that's why Keelyn could access the Claver when she touched it." Tolen noticed how Rune's actions were always protective, never romantic.

He cleared his throat. "The Lóklana can access a *hint* of the Relic's power because their gift is connected to pure Light energy, but no, only the oldest living descendant whose bioelectricity has DNA passed down from the original Tribal Elder can actually *use* the Relic. I don't know why it wouldn't work for you." He put his hand on Macy's back.

"So Keelyn could do it because she has the Lóklana gift." Rune tapped Keelyn's arm, but she was staring at Tolen.

"You've felt it, haven't you?" he asked her.

"What?" Rune looked between the two. Tolen could feel Macy's eyes on his face, but he kept his gaze on Keelyn.

Keelyn nodded. "There was always something there. Something more."

"What?" Rune demanded.

She peeked up at him, her pale face searching his. "I'm not human."

Part of the truth, but not all of it. "Not *completely* human. You are half-human." He added.

"And the other half?" Rune's shoulders tensed.

"Lóklana. She is a child of Light." Tolen watched the concern melt off Rune's face to be replaced with relief.

He touched Keelyn's chin, "I could have told you *that*." A tiny sparkle lit her eyes, but he pulled his hand away, and the light dimmed. Tolen felt Macy's nervous impatience beside him. *Are you going to tell them?* He barely shook his head and lightly touched her hand. It wasn't the right time yet. Her face fell, and he wished he could tell her different, but she hadn't seen what he had seen in Rune's future. It *had* to wait. The weight of what Watchers must feel for their wards washed over him. Such a mantle. To know, but not share until the time was right. It was almost too much.

"So, that's why it worked for Keelyn, but the rest won't work for just any human, which is why the Dark is also after the Descendants?" Rune propped his elbow on the table.

Tolen nodded. "If the Descendants are captured and forced to turn the power of their Relics to the Dark, then Darsapean would be able to use their influence to drag the entire human race to his side."

A chilly wind blew across the table, emphasizing the warning.

"So my dad found the Relics, the humans connected to them, awakened them, and placed them under protection of one kind or another and…now what?" Macy waved her hand in the air, her eyebrows in a tight line, her dimple absent.

Tolen closed his eyes, focusing on the final memory. "This is where my sight gets foggy. There was an incident with a small band of Dark creatures. The last Relic was proving particularly tricky to find." He paused and tried to sift through the hazy pictures.

"When he finally found it the Dark wasn't far behind. They tracked him to the last Descendant. . . Sorry it's *really* foggy here." He shook his head to clear it. "He got the girl to safety, defeated the Dark, but it was a close battle. He came home seriously injured and Macy's mother finally agreed to leave, go into hiding. All the Descendants are awaiting further instructions from him."

"The injury he referenced in the note," Macy whispered.

Tolen nodded, but Rune didn't want to discuss the note. "So what did you see next?"

Tolen slid closer to Macy until their legs bumped against each other—knowing this next part would be hardest for her to hear. "Max loaded the car. He knew Macy was going to be Chosen. He'd planned to hide her mother somewhere while he completed the Awakening. The packs in the trunk have fake ID's for each of them, but then the Relic showed him a piece of the future. . ." He took Macy's hand. "He wrote the letter to his wife and put it in the notebook, hoping that since the Claver hadn't shown his wife's fate, somehow it meant she would survive." He swallowed and tapped the cover. "He gave in to Allison's pleas, decided to wait to leave until after Macy's birthday. But the Dark had figured out where he was. The Shadows came for him the same night Macy was Chosen." He winced at the memory.

"The Shadows came for *him*?" Macy's eyes were wet, but her voice was steady. "They didn't come for me?"

A lump lodged in Tolen's throat. He shook his head. "They'd tracked him—possibly from the last time he'd used the Claver. The Raksasha knew what you were the moment they broke in, but Bastian killed them before they could inform their masters. The Dark had no idea Max had a daughter or that she was one of the Chosen. He hid you well." He could still hear the echoes of Allison Burdow's screams. The idea that Macy had to carry that as her final memory of her mother filled Tolen with a fierce desire for vengeance that heated the Kuna in his chest.

"But they know now?" Rune flipped over the pocket knife, his voice gentle, filled with compassion.

"They know Macy's after the Relics." Tolen squeezed Macy's hand, pushing against the heat. "After what you did on the island we can assume they know you are Light's Aid and part of the prophecy, but they might not know you are also a Descendant."

Keelyn put her hand on Macy's arm. Tolen felt the tiny bit of light she was passing to Macy. Keelyn was dying, yet still determined to share her light—if only she could see just how much this world needed her!

Rune tapped the map on the table. "So, not to be the negative voice, but these people have been waiting ten years—what if they're no longer where he left them, or the Dark found them already, or they're dead? How is this map going to sort-of help us find the Descendants when Max hid them somewhere else? You're banking an awful lot on the out-dated information of a dead guy." He grimaced at Macy. "Sorry."

Macy ignored him, her eyes on Tolen. He pointed to the items in front of them. "Outdated but solid. Max wasn't stupid. I saw the Descendants and I'm almost positive the protection he created is still in place. Either way, we have to follow the path he set to make sure. If the Dark got there first, then we go after the Dark and take them back."

Keelyn put her hand over Rune's thick fist. "So how do we decipher the clues in the fakes?"

Tolen pointed to the two maps, Max's hand drawn one and the US topographic. "The fake Relics coincide with the real map and the US map. We just have to figure out the code." The anticipation was back, the possibility of an actual plan.

"Code?" Macy asked.

"Yes, he used the prophecy to do it. That's why we'll need the prophecy, his notes, and the topographic map." Tolen smoothed out Max's copy of the prophecy. "The capital letters tell more than what is important, and the numbers on each page of the notes, the symbols, and the numbers on the denim…It might take us some time to figure them all out and we're going to have to stay on the move, but it's all we have right now, and the fact that my Sight showed it to me means it's the right path, it has to be."

"Yeah, because it's not like we have to worry about the Fallen messin' with your sight or anything."

"Rune," Keelyn chided.

"Sorry, but being positive isn't a good thing if it makes you stupid."

Tolen sensed Macy's annoyance but she nodded. "Rune's right. Once we find the Descendants, what are we going to do with them? We can't exactly fit them all in the car with us. And I can't imagine it's the best idea to be carrying around all the Relics either."

"I'm going to open gates to the Zenith." Tolen kept his eyes on the papers in front of him. This was the one part of the plan he was most unsure of. "I don't know of anywhere else they can be protected until you Transcend and we can do the full Awakening."

Macy crossed her legs under the table. "But I thought it was too dangerous to just open gates at random?"

"I don't see another way."

Rune cleared his throat. "There might be."

Everyone's eyes turned to him, but he was pinching the bridge of his nose, his eyes closed. "There's a device."

"Rune?" Keelyn touched his shoulder.

"It can shield an entire city." Rune ran a hand over his face. "It's far more advanced than any Treasta."

"And you have access to it?" Tolen's blue eye started to shift and another tiny glimpse of Rune's past shot across his vision. A beautiful island…somewhat familiar. Rune, broken and bleeding, being tended to by someone in a blue dress.

"Yes." Rune dropped his hand and looked Tolen in the eye. Grief, regret, and doubt clouded his features. "I promised I would never share its location, never tell anyone about it." He met Keelyn's gaze and understanding dawned in her eyes. "But I don't see another way to succeed. We know the Zenith's location is no longer secret. As the Light's largest stronghold, it would be the first place the Dark would assume the Descendants would be hidden. This device can shield them as we gather them, and then we can set it up to hide wherever we choose to leave them until Macy completes the Awakening."

Macy absently lifted the pocket knife and started opening and closing it, her eyes far off, calculating. "Where is the device?"

"Arizona."

Something, a mixture of trepidation and excitement, passed through Tolen's shard and into his heart. Was this the right course? He wasn't sure. But while he could see the results they needed, right now he couldn't see the means to get there. "Okay Rune, we'll let you plan the next move."

"Just a sec. We're getting ahead of ourselves. We're being hunted by Fallen, and this Legion thing could come anytime." Macy kept her eyes on the knife, opening, closing, faster and faster. "Which makes even more sense if the Dark was onto my dad—and since I found the Claver, they probably think I know where the rest are."

"Add to that the fact that Daemon has always had an unusually strong interest in you." Tolen's chest tightened and a trickle of warmth flowed into his palms.

"Toke thought the Dark was after Macy in particular too," Rune added.

Macy dropped the knife and waved her hand in the air. "It doesn't matter. They're after all of us. And we've got to find the Descendants. But again, even if we do find them, how are we supposed to trek across the country towing them all, protected or not by Rune's device? They're not all going to fit in the car, and I really don't want to trade the 'Cuda in for a minivan."

"We'll just have to take it as it comes I guess." Tolen twisted the watch on his wrist. "We might have to create temporary holding places to bring each of them back to."

"I guess." She shrugged. Tolen could feel her doubts mirrored his, but what else could they do? Her eyes suddenly lit up. "Holy crap! I just realized why the Treasta's always seemed familiar to me. We had one! It was there. On the kitchen counter, all the time, disguised as a clock."

"Your dad was making sure you were protected even when he couldn't be there," Keelyn whispered.

"He taught me to recognize the Dark. I didn't realize it then, but that's why it wasn't so hard for me to believe when Bastian told me about it." Macy absently started twisting her shard between her fingers.

"It's more than that." Rune rolled his eyes.

"What do you mean?" Tolen threaded his fingers through Macy's, sensing her jumbled emotions—all the talk of the past was draining her, physically and emotionally.

"You're not like the rest of us, Macy." Keelyn tilted her head. "You can sense the Dark even past their shields. We used to think maybe you were a *Cathe* like Rune, but now we think it's more."

Macy's head flashed to Rune. "You're a Cathe?"

"Um, what's a Cathe?" Tolen glanced between the threesome, feeling once again that uncomfortable pang that came when he heard something from the Hidden world he should know, but because of his parents, he didn't.

Keelyn answered, "Have you ever met a human who seemed more sensitive to the emotions of those around them than normal?"

Slightly confused by the nervous thump that had begun behind his ribs, Tolen nodded.

"These are usually Cathe. But the ability remains latent, sometimes ignored, unless they are Chosen. Then the Radia Shard enhances the gift. Rune can sense most emotions a person is feeling even if they are shielding their life force from affecting the Balance. It's really hard to lie to a Cathe."

Rune waved his hand in the air. "We're not talking about me. I do still believe Macy has some underdeveloped Cathe ability—she's probably got some in her lineage somewhere, but it doesn't really matter. You've got some too." He motioned to Tolen. "It's probably part of being the Ninth, another side gift they thought you needed." He shook his head and Tolen was reminded of what Bastian had called his gift of empathy, the gift that would guide him better than any compass, map, advice, or training he'd ever receive. Could that be the Cathe?

Rune's next words crushed this curious thought to the farthest reaches of his mind. "But like Keelyn said, with Macy it's different. Toke told us Macy survived a trip to the Shadow Realm—which no human has done before, and that you defeated two DéHool wolves—*by yourself.* You're not a normal Chosen." Rune folded his arms across his chest, as if daring someone to argue.

"That's because I'm Light's Aid, idiot." Macy laughed and threw an apple at his head which he caught and sank his teeth into with a grin.

But it didn't feel the slightest bit funny to Tolen. *You're not a normal Chosen*, settled like lead in his stomach. The prophecy made it sound like Macy was to be his helpmeet in the Final Battle to come. Like a side-kick. But it had been Macy that had saved them from the Shadows, the Dark's ultimate weapon. It had been Macy's power that had destroyed the gate in the battle with Daemon. Tolen with all his gifts as the Ninth Chosen hadn't been able to do that. That feeling to protect, to shield, to safeguard Macy came back with an intensity that brought warmth to his palms and his fingers trembled where they rested on the table.

The morning sun seemed to lose some of its heat, and Tolen's watch gave one single ominous ding.

Chapter 10

THE GIFT

"WHAT WAS THAT?" Rune stopped laughing

"What's what?" Tolen replied, his thoughts still on his rising worry, his eyes glued to Max's notes but seeing nothing as he fought to pull back the heat rising in his palms.

Rune reached across the table and tapped Tolen's watch. The strange sun symbol—half white, half black—had reappeared across the face and was blinking in an odd way, like a warning. As he watched, the black side stretched farther across the little sun until there was only a sliver of white left, at the same moment it felt as if the earth realm also darkened, by a fraction of a degree, as if a wispy cloud had covered the sun, but the day was cloudless. The heat he thought he'd only imagined leaving, actually had.

"Where'd you get that?" Rune pulled his arm back, his eyes belying the casualness of his tone.

Tolen squeezed Macy's hand. "She gave it to me for my birthday. Why?"

"That's one he—" Rune's gaze flashed to Macy, "—ck of an asset."

"Asset?" Tolen and Macy asked together.

"To say the least. If I would've known you had that we could have saved a lot of time and been two steps ahead of the Fallen already." Rune shook his head and Keelyn nodded. "You want a way to track down someone or something, without having to mess with maps and codes and whatever, the answer is on your wrist."

"You've lost us." Tolen placed his other hand over the watch.

Rune leaned forward, elbows on the table. "Toke taught me a lot about Movan tech. We're pretty well equipped for what's ahead with just that car, but you add in that nifty little watch of yours and," he chuckled humorlessly, "we might actually have an advantage—even on top of you two and your freaky advanced gifts."

Tolen put his arm back around Macy. "Explain."

Rune motioned for the watch, "Can I see it for a minute?"

Tolen undid the band, and passed it across the table.

Rune's eyes swept over the watch. "See these markings around the rim?"

They all nodded.

"Each symbol represents one of the abilities the builder put into the watch." He counted them and started describing them. "This little guy has eight different special features, not including what these puppies have in them to begin with. I recognize four of the symbols, the other four I haven't seen before." He held it up to Keelyn, but she shook her head.

"I never understood Toke's abilities or much of his Movan tech— you and Connell…" She trailed off and Rune went back to describing the watch, but the mood shifted down a notch.

"By far your coolest features are these." He cleared his throat and pointed to a tiny silver sunburst. "This one stands for Light armor. During the day the watch will collect light energy from the sun and store it, sort of like the Treasta does. If the watch senses your life force is compromised—say you've been weakened in battle from using your gifts too much, or your thoughts and emotions are moving you too far toward Dark actions—the watch will send a blast of light energy wherever the concentration of darkness or evil is the worst."

Uncomfortable memories flooded Tolen's mind. "I've used that one before."

Rune grunted and pointed to another symbol, a silver oval. "This means it has a type of Treasta, only it does more than just detect the Dark and if it's coming your way. This reads the bioelectricity of everything within a half mile and can tell you the *type* of Dark creatures in that area." He chuckled at their obvious confusion and clarified. "It can decipher between Raksasha and Darkened, or any other type of demon. Rumors say the Fallen can scramble even bioelectrical waves, so I wouldn't trust it to tell us about them. But still, a great asset."

"I think the Treasta in the car can decipher between species too," Macy added.

Rune eyed the car. "Wouldn't surprise me. Makes sense actually. But the one in Tolen's watch is as mobile as we are."

I can do that too, Macy's thought pushed into Tolen's mind. She met his gaze for a split second. *I'll tell you later.*

"This one…" Rune pointed to a spiral symbol and Tolen worked on shifting his focus back to the lesson, but he wasn't the only one who was distracted. Macy kept sending images of her shard to Tolen's thoughts without realizing it. She'd seen something, but she was trying not to think about it. "…means this little button here on the side when activated can shield the wearer's bioelectricity and anyone standing within a few feet—good when you need to hide from other Movan tech."

"But by far this one is the coolest." He pointed out a solid silver triangle directly above the number twelve. "The triangle represents its bio-tracking capability. If by some chance Max has done something to these fake Relics—which wouldn't surprise me with his apparent love for Movan tech—and they store a piece of bioelectricity from the Descendants," He looked up with a grin, "then this watch can track them. We just need to put the signature into its core and tell it what to do."

"Seriously?" Tolen couldn't stop a grin.

Rune's own smile grew as he handed Tolen back the watch. "Seriously."

Macy's gaze stayed on her father's car as Tolen pulled his arm off her shoulders to refasten the watch to his wrist. Only now as it warmed against his skin did he realize the feeling of loss his life force had felt in its absence. "How do I activate them?"

Rune shrugged. "How did you activate the Light Armor?"

"I'm not sure exactly." Tolen thought back to both times he'd activated the watch. "The first time I'd lost control." His jaw clenched against the memory of almost killing Quasar. His anger and fear had caused his gifts to take over in order to save Tolen from a perceived threat. "The watch sent a blast of light into my face and I calmed down. The second time was when I was Daemon's prisoner. The shackles he had me in were blocking my gifts. I connected to my Dreamer ability, the watch sensed the darkness within me, and I directed the light energy through my shard and at the shackles. The surge of power was too much for the metal."

Rune's forehead creased and a swift burst of apprehension came from his life force when Tolen mentioned having a Dark gift, but he quickly stifled it. "You didn't have to do much more than consciously direct the power you felt."

"How does that work?" Tolen ran a finger over the symbols.

"Once you put on a Movan watch it syncs to your specific bioelectricity." Rune wiggled his eyebrows. "It communicates with your life force."

"Sort of like our Radia Shards." Macy stifled a yawn and dropped her chin in her hand. "So, how is bioelectricity different than what we feel in the Balance?"

Rune shifted on the bench. "Bioelectricity is species specific, not good or evil vibes—the things that effect the Balance. Get me? A Treasta senses the shifts in the balance of Dark or Light. But cells, tissue, use ion fluxes, or charged atoms, to communicate electronically, to function at their most basic purpose." He waved a hand at their dubious faces. "Humans only understand a fraction of what it really is. Only Movan, who can read and sync to the bioelectrical signals of every organism really get it. But it's tricky because everything is giving off electrical signals, even rocks and plant life. After centuries of work, Movan have managed to catalog it by species and put it into their most valuable tech—expensive tech."

"Dude, I had no idea you were so smart." Macy chuckled. "I only got, like, half of that."

"He's a genius." Keelyn said proudly.

Rune rolled his eyes, but Tolen knew she spoke the truth. He'd seen the evidence in Rune's mind and in flashes of his past. There was so much to this young man, more than Macy or even Keelyn knew. He hid a lot, and hid it well.

"What did you trade for it?" Rune asked Macy. "It must've been pretty significant."

"Nothing," Macy shrugged. "When we were in the Light Realm I wanted to get Tolen something for his birthday. Well, it's not like they have malls. Bastian suggested I meet with the Movan who serve there. I did, and they suggested the watch. I asked how much, but they wouldn't let me pay anything. Said it was an honor to aid the Ninth and all that."

"Huh, Light Movan must deal differently than those in this realm." Rune feigned nonchalance, but Tolen could sense underlying concern.

"Think your Watcher could have something similar?" Macy asked.

Rune's expression darkened. "Possibly. Tech like this is rare though— as smart as Movan are, only a handful have the skill and knowledge to put such a piece together."

"Does Toke?" Tolen asked.

"Definitely." Rune leaned back with his hands behind his head. "The Dark has been after him for years."

"How do we see if the fakes have bioelectrical signals?" Tolen reached for one of the fake Relics. His shard pulsed a combination of drive to move forward and warning. As helpful as using the watch could be, it was also extremely dangerous. If the Dark somehow got hold of this watch, with a link to every Descendant inside…he shuddered. He paused before his hand closed over the piece of fool's gold. "Is this a good idea? What if the Dark somehow gets the watch from me?"

Macy squeezed his fingers. "That's not going to happen."

Rune grabbed the fool's gold. "She's right. Besides, it's linked to your bioelectricity. It won't work for anyone else."

Tolen shook his head. "Anything can be hacked."

Rune sighed, glanced at Keelyn and held the fool's gold out to Tolen. "Yes, that's true. Even Movan tech can be hacked by a smarter Movan, but with all that's after us, it's the best, or at least the fastest, option we have." He motioned for Tolen to tap the triangle, "Focus your thoughts on the gold and the watch, imagine them combining, becoming one."

Tolen closed his eyes, focused on the stone in his hand, its rough texture, its glittering angles, the deception of its entire being, and imagined it melting into the watch, liquid gold seeping through the face and into the inner workings he couldn't even begin to understand.

Warmth flowed from his wrist, up his arm, and connected with his Watcher's eye. It shifted and behind his closed lid he saw an image of an old woman sitting on a porch, knitting needles swiftly moving, a flowing golden afghan growing across her lap. "I see a woman. She's knitting."

"Good, connect that image to the power you feel emanating from the watch."

Tolen tried to do what Rune asked. It took a moment, but then the watch dinged, and he knew he'd done it. Rune passed the other objects to his palm one at a time. Each time Tolen would get a flicker of the person, and push the image toward the watch. After each ding, Rune would pass him another one. When Rune finally said he was done, Tolen pulled back from the watch, opened his eyes, and pain lanced across his forehead. He pushed his thumbs against his temples. Heaviness weighed against his eyelids, a weakness in his muscles begged him to lie down on the ground and sleep.

"It'll pass." Rune put the fake Relics back in the bag and tightened the strings. "The watch accessed your gifts to connect to the bioelectricity in the fakes. When a Movan device forcefully triggers a gift its more draining. You'll get used to it with practice."

Tolen swallowed, unsure if he liked the idea of the watch accessing his gifts—it seemed sort of like a violation. It better be worth it.

"Tap that button and see if it catalogued them." Rune pointed to a tiny button above the triangle symbol.

Tolen did as he asked and a sort of shutter moved across the face of the watch changing the time hands to a screen, where eight little blue blips blinked along a squiggly line.

Rune pointed to the brightest blip. "This is you. The other dots are the signals of bioelectricity coming from the Descendants. Tap the nearest one to your blip."

Tolen tapped the blinking dot and words flashed across the screen. *Baskin Robbins, 1473 North Queensville, Ohio.*

"Looks like our Descendant likes ice cream." Rune smirked.

Macy smoothed out the map of the US. "We're not that far from Ohio. Should we get the Descendant first, or go to Arizona for Rune's device and then back track?"

"Let's ask the guy with the *sight*." Rune leaned across the table and thumped Tolen on the shoulder, a hint of a smile lifting the scar on his cheek.

CHAPTER 11

KINDLING

While the respite from the close interior of the car had been nice, it felt good to be back on the road. Tolen's head still ached so he was grateful that Macy wanted to continue driving. Rune's confidence in Tolen's sight, while reassuring, also made him nervous. The visions were there, but the intensity was different than just a few days ago. A dark haze of foreboding and doubt had settled over his Second Sight, making the images less vibrant, less clear. And with it came a fear that he was missing something. Something important had become lost in the haze and was waiting to be found.

His sight had shown him the Descendant in Ohio, he'd caught a glimpse of the young man's deepest concerns. He was waiting for Max, but could sense the Dark closing in. He was afraid, and ready to run—to where he did not know. Tolen decided they would go to him first—before he bolted, then head to Arizona. There were two more Descendants along the way they could stop and get, but for one, they'd never all fit in the car, as Macy kept pointing out. For two, they weren't sure what was going to happen when they went for this first one. This would be a chance to see if the Dark managed to track them again despite using the Treastas, as well as discover what kind of protections Max had placed around the Descendants.

His head throbbed and he pinched the bridge of his nose. He leaned against the window ledge and let the wind blow across his face.

Macy started musing about the government and the Fallen, but his eyes were getting heavy, the not-so-great night's sleep catching up to him.

He woke up just before noon when Macy's thoughts broke into his consciousness. She was thinking about him, assuming he was still asleep. He kept his eyes closed and let his mind flow with hers, a more peaceful place than his own thoughts had been, enjoying the feel of the love she had for him. It was shifting, strengthening every minute they were together.

He barely peeked at her to see a tiny smile playing around her lips, her dimple winking. Her thoughts were getting increasingly louder. She was thinking about his looks. The fact that he knew she liked what she saw was doing funny things to his insides. Her mind was completely open to him now.

She was contemplating the changes in their emotions, comparing them to a car—no surprise there.

Something's different between us—like shifted gears. Before, we were content to stay in first gear, get the lay of the land, find out where we were comfortable, kissing without setting each other on fire… Her memory of their first kiss passed through her mind and Tolen's stomach gave another funny flip. *It used to be just pleasant flame when he touched me, but now it feels more like a raging wildfire every time he barely brushes my skin. It's probably a good thing we haven't really kissed since we left the island. If he kissed me now, I would probably not just set him on fire, but everything surrounding us within a 10-mile radius.*

He shifted in his seat anxious, not because of what she was saying, but because of what she wasn't saying, what he could feel behind the words she was thinking. She wanted him to kiss her. And right now he wanted to. He really, *really* wanted to.

"Ugh, can you two please stop. I'm getting nauseous back here." Rune grunted from the back seat.

Tolen's eyes snapped open. Macy's cheeks reddened.

"Oh, leave them alone." Keelyn whispered through a yawn.

"Rein in your Cathe dude. We're not doing anything." Macy's teasing tone couldn't entirely hide her guilt and Rune laughed. Tolen couldn't hold back a smile of his own.

"That's the problem." Rune chuckled again. "It's only going to keep building and I don't know how much more I can take of it floating around in here."

Keelyn slugged his arm. "Stop."

"You know what? I think it's time for a stretch break." Tolen sat up. "Macy pull into that rest stop." She pulled the car off the highway into a rest stop advertising picnic areas and walkways. Only one car occupied the lot, its owners an older couple waiting for their dog to do its business.

Macy parked and Tolen ignored Rune's laughter as he got out and walked to Macy's door, took her hand and helped her out of the car.

"Hey, you two—" Tolen slammed the door before he could hear Rune's remarks. The hot summer sun bore down on them as he led Macy down one of the shady walkways, past the old couple, until the car was no longer visible through the trees.

He started with the intent of asking her about what she'd said she would tell him later, but curiosity couldn't compete with the heat pushing through his chest. He led her off the trail and deeper into the trees. "Rune's right."

"About what?" Her cheeks were still pink.

"You're driving me crazy."

"What?" Her eyebrows lifted and her green eyes flashed with hurt.

"I heard your thoughts in the car when you assumed I was asleep." Her eyes widened with embarrassment, but the look only increased the heat until it moved down his arms. "I've wanted to kiss you more times than I can count since we left the island. It keeps popping in my head when I should be focused on the mission, all the stuff we're *supposed* to be focused on. Trying to keep you out of my head, trying not to give in…it's driving me crazy." That desire to protect, to shield her from the world mixed with the other heat, the desire to kiss her, and intensified both desires until he couldn't hold back his hand. Tolen touched her cheek which was the wrong thing to do. Heat trailed from his fingers the moment they met her skin and began to glow with inner light.

He leaned down until his lips met hers and the flame that ignited thrilled and terrified him. She seemed to melt into his embrace. He wasn't sure how it happened but one moment they were standing in the shade, the next her back was against a tree, her hands in his hair. They were glowing and he couldn't care who saw, what creatures they drew to them.

"It's time to go you two." Rune's tone no longer held even a hint of teasing.

Their glow flickered out like a blown fuse. Tolen dropped his hands and stepped back, horrified and humiliated.

"I'm driving." Rune started back to the car, slowly. "Macy you're in back with Keelyn."

Macy's cheeks were bright red. Her emotions as tangled as Tolen's. Desire still flowed between them, mixed with embarrassment, and for him, a rising, sickening guilt.

No they hadn't set anything on fire, but the flame they'd kindled was far more dangerous.

o o o

"Don't you think it's weird how if one girl has to pee, so does every girl she's with?" Rune watched the girls head into the gas station, a look of frustrated worry on his face as he pumped gas into the car.

Tolen shrugged, leaned back against the single tree planted a few feet from the ancient pump, and closed his eyes waiting, uncomfortably, for Rune to start in on the lecture. A trickle of warmth surged across his skin, his life force connected to the tree, and he heard a soft baritone voice in his mind.

Hello Mindra.

Hello. Tolen replied.

You travel with Light. You must protect her—

"You know," Rune interrupted the tree's warning. "When I was giving you two crap about your annoying lovey-dovey hormones, I wasn't expecting you to take me literally. You really need to reign it in."

Tolen kept his eyes closed but his face warmed.

"She's only sixteen. You need to wait until she turns eighteen and transcends, at least, before you start down that road."

Tolen gritted his teeth. "I have *no* intention of doing anything regarding her virtue until I've sealed all the right promises."

"Look, I really don't want to lecture a guy on making out with his girl, but you were out of control and you know it. You two were swimming in happy pheromones. I could feel it in the car, and the moment you guys left it was like a trail leading right to you. Strong enough it wouldn't take a Cathe to sense it. The Balance was saturated with it." He replaced the pump and twisted the gas cap shut. "I'm not saying that just to give you crap. Whether what you were doing or thinking was *virtuous*—I had no idea people actually used that word anymore—or not isn't what's affecting the Balance. It's the *power* behind what you feel."

Rune sighed. "You said my feelings for Keelyn are too strong to block in my thoughts. Love works the same way within the Balance. It has an incredibly powerful signal. It can become so strong that it can't be blocked, just as the most evil of creatures can't hide their darkness from affecting the Balance." He leaned against the car. "The more you fuel it, the stronger its signal gets until you won't be able to shield it." He held his hands in front of him.

Tolen picked at the bottom of his shirt. "I don't know how…to stop."

Rune offered an understanding nod. "I'll tell you what I do with Keelyn. Think of her like a puppy. You pick it up and it's just so cute you want to squeeze it, but you don't because you know it could kill it."

"Are you really using a puppy analogy?" Tolen tried for light sarcasm, but Rune's words were cutting him deep.

Rune's eyes hardened before he glanced back at the station. "Your feelings for her have reached a point where they're powerful enough to shift the Balance. If you continue to allow that love to flow from you— too much joy or elation, or adolescent yearnings, whatever you want to call it—it's like squeezing the puppy too hard, and the next time you are in battle with Dark Creatures, and she is with you, and you haven't learned to contain your emotions, they will instantly turn on her. The greatest way to destroy someone is to take away their reason for existing. They will know through the shift in the Balance that to destroy *you*, they only need to kill *her*."

Tolen swallowed hard. "I've heard that warning before and I know it's true, but. . ." He blew out a loud breath. "Is that why you hold back your feelings from Keelyn? To protect her? Because it doesn't seem like you're doing her any favors by lying to yourself and to her."

Rune took a step forward. "You have no idea what you're talking about Tolen. Don't think for one second I care less for Keelyn than you do for Macy. You don't know what I've seen, what I know. When you've seen the Dark use love against their prey time and time again, when you can sense how every emotion—good or bad—affects the Balance, you learn to protect, not *project* your feelings."

"Rune, really, I'm sorry. I didn't mean to offend. I was honestly just curious. It's something I've been struggling with since I first realized I was in love with Macy." He dropped his head back against the tree. "You're one hundred percent right. My ignorance has put Macy at risk more times than I want to admit. The Dark already knows how I feel about her. She's a target because of me."

"Dude, not *just* because of you." Rune's pale blue eyes held knowledge beyond his years. "You know exactly what I mean. She's different. We all sensed it the first time we met her, I'm sure every Dark creature she's ever faced has sensed it. Maybe it's because she's Light's Aid like she said, and maybe not."

Unable to argue, Tolen whispered. "Even more reason to get my feelings under control. The less attention she gets the better. But it isn't just adolescent hormones." His face warmed again. "There's something else. Something *other* that pulls me to her. It's beyond my love for her, it feels even beyond the prophecy. It gets tangled up with my feelings for her and intensifies everything, and I mean everything. My every emotion is heightened when I'm around her. It used to just be my gifts that surged when she was around, now," he shook his head, "It's so much more." His cheeks warmed again.

"Well there's that combined destiny thing you two got going and she's less than two years from Transcendence, maybe that has something to do with it."

"Maybe." Tolen swallowed against the fear that crawled from his chest to his throat.

"Virtue?" Rune chuckled and the mood lightened *slightly*.

Tolen lifted his shoulder. "It's what my mother called it."

Rune tipped his head with a trace of a smirk, "And isn't your mother like a thousand years old?"

"Touché." The corner of Tolen's mouth twitched. "But at least she raised me right."

Rune chuckled again as the girls walked out of the station arm-in-arm—Keelyn leaning just a little too much on Macy—his eyes softening as he took in the scene. "As much as I'd like to, I can't argue with that." He rushed forward to take over guiding Keelyn whose complexion was even grayer than just minutes ago. Every hour more of her light faded.

He thought of Rune's Cathe, him being able to sense how every emotion affects the Balance. If that were true, then he must know what Keelyn feels for him—he must know that she loves him too. Then why hold back? He stifled the desire to search deeper into Rune's past. If the Balance showed it to him, then that meant there was something he was supposed to do for Rune, as the Ninth. If he went searching for it, it would be an intrusion. If Rune wanted Tolen to know, he would tell him. The flash of Rune's possible future hit his sight and he took a slow breath. That future was something he would do all he could to change, Ninth or not.

He'd first thought it strange how intense Macy's feelings were toward these two, that they could have such a strong bond after knowing one another for such a short amount of time. But the longer he was with them the more his own feelings intensified. Rune and Keelyn were *good* and motivated by only that goodness. There was no thought of glory or reward for the sacrifices they made every day to protect the human race. While the desire to protect them wasn't nearly as powerful as it was to protect Macy, it was still stronger than he'd felt toward anyone else. Different, and vastly important. Whether it was because they too were part of the prophecy as members of the eight, or something else, he wasn't sure. But there *was* something there, something he couldn't explain.

As Macy returned to her place in the back seat, she met his eyes, her cheeks pink, and Tolen knew he had to do something about his feelings—but this time he and Macy would talk about it, not act on it.

CHAPTER 12

THE FIRST DESCEN-DANT

AROUND FOUR O'CLOCK they pulled into Queensville, Ohio. Macy had traded off with Rune to drive a couple of hours ago. What had happened between her and Tolen was embarrassing, and a little bit scary. When she'd suggested Rune take shotgun while she drove so Tolen could get some sleep, Tolen didn't argue. She knew he felt the same as she did. That a little distance would probably be a good thing moving forward. Her and Rune had enjoyed casual conversation while Keelyn and Tolen both slept for the remainder of the drive.

"Think we need to have Tolen check where he's at?" She asked Rune as they passed the city limits sign.

Rune reached back to pinch Tolen's leg. "We just entered the town, you wanna check and see where he's at?"

Another check in the rearview and she saw Keelyn sit up and rub her eyes and Tolen yawn while checking his watch. "He's still at the Baskin Robbins. He must work there."

It took them a few minutes to locate the business in an under construction street mall smashed between a tiny grocery store and a run-down pawn shop. They pulled into the crowded lot and parked next to a beat up yellow Volkswagen Bug, and a sweet, cherry red, 1965 Ford Mustang.

"You guys feel that?" Rune paused with his fingers on the door handle.

A subtle thrumming, like a mirage hiding the truth behind it, barely swayed in the Balance. Almost undetectable.

"I can't feel the kid's life force or access his thoughts." Tolen leaned forward. "Max's protection?"

Rune grunted. "Let's hope that's the extent of it. I say we get some ice cream, make sure the guy is really here." He hopped out of the passenger seat and popped the seat forward for Tolen and Keelyn to get out. Macy eyed the 'Stang as the four of them walked into the building waiting for Tolen, but he went around the other way, and she ended up rushing to catch up.

Rune held the door open for her and Keelyn, Tolen had already gone in. Rune wiggled his eyebrows as she passed. Macy paused long enough to elbow him in the ribs. A grunt, then a chuckle, and he followed them inside the cool interior.

Once inside, the thrumming in the Balance increased to a persistent hum that quickly became annoying. Macy had a strange desire to leave and forget she'd ever seen the place. She looked at the others to see lines between their eyes as if scrunched because of the noise. Rune stuck a finger in his ear and wiggled.

She shook her head and looked around. White covered everything in the little shop: the floors, the countertops, the tables, chairs, even the cash register. The only color came from the menu board, the workers' pink shirts and blue aprons, and the barrels of ice cream under the glass covered display.

Tolen tilted his chin toward a young man behind the counter wearing a name-tag on his blue apron that said River Hok'ee. Tall, thin, dark hair and eyes, high cheekbones, prominent nose—likely Native American heritage.

River did a double-take as they walked up to the counter. His eyes kept flicking to Macy as they placed their orders, and after they each got their ice cream he continued to shoot glances her way where they sat at a table near the door. Tolen sat across from her, and had not-so-discreetly placed his chair in the guy's direct line of sight. To see Macy, he had to move all the way to the end of the counter, which he managed to find reason to do more than once.

The line between Tolen's eyebrows deepened the longer they were here. Macy began to doubt it was the weird hum in the Balance causing his scowl from the looks he kept shooting at River and was surprised to find she kinda liked jealous Tolen.

"That noise has passed annoying to downright obnoxious. Can we just grab him now?" Rune whispered over his double-decker of Rocky Road, snapping Macy out of her thoughts.

"No, let's wait for him to get off and follow him home." Tolen stuck his spoon in the chocolate side of his banana split. "Fewer witnesses."

"Fine. But eat fast. I want some distance from that sound." Rune took a big bite off the top of his ice cream.

"You do realize it's coming from River so it's probably going to come right along with us." Keelyn picked the cherry off her sundae and licked away the whip cream as Rune groaned, her eyes on the family two tables over, a tiny smile lifting her cheeks. Purple tinged under her eyes despite her long nap, and unless the florescent lights in the building were playing tricks on Macy's eyes, her skin had a grayish tint to it. Macy took a bite of her cookies and cream and tried not to think about it.

Despite Rune's annoyance, they took their time finishing their treats before heading back out to the car to wait. Macy and Keelyn in back, Tolen and Rune in front.

Two hours later Rune's complaining became more obnoxious than the buzzing. "It's hot in here. He better not be working until closing." Rune dropped his head onto the seat back.

"If you plan to whine the entire time be prepared to have all that pretty hair singed off." Macy lifted her head off the seat to glare at Rune before resuming her position, head back, eyes on the ceiling, trying not to think.

"Aw, you think I'm pretty?" He thumped her foot where it sat against his seat.

"Shut up."

She wished Tolen would talk to her. She knew he could hear her thoughts by the occasional glance he would send her way, but he was choosing to ignore them. Was he mad at her for wanting to kiss him? Or…maybe he was mad at the thoughts that had shot through her mind in the heat of the moment. Surely he had heard them. But, didn't he know she would have never, could have never let it go that far? Her thoughts rushed back over the kiss, the intense emotion she'd experienced that had seemed to take on a life of its own.

Bastian had raised her with the values of the Light. They taught that physical intimacy was a gift meant to be shared between husband and wife who had made all the promises and links to one another set in the Book of Light's Decree. He'd made it sound so important, so beautiful and precious. Those promises, which she'd never questioned, would wait until she was married to go down that road.

But it's not like she'd had a lot of dating opportunities as a Chosen. Tolen was really the first person she'd ever even been attracted to in that way, and when she met him she never dreamed he'd be the one she'd want to make those kinds of promises to. But that's exactly what had happened, and she did want to be with him, and only him, forever.

She didn't realize her eyes had moved off the ceiling to stare at Tolen's profile until he flashed a look her way.

"I'm going to check around the building again. You guys stay here." Tolen left without asking if she wanted to come.

Rune chuckled.

"What?" Macy folded her arms across her stomach.

"Poor guy." Rune shook his head side to side.

"What's that supposed to mean?" Heat pushed toward her hands but she pulled it back.

Rune lifted his palms up. "Nothing. But, you might want to reign in those thoughts of yours so he can focus on what he's supposed to be doing."

"You have no idea what I'm thinking." She leaned back against the seat, resisting the urge to let the heat come to her fingertips, just enough to singe his eyebrows.

Rune shrugged but it was Keelyn who replied, her eyes fixated out the window. "Rune usually knows what people are feeling often before they recognize it themselves." Her voice trailed off.

Macy repressed a snort. "Freaking Cathes."

Rune turned back around. "Takes one to know one."

She was both annoyed and intrigued. Cathes were extremely rare, especially among humans. Maybe she did have some of the gene in her, maybe not. Either way it wasn't as attuned as Rune's seemed to be. Cathes were known to be volatile, smacked with emotions from all sides of the Balance, none of which belonged to them. It was a lot to process. It also explained why Rune was so protective of Keelyn—he would sense her innocence, her purity. It also meant he knew how much Keelyn loved him, and from the downward turn of her mouth, she knew he knew. But he wouldn't act on it. Why?

Focus on the mission, Macy. The Dark is nearby.

Macy glanced out the windows as her Watcher's voice entered her mind. The sun had lowered behind the wall of businesses, casting the parking lot in blessed shade. The traffic had lightened considerably, the number of cars coming and going from the lot getting fewer. People walked up and down the sidewalks hardly aware of each other. A typical city night. *Bastian?* Her eyes flicked to the screen on the dash. *The Treasta doesn't show anything.*

You are relying on technology—it may be good, but it is not perfect, turn your focus to your life force. Trust the gifts the Light has given you. Focus.

As Bastian's voice trailed off Macy pushed her palms together in her lap and closed her eyes, allowing the Kuna to flow back into her hands. *Focus.* Push aside the thoughts of kissing Tolen, the worry for Keelyn, the curiosity for Rune, the stress of the mission. *Focus.*

The thrumming in the Balance increased as if the shield were being tested. And then there it was. Subtle, the tiniest of ripples, a separate powerful shield trying to block it, but with a tiny chink, a single tear in the armor—immense power hiding behind the veil. The Dark was close. Incredibly close and gaining.

"Crap! We're so stupid. We should have got the device first!" She pushed on Rune's seat, "Let me out!"

"What are you freakin' about?" Rune yawned.

"We led the Dark right to a Relic and a Descendant! They're almost here! I gotta get Tolen!"

Rune jumped out and popped the seat forward. "Use your shard!"

"I don't know how!"

"Didn't your Watcher—" The panic must have been obvious on her face because he quickly added, "Never mind, I'll do it."

Prickles rose on Macy's arms. *The Fallen.* "No, Rune! Wait!"

Too late, she saw his shard light up and the ripple in the Balance rolled into a monstrous wave.

Tolen came sprinting around the building. "You guys feel that?"

"We're in big trouble." Macy rushed to his side.

"Rune, go around to the back door. Macy and I will take the front." Tolen's hands trembled as Keelyn climbed out of the back seat, he glanced over her chalky pallor. "Keelyn, go in and lure the kid out any way you can."

Rune paused long enough to ask, "Tolen, what are they?"

Tolen tapped his watch. "It says Darkened."

"Which means Fallen." Rune's face paled.

Macy dived back in the passenger seat and started tapping on the keyboard.

"What are you doing?" Tolen asked.

"The car's got a self-defense mode. I've just got to set it, up." She could sense their impatience—just a few more taps. "Done! Keelyn, just get the kid to the car, we'll hold off whatever's coming. He should be safe once you get him inside."

"Too late!" Rune rushed forward as another sleek black car—identical to the one that had chased them from Whisper—screeched into the lot and skidded to a stop right in front of the shop doors, blocking both entrance and exit.

CHAPTER 13

IMPROVISE

"RUNE WAIT!" TOLEN's blue eye flashed showing him a flicker of the future. "Take Keelyn, go through the back, get the kid. Macy and I will draw the Dark."

Rune yanked his sword from the weapons bag and tossed Keelyn her bow and arrows. Tolen tried not to worry whether she'd have the strength to use them as they ran the length of the mall to the back.

Tolen wanted to grab Macy's hand but with Rune's reminder still fresh in his mind he only beckoned her to follow him.

"Tolen! The humans!" A few people in the parking lot had paused to watch the screeching car, and now four teens ran across the lot, one carrying a glowing sword.

Tolen's palms tingled as he called his gifts to the surface, visualized what he wanted, and pushed the power from his body.

"*Vin'akra, win'tashta, tin'ruhl!*" A powerful gust of wind swirled into the lot carrying dust and bits of debris. He twisted his fingers as he ran and a fire hydrant across from the building burst open, flooding the lot. Another twist of the fingers and the water increased in pressure, hitting a pile of dirt heaped high by construction crews sending mud everywhere and successfully distracting the parking lots occupants.

They neared the black car as its doors opened. The driver stepped out first—a woman clad in skin-tight black leather, black army boots, and an ankle length black jacket. A black scarf covered her head and face. She took in the mess in the parking lot before looking toward them. Tolen's steps slowed when he saw her eyes. Light sapphire blue, almost translucent, *Watcher's eyes*, but it was the malice in them that caused his steps to falter.

Her companions climbed out of the car. A brunette woman and three men with hair varying shades of gray. All dressed in black. The brunette and one of the men also had Watcher's eyes. Both Fallen? Thankfully no Gungruin disguised as Connell this time. The other two men must have been the Darkened. A hint of gray tinged their skin. Their eyes were flat black, no whites. When they saw Tolen and Macy they bared their mossy, rotten teeth.

"Gross." Macy stopped beside Tolen, her feet planted, her hands out front, the heat building in her body swirling around them.

The woman with the scarf laughed. "Ah, two little Chosen." She flicked her gloved hand and the Darkened men walked forward.

"Do Darkened have powers?" Tolen whispered.

"I guess they could if they were once Chosen…but I don't intend on waiting to find out."

The woman and the other Fallen moved to where a group of patrons were trying to squeeze past the car to get out of the building. Tolen twisted his fingers and a burst of wind slammed the door shut. Scarf woman put her hand on the glass and shoved until the glass shattered. She and her companions forced people to the side and started walking through the gaping metal frame.

The Darkened sashayed closer. The smell of eucalyptus and roses filled the air and Macy flicked her wrists. Both creatures went down one after another, each with a hole burned through their chests.

Scarf face paused and looked back, her eyes narrowed. She hardly spared a glance at her dead Darkened as she fingered the shard around her neck. The other Fallen returned to flank her sides and did the same as scarf face spoke. "There's a hefty price on your head, little Chosen."

Tolen's hands trembled. He tried to read their thoughts but he couldn't sense a single thing. Scarf's gaze flashed to his face. "I see your eyes young one—*Ninth Chosen*." She tilted her head at Macy.

Tolen heard a whispered voice echoed from Macy's thoughts at the same moment he felt a funny pulse from her shard.

You cannot win. Give up now and I will spare your friends. Join us Chosen one. We will show you the true power of that shard you wear.

Macy's hands trembled and she took a step toward them, then glanced at her own feet, as if surprised at what she'd done.

A flash in the corner of Tolen's eye had him glancing right to see Keelyn and Rune running at a crouch, using the water rushing from the hydrant as cover. The boy, River, ran between them.

Scarf's head whipped to the side and she pointed a black device at Rune and Keelyn, "Stop!"

They both stopped in their tracks as if something had taken control of their limbs, but River's body began to shimmer out of focus.

The driver's side door of the yellow bug swung open and the old engine coughed to a start. A few rev's and it took off, seemingly without a driver. River had escaped—for now.

Scarf watched Rune with an odd expression in her eyes. Tolen nudged Macy's arm and pointed his chin toward the Barracuda.

You want me to get the car? Her voice filled his mind and he nodded.

She ran at the same time Tolen headed for Rune and Keelyn while twisting his fingers, raising a wall of mud and water between them and the Fallen.

Scarf face waved the device again and a tube-like opening, large enough for her party to pass through, broke through the wall of muddy water. Her eyes fixated on Rune.

She would reach them first.

"Ah, it is you." She sounded amused.

Rune's eyes narrowed in anger and she grinned. "Surprised to see me? Believed me dead?" Her hand dropped to her hip. "It's no use fighting us, Rune. You know I always get what I want."

Rune's jaw flexed. "Not always."

Her grin twisted into a scowl. Tolen focused on breaking the power holding Rune and Keelyn in place. It felt like a wall of stone, blocking his gifts. He pushed hard against the force until he finally felt it crack.

Rune grunted and stepped left to shield Keelyn from the Fallen.

Scarf face laughed, "As sensitive as ever. Always protecting the weak."

Tolen heard the roar of the Barracuda coming to life. The group of Fallen jumped left as it screeched to a halt between them. Tolen, Rune, and Keelyn dived in on top of each other and Macy squealed out of the lot. A jumble of limbs, it took several seconds before Rune was in back with Keelyn and Tolen buckled himself in the passenger seat.

A check over his shoulder showed the Fallen dragging the dead Darkened into their own car. They'd be following in seconds. "Step on it Macy!"

The car growled as she shifted gears. "Which way did he go?"

Tolen tapped his watch and saw the blip showing River just ahead. "Left on Main Street."

"He won't get far in that old car." Macy pressed her foot to the floor and swerved around and through the light evening traffic.

Soon the rusty Bug appeared in front of them, black smoke billowing from the tail-pipe.

"If he pushes that thing any harder it's gonna blow." Macy pulled the car up to his passenger side as close as possible. River had rematerialized. "Hey, kid! KID!"

River looked over and his face blanched. It sounded like he tried to speed up but the car only blew more black smoke.

"Pull over! We're not going to hurt you!"

More black smoke, a sputter, and steam hissed out the trunk lid. He pulled over to the side of the road, jumped out, and started to run, his image shimmering again.

"Seriously?" Macy squealed to a stop. "Come on!"

Tolen jumped out, shouted "*Mignata!*" and took off, pushing the strength surging from his life force to his legs. He caught up with River before he reached the sidewalk. The guy was as tall as Tolen. He moved to wrap his arms around him just as another set of beefy hands gripped River's neck. Seconds later he fell limp against Tolen's chest.

"What did you do?" Tolen asked as Rune tossed River over his shoulder.

"He'll be fine. He'll have one heck of a headache when he wakes up, but he'll be fine."

"Hurry!" Macy shouted through the window.

Rune shoved River in the back beside Keelyn, and dived in. Tolen barely had the door shut before Macy hit the gas.

The black car skidded around the corner and Tolen's hands tingled. "They're coming."

"Let's hope we got a drop of NOS left." Macy pushed the red button but there was no burst of speed. "Empty! Tolen do your thing!"

Tolen put his hands out the window. The black car weaved in between traffic. Gaining. They passed a landscape company with large rocks on display out front. He twisted his fingers and one of the rocks rolled out into the street. The car—going too fast—plowed right into it.

Once back on the highway Tolen released his tense grip on the door and tried to calm his racing nerves. "How long will River be out?"

Rune sighed. "Could be awhile." He stowed his sword and Keelyn's bow back above the seat. "Well, at least we know which Relic the kid's got."

"*Dicernan*—unseen." Macy pushed her sweaty hair off her face. "I didn't know it would work like that. It must be some sort of self-defense thing. If he feels threatened it activates."

"Which means he's carrying it with him. *Dufus*." Rune leaned his head back.

"Was that Sorsha?" Tolen used the collar of his shirt to wipe the sweat from his eyes.

"Yeah." Anger and frustration laced Rune's tone. "Which means I was right. Treasta or no Treasta, she's been tracking me since we left the island."

"Or tracking my shard." Macy fingered her necklace. "She talked in my head again. Saying she could show me its real power."

Tolen waved his hand. "It doesn't matter how she's doing it. It just means we have to assume she's always going to be one step behind us. I also think we need to be careful about connecting too much to our shards—just in case." Tolen clenched his fists in his lap. *There's a hefty price on your head, little Chosen.* Had she meant both of them, or just Macy? A growing dread in his heart seemed to answer for him.

"We need to get to Arizona." Rune growled from the back seat. "That device is the only chance we've got to hide from *her.*"

"She really is bad isn't she?" Macy whispered.

Tolen could feel her fear as she too thought of Sorsha's power over her, the way she seemed to know too much about them. The heat increased in his palms and he had to take three slow breaths to calm down.

"You have no idea," Rune said softly.

"Maybe you need to tell us a little more about her, so we know what we're up against," Macy suggested gently.

"It's a long story."

"We've got a long drive ahead," she prodded.

Tolen agreed knowing more about Sorsha may help, but knowing what he did about Rune, and his possible future, it didn't seem like the time to push. Rune needed to reveal when he was ready. He reached over to grab Macy's hand, get her attention so he could send her a signal to wait, but Rune's panicked shout had Tolen spinning in his seat.

Rune shook Keelyn, but her head only flopped to the side. "Keelyn!"

Macy pulled onto the shoulder. Tolen placed one hand over Keelyn's heart, the other on her head, "*Lonadras chan'ta. Vast don da'bay,* Keelyn. *Chan'ta.*" His heart thudded in his throat as the warmth left his palms and seemed to hit a wall just before it could enter into Keelyn's body. He pushed harder, sweat beaded on his upper lip. *Come on Keelyn, let it in!*

Rune's pain was palpable as the seconds ticked by. "Come on kiddo, wake up." He urged with a crack in his voice.

A line of heat finally broke free of the wall and shot into Keelyn, but it was a small trickle, a tiny flame of healing. Tolen sat back, knowing it wasn't enough, but…Keelyn's eyes fluttered. A tiny cough.

"Wha—what happened."

"You passed out." Rune tucked her hair behind her ear.

Macy met Tolen's eyes, and the terror there told him she knew. Keelyn hadn't passed out. They'd lost her, for those few seconds she'd really been gone. What Macy didn't know, what Tolen did, is that Rune's voice had broken through the wall and allowed the tiny bit of healing inside. Somehow, his plea had called her back.

Tolen put his shaking hands on his lap. His blue eye started dilating again showing him flashes of future and past that sent his stomach plummeting into the vicinity of his sneakers. Sorsha…Rune…Keelyn… "Change of plans. We can't go to Arizona yet."

Rune met Tolen's eyes in the rear-view mirror. His face was drawn, all earlier humor forgotten, resignation taking its place. "Where are we going?"

"We're going to find Jonas."

CHAPTER 14

WHEN ONE BECOMES TWO

THE PRISONER SHIFTED on the blanketed wooden frame that served as his bed, watching the single star that winked from the tiny window above him. A pinprick of light in the coming night that brought with it an image of his daughter, pushing against the wall he'd constructed within his mind. The tactics used for the last ten years to control his thoughts and memories were no longer working. He tried again, begging his deprived physical needs to overtake his thoughts. The rumbling stomach, the craving for sunlight, the desire for running water and clean skin. He focused on his empty stomach and the one thing he'd allowed himself to wish for all these years—a big juicy cheeseburger.

He remembered the smell of the thick meat, grilled to perfection, the feel of his teeth sinking into the soft bun.

Daddy, can I have a bite?

He grabbed the sides of his head and pulled his hair. *Stop.*

But she was there, giggling in his memory as he flipped burgers on the grill, dancing on her tip-toes as he piled a bun high with her single favorite trimming, pickles and more pickles. Sitting on his lap as they ate, the sunlight danced in her eyes, across her pink cheeks, and highlighted the tiny dimple beside her mouth.

He bit down hard on his lip drawing blood, dragged his chipped fingernails across his arms, focusing only on the pain as the skin tore. A moan escaped his lips, but it was working. He dropped to the floor, his knees slamming onto the warped and splintered wood.

A sound cut into his ears. Someone was coming. They paused beside the table where his guard sat, he could just see the tips of their dirty boots under the edge from his spot on the floor.

"What do you want?" His guard asked.

"New arrival." A grating voice replied.

"So?"

"So, he goes in with the other one."

"This scum was to remain in solitary. No contact with other prisoners."

"Things change."

"Says who?"

"Says Soveryn. You gonna challenge him?"

"Soveryn is here?"

The prisoner's head snapped up. Soveryn. The leader of the Fallen. Here. *He knows.* His heart thrummed behind his bruised ribs. The time had come. He would fight them. Fight them until they had no choice but to kill him.

A grunt and the sound of metal clanking against metal. He pushed to his feet, curled his hands into claws, poised to attack, and allowed the hate to pool in his extremities.

The heavy door grated open. Two Darkened walked in, took in his stance and dropped a nearly unconscious man to the floor to block the attack. But the prisoner's gaze had fallen to the man on the floor. His knees wobbled and he fell down beside the newcomer.

The tallest Darkened laughed, kicked him in the ribs once for good measure, the second spat on the floor by his head, then they left.

The prisoner dragged himself closer to the newcomer. The beaten man lifted his head. His swollen face was covered in blood and bruises, but the purple hair, the tiny tattoo beside his orange-brown eye were all achingly familiar.

"Toke?"

The tiniest of smiles lit Toke's damaged face. "Hey Max. Nice to see you alive."

CHAPTER 15

OLD FRIENDS

Forrest Bastian landed beneath a tall coconut tree. The sand beneath his feet glittered blue in the light from the rising moon as he tucked the tiny jewel beneath his robes—a gift from his friend that allowed him to come to this hidden place. He glided forward, his wings pulled tight against his back, his sandaled feet barely shifting the sand. The guards in the trees above watched him, their emotions clear on their faces. Fear. Concern. What would bring a Guardian *here*?

What indeed?

He nodded up at them and continued on the barely discernible path. He approached the tiny hut, waved to the young Hawaiian man standing sentry, and entered through the slatted door.

The ravaged man sitting on a chair inside looked up from the book in his lap. "Bastian?" His single sapphire eye widened with shock.

"Nahmala."

"Wh—?"

Bastian raised a palm and Nahmala closed his ruined mouth. Heaviness settled over the hut, blocking their voices and thoughts from the people outside. Bastian walked forward and placed his hand on the sitting man's shoulder. "It is good to see you my friend."

Nahmala motioned for Bastian to take the seat opposite him and laid his book on a side table. "And you."

"I do not have much time." Bastian looked over his friend. "Nor do you."

Nahmala sighed. "Being a Guardian has its drawbacks."

"It does."

"How is your ward?"

Bastian took a slow breath. "Still unaware."

"And you believe this is wise?"

"For now."

"I…" Nahmala folded his hand over the stump of his left arm, "will not disagree with you. You are her Watcher, but between her trip to the Shadow Realm, and the events on the island, the Dark will have deciphered she is no mere Chosen. You knew it the moment you received the call to find her, I knew it the moment she first showed up in my thoughts. Add that to the task given her by the Seraph and she is in far more danger than ever before."

Bastian stood and began to pace. "The danger is greater than either of us had thought. Darsapean means to release Legion, and Soveryn will lead it to them."

What little color there was in Nahmala's melted features drained away. "Legion…" He ran his good hand over his face. "Is Soveryn tracking them through Rune?"

Bastian paused and faced Nahmala. "Partly. As his fear for Keelyn grows there are moments his anger opens the connection, but he has mastered his emotions better than he realizes. They are mostly following Macy. Now that her shard is united with the more powerful Watcher half, my half, she cannot fully shield its strength. Soveryn is using that tiny link to track her."

"Soveryn has done well at deceiving us. Blocking our Sight." Nahmala fingered the blackened shard at his throat. "I did not see him until my fate crossed with Rune's."

Bastian looked down at his sandaled feet and nodded. "Nor did I see him until he began to actively pursue Macy. The task of hunting her once belonged to Daemon, but his failure to bring Darsapean into the earth realm has lowered his favor with the Dark King. Daemon has been demoted to recruiting demons and building the army. The hunt has been handed over to Soveryn which allowed me to see him in her future. As the leader of the Fallen he has many assets and connections." His hands twitched beneath his robes. For so long he had tried to protect his ward, tried to save her from a possible fate that had haunted him from the day he found her—the closer Soveryn got to her, the closer he was to failure. He had to trust Tolen, he had to trust what little he understood of the prophecy.

Nahmala shook his head slowly. "Which means Daemon will be even more intent on catching her first, to regain his honor. Soveryn's intent is clear then?"

Bastian's fingers twitched. "That he is after Macy, yes, and not just because the Dark believes she will lead them to the Relics."

"I have seen that he still desires Tolen, as well as Rune, by his side as well."

"Yes, there is a connection." Bastian returned to pacing the small hut. His wings fluttered, stirring up a puff of dust from the wooden floor. "This…connection…is why I am here. Soveryn's presence remains veiled from other Watchers, even those among the Guardians. Right now, only you and I *see* glimpses of him because of our bond to Rune and Macy." The muscles in his back tightened. "There is something I did not discover until Soveryn appeared in Macy's future. I still do not fully understand and neither do my brothers on the Guardian council. We have petitioned the Light, but so many things are in motion. Free will cannot be interfered with." He stopped and stood in front of Nahmala. "There is more to the prophecy, a hidden piece that will soon be brought to the open—if my Sight can be trusted in times such as these—a truth that could change the tide of the war."

He eyed the broken man before him, not wanting to ask, but knowing he must. "Keelyn will leave this world in a matter of days. Tolen has seen it—as well as what will happen to Rune if she dies. He is taking them to Jonas in the hopes that he will know how to heal her. I cannot see the outcome. But the Relics, the Descendants, the Pact, and Macy's path forward cannot be ignored. The Dark is gaining too much ground. They must not get the Relics—and it is too dangerous for Macy to go after them alone. She needs Tolen's protection, Rune's strength, *and*

Keelyn's light. I can think of no other way." His jaw clenched and he pulled in a breath between his teeth.

For a moment Nahmala watched the trees blowing in the breeze out the window. He took in a deep breath of ocean air. "You need not ask my friend. I see what you need of me, and there is no other way. It will be done."

Bastian gripped Nahmala's hand waiting for his friend to meet his eyes. "It will be more than just a risk to those you protect. It goes much deeper. Are you certain?"

Peaceful resignation twinkled in Nahmala's sapphire eye. "Yes. Perhaps when it is done, it will have been enough." He fingered the black shard again.

Moisture pooled in Bastian's eyes, blurring his vision. "Your physical body may mirror your past mistakes my dear friend, but the marks upon your life force have long since faded. As a Guardian I can assure you of that." He squeezed Nahmala's fingers. "Thank you."

Nahmala tipped his head. "What of you?"

Bastian straightened up, his hands clenched by his sides. "I must hunt Soveryn."

Nahmala's fingers stopped twisting the shard and curled into a fist around it. "But with the growing darkness, you cannot stay in the earth realm long enough to fulfill a task such as that."

"I am the *only* one who can."

Guilt and shame covered Nahmala's face, but Bastian gripped his shoulder. "The path forward requires much from us both. There is purpose to everything. I will do my part and you will do yours. One purpose is not more or less than the other. It is as you once taught me: there comes a time in every Being's life when they will be asked to sacrifice something great for the sake of something greater."

CHAPTER 16

OUT OF SIGHT OUT OF MIND

"Jonas is no longer in the Light Realm, then?" Macy reached for the knob to turn down the air conditioning, her eyes focused on the strip of asphalt beneath them. Light slashed across the road in long ribbons between the trees as the sun dipped toward the horizon, but the summer's evening had lost its heat. The momentary joy from escaping the Fallen again, and getting River and the Relic had become lost to the shadows.

Tolen shoved his arm behind his head, a makeshift pillow, his eyes drooped and his voice came out low, exhausted. "I saw him in another forest. It didn't match the one in the Light Realm. Based on the position of the sun and the types of trees, I don't *think* it's too far away."

She squeezed his shoulder once before putting both hands back on the wheel. "So what's your plan? And what do we do about the kid?" If Tolen had thought of a way to save Keelyn, the mission could wait. It had to.

"You continue driving southwest while I keep trying to get a better picture of where Jonas is. *If* I can get through the haze over my Second Sight I'm going to open a gateway, and then we're going to let the Light guide us the rest of the way." Doubt lingered in his tone despite his efforts to sound confident and Macy wished she knew how to comfort him. But her own fears were too close to the surface to have a clue what to say.

"No." Keelyn pushed herself up in the seat. "No, don't risk it. You'll just lead the Dark to us faster. Stay on the mission. I'm fine. Really." Macy caught her fake smile in the mirror and her stomach tightened.

Tolen pinched the bridge of his nose and Macy *almost* smiled, it was usually her that caused him to do that.

"You're more important than any mission." Rune cradled her chin in his massive hand. "Got it?"

Keelyn tugged her chin out of his grasp, folded her arms across her chest and stared out the window, her lip trembling.

o o o

Macy drove southwest while Tolen used the time to focus. Two hours later and the tension inside the car was still palpable. They were all exhausted and stressed to the limit. And she couldn't get her head to stop playing their predicament over and over. The Seraph gave them a job. She made Keelyn one of the eight. There was a purpose for Keelyn and they couldn't let her die, but was it safe to leave the Relics and their wielders out there with the Dark after them? Would it be better if Tolen just sent Rune and Keelyn through the gateway themselves?

She tapped her fingers on the wheel, wishing Tolen could listen to and answer her questions, but his eyes were closed and she shouldn't want to interrupt whatever process he was going through to figure out where Jonas was. He'd probably thought of all this already anyway, right? Another fear wiggled around in her mind and caused her stomach to writhe with guilt.

What if she wanted to send them off alone because, selfishly, she just couldn't handle watching her friend die?

Her stomach twisted again and she fought to shift her thoughts to mindless things, but as the miles passed and Tolen remained silent, the harder it got. Keelyn drifted to sleep after a while, but Rune stared out at nothing for at least an hour, a muscle in his jaw twitching, before he finally dozed off, his cheek resting on the window. River still hadn't woken up, but the move Rune used could leave him out for hours. She'd always wanted to try that move, but the creatures she usually fought had to be killed, not taken prisoner. She wondered for a moment if it was a move he'd been taught by his creepy Watcher and shuddered. How awful it must have been to be trained by such an evil woman.

She rubbed a thumb over her eyes. This wasn't at all what she'd expected as they'd left the island together. The four of them chasing down leads, fighting back the forces of darkness, bloody battles and close calls, yes. If she were to admit the truth, she would rather be engaged in a daily fight to the death with a hundred Dark creatures than be driving toward an invisible goal with her friend dying in the back seat and carting around some stranger they had to protect with their lives.

Her fingers started to shake on the wheel and the smell of warm plastic filled her nose. She fought against the heat building in her fingers.

Tolen whispered a Hidden word she couldn't quite make out and touched her hair. Calm coursed through her body and the Kuna cooled. She flashed him a tiny smile, *Thank you.* For the first time since their kiss he was looking at her, letting their eyes meet. He dropped his hand, she turned her eyes to the road and cleared her throat. "What did you see?"

Tolen hesitated before answering. "I can see the place in my mind where we need to open the gate, but it's still hazy. Just keep driving. I'm pretty sure I'll know it when I see it."

"Will that be far enough away from the Fallen?"

His eyes searched the growing shadows out the windshield. "We're out of time." He spoke quiet enough he may have been talking to himself. "There's a tribe of Spheres near the place I see in my mind. The area is heavily shielded."

"So hopefully we can stay under the radar."

"Hopefully." He cleared his throat and she sensed his discomfort. He checked the three people sitting in the back as if making sure they really were asleep. He sighed and his shoulders drooped. "We need to talk."

Macy's stomach fluttered. "Right."

"I love you." Tolen pinched his nose again.

She bit her lip. "I love you too."

He reached over and after only a slight hesitation touched her cheek.

Like a match to dry tinder the fire ignited in her chest, her mind flew to their kiss, and the cover on the steering wheel started to smoke leaving an acrid scent in the air. Tolen pulled his hand away from her face and the intensity of his emotions forced a small crack in his window. Color flooded his cheeks at the same time warmth rose in her own.

Her breathing increased in tempo, her heart galloped behind her ribs, and tingles ran from her toes to the top of her head. "What's happening to us?"

"I'm not exactly certain." He ducked his chin. "Remember what I told you about when the Shadows had me in their veil?"

She nodded, her heart clenching at the memory—Tolen held by the Shadows, dying. . .

"When they were torturing me, trying to break me, they showed me images of you." He swallowed loudly. "Dead." His voice cracked and it took him a moment to go on. Macy placed her hand over his and squeezed his fingers. She felt his eyes on her face and met his gaze for as long as driving would allow. "The Dark knew that to get to me they only needed to hurt you. The longer we are together the stronger my feelings for you are getting. Even my gifts are responding in ways they never have before." He ran a hand over his jeans. "It's hard to explain. . ."

"Tolen, the Dark wants me dead just like every other Chosen on the planet. They will try to kill me no matter what you feel or don't feel." She couldn't help but be a tiny bit relieved. He wasn't mad at her after all. He was worried. Typical Tolen.

He reached over and put one finger on her cheek. "I know that, but I can't *know* I'm making it worse—making you more of a target. Do you understand?"

She sighed. "I do. Only because it goes both ways." She swallowed again, the words hard to say aloud. "If they killed you, it would destroy me."

"And we can't have that."

"We can't have either." She twisted a lock of hair around her finger. "So what do we do?"

"I've been thinking," he sat a little taller in his seat. "Quasar was going to teach me how to block my mind from intrusion of unwanted forces."

"You're going to block me?" It hurt more than she knew it should, even if it made sense.

"Not exactly." He met her gaze for a single second and butterflies bloomed to life in her stomach. "I want you to block me—sort of. I want you to try to um, keep *certain* thoughts out of my head. I don't want you to stop communicating with me, just maybe guard your more private thoughts a little more." His cheeks warmed again. "I know you can do it. You used to do it subconsciously when you weren't my biggest fan. I only heard you when your emotions were heightened and you couldn't focus. But since you admitted you love me," his Adam's apple bobbed, "you let me see everything, probably even some things you don't want me to. That connection continues to grow as I feel the love you have for me in your thoughts and the emotion I feel coming from your life force. It amplifies how I feel for you. Love reciprocated is an incredible high."

He shook his head. "But love reciprocated when the recipient isn't speculating, but actually feels *exactly* how much they are loved in *perfect* detail, with every emotion attached to it, even those triggered by adolescent hormones," he gave an embarrassed chuckle. "It becomes intoxicating, overpowering. This continual feedback from each other is making our emotions uncontrollable, volatile, and our judgement is weakening making us easier targets for the tactics of the Dark."

She met his gaze and what she saw there sent the butterflies in her stomach into a frenzy. "I love you Macy, so much. I wish for a single moment you could feel what I feel so you would truly know." He reached his hand out but stopped just shy of her lips. "I need us to put our deepest feelings aside for a time so we can focus and I can keep you safe. I refuse to be the reason the Dark comes after you."

CHAPTER 17

TROUBLED

Tolen could feel Macy's conflict of emotions. She was trying to block him, but after weeks of just letting him in, it was difficult for her. She was trying to ignore the emotions running through her body so they wouldn't ignite his. But she was thinking of what he'd said. He tried to block her, but she was more powerful than him in this case. If she wanted in, she got in. End of story.

"Um, Mace?"

"Sorry." She bit her lip in her customary way. "Is this part of the reason we can't just leave Rune and Keelyn with Jonas and get going with the mission?"

Tolen shook his head and squeezed her hand. "I don't think so. It's something else, something I don't quite understand yet, but I know that they have to come with us." Should he tell her what he'd seen? He couldn't really be certain Rune was asleep. He switched what he wanted to say to something less revealing…or complicated. "You know how Keelyn called Rune a genius? It wasn't just her affection for him. He was declared a child prodigy at age five. Advanced memorization, retention, problem solving, and mathematics skills."

Macy's eyebrows shot up. "*What?*"

Tolen nodded and rubbed his eyes. The sun had passed below the horizon, the first stars winked back at them, and the gentle purr of the old car was soothing despite his tight nerves. He hadn't slept well for

what seemed like weeks, and the emotions rolling through his body—
fear for Macy and what the Fallen knew about her, fear for Rune and
Keelyn, fear that he would fail this mission—were draining not just his
physical body, but his gifts too. He'd need to rest soon and fully regenerate if he was going to be of use to anyone.

"Wow…"

Tolen resisted the urge to smack his cheeks. He needed to stay
focused. Who knows what might happen when he opened the gate?

"And all this time I thought he was more brawn than brains." A trace
of regret and chagrin laced her tone.

The landscape out the window changed, giving him a spark of energy,
and he pointed out the window. "We're almost there. I recognize the
trees." They passed through an old town and came upon a square brick
house turned store with a peeling sign that read, *DeeDee's Donuts*. "Stop
here and pull around to the back."

Macy guided the car around the neglected donut shop and parked
in the darkest area of the abandoned lot. She tapped the screen on the
dash, "Looks like it's pretty clear here, no Dark creatures nearby."

Tolen leaned forward, his eyes on the dark sky out the windshield,
feeling her tension mix with his own. He wondered if she realized just
how much she could sense even more than the Movan tech. "I trust you
more than any Treasta." He shook his head more to dislodge the sleepi-
ness than anything else. "We won't have much time once I open the gate.
The Spheres nearby are going to know what I've done, I don't want to
worry them any longer than necessary."

Macy revved the engine. "Open the gate. We'll be through in nothin'
flat."

Tolen rolled the window down, pulled himself halfway out, closed
his eyes, and took a few deep breaths before raising his hands and speaking the string of words to open the gate, his mind on the image of the
place he could see in his mind.

His gifts were running on fumes, he could feel it. Opening the
gate was taking more out of him than it should. He opened his eyes
and focused harder. The air in front of them, almost to the line of trees,

began to shimmer like rippled glass. To fit the car the gate would have to be larger than most he'd opened, and it seemed to take forever. When at last the gate was as tall as it was wide, Tolen sensed an incoming evil that forced him back into the car.

"Go now!" He shouted.

The engine roared, and the car barreled through the gate. Tolen spun around, aimed his hands back out the window willing the gate to close as a wall of Kinchomen, Raksasha, and Kezgani rushed toward them.

○ ○ ○

"How'd you do it? How'd you find me?" Max stared at Toke, the right side of his face highlighted by the tiny strip of moonlight passing into the cell, trying to convince himself this wasn't another dazed illusion brought on by the attempt of a Tormentor attacking his mind.

"It's a long story and we don't have much time." Toke wiped at the blood on his lip while Max sat shaking his head. *Toke.* His oldest friend. Sitting across from him. "Let's just say I had a lot of help from the Light and an old friend of yours." A fluttering above and Max saw two beady eyes surrounded by feathers peering through the bars over the tiny window.

"Macdara?" He whispered.

Toke smiled. "Yep. Your owl came to us. It took some time to figure out what she was trying to tell us, but eventually we just started following her and ended up here." His eyes searched the cell. "I've got more help outside, but we've got to time this just right." He moved to the corner where a single wire trailed from the camera installed in the upper left corner of the tiny room. He touched the wire, it glowed blue, his eyes lit up and it was like looking into the past.

How many times had he watched Toke work?

Toke released the wire. "We've got three minutes." He glanced up at the high window but Macdara had gone. "The blast will come from that side, we need to be ready." He looked back at Max and there was pain in his eyes. "I was certain you were dead. I went to your house right after I felt M—"

"Don't say her name!"

Toke tilted his head, then nodded. "I'm so sorry. I accepted your death, I mourned for you both."

Max squeezed his eyes shut. *Alli.*

"How did you end up in here?" Was it his imagination or was there accusation in Toke's eyes?

"The Shadows killed Alli—" His voice hitched and he looked away from Toke's gaze. "Then they brought me here."

"They knew you had information." There, again, accusation.

"You still think I was wrong to search, to learn more?" Max met Toke's eyes. "I was only doing it for her. To protect her."

Toke shook his head. "But at what cost Max? Now they have your secrets and they *are* hunting her."

Max was shaking his head before Toke finished, his eyes squeezed shut. "No, not because of me. They have some knowledge, pieces of information, but not all. I never told them everything."

"You were able to resist the Tormentors all these years?"

Max opened his eyes and nodded.

"You were one of the most talented Chosen I've ever known. Stubborn, and terrible at taking counsel, but talented." Toke tilted his head, his expression awed. "That's why the Seraph led us here."

"What?"

"Sorry, it's that long story that has to wait."

"You never change."

"Sixty seconds. Get ready."

Max quickly crawled under the bed and brought out the planks he'd scratched with his secrets. "Scan these."

Toke closed his eyes for a brief moment, his fingers suddenly glowed blue and he ran them over the scratches. They too began to glow, and then a mirror of them curled into the air forming words and patterns that flashed swiftly by before funneling into Toke's left temple. His strange eyes brightened with orange light again for a split second. The blue light faded from the wood leaving just the strange scratches, pock marks, and age lines. Max tossed the planks back under the bed and met Toke's measured gaze.

"I don't doubt you know the Prophecy forward and backward from all your years of study, but is all that really true?" He gestured toward the planks.

Max looked out the cell bars at the darkening hall. "It has to be."

"This will change the tide." Toke whispered.

"I know."

"We need to get back to her. Now."

Max's fingers twitched, the anticipation painful. "Waiting on you my friend."

Toke touched the wire again. "Brina, one of my Lost Ones, will be here in three seconds. Three. Two. One…." A series of explosions cut through the air, the light out the window glowed fiery red, and the wail of sirens ripped apart the silence of the night. The windowed wall exploded inward, knocking the two to the ground. Macdara was there suspended strangely as if on an invisible perch, and then a young woman appeared where seconds ago there'd only been falling debris and a dusty view to the outside, Macdara sitting on her shoulder. The girl's long black braids still quivered from the aftershock. A Dicernan. *Nice.* Flickers of orange reflected off her dark skin as she gestured for them to follow her out the blast hole.

"Hurry. The others are guarding the escape route, but either way we'll be lucky to get five minutes on it before its overrun. This place is insane." She grabbed their hands to help them up.

Max climbed over the rubble, hardly caring about the sharpness of the broken stone under his bare feet and hands, and Macdara fluttered to his shoulder. He had one glance at the chaos, prisoners rushing about, the pop of gunfire as the Darkened took them out, before the girl tugged on his sleeve and he followed her into a dark tunnel beneath the ground—from the smell, it was the makeshift sewer.

Macdara fluttered ahead and after ten years and no hope of ever leaving this place alive, Max rushed behind her eagerly, his weakened body filled with hope, the adrenaline firing through his veins masking the pain of his injuries. His every fear overwhelmed by the desire to move. To see her. To know she was alive and safe.

Macy, I'm coming.

CHAPTER 18

FAMILIAR

Tolen leaned back against the seat as the gate hissed shut blocking the Dark creatures from sight. Macy slammed on the brakes as they took in their new surroundings. The car idled on a stretch of abandoned highway surrounded by forest. The Dark felt farther away, but still too close. They needed to find Jonas' camp, and fast.

"Where to now?"

Tolen took a slow breath in and out through his nose and closed his eyes, trying to push past the tumult of everyone's emotions and his own exhaustion so he could search out the vibes of the Light. Jonas would be shielding the camp from affecting the Balance, but the Light could still guide them, if he could just focus. Rune cleared his throat and Tolen's concentration broke. "Gimme a second." He left the car, very aware of the danger, and walked fifty feet left of the beam from the headlights into the dark tree-line.

Once in the shelter of the trees he pressed his palms together and allowed the life forces of the forest surrounding him to calm his mind and body. The Honitahai within him awakened and his life force connected with the trees closest to him. He felt their concern for his welfare, their joy at his presence, and their protection.

Several of their voices filled his mind. *Hello Conchla Mindra—Ninth Chosen, you are safe here, we will watch over you.*

Peace replaced some of the anxiety Tolen felt. *Please watch over my friends on the road as well.*

As you wish. There was a tense pause. *You carry Light with you, you must protect her.*

That's what I'm trying to do. She needs help. He paused, searching their light to make sure they could be trusted. *I'm looking for a Radia Warrior training camp nearby, led by a Sphere named Jonas. Do you know of such a place?*

Rush of whispers like wind, another ten-second pause. *We have been sworn to secrecy to all but you, Conchla Mindra. Ianda will guide you, follow his life force.*

A pale blue light appeared in the tree to Tolen's left and flitted quickly to another tree about fifty feet from the roadside. Tolen understood that once a tree's life force left the place of its birth, its life was shortened considerably—Ianda was making the ultimate sacrifice. He was grateful he didn't have to speak his gratitude over the sudden tightness in his throat.

A sacrifice for the light is never truly a sacrifice, Ianda replied in a deep baritone. *As I pass through Light's door, I shall be rewarded in the Light Realm to dwell with my ancestors forever. There is no greater gift to seek.*

Tolen walked back to the car and knocked on Macy's window. "We've got a guide. I need to drive."

Macy paused with her fingers on the door handle. "Tolen, you're dead on your feet."

"I'm fine." Tolen lied.

Macy vacated her seat, squeezed his elbow as she walked by, and climbed in the passenger side.

They drove in silence, everyone but Tolen drifting off occasionally, although not without effort. He smacked his cheeks and even pinched his leg several times.

River remained out, his chest moving evenly up and down, his head on the back of the seat, his mouth slightly open, the occasional soft snore punctuating the quiet.

Had he left a family behind? Did he have any clue why they'd taken him? How much had Max told him when he'd awakened him? Were they doing the right thing abandoning the mission to take Keelyn to Jonas? Tolen knew he needed to be calming his emotions, staying focused, doing his duty as the Ninth, but the questions continued to build within his mind, roiling and twisting, messing with his focus and increasing his frustration.

A little past two in the morning Ianda spoke in Tolen's mind. *You can go no farther by vehicle.*

Grateful for the intrusion on his thoughts Tolen pulled off the crumbling road and into the tall grass at the side. "Hey guys?" He waited until all eyes except River's were on him. "Sorry, it's time to walk."

Rune glanced pointedly at Keelyn.

Tolen tipped his head in apology.

"What about him?" Macy pointed her thumb at River.

Tolen killed the engine, pulled out the keys and handed them to Macy. "We can't exactly carry him. We'll have to wake him up."

"Think he'll try to run off again?" Macy pulled a handful of suckers from her bag and held them out to the others.

They each grabbed a purple sucker, needing the burst of energy, especially if they ended up needing to use their gifts before they reached Jonas' camp. Tolen hoped they'd be allowed a brief reprieve with Jonas— he really, really needed to sleep.

Rune poked River in the arm. "Hey kid, time to wake up."

River continued to snore.

Tolen reached back and placed his hand on the young man's forehead wondering what words he needed to hear to choose to wake. *Bring him peace Tolen.* Bastian's voice whispered. *He is a troubled child. His surname means 'abandoned'.* Tolen closed his eyes and whispered, *Pench Ni'yalo River Hok'ee. Ladonra un da'bay. Be still. Peace my friend.*

River blinked several times before his head snapped up, he took in his surroundings, the faces watching him, and the color drained from his face. His eyes flicked most to Macy. A flicker of annoyance flared in Tolen's chest. "What do you want with me?"

"To protect you." River's eyes locked on Tolen and he got a tiny glimpse of his thoughts. "You were told someone would come for you, but you expected it would be a long time before now."

River's eyes widened. "How do you know that?"

Tolen sighed, pushing aside the petty jealousy he felt, focusing on the compassion this young man needed. "The man who told you about the Dark, who gave you the Relic and told you to protect it and keep it safe, this is his daughter. We've been sent to find you." He pointed at Macy and relief washed over River's face.

"You look like him." His pale face flushed with red. "I mean—not like a man, you're pretty." The red deepened and Tolen had to bite his lip. "You just, um, have his eyes."

Rune laughed and quickly turned it into a cough. "Well, let's see it."

River looked around at their anxious faces. "See what?"

"The Relic. We know you've got it on you. We saw it activate." Rune waggled his fingers in River's face. "Let's see it."

River glanced around at them all but didn't reach in his pocket until he got Macy's reassuring nod. River pulled a ring of keys from his pocket and pointed to a curved piece of metal. "This is it."

"Dude, you keep the Relic on a keychain?" Rune snorted and color flushed River's cheeks.

Macy reached back and slugged Rune's arm. "Ignore him. He's a butt."

"Max said to keep it with me at all times," he placed the keys back in his pocket, "that it would protect me as long as I had it with me."

"Well, he was right. Wasn't he?" Keelyn said kindly. "The Fallen didn't see you, that's why they came after us."

"The Fallen?" River's eyebrows creased.

"The real bad guys," Macy added.

"So, you really are the good guys?"

"Yep." Rune quipped.

Tolen opened his door. "River, I'm sure you have a lot of questions, as we do for you, but first we need to get you someplace safe."

River spared Tolen half a glance and nodded before his eyes returned to Macy.

Tolen may have been a little rough pushing the seat forward and helping River out of the back, but he made sure it was a gentle hand that steadied him as he stood upright.

It took less than five minutes to load their gear and for Macy to set the car to stealth mode and send it off to hide somewhere they could find it later. Tolen wanted to hold her hand, a tiny voice whispered he needed to stake his claim, but knowing he had to focus he walked ahead, allowing the others to fall behind him.

Ianda, how far? We have an injured friend with us.

I sense her pain. You will reach the camp before the sun rises.

With sunrise still a few hours away this news didn't help his growing worry. The trees had promised their protection, but night was the worst time to travel. They needed to stay alert, despite their exhaustion. Tolen stayed in the lead, knowing he needed to ask River questions, but it was Rune, Macy, and Keelyn who talked to him. Tolen couldn't seem to concentrate on what they were saying and the path ahead at the same time. Minutes later he felt Macy come up behind him.

"So, River seems like a nice guy." She said once she reached his side.

Tolen grunted.

"He was only seven when my dad found him. He was living in a group home on a reservation. Dad took him to Ohio, placed him with some person he trusted, put protections in place, and told him he would be back soon. River had a terrifying childhood, seeing the Dark, but having to pretend he didn't. Disappearing and reappearing for reasons he didn't understand."

Tolen grunted again.

"You know, you're really cute when you're jealous."

Tolen's foot caught on a root and he stumbled. "Is it that obvious?" He caught Macy's grin and sighed. "I'm trying not be a jerk."

She wrapped her arm through his and leaned into his side as they walked. The warmth of her touch seemed to lessen the weakness in his steps. "You're doing fine Tolen. You're too nice a guy to do anything too irrational." Her grin widened.

He tugged her close and kissed her forehead as they walked, the tiny voice in his head hoping River saw it.

Tolen pulled away from his feelings for Macy, turning his thoughts to the forest around them—hard to do with her so close to his side, her touch on his arm, but he would do it.

They walked for less than thirty minutes before Keelyn became too weak to continue. Rune pulled her onto his back, but Rune needed to regenerate as much as Tolen did. They needed rest. He offered to take turns but Rune refused. Two and half hours later no one talked. The effort to keep putting one foot in front of the other took all their energy. Finally when the first hints of daybreak brightened the sky, Ianda finally had them stop.

Wait here.

Enough time passed to allow a pink sunrise to gild the sparse clouds above their heads with gold before a familiar face stepped from behind the trees.

"Incrah!" Tolen rushed to grip the arm of his friend. "I can't tell you how glad I am to see you. We need your help."

Incrah's gaze paused on Keelyn, her cheek pressed against Rune's back, eyes closed, breathing shallow, and rubbed a thumb across his brow. "Well, this is familiar."

The first time they'd met, it had been Tolen cradling an unconscious Macy. He shook the memory from his thoughts.

Incrah gestured with his hand toward an almost invisible trail into the trees. "Follow me."

CHAPTER 19

SHOCKWAVE

"You managed all this with just the two of you?" Max kicked at a rat sniffing his bare feet and tried not to think about what sloshed between his toes.

"Not quite." Toke pointed to a tiny dot of light ahead. "We ended up with some help along the way."

They traveled another ten minutes when Toke stopped and lifted a finger to his lips. Brina went invisible again, only the small ripples in the sewage showing where she placed her feet.

Muffled grunts and clangs met their ears, then a large splash and a huge shadow stalked toward them. Max poised to fight as he watched the creature, a Fallen, a Darkened?

"Mahto?" Toke asked.

"Yeah, man, it's me." A deep voice replied.

Toke breathed a sigh of relief and Brina reappeared.

"We better hurry. Sienn is holding off a small group of Darkened headed our way, but she'll run out of arrows soon."

Mahto. "Bear" in Hidden language. The name fit the huge boy with his thick dark hair and warm eyes, lit up by a glowing satchel tied about his waist.

Macdara flew off, letting her wing just brush Max's cheek. She'd done her duty and he sent a thank you to the Light, hoping he would see her again someday as Mahto helped them all out of the sewer.

Topside a pretty blonde elf, well, half-elf, stood notching arrows as fast as she shot them.

"Brina, my bag please." Toke said in his eerily calm battle voice.

Brina pulled a large backpack from her shoulders and handed it over. Toke searched for a few seconds and lifted out a familiar object.

"Still up to your old tricks I see." Max almost smiled.

"If they work you don't stop using them." Toke placed the device on the ground. "Everyone run at the count of three. One. Two—" They were all running before he finished three.

Max, clutching an ache in his side, the shockwave pushed from behind shoving him forward to his hands and knees. Mahto grabbed him as he tried to stand and tossed him over his shoulders. The world went black.

o o o

"We should be safe to rest here for a bit." Max woke from a spot on the ground. The palm trees surrounding them were thicker and older than those he knew dotted around the prison. The sky here was light, the sun fully risen. How far had they traveled? The elf/girl Sienn was tugging her bow and quiver off her shoulder and laying them on the ground.

Toke twisted his ancient Treasta in his fingers, twiddling the buttons and knobs. "We've got eight hours." His head dropped onto the tree behind him. His cheek was bleeding again.

Max moved to help him, but Brina got there first. "You need rest too. Let me."

"Max, you've heard their names but allow me to officially introduce you to your rescuers." Toke pointed around the group as Brina wiped at the blood on his face. "Brina, is one of my Lost Ones. Mahto and Sienn are Honitahai, we have fought together in the past."

"Thank you for risking your lives to save me." Max swallowed past the emotion thickening his throat. "I was sure I would die in that place."

Mahto finished stoking a small fire and then walked over to Max, opening a large backpack and handed him a set of clothes and pair of boots.

"They'll be a bit big, but you can't travel like that, man." He gestured to Max's ragged shirt, shredded jeans, and bare feet.

Max took the clothes with another word of thanks and excused himself to hide behind a copse of trees. As he changed the excitement at seeing Macy again began to twist into a heavy knot in his stomach. Once she knew he was alive, would she forgive him for not coming for her? For the danger he'd wrought upon their family? For the fact that it was his fault her mother had died? He pushed his dirty feet into socks, slid on the overlarge boots, and tied the laces—the movements methodical, his thoughts racing. He shook the exhaustion from his shoulders, ignoring the pain that shot through his body and moved back to the group. "We need to get to LadonRyn."

Silence. Even the wind seemed to have hushed.

"That place is a myth," Brina murmured as she wiped medicine over Toke's face, but Mahto's back went rigid.

"It's not. I've been there." Max looked at Mahto. "And so has he."

Mahto met Max's gaze. "And I promised myself I would never go back."

"As did I, but we must."

"That place isn't a haven. It's a refuge for cowards." Mahto shook his head.

"That depends on your perspective." Max ran his fingers through his tangled hair.

Sienn put her hand on Mahto's broad back. "Why must we go there?"

Brina held out a brush and Max ripped it through his hair, ignoring the clumps that came out as he pulled. "Because that's where Macy will go."

"How do you know?" Toke asked.

Max finished with his hair and started trying to untangle his dirty beard. "I heard them. The Dark knows the location of the Zenith. Which means LadonRyn is the last safe place to hide the Descendants."

"Descendants, as in the Nine?" Sienn's hand moved to her bow. "The Awakening?"

Max nodded. "The Final Battle has already begun. The followers of Light just don't know it yet."

CHAPTER 20

FAILING SIGHT

Tolen held tight to Macy's hand as they followed close behind Incrah. Sunlight filtered down through the leaves as dancing patches of gold along the path.

"You couldn't have come at a more difficult time." Incrah held a branch aside and waited for them to pass through. Once the others were farther up the trail he continued, "All but one of our Housemen and women have been dispatched to other camps, and the state she is in…" His eyes flicked ahead to Rune carrying Keelyn on his back. "I do not know if he can help. And Jonas is under great strain."

"Is Jonas okay?" Macy twisted her hair around her pinky as they walked—a nervous gesture Tolen recognized. He squeezed her other hand.

Incrah tapped the sword bouncing at his hip. "Fit as a thousand year old sword." His jaw clenched. "But the growth of Dark is requiring him to use most of his energy to keep us hidden. Occasionally another Sphere will come and give him relief, but with so few of them and so much need, we can hardly train warriors fast enough to send out."

A wave of cold that had nothing to do with the weather passed through Tolen's body. "Why haven't I *seen* any of that?"

"Second Sight continues to fail. The Fallen have always had ways of subduing the vibes in the Balance. But as Darsapean's power grows in the Shadow Realm, it also seems to be furthering his reach here, the

Fallen are getting stronger. We've received word that even Sashan is struggling to *see*."

What happens in one realm is mirrored in the other. The image Tolen saw when they first left the island came back with vivid clarity. Darsapean, sitting on his silver throne, confident, almost smug, certain he would not fail in his plan. As his power grew, so did that of his followers here. *Shadowing the light.*

If the Dark could cover the Sight of even Sashan, the most powerful Watcher, they would be rendering all followers of Light blind. Sashan's ability to connect to the Second Sight of all other Watchers gave them a huge advantage, a glimpse into the future of the Dark's plans from thousands of different views of the future. Without his ability, how would they prepare? How would they even know where to begin?

The idea of severing the Pact so humans would be able to *see* the monsters of the Dark, enabling them to fight back, was beginning to seem more and more necessary. There simply wasn't enough Chosen around the world to do it alone anymore. They needed the Descendants wielding their Relics, leading, they needed the help of the whole human race. The Seraph said the full Awakening could not take place until Macy transcended—but that was almost two years away. If it was this bad now, in two years the human race could be nothing but Darkened.

A cold sickening dread clawed at Tolen's heart and he shivered. They needed to help Keelyn, and get back on mission as quickly as possible.

"So who are your friends?" Incrah asked in a low voice snapping Tolen back to the moment. "I sense the two are Chosen ones, but the third?"

Tolen cleared his throat. "Rune, and Keelyn are the Chosen ones. They're friends of ours. We're on a mission from a Seraph…" Tolen paused. "River Hok'ee is one of the Nine Descendants."

Incrah's steps faltered. Tolen met his concerned gaze, but shook his head slightly when River glanced back at them, curiosity warring with fear in his expression. This was enough of a clue for Incrah to know what their mission was, but this wasn't the place to discuss it.

Tolen tugged Macy closer to his side. "We've all sensed the growing darkness, but I just can't believe it's happening so fast."

Incrah's anxiety rippled beneath his words. "Darsapean roaming free in the Shadow Realm seems to have given all creatures of evil confidence. The Fallen especially. They may be few in number, but their ability to hide in plain sight, tempt Chosen and Watcher alike, has never been a more valuable tool. They are openly hunting Chosen—many have been slaughtered already. Word has reached us that some of their mutated spawn are massing, creating more Darkened."

"We just had a battle with a group of Fallen." Tolen's chest tightened and he kicked a rock in the path. It skipped across the dirt and slammed into a pine tree with an echoing crack. "One of them had some sort of device that seemed to take control of our friends. I was able to break the connection, but it wasn't easy."

"It's true then." Incrah pushed away more invading tree limbs. "We've heard rumor that some Movan are building new tech for the Dark. Tech that can connect to a Chosen shard, and give the Fallen power over the human carrier. The threat of the Fallen and their connection to the Chosen through their shards has never been more dangerous."

Macy stumbled beside Tolen. He wrapped his arm around her waist, the shock and fear he felt from her matched his own.

"Just a bit farther and we'll be to the Houseman's tent." Incrah added.

They picked up the pace and within a few minutes the scene before them gave Tolen a wave of deja vu. Dozens of Radia Warrior trainees—the youngest of which couldn't be more than twelve—stood in lines practicing with their gifts. But this time the focus was grim and less playful. Last time children had laughed and goofed around while they practiced, now their eyes were glued to their targets, their hands steady, their ears tuned to their mentors standing beside them. The overall feel was one of heightened urgency. These trainees knew they were needed. They knew that to lose focus was to give the Dark an edge fighters for Light could not afford. A tremor moved along Tolen's shoulders and settled in his stomach like a rock. They needed to find the rest of the Nine, yet here he was, completely off mission.

You're doing the right thing Tolen, Bastian's voice whispered.

I hope so.

Incrah paused at a tall white canvas tent with a red eagle painted on the door and motioned for Rune to take Keelyn inside. "You should be looked over as well," he said to River. "Go on in. We'll come for you soon."

Once Rune, Keelyn and River disappeared inside, Incrah led Tolen and Macy on.

Two sentries stood guard outside another tall white tent, but in place of an eagle on the door flap was a pale blue circlet of leaves with a depiction of a glowing Radia Shard at the center. Incrah waved the sentries aside. "We must only bother him when absolutely necessary and only for a few moments. Be quick."

Their old friend lay on a large bed made of hewn logs covered with a thick stuffed mattress.

A foot away from the bed Tolen paused, but Macy continued forward dragging him with her, and touched Jonas' wrinkled hand.

Jonas' white eyes focused on them. "Ah, hello McLacy. Tolen. It is good to see you both. I've been expecting you." He had more color in his cheeks, and they were far less sunken than when they'd visited him in the healing wing of the Citadel, but the strain of shielding this place was taking its toll. His white eyes and pale skin had a grayish tint, similar to Keelyn. Even the pale morning light filtering through the canvas didn't help his gloomy pallor.

Tolen put his hand over theirs. "It's so good to see you again Jonas."

Jonas raised himself to one elbow to face them. "You have come for my help."

Macy smirked. "Of course you already know."

Jonas inclined his head. "Forrest Bastian is a good Watcher."

Tolen couldn't hold back a tiny smile. Jonas had said the same thing the first time they'd met—although then both Macy and Tolen had believed Bastian to be dead and gone from them forever. "Yes he is."

Macy's fingers twitched. "Can you—can you save her?" her voice cracked and Tolen dropped her hand to put his arm around her shoulders.

Jonas' face fell, his many wrinkles deepening with sorrow. "No, I am sorry McLacy. She needs the power of her own kind, and alas, we have no Lóklana here, and even then Grief Sickness is an ancient mortal illness and successful treatment depends on many factors. The rate of survival is…not high." He tapped Macy's chin and sighed.

Pain rolled off her life force despite how hard she tried to hold it in and Tolen wished for a way, anyway, to take her sadness for her, pull it all into himself to spare her the agony. But he could only heal physical pain, and it was Macy's heart that was breaking. Instead he pulled her tighter to his side and uselessly rubbed her arm. "Do you know where any Lóklana are?" she asked, emotion thick in her voice.

Jonas nodded. "Yes. But the place the child must be taken, the place that is her only hope…it will test you and all you think you know. In more ways than you can possibly imagine. It will change you."

Macy leaned forward. "I don't care. We'll do it." She rocked back and shook her head. "Wait, is there someone here who can take them? Tolen and I are supposed to be finding the Relics and the other Nine Descendants."

Jonas was shaking his head before Macy finished. "You two must take the girl and her companion. There has been a shift in the Balance, a twinge in the future. You will go and the plan will fall into place. There is no time to explain further. I need to return my focus to the protection of this camp. Just know the Light is aware of you and what you need."

"Where are we going?" Macy asked, relief mingled with doubt in her tone.

"Tolen knows." Jonas's eyes drooped.

Tolen shook his head. "I do?"

"You have seen it in Rune's mind. He must guide you there, he is the only one who can…Not even I can find it. LadonRyn is its name." His eyelids fluttered, "some…call it Nowhere. *Liosladon,* my friends." His eyes closed and his breathing resumed a steady and slow pace.

"*Liosladon,*" Tolen and Macy whispered.

Tolen held open the flap for Macy and they rejoined Incrah outside.

"Did you get what you needed?" Incrah waved to the sentries as they resumed their vigil outside Jonas's door.

Tolen had felt Macy's Kuna begin to pool in her fingers with fear and anticipation, but she'd reigned it in, her eyes showed her focus had shifted back into mission mode—save Keelyn, retrieve the Descendants and the Relics. "Jonas said he can't heal her, but he told us where we can find someone who can."

"You're going to sever the Pact, aren't you?" Incrah's dark eyes held both uncertainty and grim acceptance.

Tolen nodded and Incrah sighed. "I suppose it is for the best. Dark times are upon us. The Final Battle is closer than ever."

Tolen didn't like even thinking of that scary fact, let alone discussing it. "How's River taking everything?"

"I was told he's taking it all surprisingly well." Incrah tipped his chin at Macy. "It seems your father taught him much in the short time they had together. He will be alright." He pointed to a trail on the left. "I have tents for you both to rest."

"Is Keelyn awake?" Macy asked, a catch in her voice.

Incrah shook his head. "No, but the Houseman has given her some herbs. She is resting peacefully. You should be safe to let her sleep through one night here before you leave. Rune has refused to leave her side, I was hoping you could come and convince him to rest." He eyed them up and down. "I imagine all of you are in need of a full regeneration."

Macy nodded but Tolen put his hand on Incrah's arm. "You have no idea how nice that sounds, but there's something else I need to do. Is there somewhere quiet Macy and I can go for a few minutes?"

"Of course." Incrah changed direction. "This way. When you are finished, come back to the main square and I'll make sure someone is there to lead you to your tents."

○ ○ ○

They followed Incrah to a secluded piece of forest, Macy's hand warm in Tolen's. She wondered if he knew how much she needed the comfort of his touch, or if she was succeeding in blocking her thoughts. It wasn't easy to do when they were spinning and churning inside her making her want to scream one second and vomit the next.

Incrah left them in a quiet copse of trees. Light filtered down through the leaves, dappling Tolen's hair with gold. Birds chirped in a melody that should bring feelings of peace and contentment, but the muffled clang of a sword, or thwack of an arrow hitting its target told the truth. All wasn't right with the world.

Tolen tucked a hair behind her ear, his fingers raising goosebumps where they brushed her neck. Her insides ignited, but cooled the moment she looked in his eyes. That look was back. The look he'd had when he first told her Keelyn was dying—a look that said he needed to tell her something he really didn't want to tell her. The Kuna bloomed to life in her chest and she had to fight to contain the heat.

"Tolen? Have you seen? Is she…?" Her throat closed and she couldn't finish.

Tolen pulled her against his chest. She could feel his heart beating through his shirt, his familiar smell filling her nose and bringing the tears to the surface. She bit down hard on her lip.

"I haven't seen her death, only the repercussions if she does die. Both for Rune, and for our mission. They don't feel set, like they can be changed…but," he cleared his throat. "What I have seen, what I have felt …it's not good Mace." He ran his fingers through her hair. "I didn't want to tell you. I wish I didn't need to, but if we can't save her…"

She pushed away from his chest to see his face, but stayed within the comfort of his arms.

He stared past her into the forest, his eyes shifting every now and then as he spoke. "Just after I told you about Keelyn I had a vision of Rune. A piece of his future." He winced. "What would happen to him if Keelyn…"

Macy clenched her teeth, heart pounding in her ears.

"It's bad." he winced again, "Macy, if Keelyn dies, he will turn. He will fall into darkness. He will become Darkened."

Dark, suffocating cold wrapped itself around her middle and slowly squeezed tighter and tighter. "He wouldn't. He…" but she knew it was true. She'd seen Rune's angry side. She'd sensed his fear of his own gifts. Seen him deny his destiny as a Chosen. And she knew Keelyn was the only Being on this planet that kept him grounded. He harbored resentment toward the Light. If they took her back to Them, he would see it as the ultimate betrayal. He *would* turn.

Tolen squeezed his eyes shut and Macy knew she didn't want him to tell her the rest of the vision. Deep down she knew what she would have to do to stop Rune from turning, and she would if it kept the Dark from getting him. It was the same thing she would expect Rune to do for her if the situation were reversed. She bit the inside of her cheek to keep from screaming. Why? Why did love have to hurt so much?

Tolen lowered his forehead to hers. "I will do all I can to save her, to save them both Macy, I promise."

She tilted her chin to just brush his lips, no fire this time, the sorrow was too deep. "I know you will. I know you would risk anything for them…for me." She breathed deep, wishing it were enough to guarantee success. "Thank you, Tolen."

He kissed her again then pulled her close against him, almost as if he needed the comfort as much as she did. Maybe he did.

They stood that way for a few brief moments, listening to each other's breathing, the birds, the mock battle echoes—a moment stolen from the chaos of the real world, a moment she knew she would be clinging to in the days to come.

When they knew they could stall no longer, Tolen took her hand and led them back toward the camp, between tents, past groups of trainees heading to breakfast. His pace was slow, measured, as lost in thought as she was.

CHAPTER 21

PARTING PLANS

"Supper!" A voice spoke and Tolen sat up so fast the walls of the tent spun.

A young boy poked his head in the flap. "Incrah said to wake you. You need food to help your regeneration."

Something squeaked and Tolen looked left to see Rune rolling out of his cot and hurriedly lacing his boots. Tolen must have slept right through Rune coming in. He wondered how they'd managed to convince him to leave Keelyn's side.

"I'm going to check on Keelyn. I'll meet you guys there." And he was gone.

Tolen rubbed his fists over his eyes. Maybe they did need both rest *and* food, but as his fingers fumbled with the task of pulling on his shoes he had to wonder if he really needed food as much as he needed sleep. Macy, always faster at getting moving than he, was likely already waiting outside and it was that thought that helped him to his feet.

With slow steps and many yawns, Tolen and Macy joined the line leading into the mess tent. Tolen spotted Rune leaning against one of the poles that held open the canvas flaps. His feigned nonchalance probably fooled all the people passing by him, but a tightness in his neck, the rigidity of his stance, the way his eyes kept flicking in the direction of the Houseman's tent, showed a tight wire about to snap. He caught Tolen's eye and walked over.

"How is she?" Macy asked.

Rune kept his voice low, Tolen guessed more to disguise his emotion than to keep their conversation private. "Gray skin. Cold. I wanted to stay, but they said she needed to rest and I was no good to her weak." His jaw clenched. "I know we decided to let her rest one night before we try to leave. But she looks so…I don't know if we should wait." Rune's eyes flashed around the tables without seeing. "But I don't want to take her if rest really is what she needs."

Macy's hand trembled in Tolen's and he rubbed soothing circles with his thumb across it. He led the way to the line to get food and after one more squeeze, reluctantly let go of her hand so she could fill her plate. "How's River?" He asked Rune.

"He looked fine. When I left he was being taken to meet Jonas." Rune began piling things on without paying attention to what he was doing. When he put on the fourth spoonful of corn Macy touched his wrist.

"It's going to be alright Rune."

Tolen's throat tightened. She was trying to reassure herself as much as Rune.

"Let's eat." He led the way to an empty table. "We're no good to anyone hungry and tired. We'll eat, go back to bed, and leave at first light tomorrow."

They ate silently for a few minutes, all of them more famished than they'd realized, but as their stomach's filled the tension had room to move back in.

Rune's foot started tapping a nervous rhythm under the table. "So what's the plan?"

"Jonas told us to take Keelyn to LadonRyn." Macy dabbed her mouth with a napkin. "And something about the plan coming together after that."

"LadonRyn?" Rune tilted his head.

Macy's fork-full of mashed potatoes paused an inch in front of her mouth. "Jonas said you'd been there."

Rune shook his head. "I've never heard of it."

Tolen laid down his spoon. "He also said it was called Nowhere."

The color drained from Rune's face. His fork clattered back to his plate. A flash of the place where Tolen had seen Rune in the past, injured, being cared for, flicked across his vision—a memory of pain and regret, but also hope.

"Nowhere?" Rune swallowed loudly and folded his hands in his lap.

Tolen sifted through the emotions he could feel from Rune, a mingling of despair, doubt, and again regret with traces of desperate hope. "Jonas said that this place would test us in more ways than we can imagine. He said it will change us." A few more flashes of memory. A beautiful island, the face of a man—his features melted looking, the woman in blue again.

"I promised I would protect its location with my life." Rune shifted on the bench. "I've never told anyone where it is. Not Toke, not Keelyn, no one."

"Jonas said we have to go there," Macy pleaded. "That it's Keelyn's only hope, and you are the only one who could take us."

Regret, pain, resolve—Tolen felt each emotion equally poignant and powerful as they flowed from Rune's life force, but in less than a minute he spoke with conviction. "Then that's where we will go. But it *will* test you. It'll make you question everything you know about being Chosen. And when you leave, you'll never be the same."

○ ○ ○

Tolen stared above his head at the light dancing across the canvas as it filtered down through the trees. They'd plotted and planned through supper and finally decided on their next move.

In the morning they would leave, and once they determined they were at a safe enough distance from the camp, but still under the protection of Jonas, Tolen would open a gate, but not directly to LadonRyn. Because while Tolen could see brief glimpses of the place, when he tried to connect to the spark of familiarity and connection he experienced each time he opened a gate, it would not come. Rune told them the Island of Nowhere was protected by ancient power and only those who had been invited could see it, or ever return—and since even Tolen as the Ninth couldn't seem to bend that power, Rune was most definitely their only way onto the island.

But that's where it got really tricky and dangerous. The moment they left Jonas' protection they'd be right back on the radar of the Fallen, and Tolen would be opening a gate near a small airport in the town of Kapa'a on the Hawaiian island of Kauai. An island where Sorsha had once—and maybe still—lived on occasion. But Rune had been unconscious when he'd been taken to the island of LadonRyn. His hope was that if they retraced his steps from the first time he'd left there, something would be on the path that would lead them back. It was a vague plan with a million places for something to go wrong, but after hours of discussion they couldn't come up with any other ideas. They had to trust Jonas knew what he was talking about and they had to try, for Keelyn's sake—*and* Rune's even if he didn't know it.

Macy was in the tent next door, but his shard pulsed with her energy as if she were lying next to him. Rune shifted on his cot, and Tolen knew none of them were likely going to be able to quiet their minds long enough to let them sleep as they needed.

They had to save Keelyn, for so many reasons…Tolen had spent the first ten years of his life without the luxury of friendship. Dane had been a godsend and when he passed, Tolen had realized just how valuable true friendship was. In the last couple of months, he'd formed friendships with Macy, Quasar, Blaze, Mahto, Sienn, and Belch. And now Keelyn and Rune—someone he couldn't have imagined being friends with—and now he wanted nothing more than to save them both.

Another hope that had him back in a place where concern for his friend's future muddled his judgement. He had to keep reminding himself not to jump in with his heart, his own desires. He had to weigh the options. He had to pay attention to his role as the Ninth—everything done at the right time and for the right reasons. He shoved his hand behind his head and forced his eyes closed, concentrating on the patterns of red behind his closed lids, begging his thoughts to silence and let him sleep.

o o o

The cot wiggled beneath him and it took a moment to realize some-one was shaking his arm. He sat up so fast his head swam, blurring the image of the person standing above him. He rubbed his eyes with his fists. "Incrah?"

The only light came from a small lamp in Incrah's hand. He peeked at his watch, 3:16 AM.

Rune bolted upright, "Keelyn?"

Incrah lifted the lamp. "I need you both to come with me, now."

Macy waited outside under a star-filled sky. Tolen grabbed her hand, welcoming her warmth. The three of them followed swiftly behind Incrah who led them through the sleeping encampment back to Jonas's tent.

Contrary to the last time they'd visited, this time Jonas paced, his cane clunking with each step. "Ah, you're here." Fatigue had carved new lines beside his eyes, eyes that looked just as exhausted as before, but the determination Tolen could feel swirling from his life force must be fueling his gait.

"What's wrong?" Rune's voice held no emotion, but the inward curve of his shoulders, the tremor in his hands, and the dark rings beneath his eyes showed the despair of the man inside. Rune was one thread of bad news away from snapping. In this moment he looked far too close to the Rune Tolen had seen in his vision—the Rune who would become Darkened. Tolen fought to pay attention to what Jonas was saying, but it only brought the fear closer.

"Keelyn has taken a turn for the worse. You cannot wait any longer." Jonas continued to pace, barely sparing them a glance. "You have a plan to get to LadonRyn?"

The heavy rock had rolled back into Tolen's gut. "It's a lot of guess-work. We're going to open a gate to Kapa'a and retrace Rune's path when he left. We're hoping we'll find something that will lead us back."

Jonas paused, his white eyes trailing over each of them. "When on the right path, you need not fear. Trust the Light." He resumed his pac-ing. "You must leave now. I will ensure that River will be safe here until you can come back for him. Travel ten miles outside camp, then open your gateway."

"We have a car stashed. We can go farther than ten if need-be." Macy's voice sounded like she was talking through a cold. Tolen pulled her to his side, trying to send some comfort to her life force, but his own worry interrupted the flow.

"Ten is the maximum I trust my ability to shield you." His brow furrowed and the lines around his mouth deepened. "I wish I could offer you more…" He stopped in front of them and ran a shaky hand over his eyes. "Your window will be short. It takes tremendous effort for me to shield a gate, and even more so with the power that will be traveling through it." He pointed to Tolen's watch, "Pay attention to the time. I will focus my projection over you for one hour, then you're on your own."

Tolen looked at the man who had done so much for them, a man he trusted more than he trusted himself. "Thank you Jonas. For everything."

CHAPTER 22

STAY CALM

MACY STAYED CLOSE beside Tolen as they hurried back to the med-tent with Rune in the lead. Incrah passed around cold biscuits and slices of ham, telling them to eat, but she hadn't been able to put it in her mouth. Instead it became of mash of crumbs and slime in her fist.

Rune went in to get Keelyn while Macy paced and Tolen watched, sympathy mixed with something akin to guilt in his features. When they emerged from the tent Macy realized how much she'd hoped coming to Jonas would save Keelyn. A hope that dissolved to ash as she looked over her friend strapped to Rune's back in a sort of adult-sized baby carrier. Keelyn's skin looked like it'd been painted gray. Even her hair had lost its vibrancy. It now resembled the dull matte of dirty bricks. Her eyes had a strange darkness to them. The irises no longer held a gentle hazel, but flat black, the whites the same grayish tone of her skin. When she lifted her head to meet Macy's gaze it was like looking at a stranger.

Macy swallowed and put on her best pretend smile. "How are you?"

One corner of Keelyn's mouth lifted but her voice came out in a low rasp. "I've been better."

○ ○ ○

It took several long minutes to get to the northeast exit, and none of them spoke, the undercurrent of urgency keeping their pace steady and their thoughts occupied—and making the journey seem all the longer. Once Incrah told them they were at the camp boundary, Macy focused her thoughts on the car and felt it instantly connect to her life force, but they had to walk nearly a mile before it appeared.

They unstrapped Keelyn from Rune's back and he gently positioned her on the seat before hoisting his bulky frame in beside her. Tolen opened the driver's side door for Macy and after buckling in the passenger side, closed his eyes and started tapping his temples. "Keep heading northeast for the nine miles. Let me know when we're almost there."

"Okay." She double-checked the on-board Treasta. It showed nothing, but as she drove down the narrow dirt road she focused more on the feelings pulsing from her shard, trying not to connect too much, but enough to catch something the Treasta might miss. The usual pull to fully link to the shard pushed outward, a call to her gifts, but she held back, Incrah's comment about their shards still fresh on her mind. Maybe it was his warning, or maybe it was her own overactive imagination, but she could swear something felt different. A tiny tremor of something *other* she couldn't describe seemed hidden within the normal warmth she always felt when she connected. There weren't any intense stirrings of the Dark, but a warning pulse to stay alert and on guard sent tremors up and down her arms.

Nine miles later she touched Tolen's knee. "One mile left."

He opened his eyes but they remained unfocused when he glanced her way, the blue eye dilating and contracting.

"What do you see?" She whispered, aware that Rune was wide awake and listening.

Tolen winced, blinked, and his eye settled back to normal. He checked his watch. "Just about fifteen minutes until our hour is up. Let's stop here."

They climbed out, helped strap Keelyn to Rune's back again, and shouldered all their gear. Macy locked the doors and patted the car's hood. "Go home boy, I'll come back for you soon. I promise." The engine revved once before going silent and slowly trundled back the way they'd come. Tolen raised his hands, spoke the words to open the gate, and for once they passed through without a hitch.

o o o

"Man, even at night Kauai is beautiful." Macy ran her fingers along the spiny bark of the closest palm tree. The smell was amazing, floral, earthy, with a hint of brine. Even the trace of oil fumes from the dark and deserted airport in which they stood couldn't detract from it. "What time is it?" Through the darkness she could just make out a squat signal tower on their right.

"Around 11PM." Rune grunted before Tolen could consult his watch. "We passed through two time zones and over an ocean in seconds."

Macy knew that to them, it still wasn't fast enough. "Where to Rune?"

Rune grunted again and took off at a quick pace, despite the added weight of Keelyn on his back, to a small shed at the side of the airstrip beneath the signal tower. He walked in a circle around the shed, even opened the door and peeked inside at a crusty old motorcycle.

Her Kuna started to tingle in her palms. "Well?"

Rune slammed the door shut. "Stop pestering me, and let me think."

A tiny plume of smoke lifted from her fingers, Tolen stepped between them and put a hand on her shoulder.

"Mace, let him focus."

Macy clenched her teeth, doing all she could to keep her eyes off Keelyn, who in the lack of sunlight seemed more like a lumpy shadow than a human across Rune's back.

Tolen dropped his other hand to Rune's shoulder. "You said this airstrip is where you landed a plane you flew *from* LadonRyn. Could the plane have something Movan on it like the car, could it know the location and only work for those who have flown it before?"

Something akin to madness lit Rune's eyes. "Yeah, maybe! This way." He jogged left, both arms around the strap holding Keelyn against him. He paused beside a small hangar and yanked on the lock which ripped in half in his fist. He dropped it to the ground without another glance, but Macy's Kuna zinged hotter. She'd heard Darkened could do things like that, access a freaky amount of strength without ever speaking the Hidden word—because Darkened functioned like the animalistic version of a human, a human who moved on instinct, driven only by emotion and fight or flight thought patterns. Her fingers trembled and she welcomed Tolen's cool touch as it wrapped over her hot fist.

"We have to stay calm so he stays calm, alright?" He whispered in her ear as they entered the dark hangar. She nodded, but kept the Kuna burning in her palms, the smell of eucalyptus and roses a comfort and a ready weapon in one.

A single yellow bulb popped on, barely illuminating a tiny blue and yellow plane. "Help me." Rune started to unstrap Keelyn and Tolen rushed over. He cradled her in his arms while Rune climbed into the cockpit. Macy walked around the small space, letting her life force sense the vibrations around them, alert and focused—a better plan than looking at Keelyn and her shallow breathing. She would only focus on one thing. *Protect.* Be the look out. Don't think of anything else. A lump rose in her throat. *Stop. Don't think.*

A sputter and a cough and the front propeller started to spin. "I've got it!" Rune leaned out the door taking Keelyn from Tolen who jumped up and held out a hand to Macy.

She made to jump but something grabbed her foot and pulled causing her to stumble. Tolen yelled and she rolled out of the way just before the wheels of the plane would have crushed her legs as it passed.

She looked down to see a dozen Kinchomen swarming her legs and dragging her toward the hangar door, their lizard like scales making a rasping noise across the pavement. Tolen continued shouting but she couldn't make out his words over the din of the engine and the wind from the propeller on the plane. She twisted her fingers and sent a volley of tiny fireballs toward the creatures, aiming with her mind, and knocking each one back in a shower of ash.

They'd managed to drag her just outside the hangar door, she saw the plane turning, coming back for her, it was only a few feet away when something huge and black rose up from behind it, from the darkest shadows of the airport, yet it seemed to be made of shadow. Its dark edges blurred the night around it so she couldn't make out its shape, but the amount of evil flowing from it sent her Kuna into a frenzy, light burst from her palms, and the creature reeled back. Tolen grabbed under her arms and hoisted her up into the plane.

Macy's hands continued to glow as the plane door shut and an ear shattering roar echoed outside.

"Punch it!" Tolen shouted.

Rune guided the plane onto the strip and picked up speed. Macy tried to look out the windows, but could see nothing but darkness. The pulse of her shard and the roil of her gifts said the shadow creature was responsible for the rumbling beneath the tires and the rocking of the plane as it chased them.

"Come on, come on!" Rune growled. Too slowly the plane's nose lifted. Something slammed them from the side and the back of the plane shifted.

Tolen thrust his hands toward the window. "*Vin'akra!*" A gust of wind lifted them higher. Tolen kept his eyes closed, the tendons standing out on his arms, a vein pulsing in his temple, his face turning purple. The wind moved to a gale and suddenly the plane shoved forward as if it had a NOS button. Another roar, but this time below them, farther away.

Macy collapsed back against the seat. "I think I just got my first look at Legion."

CHAPTER 23

LADONRYN

T OLEN RAN A shaky hand over his face, wiping away the sweat, flashes of images trying to form in his mind, but again covered in haze. Only a few key things were decipherable—and enough to bring heat to his chest and a tingle to his palms.

"If that was Legion, it must not be as bad as it sounds," Rune mumbled as he checked gauges and flipped switches.

"You didn't see it. Or feel it." Macy shivered in the seat beside Keelyn. Sweat poured down her face and back, but still she felt cold.

Tolen sorted through the images in his mind feeling sick. Rune's anger and fear had opened up the connection between him and his watcher once again. "It *was* Legion." He knew his next words would hurt but he had to tell them. "Sorsha has been getting glimpses of Rune again. She knew he was coming. She told her master we can lead them to LadonRyn." He caught the tightening of Rune's jaw but plowed on. "Legion let us go. It had orders not to harm us, but follow us. If it lost us, they've put something on the plane, a way for them to track its trajectory. Legion will not be far behind."

"So? The power over Nowhere can't be hacked." Rune waved his hand in the air, and Tolen's neck prickled. Rune's skin seemed to lack some of the color it had an hour ago.

Tolen sighed. "No, but giving them the general location still isn't good."

Rune's mouth hardened into an angry line. "I'm not turning around."

"I'm not asking you to." Tolen could feel Macy's tension rise as Rune's anger filled the space. "I trust Jonas and he said come here. We'll take the rest as it comes. But we need to be aware of the fact that Legion is going to be the toughest enemy any one of us has ever faced. The toughest any fighter for Light has *ever* faced, and it will be doing all it can to find a way into LadonRyn."

○ ○ ○

They flew in silence for nearly an hour before Rune whispered, "That's it."

Tolen had been sitting with his eyes closed, trying to piece together the mess of hazy images to no avail. None of it made sense and some of it was so blurry he couldn't even guess at what he was seeing. He searched the glittering sea out the window, a mirror of the star-speckled sky above, and then he saw a mass of black among the sparkles. The night remained too dark for him to be certain it was the place he'd seen in his visions. But he could feel a tiny tremor from his shard, he couldn't name it, but it was definitely something.

"Can you feel that?" Macy leaned between them, her gaze focused on the black mass.

Sweat ran in beads down Rune's face, his eyes flashed between the gauges, and his head twitched like he wanted to look behind him at Keelyn, but was resisting the impulse.

Macy's hand dropped to Tolen's shoulder. The contact cleared his thoughts for a split second and he was able to name what he felt. "There is goodness here, Light, but fear festers beneath. A darker power held at bay…" He pushed a thumb to his temple. "It's strange."

Macy swallowed loudly.

"We're coming up to the landing field." Rune pushed the joystick forward and the nose dropped.

Macy went back to her seat as Tolen checked to make sure Keelyn was still strapped in. His stomach rolled—she no longer resembled the pretty young girl he'd first met. A voice, not the voice of a tree or any other thing in nature, but the voice of a man he'd never heard entered his thoughts, and the reason they were here, the mission they'd left behind, and the risks moving forward all crashed back down.

Conchla Mindra, you bring Light with you. She is in grave danger, even LadonRyn cannot protect her as you can. The Dark is closer than it seems.

The plane touched down and the voice faded. He glanced at Keelyn…*even LadonRyn cannot protect her as you can.* What could the Ninth possibly do to protect her from her fate? The Lóklana were the only ones who knew how their gift of light really worked and Rune was the only one who could give her the desire to come back. Something that had to be Rune's choice. Helplessness and frustration muddled his thoughts. Would the next few hours bring about the horrible future he had foreseen, or could a miracle happen here, in this mysterious place?

○ ○ ○

Macy squeezed her knees together, her heart pounding in her throat, as the plane rolled to a stop beneath a single bright light. The Kuna tingled in her fingers both from the close call with Legion, and anticipation. She kept her eyes averted from Keelyn's sleeping form, focused instead out the window where a group of six burly teens carrying flashlights had rushed out of a small grass covered building and stalked toward them through the darkness.

"Stay here. Let me talk to them." Rune unbuckled, and jogged out to meet them. The tension inside the little space weighed heavy and uncertain, increased by the only sound—Keelyn's raspy breathing. *Don't look.*

Macy watched Rune pause before the group as one of them shined a light in his face, then the smallest young man, Hawaiian by the looks of him, pushed the light down and wrapped his arms around Rune's middle. The tiniest bit of anger had left Rune's face as he led the group back to the plane, but when the door opened she could see it hadn't cleared from his eyes. Fear, doubt, and pain clouded them as they flashed manically around, never pausing to rest on one thing, especially Keelyn. He hardly glanced at her as they strapped her onto his back. There were no introductions, just harried movements and clipped directions. The boys led them by flashlight away from the airstrip and through the tiny village. Rune's shoulders shook so violently as her and Tolen hurried behind them, feet slipping in the sand, that Keelyn appeared to be vibrating.

They ended up in a clearing with a circle of small grass and wood huts, only one lit by the shimmering light of a candle. It was from this hut that a woman wearing a blue nightdress burst out and ran toward them.

"Carsa!" Rune called when she neared. The agony in his voice sliced into Macy's chest and sucked the breath from her lungs.

The woman paused beside them, and after touching Rune's cheek, spoke to the group of boys. "Bring Fraya. Hurry!" She grabbed Rune's hand, "This way!" and led them back into the hut she'd just vacated.

The small hut couldn't hold all of them. Tolen motioned for Macy to go inside with Rune and Keelyn and he stayed back, leaning against the doorframe. While part of her wanted to be inside, another part, getting louder every second, wanted to run as fast and as far away from the situation as she could. Her fingers trembled, her shoulders shook, one foot inside the hut, the other cemented in the doorway beside Tolen.

Carsa helped unravel Keelyn from Rune's back and he laid her down on the small bed inside, his eyes manic as he brushed the hair away from her face with trembling fingers. "It's going to be all right kiddo," he crooned, but her eyes stayed closed, her breathing shallow and rapid.

Macy's foot inched closer to the door, while her body leaned awkwardly inside. Tolen touched her back, a trickle of warmth tried to push into her heart, but the fear blocked it.

"Excuse me." A gentle voice spoke from behind and Macy stepped fully into the room to let a woman pass by. Then she moved back to the door, and leaned against Tolen. His arms came around her shoulders and she pushed her body tighter to him.

"Fraya…" Relief pulsed from Carsa, but Fraya's expression didn't bring any feelings of relief to Macy.

Fraya lowered a cream-colored shawl from her face, her skin held a soft yellow glow. Fraya moved her hand from Keelyn's head to her feet, a thread of golden light jumped from her fingers and spidered across

Keelyn's body. A tiny bit of the gray in Keelyn's skin faded were the light touched, but returned the moment the woman dropped her hand. She did not wake.

"Who is she grieving?" Fraya asked without looking up.

"Her twin brother." Rune's voice cracked.

"She is fading fast. We've not much time." She grasped Rune's hand, her pale blue-green eyes searching his face. "I will need your help."

Fraya then addressed the room, her fingers still locked around Rune's fingers, a slight glow of their entwined hands drew Macy's attention and she stared at that instead of either of her friends. "We have no choice but to wait for noon, when the sun is at its peak in the sky to begin the healing." She looked back to Rune. "Until then you must use your link to keep her here."

"My link?" Rune pulled his hand free, his movements jerky, his arms trembling.

"The love you feel for her. The love she has for you. It is extremely powerful. More powerful than her grief. The *only* thing more powerful than her grief at this moment. I will do what I can as a Lóklana to coax the light back inside, but love will be what saves her."

Rune's shoulders drooped, his knees seemed to give way and he leaned against the wall for support.

"Ask what you must." Fraya's tone was gentle but firm.

"What if—" he ran a hand over his face. Where a teenager's youth should be, a mask of a thousand years' worth of pain resided. "What if she is better off if—if I let her go?" He looked at Keelyn's fading body. "She is too good for this world. She deserves a life of peace."

"That is for her to decide, *not* you." Fraya touched Rune's elbow, her fingers glowing, but he pulled away from the light she offered. "It is only fair that she hear the truth from your lips before she makes that decision. She must be told that you love her as you *know* she loves you."

Rune's head dropped to his chest and a sob erupted from deep within his chest. Macy's feet seemed to move of their own accord out of the shelter of Tolen's arms to comfort Rune, but he pulled away from her touch. "I don't…deserve her. Why would she love me?"

"Because you are more than you realize, Rune." Macy whispered, the crack in her heart growing to the size of the Grand Canyon. "Whatever happened with that evil woman, that's not you anymore. You can have a future with Keelyn. A really beautiful one."

Rune slid down the wall and wrapped his arms over his head. This time he let Macy put her hand on his shoulder, she knelt beside him and whispered in his ear. "You say I have Cathe, then trust me when I say I know you are good. I've felt it. You deserve happiness Rune, and the first place to start finding it is with her."

○ ○ ○

The tingle in Tolen's palms increased every second they were here. A mixture of worry, anticipation, and a growing fear.

While Macy soothed Rune, Fraya moved to his side, and her whisper ignited something inside him, some instinct or deep knowledge he had yet to discover but held the weight of destiny, "*Conchla Mindra*, you have brought the Child of Light with you. Her love is strong and will help in the healing. But you must protect her. She is not safe here. You should not have brought her to LadonRyn."

CHAPTER 24

DARKENED

M ACY SAT AGAINST a tree, legs pulled up to her chest, forehead pressed to her knees, eyes squeezed shut. One more hour to go until noon. Last night Carsa had told them they could sleep in the hut next to Keelyn's and that someone named Nahmala wanted to speak with Rune, but he refused to leave Keelyn's side. Carsa had given in and said he could go after the healing.

Tolen had taken Macy to the hut and told her to rest, but she hadn't been able to shut her eyes until he sat on the floor by her bed and started singing in Hidden language. Even though she couldn't understand the words, they brought a peacefulness that managed to lull her into a fitful sleep until the sun rose. When she woke Rune still hadn't come, and the circles under Tolen's eyes said he had had a worse sleep than she had. Unable to stand the close confines of the hut, she'd left to pace outside.

She'd spied Rune sitting in the sand between their hut and Keelyn's and knew she should have gone to him, but only made it to the nearest tree before her knees gave out and she collapsed in the sand, her head in her hands.

"Macy?" The sand shifted and Tolen's long legs stretched out beside her. He started rubbing her back and a shudder passed through her center. Her throat tightened and it took monstrous effort to say the words on her tongue.

"You were right you know."

"About what exactly?" Tolen continued to rub in soothing circles.

"After Bastian's Farewell funeral thingy. You said I block everyone out so I won't have to feel pain. This hurts so much, Tolen. I don't want her to die." A sob pushed its way out and she bit down on her lip so hard she tasted blood.

Tolen touched her lip with his finger and she felt the pleasant warmth of his healing shiver across her skin as the cut from her teeth healed. "Love does that." He pulled her under his arm and she leaned into his embrace.

"Causes overwhelming joy and crippling pain." She hiccuped.

Tolen kissed the top of her head. "But ask yourself Macy, would you rather never have known Keelyn in order to avoid this hurt?"

Macy's thoughts turned to Keelyn. She'd only known her for a short while, very short, but in that time she'd seen something beautiful in Keelyn, something pure, and undefiled. Anyone who took the time to know Keelyn would love her. She was impossible not to love. But it was more than her nature that made Macy love her. It was the love and acceptance she'd shown Macy from the first day they'd met. As Tolen said, love reciprocated is an incredible high. It's sustaining, comforting. True friendship was an incredible gift. And now that Macy had experienced it, it had become vital—something she no longer wanted to live without.

But despite all that, the answer still wasn't as easy as it should be. The pain was so incredibly strong. Even having nearly all the bones in the right side of her body crushed, the DéHool's huge fang ripping through her arm, none of that compared to the pain piercing her heart right now. A pain so deep she could hardly breathe. "No. At least I don't think so. I'm glad I've had the time I've had with her, but…"

"You still don't want her to die." Tolen placed his finger under her chin, pecked her lips, then held her in silence, giving her time to sort through the churning thoughts inside her head. Keelyn was dying. Just like everyone else in her life besides Tolen, Keelyn was going to leave. Love—joy and pain. It was like an addiction, a craving, a need so intense you would go to any lengths to save it, savor it, hold onto it. Once you'd had it, you could never go back to a life of indifference.

I'll miss her so much…and I don't want to lose Rune either. The tears ran again, staining Tolen's shirt.

She will never truly be gone, LaUnahi. Bastian's gentle voice filled her mind. *Surely, I taught you that.*

And I believed you, sort of. It's just so hard Bastian. I have proof of the after-life. But it still hurts so much. I'm not ready to say goodbye.

I know, LaUnahi. I know.

She let Tolen hold her for several minutes, but the tugging toward Rune couldn't be ignored. She'd been avoiding him and it wasn't fair. Her pain was overwhelming, but his was unbearable. The waves of defeat, self-loathing, and sorrow coming from his life force were like a series of gut punches—maybe she really did have some Cathe in her after-all.

But a tiny part of her was angry. Angry at Rune for not just telling Keelyn the truth, not doing everything he could to save her friend. But this was the childish side of her. The side that only thought of itself. The side that refused to acknowledge that Rune and Keelyn had a history of years together that she had not been a part of. That Rune had led a life far different than her own. That it had been a life of mostly pain and sorrow until Keelyn entered it. She took a deep breath and leaned out of Tolen's arms.

"You're doing the right thing." Tolen kissed her cheek, stood up, and helped her to her feet. "You might be the only one who can reach him."

Macy swallowed the lump in her throat, squeezed Tolen's hand, and walked the short distance to where Rune sat, his head in his hands.

"It's almost noon." She whispered and he grunted.

Show him you care Macy, give him something else to think about, Bastian whispered gently.

Macy bit her lip. *Small talk. Ugh.* But she took her Watcher's advice— the best way she could. "I didn't know you liked cars."

Rune shrugged. "I guess we have a lot more in common than we thought." He glanced her way and the Kuna inside her lit like a struck match.

His skin had a grayish tint, not like Keelyn's, but the rotting gray of the Darkened. His eyes, instead of bright blue, had turned the churning steel of a stormy sky. Pain flared her temper and she no longer cared if it was childish. How could he be letting this happen? He knew better! "Yeah, both hot tempered, stubborn, and blindly stupid at the worst moments."

"What's that supposed to mean?"

"You know what it means!" Smoke furled from her palms. "She's dying! You can save her but you're giving up. You're so damn stubborn!"

Rune spun to his feet, his fists burst into flame, and Macy's did the same, ready to pull his fire if he shot, but he did not raise his hands. "Hypocrite." Firelight flickered in his eyes, eyes that held more pain than Macy had ever seen, her own heart trembled at the sight, but the anger was stronger.

"It's the truth! I don't care if it's hypocritical for me to say it. You're being a jackbutt!"

The corner of his mouth twitched and a burst of hope surged in her chest. Then the churning in his eyes became hardened steel. "Proof that she *shouldn't* love me!"

"But she *does!*" The flames continued to crackle from both their hands, the light dancing in agonized shadows across their faces. People began to gather, Macy could feel the concern emanating from their life forces and Tolen's calming influence at the edge of the trees, holding them back.

"She shouldn't!"

"You have no right to make that decision for her." Macy twisted her fingers, and an image of Keelyn's face shimmered within the flame for a single moment. "She chose *you.*"

"I'm no good for her!" Flames curled up his arms and leapt from his palms but stayed in front of him. His eyes darkened a fraction more.

"So WHAT?!" Both their flames licked higher. "SO FREAKING WHAT! Look around you. Look at what this world has become. There's no such thing as fairytales. There's no such thing as Cinderella or Prince Charming. No one is perfect. There's no happily ever after. There's only now, and what we choose to do with it."

The flames licked up her arms to her shoulders, but the heat wasn't painful, it was sustaining, as if it were fueling her words, telling her she was on the right track. Rune's expression faltered, his flame rose and fell, mimicking the fight waging within his soul. Veins of blue pushed against the storm in his eyes. He wanted to believe what she said. She could see it, feel it. More words entered her mind, words she knew were not hers, but they were for him alone.

"No one is perfect. We've all got light and darkness within us. *Every-one* is in need of redemption, but it doesn't come to everyone. It comes to those who fight for it, EVERY. SINGLE. DAY. Jonas told me love is the only thing capable of causing two equal but opposite emotions: crippling pain and overwhelming joy. Love is rarely easy Rune, but it *is* enough. It's enough for two people to be together even if it doesn't always make sense, even if it's hard or scary, even if one of them thinks they don't deserve the other. Love is the only thing that matters. If it isn't, then what's the point to all this?" She waved a flaming hand through the air leaving a trail of light. "What's the point to any of it?"

Rune's hands fell to his sides, the flame barely a flicker, but Macy's light continued to grow, her arms and cheeks began to glow until the only person she could see within the light was Rune.

"Let the monster go, Rune," she whispered, not understanding what she said but knowing it was right all the same. "You are not him. He is not you. You are not your father, or your past. You are who you choose to be, *today*." A line of flame curled from her fingers, a thread of light, bending and straightening, until it hit Rune's chest and then he too was engulfed in light. "*Lonadras* my friend. Be *free*."

A scream from behind extinguished Macy's light and she met Rune's terrified gaze.

"Keelyn!" Rune rushed past her back to the hut, she followed tight on his heels. The sight they met inside had them both skidding to a stop. Macy's hand flew to her mouth afraid she was about to be sick. A bright beam of sunlight streamed from the ceiling and illuminated Keelyn's body. Her skin had become shiny black, her eyes and cheeks sunken in. She looked more like a mummy, a thousand year old corpse, than a living being. Fraya paced around the bed tossing herbs above Keelyn's body with one hand, chanting in Hidden tongue, while trailing

her fingers over her face and arms, but the golden threads were no longer penetrating the dark outer layer of Keelyn's skin.

Rune stood beside her, his face a mixture of horror and defeat, his
skin darkened further and when she caught his gaze, his eyes were the
flat black of the Darkened.

Chapter 25

TO LIGHT

"No Rune! Please!" Macy pleaded, her chest filling with ice instead of fire. So cold. Death's icy fingers wrapped around her heart. She grabbed his arm and shook, but the connection to her friend, the Rune she knew was slipping away, anger and hatred filling his gaze. "Please Rune, come back. Keelyn loves you! Let her decide!"

Rune's eyebrows creased and he raised his fist. Tolen's hand flashed to Rune's wrist and wrenched his arms behind his back. Rune yanked against Tolen's hold and sweat broke out on Tolen's face.

"Kill me," Rune rasped. "Macy…please…"

Lead filled Macy's feet, her chest. "No." A sob hitched in her throat and tears poured from her eyes. "You and Keelyn are part of the Eight, you are in *the* prophecy. This world needs you both. We need you both." She grabbed his face with her hands. "I need you! I love you both!"

Light burst from Macy's body and flashed like a wave around the room. It seemed to move through and around them all. A warm embrace that surrounded her heart. Rune's black gaze settled on her face, hope warring against the pain. But the darkness fought back. "I can't…lose her." He wrenched an arm free and wrapped his fingers around Macy's throat. "I won't!"

Macy's light dimmed, and a burst of wind shot through the room, flame erupted from Tolen's hands where he fought against Rune's hold, but Rune's arms just soaked it in. Lights popped in front of Macy's eyes, she clawed at Rune's fingers as her oxygen-deprived body twitched.

A flash of reddish light and she was on the floor, gasping for breath. A no-legged man stood in the doorway, held up by two of the boys they'd met earlier. His one arm—only arm—held high, a black shard clasped in his fingers. Another flash of red light and Rune fell down beside her, Tolen still wrestling for a hold.

"Lift Rune to his knees." The man said and Tolen fought to hold Rune up, Macy shifted to help, her throat aching. The boys lowered the man to his right knee but stayed there to balance him as he placed the black shard on Rune's forehead.

A bloodcurdling animalistic scream left Rune's throat. Tolen had seen this moment, Rune becoming Darkened. Was she about to lose both Keelyn *and* Rune? Then the gray in his skin began to recede, flowing toward the shard pressed to his forehead, darkening it.

As the shard darkened something happened to the man holding it. His melted features blurred even more, almost completely obscuring his one eye. The knee he rested on shriveled and shrunk until both legs were but short stumps. Three of his fingers dissolved until all that was left was the first finger and thumb holding the shard.

Rune's body began to twitch violently, it took all Macy and Tolen had to hold him up, only his head remained still, seemingly held in place by the power of the shard on his forehead. His face contorted, and a cry of pain escaped his throat.

"Let the darkness go Rune, it is not you and you know this." The man whispered and pulled away the shard—now black as tar.

The shaking in Rune's body increased and Tolen and Macy were thrown backward. Rune's head reeled back, another heart-breaking scream erupted from his throat, tears fell from his eyes and he fell forward onto his hands and knees, his sobs bouncing around in the tiny space. Macy crawled to his side and touched his arm. "Please Rune. Come back to us." A shudder ran across Rune's shoulders, the gray in his skin faded back to his suntanned brown, and slowly the sobs subsided. Seconds passed while no one dared breathe. Finally Rune lifted his head, blinked, and the black faded from his eyes. "Wh—Nahmala?"

The ruined man's face seemed to lift in a semblance of a smile. "Welcome back Rune. Come now. You must save the girl. If not for yourself, then for the purpose to which she was put on this earth. The world needs her light. She has a mission to fulfill and only you can make sure she fulfills it. *Rise.*"

Rune rose unsteadily to his feet, only now seeming to realize Tolen and Macy had been on the floor beside him.

The boys lowered Nahmala to the chair beside Keelyn's bed as Rune walked to her. Fraya had paused in the herb tossing, her gaze flicking from Nahmala to Rune and back again.

"Rune, forget who you *think* you are, and be who you *know* you are. Redemption is yours if you but accept it," Nahmala whispered. "This is the moment for which you were born, the moment that will determine your path for the rest of your life. *Rise to it!*" The command seemed to reach inside Rune, and Macy felt the shift take place in his life force. The fear and the doubt remained, but it had shrunk beneath his acceptance of Nahmala's words. Finally, for the first time in probably ever, Rune had seen a glimpse of the incredible person he truly was and had begun to accept it.

Rune sank to his knees at Keelyn's side, laid his cheek against hers. The self-hatred had left his expression, to be replaced with determination. A flare of hope heated Macy's chest.

"Keelyn…" Tears flowed down Rune's face and dripped in her hair. "If you choose to leave this world because it is what you want, because you want to be free, then go. Be with Connell."

Keelyn's breathing became shallower. Macy's Kuna flared and Tolen grasped her hand, coaxing calm into her heart.

"But, before you go, I have to tell you that…" He rested his forehead on hers. "I love you." He chuckled sardonically. "I'm so sorry I never told you before. Stubborn as always, eh." He cupped her blackened, crusty cheeks in his hands. "I didn't know I could ever love anyone. Didn't know it was in me. But you…you showed me that I can experience love, real love. I love you Keelyn." He pressed a kiss to her waxy forehead. "If you choose to stay, I promise to love you until my dying breath. And if

I'm lucky and by some miracle I make it to where you go on the other side, I'll love you forever." He moved his lips to her blackened ones. She took one more breath and was still.

He dropped his head to her shoulder and shook with emotion.

Fraya stepped back, her face drawn. Nahmala sighed from his chair.

Tolen wrapped his arms around Macy but for once his touch did nothing to dispel the grief she felt. So cold. *Grief Sickness*. It made total sense. If she were Lóklana she knew she would look as blackened and dead as Keelyn.

Macy dropped her head against Tolen's chest unable to take her eyes off Keelyn's lifeless body. What would happen to Rune now? Would that guy, Nahmala's, words be enough to keep Rune from going back toward Darkened? Would her and Tolen and his other friends be enough to fill the void Keelyn left behind?

She blinked back moisture and saw something that had her lifting her head and moving closer to Keelyn's body. She rubbed her eyes, just in case it was all the salt water doing funny things to her vision. No, there it was again. Keelyn's skin rippled. She gasped and Rune lifted his head.

The ripples became waves beneath Keelyn's skin. The blackened layer cracked, the sunken spots filled out. Large scales began to flake off, revealing pink freckled skin beneath. Rune leaned back, but kept one hand on her hair, the other grasping her brittle fingers. The new skin began to glow, the light becoming brighter and brighter until it became difficult for Macy to stare directly at her. Fraya converged.

"*Conchla Mindra!*" She grabbed Tolen, dragged him to Keelyn, and shoved his hands on her head. "Speak the words to heal!"

"*Lonadras!*" Tolen shouted, and Macy knew he was directing his Sphere ability to help heal Keelyn's physical body.

Fraya pointed to Rune. "Coax her the rest of the way back." Rune leaned over and started whispering in her ear, fierce hope lighting his eyes.

"Lasan," she gestured to Macy, "put your hands over the Ninth's. Let the love you feel for Keelyn flow from your hands into his, it will amplify his gift."

Macy rushed to do as Fraya asked. The moment she touched Tolen's hands she felt the light within her surge from her fingers into his. He gasped and a burst of light blinded them all.

A second's breath, a tiny cough, a relieved sigh, the light faded to a gentle glow, and all was still.

Keelyn's eyes opened, warm hazel and filled with sparkling light, her gaze locked on Rune. "Will you Promise yourself to me now, *before* you change your mind?"

CHAPTER 26

PROMISED

Tʜᴇʏ sᴛᴏᴏᴅ ᴏᴜᴛsɪᴅᴇ Nahmala's hut, Tolen's hand wrapped tight over Macy's—relishing the joy coming from her life force. Keelyn stood tight against Rune's side, held there by his huge arm, a smile on her face that grew every time he leaned down to kiss the top of her head.

Funny that joy could be found despite the reality they faced, but it could. As Macy had said, it was the point of it all anyway.

Nahmala was carried back to his hut shortly after Rune promised they would come and see him after he had some time to regenerate. Carsa had a meal brought in for the four of them and they'd eaten in peaceful discussion, avoiding the heavy stuff, enjoying their miracle, until Carsa came back around three and told them Nahmala was ready to see them.

The amount of joy swirling between them as they waited outside the hut in the bright afternoon sunshine could have been enough to make one forget that evil existed, but the influx of blurry images pressing against Tolen's Second Sight kept the truth in focus—at least for him—and he was somewhat grateful he wouldn't be the one to burst the bubble of happiness enclosing the others. Tolen now knew it was Nahmala's voice he'd heard when they first arrived and whatever Nahmala had summoned them for would not be good.

The slatted door finally opened and Carsa stepped out, concern etched in every line of her face. "He's ready for you." She touched Rune's arm and left.

Rune led the way into the largish hut. Nahmala sat in an oversized chair inside, his stub arm and legs propped up by fluffy flowered cushions, his remaining thumb and finger twisting the black shard at his throat. Open windows punctuated each wall, letting in the briny breeze and bright sunlight. "Come in and sit down." He nodded to four wooden chairs that had been set up to face him. Keelyn scooted her chair closer to Rune and Nahmala chuckled, softening the slightly tense atmosphere.

"It does my heart much good to see you two together." Nahmala reached out to pat Rune's and Keelyn's knees. "We have much to discuss, but first, I hear you have accepted to be Promised?" He smiled at Rune, half his melted face lifting, as Rune and Keelyn smiled back.

"This is good. The bond will bring you strength and courage in what is to come. In the Hidden way, a couple is Promised to one another for one year. At the year mark of their Promise, they are Centered in a ritual that binds them as one for eternity." A gentle twinkle lit Nahmala's eye.

"The Promise ceremony is sacred and can only be performed by a person who has been chosen by the couple wishing to be bonded. Would you do me the honor of allowing me to promise you?"

"Now?" Keelyn's eyes widened.

"Unless you'd rather wait?"

"No!" Keelyn's cheeks warmed and Rune stifled a laugh. She elbowed his ribs. "I mean that would be perfect, thank you."

Nahmala looked to Rune, who smiled at Keelyn and without taking his eyes away from her face said, "Yes. That would be perfect."

Tolen tugged Macy's chair closer to his and she grabbed his hand. Her joy filled him up like he'd drunk Euphoria. She was shielding her thoughts well, and he found himself desperately missing the connection. A spark of envy rose in him. How much he wished it were he and Macy being Promised.

"Then we'll begin." Nahmala motioned them over. "Stand in front of me please."

Rune pulled Keelyn to her feet, wearing a smile that transformed his face. The deep scar seemed to disappear, the tiniest amount of fear still hid in his eyes, and Tolen could sense his feeling of unworthiness for the girl beside him, but the joy on Keelyn's face mirrored his own. If it were possible, he bet Keelyn and Rune would be floating.

Nahmala lifted Keelyn's hand and put it in Rune's where they began to glow. "Neither of you have yet to Transcend, and most Promises are not made until after such time, but given the circumstances ahead, the Light accepts your choice."

Tolen tried to listen to the gentle promises they spoke back and forth as Nahmala directed, but his mind kept changing the scene to something else. Macy standing beside him, her hand in his, his voice making the promises uttered, promising to love her, and only her, forever.

An ache started in his chest, the old ache that he had worked so hard to suppress. The ache that said even if he did marry Macy, or became Centered to her or whatever, and they lived through the battles to come, he would age as the Hidden do, living thousands of years, and if he was lucky he would get maybe a hundred of those years with Macy.

His eyes burned. He'd accepted this. He'd said he would love Macy as long as they were allowed to be together in this life and she said she would be waiting for him on the other side of Light's Door. But watching Rune and Keelyn, who would also age differently, already beginning their lives together had Tolen wondering. Would it be wrong to be promised to Macy now, before her Transcendence, so that they could be Centered in one year, and take advantage of every moment they may have together as a complete whole?

His heart pounded with the thought. A tingling started in his stomach and rushed through his whole body. Macy let go of his hand to clap and he realized the ceremony was over. He stood with her but couldn't take his eyes off her profile. That could be them, entering a phase where they no longer had to hold back the love they felt. But then reality slammed down like a sword through his chest. They *had* to hold back the love they felt. The only way they could ever be Centered was if they defeated the Dark, won the Final Battle, and who knew how long that could take. Years? Centuries? That was the real fear in Rune's eyes, not only that he wasn't worthy of the girl beside him, but that letting his feelings be known made her a bigger target for the Dark.

Rune bent down to peck Keelyn's lips, but she grabbed his face and held him there for a good long smooch. "You're never getting away from me again, buddy."

Rune laughed, picked her up to kiss her properly, and Nahmala chuckled.

Macy pulled Tolen back to his seat and caught his eye. *Are you alright?*

Tolen nodded, "I'm great." Feeling Nahmala's eye on him, he reached over to shake Rune's hand. "Congratulations you guys."

Rune shook back and Keelyn grinned so big it pushed fat tears from her eyes. "Thank you."

Nahmala sighed. "I'm so proud of you two. You have been through much, suffered much, but the step you just took shows your faith in the future." He went back to fingering the shard at his throat. "As you are aware, Legion is in the earth realm. Sorsha sensed you as your fear for Keelyn turned to anger."

"I'm so—"

Nahmala raised his hand, "No, Rune, don't punish yourself. Sorsha is wise and cunning. She has been searching for this place since long before you came here. It was only a matter of time before we were discovered."

"But as long as you are here, she can't find it right?" Rune asked.

Nahmala rubbed his brow. "Alas, I will not be here much longer." He waved a hand over his ruined body.

"You took the darkness from me and added it to your shard—now it's even more poisonous than before, isn't it?" Rune gripped the sides of his chair. Macy looked from face to face as confused as Tolen was.

Nahmala nodded. "A worthy sacrifice to save you, Rune."

"I'm sorry, I don't mean to be rude or anything, but I'm totally lost. Can someone fill us in?" Macy leaned forward, gesturing to her and Tolen.

Nahmala tilted his head. "Do you know how a Watcher becomes Fallen?"

Macy nodded while Tolen shook his head. "A Watcher becomes Fallen if they are responsible for the death of their ward. Right?" She looked to Rune for clarification.

Rune's jaw clenched. "That's the gentlest way to put it. You don't have to tell them." He said to Nahmala. "They can see that you're a good person."

"Tell us what?" Macy's fingers trembled and a sick twisting started in Tolen's gut.

"That I am Fallen." Nahmala dropped his head.

Rune's face flushed. Tolen could sense his desire to defend his mentor and friend, even as Macy recoiled. "He wears the shard of his dead ward as a punishment. It's been slowly poisoning him to death. And by saving me he gave up what little was left of his life."

Nahmala shifted against the pillows, his features distorted with pain—whether internal or external Tolen couldn't be sure. The only thing he did know, even his Sphere gift couldn't heal the man before him. "I have but days left in this body. After that the power protecting LadonRyn will disappear and Legion will come. But this is not the most troublesome effect my demise will bring."

He lifted a small book, bound in leather, cracked with age, from the table beside his chair. A funny feeling rose in Tolen, almost as if he knew the book. Nahmala leaned forward, his blue eye piercing, and another rush of images flashed across Tolen's mind—a hazy black form, Legion? A mass of people running, screaming. A million demons facing a million more humans and Hidden kind alike. Was Nahmala saying his death would begin the Final Battle?

"Nearly two thousand years ago, on this very island, at a place once called Gyeesta—meaning Dark Earth—Darsapean received his form and Daemon the Demon Master became the monster he is today. The force that lived within Gyeesta and birthed the King of the Dark was defeated in the Revolution, its power trapped again beneath the earth when Darsapean was sentenced to misery. This island was separated from the whole of the American continent and hidden from all sight— even that of the Watchers. After my betrayal I was sentenced here. My life force is bound to this place as a shield and protection. While I live, the evil beneath the earth cannot rise. But upon my death, whether by accident or design, the evil can be set free. *Gyeesta*, can rise again."

CHAPTER 27

ALLIES

Goosebumps rose on Macy's arms. "Gyeesta? I thought that was a myth."

Nahmala tapped the book in his lap. "It is not. When this earth was being formed the Dark sent a piece of itself into the belly of the planet. For centuries it waited, tempting those who came too near. It seduced Daemon and he helped it create Darsapean, a portion of itself in physical form. Gyeesta knows Darsapean has escaped Misery. It has become restless; its power grows as evil increases in the earth realm. Even now it fights against me."

Macy raised her palms up, the Kuna heating in her chest tingling in her fingers. "Wait. You said 'can' rise again. Does that mean we can stop Gyeesta from rising?"

Nahmala thumbed the edge of the pages. "The only thing Gyeesta needs to rise is a connection to pure evil, a piece of itself to latch on to. Darsapean cannot yet enter the earth realm, the Balance has not yet shifted enough to his favor. But, the amount of darkness that exists in Legion means that creature would need to set but one foot, one claw upon this soil, and Gyeesta would be free, the Balance would tip exponentially and Darsapean would be able to leave the Shadow Realm."

"Then we'll kill it." Rune leaned forward in his chair and Macy's heart picked up its rhythm in agreement. "We'll hunt Legion down and kill it."

Nahmala raised his fingers. "Once I am gone this island will be visible to all, human and Hidden alike. Even if you went after Legion, defeated him, others will come, hordes. Gyeesta will call them."

"Then tell us what to do," Tolen pleaded.

"Let evil rise, so we can destroy it once and for all."

o o o

The sun had passed below the tops of the trees when their chat with Nahmala ended. The young Hawaiian boy, Oki, came to take them to another hut at the edge of the village where they could rest for an hour until dinner. *Rest, ha!*

Oki was a chatterer but Macy couldn't bring herself to join in the conversation. Tolen absently stroked the cover of the book Nahmala gave them as they walked. He told them it was a journal that had belonged to Tolen's mother. She could tell he was itching to read it.

Weren't any of them as freaked as she was about the whole "let evil rise" thing? Rune had asked Nahmala about the device in Arizona, since apparently Nahmala was the one who originally gave it to Rune. Nahmala said that if not for his impending demise, LadonRyn would have been the perfect place to hide the Descendants, but now agreed that the device would be the best option to protect them. Even they, Tolen, Macy, Rune, and Keelyn, could live under its protection until Macy transcended and finished the Awakening. He'd then become too exhausted to continue discussing their plans and asked them to return in the morning for final counsel before heading out the next afternoon.

But could they just up and leave this place and all its people when Gyeesta could rise in days and…

Oki paused at the door of the hut and pointed out a water pitcher and something called *Haupia*—little white squares on a tray that they could eat, a couple of chairs, and four bed rolls pushed against the wall if they wanted to take a nap.

The second he left Macy's thoughts burst from her mouth. "This is nuts."

Rune paused with a white square halfway to his mouth. Tolen hesitated above the chair he'd been poised to occupy, the journal already open in his hands. Keelyn stopped filling a cup with water, and they all looked at her with varying expressions on their face from amusement, to sympathy, to resignation.

"I'm sorry Rune, I know you look up to that guy and all, and he really seems awesome *and* smart, but this is crazy! Let Gyeesta rise?" She grabbed Tolen's arm. "Please tell me you think this is crazy."

His eye dilated, but only a couple times, and slow, much slower than she'd ever seen it. He must still be having trouble with his Sight. She dropped his arm and he sat down, answering carefully, as if measuring his words. "Crazy enough to be right," he said apologetically running a hand through his hair. "There's so much happening beyond what we can see in front of us." He tapped his temple. "Something has been at the edge of my *Sight*, something hidden behind the haze, the fear and the stress. A change, a piece that will affect the tide."

He motioned out the window to where the surf billowed and rocked, sea birds squawked, and palm fronds swayed—beautiful *and* deceptive. You'd never know what lurked beneath this island's shores. "Despite being relentlessly hunted, the Chosen are gathering, waiting for direction from the Ninth. The Descendants are *waiting* to be found. Followers of Light are waiting to be led. Humans who are in tune to the vibrations of the Balance can sense something coming, they may not recognize it, but their souls are waiting for the truth. Even the Dark is waiting, waiting to see if Legion succeeds, waiting for Gyeesta to rise and Darspean to return. I think Nahmala has it right." He met her gaze with regret and determination. "The Final Battle is inevitable Mace. If we let evil rise, maybe we *can* finally eradicate it once and for all."

"Well…then…" She stuttered. "Why not destroy Gyeesta in the earth before it comes out?" Even as she said it she knew it wouldn't work. Somehow, she just knew. She didn't need Rune's scientific statement or Tolen's affirmation that his *Télora*—earth connection power—told him it was impossible.

She yanked one of the white squares off the tray, dropped into the other chair, and shoved the square into her mouth, one part of her mind noting the pleasant coconut flavor of the wafer cookie, the other part stewing over the tasks ahead. They had to get that device in Arizona so they could find and protect the Descendants, but they couldn't just let Legion come, free Gyeesta, and kill everyone here.

A knock sounded by the window and everyone jumped. Fraya stood outside, sweat dripping off her cheeks onto her shawl. She twisted her head, searching behind and around her before beckoning Tolen forward, "*Conchla Mindra.* You must go, you must get her out of here."

"What?" Tolen gripped the windowsill and leaned out, the better to hear. Macy moved to his side.

"*Lasan*—The Gift of Light."

Keelyn stepped closer to the window but Rune wrapped his arm around her shoulders and pulled her back. "Why? She's no threat."

Fraya shook her head, "Not her. *Her.*" She pointed a finger at Macy and bowed her head. "It is not safe for you here, *Lasan.*"

"Wait," Macy looked from Tolen to Fraya. "What?"

"Yes, *Lasan.* There are some—" she looked over her shoulder again, "devising a way to destroy you."

Heat rose to Macy's fingertips but Fraya reached through the window to clasp her hands. "No child, hold it back." She looked around again. "Come with me. I will help you escape. But we must move quickly."

"We can't leave LadonRyn with Legion so close." Rune raised his palm.

Fraya was shaking her head. "Protecting the *Gift* must come first. Please. Trust me."

"Why would anyone here want to hurt Macy?" Steel laced Tolen's tone. He grabbed Macy's hand and she could feel his confusion matched her own, but she also sensed something else, a growing fear he'd been working to suppress.

Fraya closed her eyes briefly. "No one here is evil *Conchla Mindra.* But the evil beneath the earth has touched some, festering their fears, edifying the misconceptions in their hearts. They want to stop the Awakening.

They mistakenly believe that allowing the human race to die out will protect their way of life—keep them safe from the ways of the Dark. They think they can make this island a haven that can outlast the Final Battle, but this is madness, they do not understand the power of Gyeesta."

Rune gripped the window frame above Macy's head, Keelyn still shielded behind him, the tendons on his arms popping out. "Why didn't Nahmala tell us this? Or better yet, why haven't *you* told him about it?"

Fraya looked down. "Not even Nahmala knows all things, *Mindra*. He trusts some that he should not." Regret and sorrow lowered her voice. "I do what I do to protect my loved ones. But I cannot stand by and let them harm *Lasan*." Hand shaking she lifted her shawl to wipe the sweat away from her eyes.

"One moment." Tolen pulled Macy and Rune back from the window, out of ear shot, and whispered, "What do you guys think?"

"I think she's nuts." Macy tried to hold back a shiver. Nuts, but her words still raised chills on the back of her neck. Gift of Light? Was that some other name for Light's Aid?

Tolen gripped Rune's shoulder. "What does your Cathe tell you?"

He chewed the side of his lip. "That she believes what she says. I sense no deception in her."

"I feel her light too. Her heart is pure." Keelyn added with a nod.

Tolen touched Macy's arm, a battle waging in his eyes. He was afraid for her, she could feel it, which only made her heart race faster. "My Sphere ability says the same. Her character is honest. She's kept her secrets to protect her family. She's taking a great risk coming here to help us." He pinched the bridge of his nose. "I hate to do this, especially with the Fallen so close…"

"What?" Macy tugged his hand down.

"I think we need you to connect to your shard. My sight is so unreliable right now." He grabbed a fistful of his hair. "It's dangerous, but I think you are the only one who can determine our next steps…"

"Sorsha—" Rune started, but Tolen raised his palm up.

"One of the only crystal clear images I've seen, and I've seen more than once, is of Macy using her shard to guide us. She senses beyond the

Balance, you know this. I can't tell why, or how, but I think the time for her to use it is now, Fallen or no Fallen."

Macy bit her lip and met her friends' eyes. Tolen wouldn't quite meet her gaze. The mention of connecting to her shard seemed to have woken it up. The persistent urging she'd been consciously and subconsciously pushing back, rose to the surface, calling, almost begging. "Are you sure, Tolen?"

His Adam's apple bobbed and his jaw clenched, but he nodded.

Macy touched her shirt where it hid the Radia Shard, and felt it warm up. She took a slow breath, allowed her life force to connect just the tiniest bit. It zinged with joy and anticipation. It fought to connect fully, tempting her with its warmth and light, but she resisted, focused only on the need to know their next steps. A thought rushed to her mind, not an image, but as if someone spoke the words and she knew them to be safe and true. "We need to go with Fraya." The words burned as she thought of leaving the people here unprotected, but the next image gave her a tiny measure of peace. "But we're to get a message to Nahmala. He must know there are traitors in LadonRyn and prepare a way for his people to leave, if they choose, before Legion arrives."

o o o

Fraya didn't like the idea of waiting for Rune to go see Nahmala, but in the end helped him sneak over while the others packed their bags. They returned in less than ten minutes, Rune's complexion pale, sorrow emanating from his life force. "He agreed with Fraya and wants us to leave right away without telling anyone. He was aware there was some discontent rising among his people, but not that it had reached such a peak. He said he'll do what he can to change their hearts, but there's not much time. He's more concerned with getting the people off the island before he…dies. He's had some local Movan working on a gateway device that he plans to use to evacuate the people who will go. But he looked *bad*. His entire left arm is gone to the shoulder. His mouth barely opened. I don't know how much he'll be able to do before…." Rune swallowed and Keelyn put her arm around his waist.

"Come, we must hurry," Fraya urged in a shaky voice, her eyes red-rimmed and brimming with moisture.

They ran behind Fraya, keeping to the thickest shade of the Palm tree jungle, their packs bouncing on their backs. Tolen gripping Macy's hand so hard it hurt.

As the sun fell toward the horizon Fraya began pausing more often to check around trees, her body trembling, her light dimming—because of her stress, or to blend better, Macy wasn't sure, but it made her even more nervous. Fraya had helped them save Keelyn, they all sensed her goodness. She wouldn't be trying to hurt them, right? But what if Macy'd misread the feelings from her shard and this wasn't the right move? What if it wasn't her shard at all she'd sensed, but the Fallen? She shivered and Tolen squeezed tighter.

Fraya led them to a rocky hill and motioned for them to huddle close together against its western face. "We need be extra careful now. The darkness has more power over failing hearts while the light sleeps, but we must wait here until the sun passes below the water."

"Why do we have to wait?" Tolen panted, his eyes kept flicking to Macy, the fear in them made her stomach flip-flop uncomfortably. The set of his jaw, the tenseness in his grip. His fierce protective instincts had taken over. Rune stood over Keelyn as if trying to shield her from sight.

Fraya wiped across her brow. "For the symbol to appear."

They met each other's confused looks, but Fraya didn't elaborate.

Forty-five minutes later the sun finally dropped past the horizon casting the jungle in shadow. Fraya motioned for them to move cautiously into the open, and pointed west. "One hundred yards through there you will find a large tree with a tiny star glowing in its bark. Wait there until your guide arrives. They will lead you off the island."

They whispered their thanks and squeezed her hands, then slipped across the sand trying to keep their packs from clanking.

It didn't take long to notice the tree, the star shimmering blue in its bark. Four feet away they all stopped in their tracks as they spotted their guide.

"Toke?" Keelyn ran forward and embraced the little man. "You're here? How'd you—?"

"Inside, quickly." Toke held out one of his many devices, tapped a few buttons, and the tree in front of them split down the middle. Macy was reminded of when she went into Toke's "home" within a tree. But this time as she followed behind her friend it wasn't a constructed set of stairs they walked down, but a sloping hill of sand, and no bright incandescent lights illuminated a fully furnished room at the bottom. Instead the sand dropped into a wide stone hall, roughly cut, and the opening at the end flickered with what appeared to be candlelight from the space beyond.

Toke paused in the hall. "I hear congratulations are in order." The smile on his face was genuine, but his shoulders were tense and he didn't lead them forward.

"About time too." Brina stepped out of the darkness. Keelyn squealed and rushed into her arms.

"Hey! Good to see you man!" Mahto and Sienn followed behind Brina, Mahto's big frame almost completely blocking the light at the end of the hall, and making what had seemed like a wide space feel much smaller.

"What?" Tolen gripped their arms. "This—what?"

"What are all of you doing here? What's going on?" Rune seemed to realize the tension Toke was trying to hide, same as Macy, but then he was a Cathe.

Toke's gaze fell on his reunited family, then Mahto, Sienn, and Tolen, his eyes coming to rest on Macy and the look there—a mixture of concern, fear, and sorrow—sent her heart into a painful gallop. "Much has happened since our parting and I promise to explain it all, but first we need to continue the reunions in a much bigger space." Mahto chuckled and Toke held out his hand to Macy. "There's someone who is very anxious to see you. He's been resting, but I won't make him wait any longer—"

A shuffling met their ears and Mahto moved his bulk to the side. An emaciated body, scratches and bruises covering his arms, moved into the square of light at the end of the hall. But the flickering at his back shadowed his face. Toke took her hand and led her past the group toward the man, her feet dragged through the sand as her heart continued to sprint and her shard zinged with strange energy—excitement?

They reached the end. The man was close enough to touch. She raised her eyes, both scared and anxious for what she would see. A dark dreadlocked beard cascaded down his chest, a ponytail of scraggly gray-blonde hair hung over his shoulder. She swallowed and forced her gaze to his face. More scratches and bruises, wrinkles creased with dirt, and…emerald green eyes. The same eyes she saw every time she looked in a mirror.

"Macy." He said it as a breath of release of both pain and joy. "Macy!" he stumbled forward and his thin arms came around her body. His torso trembled with suppressed sobs. But it couldn't be. Her body seemed unable to move, her mind unable to process what was happening. Her arms stayed limp by her sides even as the man seemed to be trying to crush her with his weak embrace. This couldn't be real. It *couldn't* be.

She pulled back. His eyes searched her face, the candlelight shivered, and she saw it. A familiar twinkle and a gentleness she had no idea how much she'd missed until it was there again, tangible, inches away.

"Dad?"

CHAPTER 28

SCARS OF THE PAST

"I NEVER THOUGHT I'D see you again in this life." Max lifted his hand to touch Macy's cheek but she stepped back. Hurt creased his brow but he dropped his hand. "You look so much like your mom."

Macy chuckled nervously, suddenly aware the others had moved in close behind waiting to go into the room her and her father were blocking. *Her father!*

She reached back where she could feel Tolen closest to her and grabbed his hand, pulling him forward. Max's eyes flashed to their clasped hands as he moved out of the way deeper into what appeared to be some sort of work room—a long bench covered an entire wall and held a various array of ancient tools and gadgetry. His brows drew closer together, but she did not let go of Tolen's fingers. "Um this is Tolen, he's, um…"

"He's her boyfriend." Rune offered helpfully as they all filed into the small space.

A light chuckle passed through the stone room softening the tension. Everyone started to find places to sit, either on the work bench, or wooden crates, or on the sandy floor. Candles cast their light from rows of dusty shelves that lined the walls. Toke grabbed two of the candles, walked to Macy, and gestured with his chin to their right. "There's a cellar over there. Why don't you guys go and catch up for a bit?"

Max and Macy met one another's gaze, Macy quickly looked away, but could feel her father's eyes on her as they took the proffered candles and stooped into the dark opening on the right. She didn't let go of Tolen and instead dragged him into the small cellar with her.

There were also a few shelves in here lined with blackened bottles, but no boxes to sit on. Her father sat down first and she sat with her back to the door, as far as the space would allow, and tugged Tolen down beside her. They were still close enough all their knees almost touched. She resisted the urge to move into the doorway. She didn't know why she didn't want to touch her father, she just knew something large and wriggly had settled in her stomach and she was afraid if she gave in, if she touched him willingly, she'd lose her lunch in the sand.

A few snatches of the others' conversation filtered into the cellar and Macy knew she should say something, anything, but only a rush of inappropriate expletives came to mind, ranging from shocked, to happy, to outraged. Sweat beaded on her upper lip and Tolen squeezed her knee before leaning forward and holding out his hand to Max.

"It's nice to officially meet you. Macy's told me a lot about you."

"She has?" Max whispered, his eyes widening in surprise.

She tried not to look at him but the pull of his stare kept bringing her back. Joy and fear mixed in his expression. It was as if he too were waiting for her to disappear. She cleared her throat but the words still jumbled together when they came out. "What're—How're—How'd you find us?"

Max gripped his elbows as if trying to keep from embracing her again, for which she was grateful. "I thought you would be bringing the Descendants here—as it would have been the safest place. I contacted Fraya and she said you were here, but LadonRyn was no longer what it once was. She said you were in danger. She hid us, took care of you, and brought you back to me."

Another question came to mind, but she couldn't bring herself to ask. His stare made her uncomfortable. She grabbed on to a safer subject just to get him to blink. "I found the Barracuda."

It worked. He blinked in surprise. "You—you did?"

"Yeah."

"That's—how'd it run?"

She swallowed. "Perfect."

He nodded, his eyes still drinking her in, the need so strong inside him to hold her that she didn't have to feel it from his life force. She could see it in his posture, leaning slightly forward, his trembling hands and lips, the agony in his eyes a mirror of the battle waging within herself. The little girl inside her wanted to run to him, let him hold her, but her body wouldn't bridge the distance, instead she leaned into Tolen's side.

"Max, would it be alright if I healed you?" Tolen asked gently.

Max finally looked away from Macy's face and eyed Tolen curiously. "You're a Sphere?"

"Not exactly."

Max's eyes flicked back to Macy. She took a deep breath, trying to decide if she should care that Toke didn't tell Max who Tolen really was. "Tolen is the Ninth Chosen."

The blood drained from Max's face and he swayed where he sat. "You?" His head whipped back and forth between Tolen and Macy, flashed to their clasped hands and back again. He brought a trembling hand to his face, ran it over the unruly beard and left it over his mouth.

"May I?" Tolen asked again.

Max searched Macy's face, swallowed loudly, and nodded.

Tolen released his fingers from Macy's death grip, placed one hand on Max's forehead and the other over his heart. He paused for a moment as if deciding what Max needed to hear. "*Pench Ni'ya alo. To' ladon y hai. To' LaUnahi sibatha. Lon'adras* Max. *Lon'adras.*"

Macy started at the nickname Bastian gave her and wondered what Tolen was saying in the Hidden tongue.

Bastian's voice entered her mind, answering her wonder. *He is speaking words of peace to your father. He said, "Be still. The light is here. The Little Bird returns. Heal Max. Heal."*

Moisture pricked at Macy's eyes, but the tears that had flowed so freely for Keelyn did not come.

It is okay LaUnahi. Time will heal you both.

Bastian's voice faded and Max shuddered under Tolen's hands. Macy watched the bruises fade and disappear, the cuts heal and the trembling from weakness in Max's limbs slow. Tolen could not fill the needs of her father's malnourished body, but with proper food and rest, he would restore much faster.

"Thank you," Max said as Tolen sat back down and replaced his hand in hers.

A bag appeared in front of Macy and she looked up to see Toke standing there, the kindness in his eyes, the happiness despite their predicament calming her troubles for a moment. "Food. We'll regenerate here for the night and leave at first light." He smiled when she took the bag and went back to the others.

Macy passed the bag of dried meat around. Max took a piece out but only rolled it from hand to hand.

"You have a right to know everything. My past, about your mother, what happened the night you were chosen…We don't have time for me to tell all, but I can imagine what you want to know most, given you have found the car, and likely are on the Relic Path." Either he could read minds or her own needs were just as plain on her face as his were.

She bit her lip, unable to form a response as her heart throbbed painfully behind her ribs.

Max took a slow breath. "The Dark had come for me the night you were chosen. Somehow they'd discovered my knowledge of the Relics. The Shadows were summoned. They were almost to our house when you were chosen."

"So, they really weren't coming for me?" Macy took a small bite of jerky, but tasted nothing.

"No. It was a blessing from the Light that you were chosen that night. If your Watcher had not come, I would not have been able to save you from the Dark. The Watcher took you and I fought the creatures as best I could. I'd already placed the Relic in the tree so it could no longer aid me in seeing the Dark or the future, but I knew what had come. I knew what it was I felt…The Shadows…took Alli." His voice cracked and he looked down at his dirty hands. "I heard her screaming and then…" He continued methodically, as if a clinical approach could soften the memory he had suppressed. Macy wished she had the courage to say he didn't have to tell, he didn't have to relive it. But she needed to know from the perspective of someone who had shared that night. She needed to know what had happened and why.

"I wrestled with the Shadows after they stole Alli, but I could not escape them…" He pushed his thumbs into his eyes, a few tears pushed free and trickled in dirty tracks down his face into his beard. "They took me to a forgotten island, they tortured me, but I only gave them pieces of truth, barely enough to stay alive. At first I'd hoped to find a way to escape and come find you, but soon I knew I would never escape. I accepted my fate. I had brought the Dark upon us. It was my fault your mother was murdered, my fault. You were safer away from me." He placed his head in his hands. "Such a blessing. You were such a blessing." He raised agonized eyes to his daughter.

Something came to life in Macy's middle, the dormant child who suddenly felt abandoned. Despite her father's pain a kindling of anger ignited.

"Alli couldn't have children." Max spoke between his fingers. "It was why she'd chosen to be a nun. I told her I wanted to marry her anyway. Besides, who wanted to bring a child into a world this bad?" The corner of his mouth lifted but Macy could see no humor.

He looked up, the wetness on his cheeks had smeared into the dirt creating muddy splotches on his cheeks. "But then, nearly ten years after we were married, Alli discovered she was pregnant. I knew you were a gift. A precious gift. I set out to make the world safer for you. I went back to work trying to decipher the prophecy, find the Relics, begin the Awakening. I didn't know I was actually making the world more dangerous for you. I didn't know, could never have dreamed…. If I had studied enough, if I had just—I should have known the moment your name was revealed to your great-grandmother but by the time I figured out you were a vital piece of the prophecy, it was too late. You were gone and I was a prisoner. I'm so sorry. So very, very sorry." Fat tears leaked from his eyes and streamed down his face in dirty tracks.

Macy stood up so fast the bag tumbled from her lap spilling jerky onto the sand. "I need a minute. Just…give me a minute." She ignored the stares as she burst back into the main room, the concerned whispers as she fled down the hall and stumbled up the sandy slope. She didn't attempt to leave. She wasn't stupid, but she couldn't sit down there and pretend that she was blissfully happy—as she knew she should be. She knew the resentment wasn't rational. He'd only been trying to make the world safer for her, but then he'd also admitted he'd given up. He'd stayed a captive because he thought it was best for her.

But what about what she thought? Hadn't he cared about that? Didn't he realize how much she'd needed him?

CHAPTER 29

A LINK TO THE PAST

Tolen wanted to follow Macy, he could feel that she'd stopped up by the exit, but decided to let her have some space, despite the awkwardness of being alone with Max. He hadn't ever imagined he would meet Macy's parents in this life. When he thought about how he'd been contemplating asking her to be Promised, warmth rushed to his cheeks and he started fidgeting with his shoelaces. He licked his lips and tried to think of something to say, but when he glanced out of the corner of his eye, Max was staring out the doorway.

"Excuse me." Max got up and joined the others, pausing where Rune and Keelyn sat on the work bench holding hands. "I'm sorry to interrupt," he rubbed his eyes. "It may just be my head playing tricks on me, but, I think I know you."

Tolen spun around until he faced the group his back propped against the doorframe as Rune pointed to his chest.

"Yes." Max leaned forward, and squinted his eyes. "Yes…"

Rune fidgeted under Max's stare, but Max didn't continue, just continued staring with a look of shock and *joy*.

Toke cleared his throat awkwardly. "I guess we skipped the introductions, didn't we? Max, this is Rune and Keelyn, my other two Lost Ones."

Max raised a hand to his mouth, ran it over his scraggly beard. "Rune." A tiny smile lifted his cheeks. "Your great-grandfather's name.

Now, I'm certain it *is* you. You look like your father, but the light in your eyes speaks of your mother. I can't tell you how grateful I am to know you're alive."

"What?" Rune's face hardened and Tolen felt waves of hatred swirl from his life force. He moved to his knees, ready to intervene if needed, but Max reached out and put his hand on Rune's arm, tears filling his eyes again.

"The Dark…" He shook his shaggy head, Tolen could feel his pain, and the look on Rune's face said he felt it too. Rune's arm trembled beneath Max's fingers but he made no move to pull away. The anger rolling off him was slowly turning into cautious curiosity. Barely a breath could be heard from the rest of them as they waited to hear what Max was talking about.

"Max?" Toke prodded.

"She died, didn't she?" He lowered agonized eyes to Rune. "Your mother…? And then he turned? Stoker turned, didn't he?"

Rune's voice shook. "Into a drunken monster? Yes. Not a day went by that he didn't beat me."

An image of Rune six years old and bleeding, huddling behind a pile of scrapyard junk flashed across Tolen's mind. His stomach twisted and bile rose in his throat.

Max squeezed his eyes shut and dropped his hand from Rune's arm. He swayed a little where he stood and Toke rushed over to help him sit on the other side of Rune.

Keelyn wrapped her arm around Rune's waist and leaned around him to speak to Max. "How—how do you know Rune's parents?"

Max addressed her but his gaze stayed fixed on Rune. "I knew Stoker when he was a *good* man. Strong, loyal, fiercely in love. Alexis, your mother, was special. Human, but with a highly developed Cathe ability, even without ever having been chosen. I knew it the first time we met. They'd come to see us. Alexis had just found out she was pregnant with you. While they stayed with us, the Dark…came for her."

His eyes left Rune and moved to the dark hall where Macy had disappeared. A twinge of sorrow pushed against Tolen's heart for the amount of pain Max had suffered. He'd been broken in nearly every way. Tolen had felt it as he'd tried to heal him. Years of guilt, sorrow, confusion, and pain. He'd grown up as a Lost One, a Chosen who had left the rules of the Hidden yet still chose to fight the Dark in any way he could. He'd returned his shard, returned to a human life to marry the girl he'd loved, yet when their child was threatened he'd resumed his quest to stop the Dark even though he no longer had gifts of the Light to help him fight the darkness he knew existed. Where Tolen saw bravery and sacrifice, Max only saw selfishness and failure.

Max winced and his shoulders curled inward. "I fought them off. No one could see what was happening but everyone felt it. I convinced Stoker to hide, cut off contact with everyone and everything familiar. There was a place where I thought they would be safe, a place where many Spheres lived among humans, secretly offering their protection. We never heard from them again."

He turned agonized eyes back to Rune. "I'm so sorry. So incredibly sorry. I can see your father hurt you deeply, but someday I hope you can find it in your heart to forgive him. Your mother—she was his whole world. That in no way justifies his behavior. To think that he…" He swallowed and a shiver ran across his shoulders. "Forgiving him will heal you. Take comfort that he *will* pay for what he did." His brow furrowed.

"He already has." Rune's jaw clenched. "My Watcher murdered him the night I was chosen."

A collective gasp whooshed through the room, a sick knot tightened in Tolen's stomach, and Max squeezed his eyes shut.

"I've tried to forgive him." Rune gripped the table edge. "I just can't."

Max nodded, his expression pained, yet understanding. "Each of us handles grief differently, some in far worse ways than others. Even many of the Darkened were once good people who could not deal with grief or pain and turned against the Light in anger. Free him, and you ultimately free yourself."

A wave of guilt rolled off of Rune and Tolen swallowed around the ache in his throat. He was reminded of what Macy had shouted at

Rune outside the healing hut. She'd told him to let the monster go. Be free. She couldn't have known, but it was proof the Light did, and It wanted him to be free of his past. Rune was strong, loyal, and fiercely in love…and he'd almost let himself forsake the Light and become Darkened from his grief. Maybe this comparison would eventually help him forgive his father. With Max's help to fill in the gaps, it just might be possible.

"So he—Stoker," Rune's lips curled around the name, but he pressed on. "He was your friend then?" Keelyn rubbed the back of his hand with her thumb.

Max took a deep breath. "Much more than that. He was my brother-in-law. Alexis was my wife's sister."

Rune's breath came out in a whoosh and Keelyn grinned. "That means you and Macy are cousins." She laughed. "Makes sense. Your stubbornness must be hereditary."

A tiny smile lifted Rune's cheeks. "And where the Cathe comes from."

Max winked. "Both come from your mothers' side." He squeezed Rune's shoulder.

"Thanks…Uncle Max." Rune chuckled and a flash of future crossed Tolen's vision. It wasn't much, just a jumble of images, but it instilled great hope in him. It seemed that between being Promised to Keelyn and getting a *positive* connection to his past, Rune's future would no longer be bleak.

Toke handed out more food and canteens of water. Mahto started telling a story, adding in his usual animated, hilarious antics and the mood lightened considerably. Rune kept shooting glances at Max, but Max had moved back to sit on the floor beside Tolen. He didn't speak, but after a while Tolen became so nervous he could no longer listen to Mahto and opted for conversation so at least he could pretend all the back and forth sideways glances were normal.

"Can I ask you about the note you left in the car?" He whispered.

Max blinked. "Sure." He motioned for them to go back to the cellar and Tolen nodded.

Once back inside, Tolen continued, "I've been thinking about something the Seraph said—"

"You've spoken to a Seraph?"

Tolen nodded. "Long story. But she said that Macy was the only one who could begin the Awakening, but in your note you said that you had started it. How?"

Max sighed. "As a Descendant I could *begin* the Awakening by first waking other Descendants—those whose forefathers would have served as part of the original Nine as mine did. Before I deciphered the prophecy, I assumed that at my passing Macy would take my place as a Descendant. The Claver had shown me things, pieces of the future, but it wasn't until I was in prison with months to do nothing but think that I figured it all out—what was written on the hidden fragment of prophecy, Macy's true role, and how it would affect our chances of winning the war against the Dark."

Tolen's shard warmed against his chest and that desire to protect Macy at all costs flared so fast he had to grip his knees to keep from jumping up, grabbing her, and hiding her away forever. Max spoke before he could figure out how to ask the questions forming in his mind.

"You love my daughter very much, don't you?" Max whispered, his voice trembling at the end.

Heat rushed to Tolen's cheeks. He would tell Max the truth about his feelings for Macy, but he could sense the bigger issue Max struggled with. Something that pushed against Tolen's gift of empathy and brought words to his mouth he knew the man needed to hear despite the rising turmoil in Tolen's heart that wanted its own answers first. "Macy loves you. She's grieved for you for ten years. She suppressed the memories of you up until a few months ago, but since then, I've seen the love she has for her parents in her thoughts. She just needs time. You're her hero."

Max gazed out the door. "You can't know that."

Tolen sighed. "I'm the Ninth Chosen. I know her thoughts the same as I know yours." He cleared his throat again and plowed on, pushing the embarrassment aside. "And yes, I do love her. More than my own life. More than my destiny as the Ninth."

Regret widened Max's eyes when he looked back at Tolen. "Do you understand Macy's role within the prophecy?"

Tolen swallowed, pushing against his fears. "She's Light's Aid. She's meant to help me lead the Chosen in the Final Battle."

Max shook his head, and suddenly Tolen felt the man's pain shift from his own, to pain for *Tolen*. "That is only a part of the prophecy. The part the world was allowed to know." His eyes flicked back out to the others.

Tolen's hands started to shake and his shard pulsed one quick burst of apprehension mingled with anticipation. Images began to fall into place in his mind—connections he hadn't let himself make before. "The hidden fragment you mentioned," his fists clenched. "Is it that piece of leather you put in with the fake Relics with the writing on it?"

"It is a piece of the prophecy, torn from the original and sealed away for protection." Max rubbed his beard. "The Claver led me to it a few weeks before Macy was Chosen. Few knew of it and even fewer would speak of it. It is a truth that can turn the tide of the war."

Warmth, the *un*comfortable kind, filled Tolen's chest. "*Lasan,*" he whispered and Max grabbed his wrist.

"What did you say?"

"Fraya, she called Macy *Lasan*, Gift of Light…" His stomach rolled. The strange visions, the overwhelming desire to protect Macy from a future he could not see. Something told him he was about to find out what it all meant, and as much as he knew the *Ninth* needed to know, he feared Tolen Parks, the eighteen-year-old kid in love with Macy, didn't *want* to know. "What does it mean?"

Max's voice quivered. "The last lines of the known version of the prophecy state, '*The Ninth shall lead them with Light's Aid beside, to death or victory within the coming tide.*'"

Tolen's mouth went dry, his palms tingled, and the Kuna bloomed to life in his chest. Somewhere in the back of his mind he noted the others had fallen silent.

"But the actual line is, '*The Ninth shall lead them with a Gift of Light at his side…*'" Max's voice cracked, emotion shaking it so much Tolen could barely understand the rest of his words, "'*to sacrifice in death for victory within the coming tide.*'"

CHAPTER 30

THE MISSING PIECE

"BUT EVEN THE Seraph called her Light's Aid, not Gift of Light." Rune's huge shadow suddenly stood blocking the door.

Tolen noticed matching looks of horror on all the other's faces.

"The Seraph couldn't speak aloud the protected part of the prophecy unless the Light decreed it. She used the wording we were familiar with," Toke whispered with a hand over his mouth.

Seconds ticked by as the words fell into place in Tolen's brain. *Lasan, A Gift of Light...to sacrifice in death.*

Tremors rocked across Tolen's shoulders and down his arms. A leaden weight fell hard in the pit of his stomach and pain akin to what he had experienced as he lay in the Shadow's veil, watching Macy die over and over filled his chest. The pieces of information took shape in his mind. The puzzle he'd thought already solved for their entwined destinies had suddenly flipped upside down so the picture wasn't at all what he'd thought. His mind replayed his conversation with Kichaya just days ago. She'd been testing him—making sure he was the Ninth. He'd had a vision of Macy, she'd told him he needed to focus on his task, his destiny, that Macy clouded his thoughts, but he'd argued, said how could he not think of her?

". . . she's my trigger, the strength behind my gifts."

"Mindra, so much you misunderstand. . . you are missing the real reason you exist. The real reason behind everything. . . You have accepted you are

the Ninth, but accepted the sacrifices necessary to succeed you have not. . ." He hadn't understood. Hadn't allowed himself to. *". . . you are battling between the man you want to be and the man you are meant to be."*

His chest continued to heat until the Kuna flowed down his arms and rolled into his palms becoming painfully hot.

The recent warnings he'd been hearing echoed loudly in his mind. *You carry Light with you, you must protect her.* All this time he'd thought it meant Keelyn. Convinced himself they meant Keelyn.

To sacrifice in death. . .

"No." Tolen's hands shook and smoke furled from his fingertips. "No."

Rune dropped his hand to Tolen's shoulder. "Calm down Tolen."

Tolen flew to his feet, his head bumping the low doorframe, his arms were rigid at his sides. He stared at Max, willing him to contradict the path of his thoughts. His mind continued to sort through all he'd learned in the past weeks and started connecting the dots against his will.

His gift of empathy. A protective instinct that was magnified exponentially because as the Ninth he was to "care" for the entire world. But this instinct was a million times stronger in regards to Macy, had been even before he fell in love with her. *My Radia Shard is a piece of Macy's.* A deepened connection that kept him continually aware of her and her needs.

The pieces slowly settled into a new picture, a terrifying nightmare of an image that sparked with truth so bright he could not close his eyes against it.

The Light had created in him the ultimate protector of *Their* gift. He had everything needed to be the perfect bodyguard for Light, both literally and figuratively. The gift of the Spheres—a shield and healer, the eight elemental gifts—an all-powerful warrior, the gift of Second Sight—a watchful guardian.

"That's why she can enter my mind like no one else can, that's why she's my trigger…My gifts are meant for *her*, to protect her. *She's* the final hope for mankind." The truth tumbled from his lips, no matter how much he wanted to deny it, hoping someone else would. "Light's final offering. That's why everyone thought the Ninth would be human.

Because it wasn't the Ninth they were waiting for at all. It was her. It's *always* been her. I may be the captain, the one meant to lead the army, but she's the secret weapon, the atom bomb." The words tore his throat. He'd become as broken and weak as the man on the sand beside him. His knees gave way, he crumpled to the sandy floor and wrapped his arms over his head.

Toke and Max, Mahto and Sienn, Rune and Keelyn all knelt down around him. Keelyn touched his back, trying to send some of her light into him, but his life force had become as cold as the sand beneath his knees. Macy's life force beckoned him. He could go to her, take her away, run from this destiny and never look back. He'd accepted that they would age differently. He'd accepted that they were different, human and Hidden kind. He'd accepted that they would fight in the war to end all wars. And he'd accepted the possibility that either them could die in that fight.

But never, not in a million years, did he see this coming. How could they expect him to go forward knowingly, *willingly*, and sacrifice her for the cause? There had to be another way.

He wrapped his hands tighter over his head. His parents had tried to change his destiny, and nearly got him and themselves killed in the process. In a way, Max had tried to take Macy's destiny for her and ended up in a Dark controlled prison, tortured for ten years. Trying to change destiny hadn't worked—had in fact made things worse. And not just for all of them but for the whole world.

"Tolen." Toke touched Tolen's elbow and an electric zing ran up his arm. If it was supposed to bring Tolen peace, it didn't work. "You've got to think above human understanding. Sacrifice in this sense is most likely figurative. The world *has* been waiting for the Ninth, *and* for the Gift of Light. Your very existence is a miracle. If we base yours and Macy's births on the human *or* Hidden understanding, neither of you should have been born. But here you are. One is not without the other. You represent the Hidden, Macy mankind. Your necessity to the fulfillment of the prophecy and the saving of the world is equal to Macy's, not more or less than. You are both the key to Redemption, for both our races."

A new empathy for Keelyn and for Rune began to well within him. *Grief sickness.* Never had he experienced such crippling grief, not when he thought his mother had died, not when he found out his best friend *had* died. *To become Darkened.* Never before had he had to fight so hard against the anger and resentment of this destiny. This *fate.*

Tolen, remember what I told you of fate and destiny—they are not as simple as you think. Bastian's voice echoed through the chaos of Tolen's thoughts. *There is choice in everything.*

And every choice has a consequence good or bad. Tolen bit the inside of his cheek to keep from screaming. *I can't change our destiny.*

No, but you can choose how you deal with it. She needs you. You must focus on your duty, not the outcome you fear. Fear is a device of the Dark in every way. Do not feed it. Replace your fear with determination. Be the Ninth. Protect her. Stop the Dark or the cycle will never end.

A conversation with Macy came back to him, one they'd had right before their kiss at the rest stop. A conversation that had been one sided, her musing while he fought against the pull of sleep. He hadn't consciously paid attention—hadn't thought about it at all since. But apparently one part of his mind had been paying attention. *Close* attention. Bastian's plea brought it back, the memory crystal clear. He could hear every inflection in her voice, and see every fleck of light in her eyes when they flashed to his, feel every flux of emotion emanating from her life force. She was so in tune with the Balance, so *aware.* Why had he never seen it?

"I've been thinking about the cycles of history." A little crease formed between Macy's eyes and Tolen yawned. Contemplative Macy was incredibly beautiful. He leaned his head against the window, letting the air conditioning blow across his face. So nice. These seats really are comfortable. Max definitely knew what he was doing.

Macy continued her musing. He stifled another yawn and tried to pay attention. "Tyranny, upheaval, rebellion, restoration. The crazy Pharaohs, Caesar and Rome, Napoleon, Hitler and the Nazis, Pol Pot and the Khmer Rouge, just to name a small few. Now it's terrorists. Bastian always taught me that those kinds of leaders were seduced by the Dark, but what if it's more than that?" The crease between her eyes deepened.

"I mean, what if the Fallen have been a part of the governments of the world for centuries, but each time they are defeated because they underestimate the light within the people. Once their tyranny reaches a certain point the people rise up, defeat the monsters, and they are removed from power. Until the next tyrant shows up."

Tolen's face slid down the window, squeaked, and he jolted awake.

Macy chewed on her lip. "In each cycle they tried to take over with one tyrannical leader and handfuls of supportive followers—but not all their followers were okay with what they were doing." She tapped the steering wheel. "Well, what if they've changed their tactics? We know the terrorist groups are sadistic. Good humans look at it and know this, but for the most part turn a blind eye. What if the Fallen are still part of every government including ours, and just using different tactics?

"What if they are being more subtle, a change here, a suggestion there, a gentle roll in of this policy or that, all the while we are blind to the monsters rising around the world gaining strength, readying for a fight? Slowly they tighten a noose none of us realize is around all our necks until they can safely pull the lever, and boom, there goes our pretend solid floor right out from under us. I hope the Light's got something up their sleeve for the day that comes. Something solid to catch us and raise us back up. Remind us who we really are."

Tolen's throat tightened. She was *the* something, the safety net—no, *rock*—that would rescue the races, raise them up, and remind them who they are and what they are fighting for. She would be the one thing, the *only* thing that could destroy the Dark once and for all. End the cycles of war and tyranny. Bring peace.

Tolen lowered his arms, clinging to one word Toke had said, and looked up into their faces, grasping to a smoky hope. *Figurative.* "Could sacrifice mean…it doesn't necessarily mean—she doesn't have to," he swallowed over the knot in his throat, "to die…for the Light to win?"

Toke and Max shared a look that didn't escape Tolen's notice. Toke had said it was *likely* figurative. But Max's fears were the same as Tolen's, he could see it in the man's tortured expression.

"The prophecy is ancient and words translated from Hidden tongue have multiple meanings." Max ran a filthy hand over his face. "It just means we don't know anything for certain."

"So, what else is new?" Macy stepped from the edge of the dark hall, just inside their little circle of light, her fists in her pockets, a sucker stick poking out the side of her mouth, trails of the tears she'd shed on her dirty cheeks.

CHAPTER 31

UNSILENCED

"THIS IS SOME sort of joke, right?" Macy looked back and forth from her father to Toke, avoiding the pain in Tolen's eyes and the mixture of sympathy and horror she could feel rolling off everyone else that said no, no it wasn't a joke.

It wasn't a joke, but it couldn't be the truth either. It didn't make sense. Tolen was the one everyone had been waiting for, the prophesied last hope for all-kind. "So, I've gotta like, what? Walk into the Final Battle and die?" It came out much more sarcastic than she intended, but that was good.

"No." Tolen took a step toward her, his voice shaking with emotion, but she couldn't make herself reach out to him.

Toke raised his palms up. "We don't know exactly what it means. But—"

"It could be?" She looked between the two men again, but her father wouldn't meet her eyes. "Sugar coating it doesn't change it. I'd rather be prepared." Blasé, yeah, that was good too. Make'm think she wasn't scared to death. They couldn't hear the racing of her heart, feel the tightness in her throat, or know how close she was to bursting into tears. Her eyes met Tolen's for half a second.

But he did.

"Let's just plan our next move and stop worrying about things we don't know for certain." Rune leaned forward.

"Rune's right." Keelyn nodded in agreement. "We need to focus on what's in front of us right now. We've got to leave LadonRyn to protect Macy."

Macy bit back a frustrated, and not very nice, comment. Her friends were trying to ease the tension, turn the focus, and she should be grateful, but she didn't like to be talked about as if she had no say in the matter. The feeling of betrayal grew as the conversation and speculation continued around her. Bastian had this saying from the human world he used—a little too often in her opinion— *Like a lamb to the slaughter.* It was what he'd said they would be doing to Tolen when they'd first found him if they let him go off on his own, unprepared and clueless.

Well, wasn't that exactly what the Light was doing to her? Sending her into battle without even giving her time to prepare for such a fate?

No, LaUnahi. Ignorance can be a protection. Remember timing is every-thing. There is always a greater purpose than we can readily see.

Bastian… A nagging ache throbbed in her chest. *Did you know?*

I did not know the full prophecy until recently. It was kept even from the Guardians. But I knew you were special the moment I first found you. A power existed in you that I had never seen in the thousands of other Chosen I had trained before you. A feeling told me to keep you separate from other Chosen, to no longer connect with other Watchers. I did not know why but I trusted the feeling, especially after reading your father's notes on the Fallen.

A tiny rumble of guilt hit her chest from asking this of her Watcher and not trusting her own father but she didn't want to hear everyone else's speculation anyway. *Bastian, am I really a Gift of Light meant to stop the Dark?*

Yes LaUnahi, I believe it is true. But you are not meant to do so alone.

Tolen. She blew out a quiet breath. *We are two halves of one whole… How do you know though? How do you know it means me?*

LaUnahi, my little bird, the same way you know for yourself. Truth, once spoken and realized, cannot be silenced.

She thought of Bastian's overprotectiveness. Rune and Keelyn's remarks while they'd studied the fake Relics. She *had* survived the Shadow Realm—unlike any other human in history, Chosen or not.

She'd resisted the Shadows when they'd been trying to take Tolen, and in a burst of power had sent them back to their own realm. She'd been selected to be the Seeker of the Last Shard, a shard with more power than any shard on earth. No human would have been able to wield it, yet she had. She'd accessed powers no other Kunamin was known to have, like the glowing eyes, the surge of light-fire that broke through Daemon's army and destroyed the powerful gate that would have released innumerable Dark creatures into the earth realm.

You are the Gift of the Light, Bastian's voice held both pride and sorrow, *saved for these final days, wielder of the only power that can ultimately defeat the Dark.*

By dying.

Bastian's silence was as much a confirmation as a spoken yes. Macy's thoughts shifted back to the conversation taking place around her. She could feel both Tolen's and her father's eyes on her, feel the almost mirrored pain from their life forces, but she refused to look at either of them—terrified that if she did she would start bawling like an idiot.

"...find the rest of the Descendants and get them under protection," Rune mused.

"And they're all over the place right?" Brina looked to Max who nodded.

"I haven't fulfilled my task from the Seraph yet either." Sienn paused while sharpening her knife. "After the rescue from the Shadow Realm, my father relocated to a Lafar colony in the north. We were on our way there when Sashan sent us word that we needed to change our course and get to Toke."

Mahto addressed Rune. "Hey man, are there any warriors left on this island who can fight Legion? Last time I was here only about twenty or so still fought."

Rune was shaking his head. "I imagine the number is pretty close to the same. The majority of the people here aren't warriors."

"Mahto and I can stay here," Sienn slid her knife back in the sheath on her thigh, "help with the evacuation while you get *Lasan* under the cover of that device you spoke of."

"Macy." A burst of heat flared in Macy's palms, intensified by worry and fear. "My name is Macy, not *Lasan*."

Sienn raised her palm. "I meant no disrespect."

Tolen put his hand on Macy's arm. "It's a term of endearment." His fingers trembled, agony pushed out from his life force and tried to take her breath away—but she pushed back.

"I don't care." Her fingers began to glow. "I won't hide under the skirts of others on a 'chance' that I'm some secret weapon that needs to be protected. Whatever the prophecy says, I am still Chosen. I will continue to fight as one."

Tolen pinched the bridge of his nose at the same time Max sighed. Both men were in pain, but she wouldn't focus on that, couldn't. She pulled back on the Kuna but it sensed her desire to fight, to leave and run into battle, right now. No better distraction.

"The Final Battle has already begun," Max whispered. "It is not one great battle, but rather thousands of small battles that began years ago and will culminate in a final stand between Light and Dark forces. It started in secret, infiltration of governments, ideas planted into the minds of the power hungry. They excelled in subtlety. And now the world is ripe for destruction. The Dark is everywhere, in every government, in every city, town, and village. They are actively hunting the Chosen, they are hunting *you*. You will fight sweetheart, because you *have to*. But in the right battles and at the right time. Until then, you must allow us to protect you."

A lump fought its way into Macy's throat. She looked away from her father, from the eyes on her face, focused on the sand beneath her feet, the flicker of light that danced off each particle. Light always overtakes darkness. Light would win—if she succeeded. If she went into the battle at the right time and sacrificed herself in the right moment.

Tolen's head snapped toward her—had she accidentally sent her thoughts into his mind? The tightening of his jaw said yes, but in this moment she couldn't care. The weight was too heavy to bear alone. He reached over and took her hand. This time she didn't resist, but it became ten times harder to hold the emotion in check. She kept her eyes on the ground.

Tolen ran a hand through his hair. "My *sight* is getting worse, most of what I see doesn't come together, or is too hazy to decipher, but a few of the clearer images are starting to make sense the longer we talk." He hesitated and a thrill of nerves rocked Macy's center. She didn't think she wanted to know all that Tolen had seen. "We're not ready to fight Legion—and revealing Macy at this stage, without an army behind us, would be the wrong move." He dropped her hand and started to pace in short lines. The break in the connection allowed her to watch him and pull further from the emotional roller coaster twisting around her heart.

"Nahmala said if we let Gyeesta rise then we have a chance of stopping the Dark once and for all. But we can't do that yet. Everything needs to be done in the right order." He rubbed his temples and continued to pace. "We'll continue to gather the Descendants, we'll set up a safe haven using Rune's device and we'll *all* call it home." Tolen looked at Macy. "But we *will* continue to fight, all of us, anywhere and everywhere we are needed." His blue eye dilated once before settling back to brightest blue.

"Sounds good to me, man." Mahto thumped Tolen's back.

Tolen resumed cutting a trail in the sand. "With LadonRyn gone and the Zenith compromised, we'll gather everyone to the safe haven under Rune's device. The Descendants, the Chosen, all the Light warriors, everyone on our side we can possibly fit."

Rune waved off the concern. "I don't think fitting numbers under the protection will be a problem. But finding a space big enough to hold us all, might be."

Toke spoke up. "Is this the device we buried in Arizona?"

Rune nodded.

"Arizona?" Sienn's eyebrows rose. "That's not a short distance."

"And with me and Macy leading the way for them," Rune tugged his ponytail, "we'll be making it with the Fallen tight on our heels."

Keelyn sighed. "And that device of theirs can control us."

"What?" Brina asked.

Rune waved his hand in the air again. "Later."

Toke grabbed his pack from a shelf and started digging inside. "There is a way we can get the device in Arizona in a matter of minutes with minimal risk."

"There is?" Tolen's eyes widened.

The conversation had been moving so swiftly, for a moment Macy had forgotten her frustration, but as silence fell when Toke started pulling out various things from his bag, the nerves returned, and she had to grab Tolen's hand again to calm down.

Toke pulled out a small silver disc, shaped like a CD but with no hole in the middle and a series of symbols etched in a circular pattern across the surface. "Tolen, if you direct your abilities to open a gate into this disc it can shield the location. The portal has a two minute maximum, and is only as large as this disc, just large enough for your hand to fit through, but with your earth moving ability you should be able to bring the device up without trouble."

A feeling of anticipation pushed against Macy's shard as if confirming the rightness of their planning despite her nerves. Tolen glanced her way and she wondered if he felt it too. He'd said her shard would lead them. Between his sight and her shard—if she could figure out how to be certain it wasn't being accessed by Fallen—they might *finally* have a way to be one step ahead of the Dark for once.

"We'll be able to move much faster to get the Descendants now that Max is here, too." Keelyn added.

"And they know me so getting them to come will be easy. Or easier. I don't look quite like I did ten years ago." He scratched his beard and met Macy's eyes with the humorous twinkle she remembered. Her heart skipped at the sight and she didn't look away, instead she offered a tiny smile. His return grin could have put the sun to shame. "I'm also the oldest living Descendant in the Claver line, so I'm the only one who can wield it."

"Well, now we know why it didn't work for Macy," Rune quipped.

"Relics, Descendants, uniting the Lafar, gathering the Chosen, coordinating a battle strategy with all followers of Light. That's a lot for this little group to do." Brina ticked the list off her fingers then began twisting one of her braids, her dark eyes belying the calmness in her voice.

Tolen tapped his temple. "Reinforcements… We need reinforcements. Then we're going to split up and divide the tasks."

"Reinforcements?" Toke asked.

Tolen nodded. "Quasar and Blaze. I think it's time we utilize the power of the Eight. With them in the game we'll have the power of the Last Shard behind us. Then, after we've gathered the Descendants, our army of Chosen and Light fighters, we'll come back here and face Gyeesta." A note of pain rang in his last sentence that he tried to disguise it with a cough.

"Sounds good to me, *captain*." Rune winked.

Max's brows furrowed. "Macy won't be strong enough to face Gyeesta until she connects fully to her gifts at Transcendence. And even with the Descendants wielding the Relics, the human race will still be blind, unable to fight, until she Transcends and completes the Awakening."

"Then we just have to keep her safe until then." Sienn absently ran her thumb along her knife.

Macy shook her head. "That's almost two years away. Daemon, Darsapean, Legion, *and* Gyeesta. Can you imagine how much damage they'll do in that time? How many innocent humans and Hidden-kind will die?"

"I can't see that we have another choice." Tolen closed his eyes and rubbed his temples again.

"There is *one* way to speed things up." Toke passed the disc from palm to palm.

"No, Toke." Max's fierce tone had everyone looking his way and sent Macy's heart racing again.

"Max," Chagrin and regret pooled in Toke's eyes, streamed from his life force hitting Macy in the chest. "It may be for the best."

"NO!" Max's hands began to shake. "It's too dangerous."

Macy's hands twitched, part of her wanting to go to her father, calm him with a touch or a word, but the stronger part of her, the side that had protected her heart all these years, rooted her feet to the sand.

"What's too dangerous?" She asked instead.

After another regretful glance Toke met Macy's gaze. "There is a way to," he swallowed loudly, "force early Transcendence."

CHAPTER 32

PROTECT THE GIFT

"WHY IS THAT dangerous?" Tolen asked at the same time Macy said, "Let's do it."

A burst of protectiveness rose again in Tolen's chest. That side of him, now that he understood its purpose, seemed to surge stronger than ever, jockeying for position in the forefront of his every thought, concern, and focus. *Protect Lasan, protect Lasan.* It wasn't a voice like Bastian's or Sashan's or anyone he knew. It was more like his own conscience speaking to him, reminding him of his duty.

He resisted the urge to smack the side of his head.

"The human body can only handle so much power at once." Toke's gaze flicked to Max then back to Tolen. "That's why the Balance waits until they reach the age of eighteen, when the bodily systems are strong with youth but settled in harmony and can accept the inseparable union of gift, body, and life force."

Macy's eyebrow rose.

"Puberty." Rune bumped his shoulder into Macy and she rolled her eyes.

Toke tipped his head. "Forced Transcendence was introduced during the Radia Revolution, when we needed more warriors, more *powerful* warriors. It was banned after the war, seen as a cruelty. It's never been done on a human Chosen before." He cleared his throat and a searing pain burst behind Tolen's ribs. "Forcing Transcendence pushes the body to accept the fullness of its gifts before it's prepared to receive them. The body resists and the…pain can be unbearable. But the life force is ready to accept the gifts of the Light the moment it receives them—Hidden kind at birth, human Chosen at six years old, the moment they receive their Radia Shard. The shard ignites the dormant qualities, enhancing them, and the life force soars because it finally gets to reveal a part of its true self."

Toke sat his pack back down and started twisting the ring on his right hand. "But it's not mature enough to recognize the need to wait until the body is ready, so the Balance guards the body until it is eighteen years old. That protection then leaves and Transcendence begins. The process can be more painful for some than others if their body isn't quite ready, but it is still far less painful than forced Transcendence."

Tolen's emotions resisted the idea even as he felt Macy becoming more and more intrigued.

Toke continued with every eye on him, "The process of constraining the will of the body to meet the will of the gifts and the life force—this is the most dangerous and risky part of Forced Transcendence. To force oneness requires a series of emotional and physical stimulants that hold the body hostage until it accepts the change. Sometimes…the body refuses."

Toke didn't have to say what happened if the body refused to accept Transcendence. It was written in every line of his face, Max's hitched breathing, and the collective horror of the group. If Macy's body refused the change, she would die. Tolen rubbed his chest and wondered if a heart could explode from hearing too much bad news in such a short amount of time.

"No." Tolen and Max both spoke at the same time Macy said, "I'll do it."

Her green eyes flashed. "It's my decision."

"But Macy, if you die. . . at the wrong time," Keelyn grimaced. "We have *no* hope of winning this war."

"And if I don't, the whole world could be gone by the time two years pass anyway." Macy's jaw was set, that little crease back between her eyes. She'd made her decision.

Protect Lasan. Tolen's little subconscious voice was back and persistent as ever.

How? Let her do this, or not? Which is better?

Protect Lasan.

Tolen fought to slow his heart and think as the Ninth, without the fear of the outcome clouding his thoughts. So freaking hard! He bit the inside of his cheek and tasted blood. "Toke, if Macy does this, is there something I can do to strengthen her body, like use my Sphere or Lóklana gift—or even Keelyn, can Keelyn help?"

Toke's orange-brown eyes lit up and his purple hair seemed to quiver in excited realization. "Yes, yes I think you both could help. Between the continual healing and light infusion, the body might be more susceptible to the change. I have a way to monitor what is going on with the body's electrical impulses which should tell us what healing component she is in need of."

"I won't need your device. I've always been able to sense what her body needs." His cheeks warmed when Max's eyes swiveled toward him. The idea was still terrifying, the side of him in love with Macy seemed to be screaming and clawing at his brain and heart from the inside, furious at the Ninth for taking this risk—but he trusted Bastian, he had to trust in the purpose of these gifts. He couldn't control Macy, he wouldn't take away her free will, no matter how much he wanted to lock her away for two years. It would destroy her. So if he couldn't stop her, then he would do everything in his power to help her.

Toke squeezed Macy's hand. "What do you want to do?"

She looked from Tolen to Max, an apology in her eyes, but her voice was determined. "I want to do it."

Max reached for Macy and after a moment she stepped into his arms. "I may not like it, but I wouldn't expect any less from you." He kissed her hair and she pulled back, a trace of moisture in her eyes she quickly blinked away.

"So, when, where, and how do we do this?" She asked.

"I need time to build the monitors and I think it would be best to do it inside the safe haven once we get it all set up." Toke started passing the silver disc between his hands again.

Macy nodded. "Okay."

○ ○ ○

Tolen tugged Macy to a quiet corner away from the others as they finished loading their packs. They'd all tried to sleep for the few remaining hours left of the night, but it soon became obvious no one was going to get more than a few winks in so they'd all gotten up and started readying to leave. With at least another couple hours to kill before sunrise, Tolen wanted to steal a few quiet moments with Macy, but it wasn't easy in the tiny space. Toke was scouring the cellar in search of usable food stores so that option was out, and Mahto kept pacing the hall, which only left the tiny corner for Tolen to try and pretend they were alone.

Half of him still wanted to take Macy and run, but he couldn't deny that they were heading the right direction. He refused to contemplate the prophecy and its implications. He would move forward one step at a time, doing whatever was necessary to protect Macy moment to moment.

He touched her hair and she put her hand over his, her eyes said what her mouth couldn't without being overheard. "So how are you going to contact Quasar and Blaze?"

Tolen laced his fingers through hers and lowered their joined hands between them. "The Seraph said the symbol would appear to them when I was in need. I was hoping I could just concentrate on them and the symbol and see what happens."

Macy nodded absently, her thoughts preoccupied. She was trying to keep them out of his head but stress made it harder for her—he was pretty sure his heightened fear wasn't helping either. He dropped her hand and pulled her to his chest. "It's going to be okay Mace." A sigh escaped her throat and she swallowed loudly.

"You say that like you believe it." She tried to chuckle but her breath hitched.

He had to clear his throat twice before he could respond and his voice still cracked with repressed emotion. "I do. I refuse to think otherwise. I spent too much time agonizing over the idea of aging differently than you, something that now seems trivial in comparison. I won't spend any moment I have with you focused on possible outcomes that don't involve us both making it to the end of this war…" the muscles in his arms flexed, tightening his hold on her. "I refuse to think otherwise."

She sniffled and he kissed the top of her head. "I'm scared."

It felt like someone had his chest in a vice. "Me too."

"I love you."

He lifted her chin and placed a quick but firm kiss on her lips—not caring who saw. "I love you. More than life."

"More than life." She repeated and tucked her head back into his chest.

While he held her he focused on Quasar and Blaze, the symbol of two hearts entwined, and the promise of the Seraph. Macy let out a startled gasp and jumped out of Tolen's arms.

Two elves stood in the center of the pool of light taking in the motley group surrounding them.

Tolen rushed over, dragging Macy with him, and ruffled the midnight hair of the younger elf. Gone was the shy boy Tolen had saved. Blaze was just fourteen years old, but his deep violet eyes held wisdom beyond his years. The mantle of Keeper suited him. He had taken the challenge of taming and protecting the Last Shard with grace and humility. Tolen felt like a proud uncle to see him standing there so sure of himself, so powerful.

"That was interesting." Quasar reached out to shake Tolen's arm, his silver hair flickering in the candle light, the scar on his cheek lifted by a warm smile. "The symbol woke us, we packed our bags, and then we were here."

"Were you still with Sashan at Hunsi's?"

Quasar nodded, "But Sashan had told us he sensed the time to come to your aid would be soon. We had everything ready to go at a moment's notice. What does the Ninth require?"

Tolen glanced around the room. "It's not going to be easy."

"I've always liked a challenge." Quasar grinned and Tolen smiled for the first time in what seemed like forever.

"I've missed you my friend."

The others moved in around them, packs strapped with their weapons strapped and Tolen apologized to Quasar and Blaze. "I wish I had time to fully explain, but you're only going to get the condensed version of what's going on."

And in as few sentences as possible, mixed with promises to fill in the details later, Tolen told them about the Relics and the Descendants, Macy and the prophecy, the problems at LadonRyn, the rise of Gyeesta, and pieces of everything else he could think mattered in this moment.

When Tolen finished, Quasar's violet eyes showed his determination. Blaze's complexion had paled, but his jaw was set.

"So, I am assuming we need to divide tasks. Where can the boy and I be of the most use?" Quasar asked calmly, hitching his pack higher on his broad shoulders.

Tolen grabbed his own pack off the sand by his feet and gave them the basics. He ran a hand through his hair. "My sight is patchy and unreliable, few images are clear. I think I know what we need to do— and Macy will be able to give us the final say if the plan is right." He glanced her way and though she bit her lip and self-doubt clouded her eyes, she nodded.

"Max, I think you should go with Quasar and Blaze to gather the Descendants and bring them to the haven. Mahto and Sienn can fulfill her mission to the Lafar, see who they can get to join the fight, then bring them to the haven as well. Brina and Rune should probably go to the Zenith and do the same with the Chosen. Toke, Keelyn, Macy and I will get the device, set up the haven, and help Macy through Transcendence." He looked to Macy for her approval, but she had a glassy look to her eyes, a light sheen of sweat on her upper lip.

"Macy?"

A funny feeling pulsed from her shard and he felt a momentary desire from her to rip the Last from Blaze's neck. He'd completely forgotten about the Seraph's warning to Macy about the Last. *You will be tempted whenever it is near you. Beware that you do not tamper again with power that does not belong to you.*

He tugged her behind his back and started rubbing soothing circles on her hand. He'd never tried to make the connection go the other way, speak into Macy's mind, but there was never a better time to try. *Macy?* Her head snapped in his direction. *Focus Mace. It's the temptation of the Last, remember the Seraph's warning?*

She shook her head, *Tolen, I want it—I miss it!*

Think of kissing me instead. And he shoved the image of their last kiss in her head with all the heat and emotion he could remember.

She gasped and everyone leaned to look. Her cheeks warmed—so did his—and the distraction seemed to work, but the battle still waged within her. She rubbed a hand over her lip. "I think the plan sounds good."

"We will collect the Descendants and lead them to their *onaepha*," Quasar added.

"*Onaepha?*" Brina asked.

"It means place of refuge in Hidden language." Max replied. "Fitting."

"Can't think of a better name for a haven than that." Rune thumped his knee in a hear-hear sort of way.

"*Onaepha* it is then." Tolen met Macy's grin and shrugged.

A resounding boom shook the walls around them and froze the smiles on their faces.

A wave of sorrow, an earsplitting screech, followed by a burst of evil so vast it reached below ground and pushed its suffocating darkness upon them.

Nahmala was dead.

Legion was coming.

CHAPTER 33

ESCAPE FROM LADONRYN

For several seconds everyone just stared at each other, each pair of eyes the same mirror of horror. The Kuna flared in Macy's chest and rushed to her palms. She felt Rune's Kuna do the same.

Tolen wrapped his arm around her waist and a million scenarios flashed through her mind—real or imagined she didn't know.

"Get out of the tree! Tolen needs to open the gate, now!" Toke shouted.

Macy's shard pulsed with each beat of her heart as they raced up the sandy incline and filtered out into the night. As she neared the top and the screams met her ears, an awareness seemed to have awakened within her. The possibility of who she really was, her role in the prophecy. She felt again that tremor of power she'd experienced the first time she'd decided to fully connect with her healed shard.

Once she'd thought the shards to be a separate entity of their carriers, but now that hers was united again with Bastian's she began to see how much it became an extension of its wearer, the shard learning from the carrier, the carrier from the shard. Her shard often exuded feelings of recklessness in its personality—just like her. Whereas Bastian's half had his strength, tenacity, concern, loyalty, and love. The older, wiser shard sought to tame the more stubborn younger half. But with this new knowledge it seemed as if the two halves of the shard were equal in one thing, their desire for her to recognize who she really was—an inner power that the shard already knew from the moment she was Chosen.

When Toke opened the tree, the screams climbed to heart wrenching pitch. The Kuna flowed in heat waves from her palms, but this time she could feel something else, something other, a power that had shown itself only a handful of times in recent days, but she could now see had only been there waiting impatiently for her to connect and set it free. She reached toward it now with her life force and felt the connection like a long lost friend. It warmed her body and heightened her senses without her even having to ask in Hidden tongue. Her thoughts flowed into actions. If she wanted to see something clearer, it happened as soon as the desire flowed into her mind.

The jungle swarmed with movement. Bodies ran from the light cast by the village into the dark recesses of the jungle. She could see each one, at least a mile in the distance, as clear as if they were inches away. The power was almost as heady and intoxicating as using the Last Shard had been. Too much. She wasn't ready for this kind of power or connection. She'd only just begun to feel safe-*ish* connecting with Bastian's shard.

She pulled away from the power and felt its sorrow as she backed away from her birthright. She shifted her thoughts to her shard, connecting to it as she had before until she could see the pinpricks in the distance, the blue depicting creatures of darkness, the yellow, followers of light—some brighter than others.

"Tolen, now!" Toke shouted as the others gathered around.

"Wait!" Macy looked back at the running villagers. "We can't just leave without helping them!"

You have to think higher than that now, LaUnahi, Bastian's voice shouted in her mind over the screams.

Bastian, not now, please.

Just as Tolen has had to learn when and how to act at the right time, *so must you. You are not ready for this battle Macy. You are the key to the Redemption. This world needs you, but you must be ready.*

I am Chosen. I've spent the last ten years training for this.

Little bird, I taught you all I knew, I trained you the best I could. But there is much you have yet to experience of the Dark and its power.

Macy thought about the time since Bastian had found the Ninth Chosen, since Tolen had become a part of their lives, and could see the truth.

Would she be strong enough for what was to come? Could she do whatever was necessary to win—even if that meant dying?

I don't think you can train for something like this, Bastian. You say the Light made me this way—a gift. If that's true then they know how I think, how I feel. I have to follow my heart and my heart is Chosen. I can't abandon other Chosen ones to save myself, no matter what life they've decided to live.

Terrified screams, guttural shouts, shrieks, clangs of metal, and the cries of children pulled Macy out of her thoughts. Her nose crinkled from the smell of battle—blood, desperation, and death. Flickers of orange and yellow danced between the trees. LadonRyn was aflame.

"Guys, please." Macy pleaded, her hand over Tolen's. "Can we just open the gate closer to the village? Maybe we can get some to come with us."

"And what if they're the ones that want to kill you?" Max growled.

"I'll go through the gate first, as soon as Tolen opens it. I—I promise, please, we can't go and just let them die." The Kuna built in her chest, molten heat, liquid flame, and she let it trickle down her arms into her palms, pooling it there until her fingers began to glow palest yellow. The smell of eucalyptus and roses brought the tiniest bit of comfort as she bridged the distance between the relative safety of the forest and the call of her heart.

The others looked around but it was Tolen's nod that sent her feet flying. They barely brushed the ground as she pushed strength to her legs, the forest became a blur, the trees gave way to the battle and her body lurched to a halt as her mind fought to make sense of what she saw.

Raksaha, Gungruin, Darkened, Daklafar, Kezgani demons. These she knew, had fought and somewhat understood. Their numbers were staggering. But it was the creatures she'd never seen, creatures she'd only ever heard Bastian tell of in stories, that almost made her lose control of her Kuna.

Half-wolf, half-man Kludde—soul trackers—ran through the throng sinking their teeth into anything that moved, the ones who ran were memorized and chased down mercilessly. A burst of flame broke free from her hand.

Giant lizard creatures, flames pouring from their mouths, igniting the huts—women and children running from them screaming, carrying blankets and stuffed toys. Thrundoon, sweat dripping off their furry faces, wielding cruel axes and swords, rushed toward the escaping LadonRynians.

Macy watched as if in slow motion as a child, no more than seven or eight tripped, her little stuffed bear flying out of her hands as she tried to catch herself on the sandy street. The mother started to run back, but a Thrundoon would get there first, his ax aimed for the little girl.

Heat burst through Macy's body, her vision turned white hot like the flames that loosed from her fingers. She twisted her hands to control the inferno and directed it at the Thrundoon. The tendrils of flame flashed forward, a lightning strike, engulfing the creature, but his ax was falling, already falling. Macy pushed harder, twisting her fingers until the flames wrapped around the ax, she yanked back and the ax fell inches from the child's head. The mother reached her child, looked over, her eyes narrowed as they took in Macy. She nodded once, then grabbed the child and ran.

Macy flicked her hand and a fireball the size of a watermelon shot over their heads igniting the spiked creature running toward them.

A blue sphere suddenly exploded out into the darkness. Nahmala's voice boomed from its center. "My people, get into the barrier for safety!"

Macy started shoving people toward the barrier—she could just make out the vestiges of another island in the middle. Whenever a Dark creature tried to follow, it disintegrated to ash.

She heard Tolen begin the chant to open their own gate behind her. A swish of wind and she knew his gate was open. He tugged her arm, but her eyes were locked on the people rushing about, some running for the promised safety, following her directions to the sphere, others were cut down as they ran. She shot fireball after fireball, saw Rune doing the same, Keelyn's arrows, and Mahto and Sienn's swords, but there were too many.

The people of LadonRyn, what they had believed would protect them, hiding, cutting themselves off, had ultimately become their doom. Fraya, Oki? Their families? Had they made it to safety?

"Macy, Legion could be here any second! Go now!" Tolen screamed in her ear and she turned to fulfill her promise.

The ground beneath them began to tremble and Nahmala's sphere disappeared with a loud pop. A strange sucking sound drew Macy's eyes to the beach where she could just make out the waves splashing against the sand in the moonlight. The ocean's surface bubbled and frothed as if boiling, an earsplitting *BOOM*, the ground pitched, and a mammoth sized geyser exploded upward expelling a jet-black monster the size of a mountain into the sky. The force rocked across the island in a wave that knocked them all off their feet and sent them rolling across the sand until they slammed into something solid.

Lights popped in front of Macy's eyes, blinding her, the screeches and screams replaced by a persistent ringing. She'd come to a stop against the side of a burning hut. She propped herself up on her hands and knees, blinking rapidly trying to clear her vision. Warmth trickled down her cheek and she lifted a hand to the side of her head to feel a sizable lump and an open wound.

She pressed a hand to the wound and the seconds ticked by too slowly as her hearing returned, her sight cleared, and she could finally look around. She spotted Tolen about a hundred yards to her left, the open gate still shimmering beside him.

A guttural growl jerked her attention up to see the monstrous creature bearing down on them. A sleek dragon with scales that shimmered like black flame. Fire billowed from its mouth. With its wings unfurled, it spanned the length of the entire village.

Legion.

Daemon the Demon Master sat upon its back, his scaly red arm brandishing a sword, his yellow eyes triumphant, his black fangs bared, and his horns glistening in the flames from his steed's mouth.

Legion would need to set but one foot, one claw upon this soil and Gyeesta would be free, the Balance would tip, and Darsapean would be able to leave the Shadow Realm.

Macy faced the gate. . . she'd never make it without Legion seeing her. She'd killed them all.

Suddenly a gust of wind lifted a wall of sand into the sky, blocking the creature from sight. A tangle of branches wrapped around her and she knew Tolen had saved her again. The cocoon sped toward the gate, nine other cocoons soon bumped against her sides holding Rune, Keelyn, Toke, Brina, Max, Mahto, Sienn, Quasar, and Blaze.

She spotted Tolen just outside the gate waving his hands in the air, his face purple with effort, from one hand he shot back creatures to prevent them from entering the gate, from the other he directed the elements to carry the cocoons forward.

They passed through and she experienced a moment's triumph as Tolen began to wave his hands to close the gate, until a scaly, black three-toed foot with razor claws gripped onto his shoulder. Blood blossomed through his shirt as Legion fought to drag him back out.

Macy screamed and fought against the cocoon but it held her fast until the gate sealed shut. As the branches released their hold Macy rushed forward to catch Tolen as he fell, Legion's severed foot still buried in his shoulder.

CHAPTER 34

THE SAFE HAVEN

Rune leaned over Macy's shoulder watching her dig Legion's claws out of Tolen's shoulder with Brina's help. Keelyn stood back, looking slightly queasy. Nothing fazed Rune—not the blood oozing out of Tolen's wounds, the battle they'd just fought, or the deaths they'd witnessed. Macy's fingers shook and she had to refocus.

She winced with Tolen as she slid out the last four-inch long claw and dropped the foot into the shallow stream trickling beside them. Blood started to spurt and Brina pushed a thick wad of fabric over the holes left behind. Macy put her hand on his forehead. "Tolen, do you have enough strength to heal it, or do you want me to stitch it up for now?" Her stomach turned. She'd stitched up many a wound on Bastian, but for some reason the idea of doing it to Tolen cut into her heart a lot more.

"I'll do it." He grunted and with her help, leaned back against the wall of the crumbling bridge they'd taken refuge under. She held his one hand as he placed the other over the bloody bandage and whispered the words to heal himself. The rest of them had minor injuries that Brina began walking around and tending to while Toke activated a Treasta.

"We should be safe to regenerate here for a few hours." Toke ran his fingers through his purple hair and looked around. "Then we can use the disk to get the device, and get to locating a place for *Onaepha*."

Tolen hadn't been sure what state, or even country he'd brought them to, just that when the image came to his mind, he knew it would be a safe place. Macy *did* feel oddly peaceful here under the ancient bridge, where the only sounds were the soft tinkle of the stream, the quiet croak of frogs and clicking of crickets. The Dark still moved out there—but not right here, not in this forgotten place. Macy lowered her chin onto Tolen's healed shoulder and whispered in his ear. "I'm so sorry."

He looked at her. Purple ringed under his eyes and even though they only had the soft light of the moon she could still tell he was pale. "For what?"

"It's my fault you got hurt." She laced her fingers through his. "If I would've just let you open the gate right there in the jungle, not insisted we run to the village, it wouldn't have happened."

Tolen sighed and kissed her forehead. "Macy, that was a horrible thing happening. It's your nature to help, to protect. Don't punish yourself for being *yourself.* We got out. I'm fine. And soon," he paused and his hand twitched in hers. "Soon we'll go back. We'll make sure Legion and Daemon and the Dark all pay for what they did to those people. For what they've done to the entire world." The vehemence in his voice had her wondering if he'd wanted to stay and fight as much as she had.

Rune and Keelyn arrived with water and food to share and sat down on Tolen's other side. Rune addressed Macy as he helped Tolen sit higher against the cement wall, and placed a blanket over his shoulders. "So, did you hear the news about you and me when you were eavesdropping?"

"You and me?" Macy took a bite of biscuit feeling warmed by both Rune's kindness toward Tolen and Keelyn's light. It had been far more palpable since the moment she and Rune had been Promised.

"We're cousins."

Macy chuckled, went to rub her eyes, noticed Tolen's blood still on them, and leaned over to rinse in the stream. "Yeah, right."

"It's true." Keelyn handed Macy a sucker and some jerky when she sat back up. "Your mothers were sisters."

Macy dried her hands on her jeans and caught Rune's quirky grin. *Huh.* A few days ago that revelation would have probably evoked more emotion, but with her present exhaustion all she could manage was, *huh.*

"Yep, so now every time you insult me, you're also insulting my mother—your aunt—which means you're insulting her genes, the same genes of your mother *and* you. So, in essence you're insulting yourself." His crooked grin lit his eyes and a tiny smile lifted her cheek. He'd changed too since being promised to Keelyn—like all along he'd had this humorous side but the shame and the pain had kept it from ever fully surfacing. If times were simpler she'd probably really enjoy hanging out with this new Rune. *My cousin.*

"Your logic never ceases to amaze, Rune." She leaned her head back against the cement, her shoulder bumping against Tolen's arm.

What seemed like seconds later someone shook her awake. The tiniest bit of light touched the sky above and turned the stream navy blue—cricket song now mingled with the trill of early birds. "It's time to go." Max helped her to her feet, his fingers staying just a fraction longer on her elbow than necessary.

Tolen already stood in the ankle-deep water, his hand over Toke's disc thing. He still looked tired and pale. A few seconds later the disc began a countdown ding and a shiny something zoomed into Tolen's palm, born by the wind he conjured. The portal closed, Tolen handed the jewel to Toke and everyone leaned in to get a look. Macy moved to Tolen's side and looked down at the Movan device that was unlike any she had ever seen. It didn't look like tech at all, but a large piece of jewelry. A fat, palm-sized, tarnished silver oval, with twelve white stones around the outer edge and a huge glimmering ruby at the center. A thick chain dangled from a silver hoop at the top.

"An *Athstazia.* Beautiful," Toke spun the jewel round and round in his hands. "I haven't seen tech like this in a long, long time." His eyes twinkled with memory and he held the device out to Rune. "I'm not exactly sure how to use it."

Rune took the *Ath*-thingy and a series of emotions from sadness to joy pulsed from his life force and affirmed something in Macy's tired brain that brought moisture to her eyes and a joyous warmth to her chest. Rune was *family.* "If I push this stone, we'll be shielded before Tolen opens any gates." Rune pushed one of the stones, she couldn't see exactly which one, and a heaviness settled over their little group. Not unpleasant. Sort of like cuddling in a heated blanket on a cold winter day. *Cozy.*

"Rune and Brina each have one of these, but you'll need them as well." Toke handed small orb like devices he called *Comms* to Sienn and Quasar and directed them to speak their names into the sides and press their thumbs to the screens. "They are now synced to your bio-electricity. Once Tolen activates the device over *Onaepha* you won't be able to locate it. Keep these with you at all times. When it comes time for you to find us, you can speak into the Comm and your message will go directly to my brain. Once I get set up in *Onaepha,* I will work on creating a portal machine similar to the disc, but larger, and Tolen will be able to let everyone you find inside the protection."

Macy stood back as Tolen turned to their friends. The time had come to separate—each one heading to another task. Necessary, but it still made her heart feel heavy. There was a chance—a really good chance this would be the last time they ever saw one another. The catch in Tolen's voice told her his thoughts were probably on the same thread as hers. "Sienn, Mahto, are you ready?"

Sienn described the place where her father was supposed to be and Tolen opened a gateway. Mahto clapped him on the shoulder and Sienn squeezed his arm once before they passed through. Macy wondered if the rift between the Lafar and the Hidden race could finally be set aside. Could Sienn as a half-human, half-Lafar be the bridge, as the Seraph had said, to get the Lafar to help them in this fight, despite the preju-dices they had been forced to endure for centuries?

Tolen's sadness touched her life force and she put her arm around his waist.

Tolen called Rune and Brina forward next—off to the Zenith to bring in the Chosen—and Macy's heart twisted in her chest.

Rune looked down at Keelyn who had both her hands wrapped around one of his in a death grip. "We'd like to go with you to *Onaepha* first, if that's okay?"

"Of course." Tolen nodded and Macy felt his relief mirror her own.

"Quasar, Blaze, and Max, that means you're next. Get River first. I'll send you right outside Jonas' camp. It will probably also be a good place for you to plan out your next moves—but I would take Jonas' advice over mine," he chuckled nervously. "Max, do you need my watch?"

Max shook his head. "No. I'm already connected to their bioelectricity through the protections I set up. I'll find them."

A heaviness settled in Macy's chest and she hurried to grab her pack and walked back with one hand digging inside. She pulled out her father's notes, the bag of fake Relics and held them out to her father, not quite able to meet his eyes. He'd cleaned up in the stream, must've used a knife to cut some of his hair and shorten the beard. Even in a ponytail his silver-brown hair looked pretty crooked, and there were a few nicks on his cheeks. He seemed shorter than she remembered, but then again, she'd been at lot shorter at six. Maybe it was just because he was standing by tall Tolen and huge Rune.

He took one step toward her, but she couldn't bridge the distance. "You'll do fine with Forced Transcendence. You have that Fairchild determination from your mother."

"And the Burdow stubbornness." She flicked her eyes to his then wished she hadn't.

He half smiled, but his green eyes were wet. "Right." He took another step toward her but paused. "I should be there with you during your Transcendence. I should be there to comfort you, protect you, and celebrate with you when it's over. I should have fought harder to escape that prison so I could have been there for your last ten birthdays. Macy, I'm so very sorry."

Macy looked away. "It's okay."

He reached out a hand but dropped it when she didn't take it. "Bye sweetheart."

"Bye dad."

Tolen raised his hands and the weight in her stomach did an uncomfortable flop. The air began to shimmer, the gateway cracked open, Quasar stepped through, then Blaze.

"Dad, wait!" she ran forward and wrapped her arms around him. "I love you."

Max buried his face in her hair. "I love you, kiddo."

She bit back a sob. "Come back."

His voice cracked. "I promise." He let go and he was gone, *again*.

Tolen pulled her into his arms as she fought the tremors rocking through her center.

"Tolen, have you seen where to put *Onaepha*?" Toke asked gently patting her shoulder.

Tolen's arms tightened around her waist. "I *think* so. It's not completely clear."

"Why don't you ask your girlfriend?" Rune quipped and Macy stuck her tongue out at him under Tolen's arm.

"Shut up, *cousin*."

Tolen leaned back to better look her in the eye. "Will you check?"

"How?" Heat rose in her cheeks, aware of Rune's sympathetic smirk.

Tolen's blue eye dilated black to blue once. "I'll push the image into your mind, you let it connect to your shard and see what you feel."

Macy bit her lip. "Isn't that dangerous with the Fallen?"

"The *Athstazia* should keep your thoughts hidden." Toke answered.

"But make it quick," Rune added.

Tolen took her face in his hands and for a moment she was able to ignore their remaining audience and just focus on the feel of his hands on her face, the love in his eyes. He leaned his forehead on hers, she shut her eyes and an image exploded to life behind her closed lids. It was hazy but still somewhat familiar, and then she remembered a photograph from an old book. "It's the Salmon National Forest." Macy opened her eyes. "Idaho."

She rubbed her temple. "Bastian had a book that talked about a settlement not far from the River of No Return. Abandoned gold mine, I think. He said at one time a tribe of Kunamin lived and worked there alongside a small number of humans who accepted them. I'm sure it's the same place. You can only access it from the river or by plane. It's very well hidden and covers at minimum a thousand acres."

"Are there other humans there?" Toke asked.

She nodded. "There's a few small settlements and tourist attractions scattered about, but it'd be okay to put them under the protection too, wouldn't it?"

Toke twisted his ring. "If we need to expand far enough to include them we'll just be sure to investigate their character first. We don't want to let any Dark sympathizers inside with us if we can avoid it."

"Alright." Tolen squeezed her hand and stepped back. "Everyone ready?"

The nerves they all experienced were evident on their faces and flowing from their life forces but everyone nodded.

Tolen raised his hands in the air. A sliver of pink pushed the last of the night away, a ray of sunlight filtered beneath the bridge, glittered off the stream and danced across their faces. With it came a surge of hope that fought against the doubts that competed for place in Macy's exhausted brain and wearied heart. The gate shimmered in front of them, opened to a darker sky—the sun had yet to rise above the forest—and they stepped through into another piece of their destiny.

CHAPTER 35

ONAEPHA

Tolen called up more bricks and rock, using the wind to help repair the back wall of the old bar—the only remaining single-story structure that needed the least amount of work to be habitable. In the time he'd been working the sun had fully risen, its warmth taking the cool mountain chill and turning the air hot and dusty.

Once he finished it should be sufficient enough a place for Macy to stay and complete her Transcendence. There were a few other structures he would work on once she was settled and the process had begun so there would be actual places for people to stay as they arrived. If he could force himself to leave her side.

Eventually they would worry about building better permanent structures—as who knew how long they would be required to stay here. How long before the final battle of the Final Battle would end? He shook his head from this thought and went back to stacking bricks.

This place shouldn't be too bad once he finished. It had a nice front area where the main bar and restaurant used to be, but the back had a living quarters with two bedrooms and a tiny kitchen. The outhouse would have to be rebuilt as well, something none of them were thrilled about. Toke told them he could rig something that would resemble plumbing, but the portal and preparing for Macy's Forced Transcendence had to take top priority. For now, they'd be roughing it, something Tolen hadn't entirely gotten used to in his time living a Chosen life. Macy handled it with dignity, but he could sense her dislike.

Rune and Brina would help them get set up, stay one night, then Tolen would open a gate to the Zenith for them at first light, just before Toke began the series of trials to force Macy's Transcendence.

Rune's boisterous laugh carried from the opposite side of the building, thankfully pulling Tolen's thoughts from the dangerous event facing Macy.

He caught snippets of Macy and Rune's banter and smiled. They were supposed to be clearing away the forest that had begun to reclaim the abandoned settlement with controlled burns. The lack of smoke and increase in laughter said they were mostly goofing off, but he was glad for the distraction her friends provided. Keelyn didn't realize it, but it was pretty much her that held the despair relating to the events on LadonRyn and the fears of the prophecy at bay. Her blissful happiness at being promised to Rune had strengthened her Lóklana, which spilled onto everyone around her. Rune's freedom from his past and openly loving Keelyn made him almost inappropriately giddy. Tolen twisted his fingers to wedge the last brick just under the crumbling facia and walked in the side door. Only he couldn't seem to find reprieve in Keelyn's light or Rune's humor.

Well, maybe he wasn't the only one. Toke, his purple hair in disarray, the sun tattoo by his eye scrunched in concentration, the *Athstazia* dangling from his neck, stood hanging various diagrams on the newly repaired wall. He'd dragged a lopsided table over and across it laid a myriad of gadgets, and at least a dozen rolls of wire. Tolen wondered how the little man had managed to fit it all in his backpack, let alone carry it.

Toke's emotions fluctuated swiftly, his thoughts, ancient in their wisdom, were guarded, but always thinking. He didn't seem quite as agitated or worried as Tolen, but he wasn't easy to laugh either. Perhaps it was age or experience, but he seemed to sense the gravity of their situation.

Brina sat closer to the front doors, flipping through a stack of notebooks piled on a rotting rectangle, probably what was left of the counter, her tongue between her teeth. She too was a deep thinker, and pretty good at hiding her thoughts, but the depth of love she had for her family couldn't be hidden. She'd hoped her "father" would have been the one the Seraph told them to find, and was deeply saddened by the information they'd uncovered that indicated he likely hadn't survived, but she was genuinely happy that Max and Macy had been reunited.

Not the tiniest bit of jealousy or resentment existed in her. Toke filled much of the void left by her father and she was truly happy to see the people she cared about happy. But her heart did long to find a love like she saw in Tolen and Macy, Rune and Keelyn. There was an underlying ache for Connell that she had hidden from the others. Her feelings for him hadn't been entirely sisterly and she held a deep regret inside for never telling him. A regret that kept her from fully benefiting from Keelyn's shared light. Tolen hoped for her sake the day would come when the Dark was defeated and she could find love again.

As the hours went by, the closer they were to Toke beginning Macy's forced Transcendence, the harder Tolen had to fight to keep his fears at bay. So much risk. He heard Macy laugh again and heat trickled into his palms. "Hey Toke," he called. "I'll be right back."

Toke nodded without looking up.

He walked out of the building to see Macy and Rune standing in the middle of the overgrown road tossing a fire ball back and forth. Macy noticed him and pulled the fire back into her palm. Did she have any idea how beautiful her gift was? And the incredibly selfless way she used it only made it more so. He swallowed. "Will you take a walk with me?" Her eyes narrowed with concern but she nodded.

"Behave." Rune called and Keelyn slugged him. He laughed and swung her around before planting a kiss on her lips.

Tolen took Macy's hand and led her down the dusty road, past the crumbling remains of the main square, until they hit the line where the settlement ended and the bigger trees began. He paused under a pine tall enough to stand under and pulled her around to face him, gripping both her hands.

"Toke wants to start your Transcendence in the morning."

"Yeah, right after Rune and Brina leave." She scratched her nose.

"I was wondering if we could do something before that. If—if you want to." He hoped she didn't notice his sweaty palms.

"Okay?" Her cheeks warmed and a flash of kissing him went through her mind, but he didn't lean in.

"I—I'm not really sure how to do this." He chuckled nervously and ran a hand through his hair. "Being raised in the human world, I don't know the Hidden way, but maybe that's the right way to do it anyway, since you're human." He was rambling, but every word he'd wanted to say fled the moment he went to actually say it and he had to scramble through his brain to remember.

"I'm lost…" She bit the side of her lip, but excitement and anticipation swirled from her life force. Her thoughts didn't reveal if she knew what he was up to, but either way her excitement spurred him forward.

He took a deep breath. "We've only known each other one summer; one horrifying, yet glorious summer. We've been told our love was wrong, then that it's okay. We accepted that we're different, that we won't age the same—the possibility that I will outlive you by hundreds of years." He paused and fiddled with her fingers. "But through it all we chose to love each other anyway. Now it's a line in the prophecy that threatens a future together." His throat tightened and he had to swallow twice before he could continue. "I started to think, if I knew the very day I would die, which would be better? To fully accept my fate determined to be true to who I am, and enjoy every single moment I had left to its fullest, in the *right* way? Or fight against the truth, grab onto my most selfish desires and possibly lose myself in the process?"

He squeezed her fingers. "We *could* choose to run from our destiny Macy, live a short life together before evil destroys the world." Her eyes danced with the same thrill at the idea fighting against duty that battled within himself. "There is a side of me that longs for that selfish existence, to hide away and have you as mine for however long that I can." She ducked her head and the sunlight that filtered down through the spiny branches lit her golden hair like a halo.

He touched her chin until she looked back at him and ran his fingers down her jaw leaving a trail of light, whether from her or him he did not know, but the feelings it stirred in him seemed to intensify the battle he'd been fighting within himself from the moment he'd fallen in love with her.

Protect Lasan. Follow your heart.

He resisted the urge to kiss her, to give in to the side of him that was crazy in love, to balance Tolen Parks and the Ninth Chosen. He lowered his hand, "But as appealing as it may be to take you away, if we denied our destiny, you could never be truly happy. And if I'm honest with myself, I couldn't be happy either, because the thing I love the most about you is your passion to do what you know is right." His voice caught. "Macy, you're my hero. You fight the Dark because it's the right thing to do, not for praise, or power, or glory. It's just who you are. No matter the temptations you face, or the obnoxious comments, or attitude you give," she chuckled but her eyes were wet, "you always do what you know to be right. You are truly a gift of light and I never dreamed I could ever love someone as much as I love you."

He pushed aside the nervous flutters in his stomach and dropped to one knee. Her mouth popped open in a giant *O* and his widened into the first full smile he'd had in what felt like forever. "Whether it be a single hour, day, month, or a year, I wish to spend every minute of it Promised to you, in the *right* way. If my hope, my dream, becomes reality, then in one year I want to be *Centered*, bonded to you for all eternity."

He twisted his fingers and a flash of gold shot up from the ground beneath them, it swirled and spun in the air splitting into several tiny strands of golden vines speckled with leaves and glittering flowers with flame-like petals. The ends met forming a small shimmering circle. Tolen plucked it from the air with his thumb and forefinger and slid it onto Macy's left wrist, "I love you Macy. Will you marry me?"

A soft yellow glow flared from Macy's left hand, spread up her arm and covered her whole body, her face lit with joy that burst from her heart and slammed into his. She leaned down, cupped his cheeks, and just before placing her lips on his, whispered, "Yes."

CHAPTER 36

A FUTURE HOPE

MACY HAD TO push hard against the joy to get her hands to stop glowing as they walked back to the village center. She wanted to run, go straight to Toke and ask him to perform the ceremony, but Tolen seemed to want to take their time, content to be alone together, stop to steal a few kisses on the way back. Which was nice, but she had never been the patient one.

When they reached the spot where Rune had taken over clearing away the bits of forest from the settlement, Keelyn hopped down from the log where she'd been waiting. "You're going to be Promised?" Macy held up her wrist and Keelyn threw her arms around them both.

Rune clapped Tolen on the back. "Nice work. Setting a high precedent there though aren't ya?" He gestured to Macy's bracelet.

Tolen chuckled and led the way back into the main building where Toke was putting the finishing touches on a lunch of hard biscuits, dried fruit, and jerky onto one of the few wobbly tables surrounded by mismatched rickety chairs.

"If we survive this, I'm really going to have to introduce you guys to trail mix and protein bars," Tolen said before biting into a biscuit.

"Don't bother." Rune snorted. "I tried that years ago. No go."

Macy had to cover her laugh or spray the table with raisins. "Bastian let me indulge in the occasional cheeseburger, but I could never get him away from Hidden food either."

"Nothing beats the food of the ancestors." Toke wiped his mouth and grinned.

"That's a nice addition to your wrist Macy." Brina pointed and Tolen choked.

Macy chuckled again, and pat his back, feeling almost ridiculously giddy. "Thanks. Tolen asked me to be Promised."

Light sparkled in Brina's eyes, but a trace of pain pushed from her life force, and Macy instantly felt guilty for reasons she couldn't name.

Tolen wiped his mouth. "We were hoping you would do it for us Toke, before Rune and Brina leave, and Macy begins Transcendence."

Toke set aside the piece of jerky he'd been gnawing on, a warm twinkle in his orange-brown eyes. "I'd love to." He stood up from the table, taking his jerky with him. "Just a few more things to tweak. How about after dinner?"

Macy and Tolen both nodded and they finished the rest of their meal chatting with Brina about Keelyn and Rune's ceremony. Macy knew their little group was stealing a short reprieve of joy amongst the chaos, ignoring for a small moment the fact that dozens of people had lost their lives on LadonRyn. If Gyeesta *had* risen, Darsapean was likely on his way back to the earth realm, and while they sat here the entire world could be falling apart.

But all of them were willing and ready to sacrifice their lives for this little blue planet when the time came. She couldn't imagine the Light begrudging them this one day to sit together and enjoy one another's company.

∘ ∘ ∘

They stayed busy and accomplished a lot, but the day still took far too long to go by in Macy's opinion. There were now four buildings that would at least provide a roof overhead for newcomers, and the bar that Rune had playfully dubbed Moony's in reference to the outhouse in the back now resembled a somewhat cozy backwoods brick home. They'd rebuilt the counter using some tools they'd found in an old shed. Apparently Kunamin made good blacksmiths. They pieced together several broken pieces of furniture and built one decent table and four fairly sturdy chairs.

Tolen had used his Animashta to ask some birds to gather feathers and before long they had four bed frames repaired—and after thoroughly washing the material—had re-stuffed four fluffy feather mattresses for the two bedrooms. Toke and Tolen would share one, Keelyn and Macy the other.

Once everyone began to arrive, this place would be perfect to use as headquarters for the followers of Light.

Finally the last of dinner was cleared away and Macy looked at Toke expectantly.

"Wait." Keelyn wrapped her tiny hand around Macy's elbow. "Macy, you know I love you, right?"

Macy's eyebrows rose at the sternness in Keelyn's tone. "Yeah."

"Then please don't take offense to this." She pinched her nose. "You stink sweetheart. And so do you Tolen. Brina and I are taking Macy to the well to clean up." She gestured to Rune and Toke. "You boys take care of Tolen. We'll meet back here in twenty minutes."

Rune saluted and Toke bit back a chuckle as Keelyn ushered them all outside.

○ ○ ○

Twenty minutes later, totally scrubbed clean, Macy stood fidgeting in front of Moony's, wearing a fresh pair of dark gray cargo pants, a pale-yellow shirt Keelyn had loaned her, and twisting her bracelet around her wrist. Keelyn had insisted on braiding Macy's hair and dotting it with a handful of some tiny yellow wild-flowers she'd found beside the river. She'd looked at her reflection in the murky water, at the most done-up version of herself she'd ever seen, and even though she was in her usual attire, she *felt* pretty. The joy swirling inside her body danced in her eyes and softened her typically serious gaze.

Tolen wasn't back yet, but Toke was and he'd told her to wait outside while he finished up a surprise inside. She shoved her hands in her back pockets and jumped when arms slipped around her waist. Tolen placed a quick kiss beneath her ear.

"You look gorgeous." His breath raised goosebumps on her neck.

She peeked over her shoulder. He wore a deep blue t-shirt bringing out the brightness in his blue eye. He'd combed his hair back away from his face and tied it in a ponytail at his collar, a few waves hung loose by his cheeks and she reached up to tuck them behind his ears. "So do you."

He smiled her favorite smile and took her hand when Toke opened the door to Moony's. They stepped inside to see he'd completely transformed the dusty space. Flowers covered every surface and he'd used his crazy genius to somehow create a version of twinkle lights that dangled from the ceiling like stars. Rune, Keelyn and Brina must have entered through the back door as they all stood in a smiling line at the counter strung with more twinkle lights. Rune beckoned them forward.

"Ready?" Tolen squeezed her fingers and her shard zinged with joy that intensified what she felt in her heart. She nodded vigorously and he chuckled as he led the way to the counter.

Toke joined the line beside Brina and directed Tolen and Macy to face them. "I have one more surprise." He raised one of his many devices, tapped a button on the side and a hazy image of Max's upper half appeared in the air above it.

"Dad?" Macy pulled Tolen forward and raised her fingers to the image. "Hey baby."

Toke adjusted a few knobs and the image cleared. Macy would almost believe her father stood there with him—if not for the slightly see-through quality of the image and the fact that his bottom half was missing. "The connection won't last long, it takes a lot of power to send and receive the signal and cloak it at the same time, but I thought it would mean more to you if it was your father who performed the ceremony."

"Even though Tolen didn't ask me first." Max winked when Tolen began to stammer. "I'm just teasing. I couldn't have picked a better future, and I stress the word *future,* husband for my daughter. Toke will physically conduct by proxy but I'll be the one prompting you through the promises. If that's okay with you?" He met Macy's gaze, but her throat was too thick to do more than nod.

The ceremony couldn't have been more perfect or beautiful, her father speaking the same promises Nahmala had given to Keelyn and

Rune. Something seemed to come to life inside her connecting all the pieces that made up McLacy Allicandra Burdow—human, Chosen, Kunamin, Gift of Light—and fused them into one, no more cracks separating the pieces, as if Tolen were the glue she'd always needed to put herself together in one glorious whole.

∘ ∘ ∘

Tolen's gaze stayed locked on Macy as Max began. This time he determined to listen to every word, relish every single second of this moment focused only on Macy and the love he had for her. This moment was theirs and no matter what happened going forward it always would be. A moment of brightest day before darkest night.

"Tolen Daedal Parks, you have asked McLacy Allicandra Burdow to be promised to you." Max waited for Tolen to meet his eyes. "The Promise covenant is not a trivial thing. It is second only to being Centered, the highest covenant a couple can make. When done in the proper way, and at the proper time, both the Promised and Centered covenants can be sealed by the Light making them an eternal bond that will extend beyond death." Toke lifted Macy's hand, placed it in Tolen's, and both their hands began to glow—but whereas when he'd watched this happen with Rune and Keelyn he'd thought it'd been them causing it, now he knew it came from somewhere else.

"The Light has accepted your choice." Max motioned to the light coming from their joined hands. "That is Their message to you."

Tolen's eyes filled and silent tears started to fall down Macy's cheeks.

Max's voice cracked. "Tolen do you promise to stay true and loyal to Macy every single day of your mortal life? To love her despite her faults and follies, always forgive your differences, value her opinions, support her dreams, and help her in her goals?"

Tolen swallowed behind a watery smile, he'd never experienced joy like this. "Yes."

"And do you promise, until the day that you are Centered, to protect her virtue—" Rune caught Tolen's eye and winked, "to never do anything that disparages the value and importance of it? And even after you are Centered to *respect* her virtue *as* a precious gift that has been shared with you?"

Tolen answered firmly, "Yes."

"Macy do you promise to stay true and loyal to Tolen every single day of your mortal life? To love him despite his faults and follies, always forgive your differences, value his opinions, support his dreams, and help him in his goals?"

She wiped her face, "Yes."

"And do you promise, until the day that you are Centered, to protect his virtue, to never do anything that disparages the value and importance of it? And even after you are Centered to respect his virtue as a precious gift that has been shared with you?"

She smiled and the dimple Tolen loved winked beside her mouth. "Yes."

Toke placed his hands over theirs as Max spoke, "As your father, and with the permission of the Light, I pronounce you Promised to each other and only each other for the period of one year, in which time you will prove your love and worthiness to be Centered and bonded together for eternity."

CHAPTER 37

AGING

TOLEN LEANED BACK in the squeaky rocking chair on the front porch watching the sky slowly lighten while everyone else slept, reading his mother's journal and sipping a cup of *Whosays*—a concoction of Brina's that closely resembled hot chocolate. Keelyn told them Brina called it "Who says it ain't chocolate?" but they'd shortened it to Whosays.

He'd learned a lot about his mother from her written words that he'd never discovered during his time with her. In a lot of ways, she reminded him of Rune. A difficult upbringing had led her to make some poor choices that culminated with the terrifying experience at Gyeesta—witnessing the creation of Darsapean, the mutation of Daemon—all of which ultimately broke her heart. He was glad she'd at least found some peace and joy with Tolen's father. But mostly he was glad Nahmala had decided to give him the journal that had somehow made its way back to its home. Because for the first time since Tolen had learned who he really was, he knew he could truly forgive his mother for her secrets.

To read her heartfelt words, to look at her actions from the distance of one with a mantle he did not want to carry, he knew without a doubt her actions were out of love. Motivated by fear yes, but at the heart of his mother's every action was either the need for, or the expression of, deep and abiding love.

A lone eagle swept low over the quiet settlement, landing in a nest atop one of the barns and Tolen's thoughts shifted to the previous night—the best night of his life. After the ceremony ended and the connection to Max lost power, Toke explained to Tolen what normally took place after a couple had been Promised. Customarily, their parents took them on a four day road trip where they spent time learning the traditions of one another's families and laid out the plans for the four seasons of courtship.

But as that wasn't a possibility, Tolen and Macy instead stayed up late into the night with their friends. They talked about their years growing up, the similarities and differences, and Toke occasionally filled in other little details from what he knew of Macy's family. Rune, Keelyn, and Brina asked questions that helped Tolen remember the good things in his past and recognize even more Hidden things his mother had raised him with.

They couldn't exactly plan a four season courtship because none of them knew if they would survive the next week, let alone the next year, but they did talk about what they would do if they'd had that option. Things like sharing birthdays and holidays, and beginning new traditions together.

It had been a glorious evening filled with more joy than he could honestly say he'd ever experienced, marred only by the fact that their parents hadn't physically been there to experience it with them, and Tolen's parents hadn't even known about it. He found himself desperately missing them and when he'd woke that morning he'd taken the journal from his pack, hoping some time reading her words would help him feel closer to them. He stroked the cracked leather cover, grateful he'd followed the hope.

He'd gone from being a kid told to hide everything to an adult expected to know everything. And in truth, he was terrified at what was to come. But he would do as he promised, he would love Macy for whatever was left of their lives, and then he would bank on that line in the ceremony that said their promises would extend beyond death.

A shiver ran across his shoulders. The next few hours could put that promise to the test.

Hearing voices through the open window, he stood up and stretched, tucked the journal under his arm and carried his cup inside.

Rune leaned against the counter, Keelyn's face buried in his chest, his arms tight around her shaking shoulders. Macy stood next to them biting her lip. When Tolen walked in and sat down the cup and journal she hurried to his side and wrapped her arm around his waist. He could feel her effort to keep her own emotions in check as Brina and Toke added a few more supplies to hers and Rune's packs.

Tolen kissed the top of Macy's head, checked his watch and met Rune's eye.

Rune took a deep breath, and ignoring their audience, lifted Keelyn off her feet to plant a good long smooch on her lips. When he finally set her down she wrapped her arms back around his waist, he laid his cheek on top of her head, and ran his hand over her hair. "It's okay beautiful. I'll be back. I promise."

Toke cleared his throat. "You'll need to open the gate outside Tolen so it doesn't interfere with the progress I've made on the portal."

Tolen nodded, not trusting his voice and led the way outside. Once everyone had joined him he swallowed several times before he could address Brina and Rune. "I'll open the gate a few miles from the Zenith since we don't know what kind of protections they'll have in place." He reached out to shake Rune's arm but Rune pulled him into a one armed bro hug, which ended as a big group hug when everyone joined in.

"We got this Tolen." Rune gruffly whispered over their heads.

"Thank you." The hug broke apart and Tolen stepped back beside Macy. "I don't know if this is what the Light had in mind when they picked all of us, but I'm proud of everything you guys have done and continue to do and I can't imagine a better team."

"If it looks like a good idea once we're out there," Brina added softly, "maybe I'll see if I can reach some of my father's connections. See what humans we might already have on our side."

"That sounds like a good plan." Tolen lifted his hands and a gate shimmered open in front of them to a very distant forest.

Rune kissed Keelyn one last time and then put his hand on Brina's shoulder as they passed through the gate.

It was a slow walk back inside, but the sorrow Tolen had from their friends leaving was quickly replaced with anxiety for what was to come.

"So, how do we do this?" Macy's fingers warmed—her Kuna reacting to her nerves. He gave her hand a reassuring squeeze, not sure who he was trying to reassure more as Toke pointed to Macy and Keelyn's room.

Toke pushed Keelyn's bed against the far wall and had Tolen help him carry in the table. He then spent the next ten minutes setting it up with various gadgets and medical supplies.

He noticed Tolen's surprise at the medical supplies and elaborated, "I used the disk to procure some emergency supplies. They may not be necessary."

Tolen looked at the thin clear tubes, bags of blood, array of needles, and wished he hadn't drunk that Whosays. Toke knew Tolen had Sphere ability. He could heal Macy's every injury, but he couldn't force in nourishment, or restore excessive blood loss. Macy trembled beside him and the turning of his stomach increased.

Finally, Toke brought in a chair and sat down, motioning for the rest of them to sit on Macy's bed. Tolen wasn't sure whose knees were shaking the most, Macy's or his. Macy dropped her arm over Keelyn's shoulders who continued to wipe away tears she couldn't stifle.

Toke leaned forward and began twisting a strange ring he wore on his middle finger. "Tolen you may remember the three phases of Transcendence: The Source, the Meridian, and the Crown?"

Toke's face seemed to fade away as Tolen's memory pulled up another face, that of Lynd the Sphere who had explained what Tolen would experience in each phase of Transcendence.

"Mindra, there is something you must understand as you go forward. The person you are now will cease to exist in its current form. You will retain your memories, desires, loyalties, every feeling and experience you've ever had, but your perception of them will change, intensify.

"In a transcended, metaphysical body, your gifts will strengthen as will every emotion you've ever felt, every connection to every experience and person you've ever had. Your current body is incapable of withstanding such an emotional climate. Your new body brings an ability to love fuller, learn faster, see more clearly." He touched Tolen's arm and a zing of warmth passed into his heart. "Allow the change to come, Mindra. Do not fight it and it will be the greatest gift you'll ever receive."

"Transcendence comes in three phases." Lynd placed his hands inside hidden pockets of his robe. "The Source, the Meridian, and the Crown. The Source will be the most unpredictable as it is unique to the individual. The Meridian will be the most dangerous as this is when the gifts reach their highest strength—the body will be tested as will the life force… The final phase, the Crown, is the settling of the Balance around your new visage—the final stage of transcendence to your true self. Everything comes together with the Crowning. It is the longest phase. It takes time for the power and knowledge within the body to equalize."

Tolen nodded and Macy's trembling increased. He wrapped his arm around her waist.

"Those are the phases of a *normal* Transcendence, but in a Forced Transcendence, a precursor, a stimulant so to speak, comes before each phase." He pointed to a round gadget with a bunch of wires sticking out with dangerous looking barbs on the ends. "The first stimulant ages the body to what it would be at eighteen. It will be extremely painful. The second will awaken the gifts." He looked up apologetically. "It too will be extremely painful. The third stimulant—"

"Will also be very painful," Macy interrupted. "I get it and judging by your emergency supplies, I expect it to be the most horrible experience of my life, so can we just skip the intro and get started?" Tolen knew she was trying for sarcasm, but it came out desperate, pleading.

Toke nodded understandingly and stood up. "Macy, lie down. Keelyn you sit on the bed at her feet. Tolen you take the chair by her head. Tolen, I know that you said you can sense everything that goes on in Macy's body, but I'm still going to attach some nodes to her head that connect to this monitor here," he pointed to a black box on the table, "and allow *me* to know what is going on in the body so I can direct Tolen and Keelyn what I need them to do. Is that okay Macy?"

Macy laid back on the pillow and nodded.

"I'm also going to insert one of these into a vein at your elbow." Toke showed Macy a long tube. "This will allow us to feed you if need be. Forced Transcendence can last hours or even days and your physical body needs to stay nourished. You should be able to eat between phases, this is just a precaution."

"I don't see any IV fluid." Tolen looked around, his adrenaline already pumping.

Toke pointed to another box, this one flat gray, beside the monitor. "We'll add food to that box, it pulls out the nutrients and liquefies them, and then we can attach Macy's tube to the box as necessary."

Macy's arms continued to tremble slightly but she didn't flinch as Toke inserted the tube in her arm and attached the nodes to her head and neck. A methodic, somewhat fast, beeping came from the box with the nodes.

"Good, it's already monitoring your heart rate." Toke tapped a few buttons on the side.

"Because Transcendence affects the ability to shield oneself and it exerts a tremendous amount of power, it usually takes place in a Capka. As we don't have one here, or a group of Spheres to shield you, I will need to monitor the strength of the *Athstazia* to ensure we remain hidden. Tolen you may also need to use your Sphere ability at times."

Tolen lifted his wrist. "My watch also has a Sphere button."

Toke grinned. "Perfect. Activate that now and it will boost the *Athstazia's* power."

Tolen tapped the button on his watch and experienced a slight prick of pain in the center of his forehead, but then an outflow of warmth toward Macy.

"I can feel it." She whispered, giving Tolen the tiniest bit of comfort.

Toke picked up the round gadget with the barbed wires. He didn't say it, but his eyes said it wasn't going to feel good wherever he put them. Macy grit her teeth and Tolen grabbed her hand as the first barb went through her pants into her left thigh and his own thigh twitched at the sting—she didn't realize how close their connection was, how he would feel every bit of her pain as forcefully as she did through the whole process, and he wasn't about to inform her. Never before had he been so grateful for the connection. He was ready to send healing and light to every part of her at the slightest twinge. He concentrated on the next place Toke was about to put a barb when Bastian's voice interrupted his focus.

Tolen, there is something you need to understand about that connection.

What? His left calf stung and he pushed some healing energy to the spot on Macy using their clasped hands as the source of direction.

Healing is one thing, you are asking the cells to align. But to take another's pain is something else all together. She will feel nothing but you will feel everything.

That's fine. I'd rather it be me than her. Toke inserted barbs in her right thigh and calf. Tolen pulled back the pain and his thigh and calf stung but she hardly twitched.

Tolen, while you can *do that, you* should *not. There is something you must understand about the laws of creation and effect.*

Cause and effect? Next barbs: left bicep, left forearm, Tolen pulled the pain inside himself.

No, creation *and effect. Each individual on this planet was created for an individual and beautiful purpose. Every event in their life has an effect that allows them to slowly begin to recognize that purpose. As they begin to recognize it they then have the choice whether or not to accept and fulfill it. But to do that, they must first believe that they can. They must believe in themselves and the gifts they have been given.*

Toke attached the last two barbs into Macy's right forearm and bicep. She barely winced.

You cannot take away her pain without also taking away the lesson she would learn from it, the strengths she would gain, which are vital for her to recognize and achieve her purpose. Focus on speeding the healing of her body so as to help her body accept the change, but you cannot take her pain. She must be allowed to discover for herself the gifts from the Light that have nothing to do with Kunamin, or prophecy, and everything to do with McLacy Allicandra, the individual. But she won't be able to do so if she does not have the experiences that will teach her to believe in herself and her abilities.

"...if we estimate one minute for every day, down to the minute you officially turn eighteen," Toke's voice ended Tolen's conversation with Bastian, "that's 443 minutes which means we can anticipate the aging process to take approximately seven hours and forty minutes give or take, depending on the exact moment I start the machine and her body reacts. As for the other phases, it's different for everyone who goes through Forced Transcendence. We need to accept that we could be at this for possibly a week, maybe even longer." Toke methodically checked every gauge and gadget he had out while Tolen fought with himself over Bastian's warning.

Could he do it? Sit here, feel the twinges of her pain and *not* take them inside himself? Could he sit there and watch her suffer, accepting that it was for the greater good?

"Ready?" Toke asked, his thumb on a shiny red switch.

No, I'm not.

"Yes." Macy squeezed Tolen's fingers. He felt her worry but also her determination. She was everything he'd told her she was, strong, always determined to do what was right. But she still doubted herself and her abilities. She doubted she could be the gift the world needed. The same way he'd once doubted he could be the Ninth Chosen. But he couldn't deny the pain, sorrow, and fear he'd experienced throughout his life had prepared himself to fulfill this role here and now, a protector for Macy, a leader of warriors. Was he as prepared and knowledgeable as he should be? Probably not, but all he *had* learned and experienced helped make him into a person he never could have imagined he would be. A much stronger, determined version of himself. If someone had taken away the pain, the horror, the sorrow, then he would never have known this version. He wouldn't know that he was strong enough to face destiny the *right* way.

Tears bit the back of his eyes, he ran a thumb over Macy's promise bracelet, and placed a gentle kiss on her forehead.

Okay, I'm ready.

But when the switch flipped and the first wave of electricity shot through Macy's body, her back arched off the bed, and tears streamed from her eyes, he knew he was about to face the greatest test of his life.

Chapter 38

TRANSCEND

Macy opened her eyes to late afternoon sun streaming in the open window. A coolish breeze played in the shredded curtains. A rush of embarrassment and guilt filled her gut. Embarrassment at the amount of tears and screams she hadn't been able to hold back as the pain gripped every inch of her body. Guilt that Tolen had to witness it.

Her muscles tingled with remembered pain at being stretched in every direction—like those people who were tortured to death in the fifteenth century by being slowly wrenched apart. But there never was a moment of release, when her arms or legs finally parted from her body and she could just lay there and bleed to death. She shivered.

"Are you cold?" Tolen tugged a blanket up under her arms, not an easy thing to do with all the wires. Dark circles ringed beneath his anguished eyes, his life force exuded regret mingled with determination. She could hear Toke and Keelyn speaking quietly from the kitchen, the smell of woodsmoke and something delicious cooking said the ancient stove was functioning.

She ran her hand over the blanket—the effort a lot harder than it should be. "I'm okay. How are you?"

"Me?"

She touched the rings beneath his eyes. "That was hard for you."

"Of course it was." His voice shook and he laid his forehead on hers. "But worse for you."

"Maybe, but I'm still sorry you had to suffer along with me."

"I'd rather be here than anywhere else."

She tugged his face down and he pecked her lips. The effort of raising her arms hurt, sort of like the next day after strenuous exercise, but bearable. "Honestly, I expected even worse."

His eyebrows rose. Was that guilt she saw in his expression?

"You're stronger than you think."

"I guess so." She tried to sit up and Tolen quickly set to help, propping her against the headboard, stuffing pillows behind her back. She'd never been one to like coddling, but it seemed to help him feel better, to be doing something, and she did feel pretty weak and rubbery.

"I see Keelyn put up some decorations." She took the cup of water Tolen offered, looking around the room at the faded pictures, and bright quilts hanging over the bedsides and chair Tolen occupied, her eyes stopped on an aged mirror on the wall directly across from her, and the cup stopped half way to her mouth.

"She found an old trunk in one of the cabins. It was full of stuff. She needed something to keep busy, she had a hard time watching…"

Macy reached up to touch her face, bumping against the nodes and wires on her forehead. Was that really her face that stared back? Were her cheekbones always that prominent, her face that thin? And wasn't her hair longer than it had been yesterday when Keelyn braided it for the Promise ceremony? She looked down at her arms, the sleeves were a tad shorter, revealing muscles that were bigger, more defined. She poked a rock hard bicep with her finger. Her fingernails were much longer than she'd ever let them get on purpose. She flipped the blanket aside. Her pants were shorter, at least by two inches, her socks tighter than she remembered them being when she'd put them on that morning.

Tolen took the cup from her hand and set it on the table. "We're the same age now. Physically at least." He leaned over until his face was next to hers in the mirror.

"I didn't think I would look different."

"You don't, just older." His mouth turned up. "I only found a couple gray hairs."

She tried to slug him but ended up wincing instead. "Anything else interesting happen while I…um…grew up?"

Tolen handed her some of Toke's hard biscuits that she nibbled slowly. "Your dad and the others found River. He didn't want to be sent here. He wanted to stay with them to help find the other Descendants. We haven't heard from Mahto and Sienn, or Rune and Brina, yet. Toke rigged a radio and has boosted signals from several stations, so we've been able to get news reports from around the world."

Macy's fingers twitched sending shocks of pain up her arms. "What's the Dark been up to?"

Tolen handed her the cup again to wash down the biscuit. "We're not exactly sure what's been happening on LadonRyn. Some sort of shield has been placed over the island that's blocking it well enough not even I can tell if Darsapean is there yet or not. A thick black sulfurous cloud has covered it. The world is reporting it as a new volcano erupting in the ocean. Since they didn't know the island existed it makes sense. They've also evacuated all the Hawaiian islands. The Fallen haven't been as quiet."

Cold shivers ran across her arms, she gave Tolen the water back and pulled the quilt to her shoulders. "What are they doing?"

"Exactly what you predicted. They've infiltrated every government, militia, and dictatorship on the planet. They are all failing as we speak. Civil war has broken out in almost every country. Europe, the US, and Canada are all closer every minute. Some odd reports have Toke guessing that even some of their mutated offspring have been sighted." He ran a hand over his eyes. "There are talks that World War Three is on its way."

She swallowed. All that in just a matter of hours? She'd been right to do this. There would have been nothing left of the world in two years. "And you, what have you seen?"

He shook his head, raked his fingers roughly through his hair. "Still hazy, but I think the reports are right. We've got maybe a few weeks, but it could be as short as a few days before the whole world will be at war. As your father said, 'they are ripening for destruction'."

The biscuit turned in Macy's stomach. "Then we need to hurry. How long before my age will trigger the Source?"

Tolen's jaw clenched. "Toke's guess was that it may begin at the hour of your birth. He knew it was close to evening, but—"

"4:35PM. That's when I was born."

Tolen checked his watch. "Then you've got a little less than an hour." She caught his fingers trembling as he lowered his hands back to his lap. "So, it's good you're awake. Toke was hoping you'd have a chance to eat before it starts."

"And does he have any guesses now as to how long it will take?"

"Still says no."

She nodded just as Keelyn and Toke came in bearing trays of food. Some sort of cooked bird and even mashed potatoes and gravy. Her stomach growled despite all the bad news.

Keelyn smiled at the look on Macy's face, but her eyes looked as strained as Tolen's. "Tolen sensed some dormant seeds in a garden behind one of the homesteads. He used his nature speak from right here in our room to coax them to sprout. I caught the bird and Toke got the stove all fixed up."

"It looks delicious you guys. Thank you."

○ ○ ○

Twenty minutes later their early dinner was cleared and Macy had a sucker in her cheek, feeling surprisingly good. Still sore, but anxious for the Source to begin. Her body had allowed the aging process to complete which meant the Balance would begin Transcendence, but despite the physical differences in the body, her brain *knew* she wasn't eighteen. The fight had only just begun. Logic could still cause the body to decide at any time over the next three phases to stop allowing the process. Or in other words, die.

She bit down on the sucker in her mouth, her teeth sinking into the soft chocolate center. Toke had used his disk to secure a few bags from some a candy store, ringing up his purchase and leaving cash in the register when no one was looking. Keelyn laughed at their stunned faces when he'd told them this, and said he'd do things like that on very rare occasions when he decided they deserved a break from his food.

A kindness for the girl who could be dead in the next hour. She shuddered away from the thought at the same moment the Kuna bloomed in her chest, Tolen jumped, and Toke's machine started clicking and beeping.

Toke jumped up from where he'd been sitting next to Keelyn on the other bed to check his gauges. "The Source is starting."

Keelyn settled back at Macy's feet.

Tolen helped Macy lay back down and started rubbing her shoulder. "It's going to be okay." She couldn't tell if he said this for her or himself.

"The Source is unique to the individual so I can't advise you on what to prepare for," Toke apologized.

"What was yours like, Tolen?" Macy licked her lips as the Kuna zinged to her palms, the heat becoming uncomfortable. She had to bite her cheek to keep the heat in her hands.

"Strange." He continued to rub her shoulder, and while it felt nice, it didn't slow the Kuna the way she hoped his voice would. "I sort of left my body and then took a trip around the world."

"Really?" Never before had the Kuna hurt like this.

She grit her teeth as Tolen started to describe what he'd seen, the world, the Dark growing above it, but soon his words disappeared as the heat hit a peak, as if her very heart had caught fire, a long earsplitting scream ripped from her throat, and her eyes went dark.

She didn't know how long it lasted, the pain. Only that one second it was there and she wanted to die and the next second it was gone and she thought she had. Her eyes saw nothing but darkness—did she still *have* eyes? She couldn't tell if she even had hands. She couldn't touch her face to make sure her eyes were still there. She'd become a phantom thought, an invisible nothing with only the thoughts and feelings of Macy Burdow. She must be dead. She'd failed. Dread filled her heart. *I'm so sorry Tolen.*

o o o

"Tolen, do it now!" Toke flipped switches and the wires began to shock Macy's body in cycles making her limbs jump. "Her heart has stopped, heal it!"

Sweat dripped off Tolen's face as he placed his hands over her heart, the heat from her body turning the room into an oven. *"Lon'adras!"* He screamed, not coaxing, demanding her heart to heal, repair, return. The fear fighting the fury to save her. "Macy!"

o o o

Something flickered in the darkness, a tiny spark. Tolen's voice in the void. She pushed her nothingness toward the sound, the spark, tried to reach a phantom hand toward it.

You are stronger than you think LaUnahi, grab the spark. Bastian's voice, not from now, but years ago, not long after she'd been chosen. The first time he'd been teaching her to use her Kunamin. He'd lit a sparkler, a firework. A crackling and spitting little stick she'd seen every Fourth of July with her parents.

"Don't touch the sparks or you'll get burned sweetheart," her mother would always say. Burns hurt, she remembered this from touching her mom's curling iron once. But Bastian wanted her to touch the sparks. Part of her wanted to, the part she'd begun to recognize as the feeling that made her shard glow. The pretty shard she wore around her neck and loved more than anything she'd ever had. She placed her little hand over it, felt its warmth, its urging that it was okay to touch the spark, that she could control it. She'd reached out her hand, the sparks had jumped from the sparkler onto her palm, her first reaction was to jerk back, but she resisted her fear and let the sparks dance around on her palm. "It tickles," she giggled.

You are stronger than you think, LaUnahi, grab the spark. Bastian spoke again, in the familiar timber of today.

She fought against the weightlessness, the nothingness, focused only on the tiny spark in the darkness.

Where the light is, darkness cannot be, Bastian whispered.

The spark brightened, its edges flicking out into the nothingness, brightening it. She imagined her hand reaching beneath it, imagined it jumping to her palm, and suddenly she saw her hand, but only her hand. She closed her fist around the spark, its warmth shot through her arm, which appeared, the skin glowing as bright as the spark. It moved swiftly up her arm, into her heart, through her whole body until she stood there, the only light bright in the darkness, the nothingness held at bay.

Tolen's relieved voice, "Macy."

Another flicker began in the distance and she floated toward it. It began as a small flame but the moment she stopped in front of it, it burst into being, a huge fiery bird as big as Legion but filled with goodness equal to Legion's evil. Its eyes held an intelligence she'd never seen in an animal. It flapped its wings slowly, the heat from them fanning Macy with the warmth she associated with her Kuna along with a pleasing scent of lilac and rain.

"I am Kunamin, McLacy Allicandra." The bird's beak didn't open, but she knew the voice issued from him.

"I didn't know you were a bird." Macy watched the flames flicker on his red-gold wings, mesmerized, awed, and all at once more proud of being Kunamin than ever before.

"I am a phoenix. In my mortal life I was a man, upon my death I rose from the ashes to become my soul form. I am the source of your gift. I gave a portion of myself to the Balance and the Balance gave a portion of me to you. Your flame is partly me, and partly you. That is why each Kunamin has a different smell, it is the blending of blood, the *heritage* of family. As you complete Transcendence our flames will unite, no longer to be separate. My strength will be your strength, my power your power. It will flow in your veins, live forever in your heart. A collective of all Kunamin, the *power* of family."

Macy's chest warmed, her fingers tingled, her life force aching for the connection. But a part of her resisted, a part she realized lay on a bed in an old house. Whispers met her ears, whispers outside the nothingness, spoken to the body, coaxing, begging. Tolen, Keelyn, Toke, they all begged her body to accept the Source. She closed her eyes, added her pleas to theirs. *I want this, please accept it. We're strong enough together, body and soul. We can do this.*

The tingle increased and she was certain if the bird could, he'd be smiling.

CHAPTER 39

THE MERIDIAN AND CROWN

"Mace, please wake up, show me you're still in there. Please Macy, please." Sunlight spilled from the window, highlighting the blue under her eyes.

It'd taken all the willpower Tolen had to only direct his healing power to her heart, to not pull the pain he could feel in every cell of her body into his. When she'd died, when her heart had completely stopped—almost exploded according to Toke—he'd nearly failed. He'd healed her heart, but her life force still floated somewhere else outside, possibly in the Between world he'd entered during his own Transcendence. That time he'd somehow managed to pull Macy there with him, but Macy wasn't pulling for Tolen, if anything it seemed like she was drifting away.

He squeezed her hand again, tried to drown out Keelyn's quiet sobs, Toke's incessant switch flipping and knob clicking. "Come on baby, come back to me." The gentlest push against his thumb. Did he imagine it? He looked at his hand wrapped around hers. No, there it was again, the tiniest twitch, soft as a butterfly's wings.

"Mace?"

Her eyelids flickered open then narrowed at the light cutting into her eyes. He raised his hand and a gust of wind closed the curtains. "How do you feel?"

"Can I have some water?" Her voice came out thick and scratchy. He gently lifted her head and helped her sip from the cup Keelyn thrust into his hand.

"Thank you." She rasped.

Tolen kissed her forehead and lowered her back down, wanting to both jump up and down and fall on the floor in the fetal position and cry like a baby.

"How—" She cleared her throat. "How long was I out?"

Tolen dabbed her cheeks with a cool rag Toke handed him trying to slow the pounding in his chest, pull back the throbbing behind his eyes.

"Almost six days." Toke's voice came out almost as raspy as Macy's. None of them had hardly slept or ate the entire time.

"You guys look awful." Macy tried for a smile, but guilt danced in her eyes.

"We're fine." Tolen brushed her hair off her face, his fingers tangling in the wires and nodes. "You just worry about you."

"Do you think you can eat?" Toke wiped his hand across his forehead.

She grimaced. "I think I'd like to, but I'm not sure."

Toke flipped another switch. "We'll start simple, just some biscuits, maybe a little bit of mashed potatoes?"

"That sounds nice." Macy smiled, just a small one, but it still had the effect of slowing Tolen's heart.

Keelyn and Toke left to get her food, Keelyn pausing to squeeze Macy's hand and push some light inside. Tolen would never be able to express how grateful he was for all they were doing for Macy. He could see in their every action, feel from the emotion emanating from their life forces, just how much they loved her. In those moments when they'd all thought they'd lost her, their agony was almost equal to his. *Almost.*

He ran his thumb over Macy's cheek, loving the fact that her eyes were open and watching him. "I thought I'd lost you. I really thought you'd gone." He touched the edge of her lips. "Those other times when my sight had shown me your possible death, were terrible. . ." his voice cracked and he had to turn his focus out the window. "But I'd been able to stop it, prevent it from happening. But this? To sit here and willingly wait and see because it was your choice to do this, it made me realize what it's going to be like to walk into battle with you. That when we ultimately face Legion and Daemon, Darsapean and Gyeesta, I may have to do it again—allow you to sacrifice yourself to save the world, because you have accepted your role in the prophecy. I know that, because if you hadn't, you wouldn't be going through this, and I can't take your choice away no matter how much I want to." He tried to hold back the tears, to stay strong for her, to show he was ready, and he accepted her will, but they fell hard and fast, dripped off his chin.

She reached a weak hand up to wipe them away and tugged his face back to look at her. "I wish it didn't have to be like this."

He caught her hand in his, held it against his cheek. "Me too."

She bit her lip and moisture brimmed in her eyes. "I do accept it. And I want to say I'm ready but Tolen, I'm so scared. . ." *of my Transcendence, of the prophecy, of. . . dying.*

This time he wiped away her tears. "Me too." He squeezed his eyes shut once. "I love you. Forever."

"Forever."

The others came back, Tolen wiped his face on his sleeve, and Macy on her quilt. They kindly pretended not to notice.

While they ate she filled them in on what she had experienced during her Source—a much better experience than they'd had watching it from the outside—and they filled her in on the state of the world and the plans that were in motion for followers of Light. Well, Toke did. Tolen just relished holding her hand, seeing her chest moving up and down, the color returning to her cheeks with every bite, and trying not to think about the next phase of horror.

"LadonRyn has grown. *It* swallowed Hawaii, and now almost reaches the coastal borders of Mexico. It floats just above the ocean on a cloud of darkness. Darsapean has announced his return to Hidden-kind and declared war. He has renamed LadonRyn, *To'Degani*, The Dark. The cloud is expanding and with it comes hordes of Dark creatures, the Radia Warriors are fighting non-stop. The Chosen who are not gathering here are fighting there. The cloud has covered California and moves farther inland every day. It won't be long before we'll begin to see it here. Humans can see the vapor, feel the Dark in its depths. Some are screaming apocalypse, others aliens, others global warming. There's been talks of nuking the island in the hopes it will seal off whatever volcano or source is causing the mist."

Macy swallowed a bite of mashed potatoes. Tolen could feel her disgust, her worry. "And the human wars?"

"They continue. Martial Law has been declared in thirteen of the United States so far."

She lowered her spoon and Tolen rubbed circles in the back of her hand trying to push some of his light into her troubled heart.

"There's Chosen here?" She sipped her water.

"Oh yeah." Keelyn twisted a linen napkin in her fingers.

"So you've heard from Rune and Brina?"

"Yes, they had another close call with Sorsha, but managed to escape again. It seems a lot of Chosen had faced some Fallen and their scary devices, but a lot of them still didn't want to listen to reason. They wanted to fight to defend the humans, *now*. Some of them recognized the need to gather, build the army and attack with combined force, but not enough." Her eyes flicked to Tolen.

He swallowed back frustration. They'd been calling for the Ninth to lead them, angry that he was staying back hidden while the human world burned. They did not understand timing, or the necessity of protecting *Lasan*. He tried to keep the frustration out of his voice as he explained. "Two days ago, a single clear image passed across my Second Sight. Me, sending out a reminder to the Chosen to gather. I knew it was a dangerous move with our shards possibly compromised by the Fallen, but I couldn't deny what I'd seen. The reminder worked. Rune and Brina have sent us dozens of Lost Ones, and for the past day and a half we've had about a hundred more Chosen arrive."

Macy's head turned toward the window as if trying to see them.

"We've got them rebuilding the small cottages along the river to keep them occupied." Toke added. "We decided for the time being to keep the full prophecy a secret. To reveal the prophecy would be to reveal it to the Fallen."

"It's not like it would help them to know anyway." Tolen cringed at the finality in Macy's tone.

Toke squeezed Macy's shoulder.

"What about dad? How's it going with the Descendants?"

"They've sent back four. They had some trouble with the most recent one. Almost lost her to a band of Kezgani." Keelyn shuddered. "Both her and Blaze were injured. They had to find a tribe of Spheres to heal them before they could send her on and continue. Your dad is worried about getting to the last two in time."

"In time?" Macy's eyebrows drew together.

Tolen sighed. "The state things are in we've decided to move forward with the plan to attack *To'Degani* as soon as you finish your Transcendence and complete the Awakening."

The implications flashed through her thoughts. All the unwelcome feelings Tolen had been trying to suppress while Macy fought for her life, stirred in his chest warming his Kuna.

She ran a shaky hand over her mouth as if almost afraid to ask her next question. "Mahto and Sienn?"

Tolen's heart plummeted as Toke and Keelyn looked his way. He leaned forward and Macy put her hand on his arm. "Tolen?"

"They—they made it to the Lafar colony. With the help of Sienn's father, the colony all agreed to join the fight. They were preparing to leave, to come here, when…" Pain lanced between his eyes and he dropped his head in his hands.

Keelyn took over the telling. "A Dark army attacked."

Mahto's smiling face flashed across Tolen's vision and his stomach rolled.

Keelyn put her hand on Tolen's arm, sending some of her light toward his heart, but the grief was still too fresh for it to do much. "We lost Mahto and half the Lafar in the colony."

Macy squeezed his hand. "I'm so sorry Tolen."

He bit back the emotion. "Sienn is here, with her father coordinating what is left of their colony. They're going to go and try to recruit any other Lafar they can find."

"They need you to lead them." She dropped his arm, frustration leaking into her voice.

"My first duty is to the Gift of Light. They'll get us both soon."

"Maybe sooner than we think." Toke's gadget started clicking and beeping at the same moment Tolen felt both Macy's and his Kuna light up again.

"It's time to stimulate the Meridian." He grabbed the round device attached to the barbs and Tolen squeezed the sides of his seat. "Be prepared for a big push of your gifts." Toke grabbed two buckets of water and sat them next to Macy's bed.

Toke flipped a switch, the barbs glowed in Macy's skin and Tolen could feel the heat building around her body again, turning the room into a furnace. "Hold on Macy. You've got this."

o o o

Heat waved off Macy's skin, rippling the air above her body. Her clothes started to smoke. Great, just what she wanted, to end up laying here buck naked and on fire. Toke threw a bucket of water but it hissed to vapor before it hit her skin, then the pain started again. Never, not once since she'd been Chosen, had fire or heat ever hurt, had she ever experienced the feeling of burning. Not so now. Every inch of her body stung like a thousand bees had pricked her flesh.

So this is what it's like when I melt a Dark creature?

It is to teach you compassion, Bastian whispered regretfully.

Compassion for the Dark?

Just compassion. Bastian's voice faded.

Flames erupted from her hands, her feet, even her mouth as she screamed. An inferno of heat and pain. The flames licked higher, she could see nothing but them. A sphere appeared, containing the flame in a dome. Tolen?

Strangely the flame twisted into images from her past. As a child playing fetch with the neighbor's dog. Sitting with her father watching an owl hunt in their backyard. Standing on a kitchen chair icing cookies with her mother. Racing Bastian in an old farm field, him pretending she'd won, rewarding her with cheeseburgers for dinner. Kissing Tolen for the first time. Her life flashing before her eyes. *Uh-oh, am I dying again? Come on body! You got this! Remember we love fire!*

Her body jerked and flopped on the bed, some awareness wondered why it didn't light up, but the other cataloged each and every second of pain and horror.

"I want this!" She screamed and her body collapsed to the mattress.

○ ○ ○

"That went better than I thought it would." Tolen's half smile lit his face. "You only scorched the ceiling and a bit of the wallpaper."

Macy chugged the fourth cup of water Keelyn held out. She'd never been so thirsty! "I'm just glad my clothes are still here." Her cheeks warmed and she glanced out the dark window.

"You are mastering your body." Toke handed her a slice of bread, warm and sweet. "I sensed from your bioelectricity the first time we met that you were extremely powerful, but I'm still impressed. You completed the Meridian in less than six hours."

"I felt really powerful. In control. The most control I've ever felt over my Kunamin."

Tolen smiled again and kissed her cheek. "You're amazing."

○ ○ ○

Toke wanted to wait for morning to stimulate the Crown, but Macy wanted to get it over with and surprisingly enough, she didn't feel tired, despite the fact that it was almost midnight. It took much convincing on her part to both Toke and Tolen, but finally they relented and only made her wait two hours and eat another meal.

After the initial surge of pain from the barbs, that had become familiar enough to be more annoying than painful, the Crown began as one not-so-simple question, spoken in one long burst of heat that held Macy in a board-like state, stiff and unmoving, but the answer took her an entire night of torture to answer.

You have been Chosen. . .Will you accept fate and fulfill your destiny?

Image after image of blood and carnage, hate and horror, never ending darkness over the earth.

Pinpricks of light, good people, human and Hidden-kind fighting the darkness.

Her friends, Tolen, her father, all fighting and dying.

One final image: a single human fighting a lone figure in a battle that would affect the outcome of all. A battle that ended with a raging inferno that burned all other images from her mind.

Will you accept your destiny?

She pulled in a deep breath and pushed out her answer with all the strength she could muster. *Yes.*

The pain fled, the flame fled, and light and peace took their place.

Thank you Mindra, Lasan Ladonradi. Thank you.

Macy opened her eyes to a new awareness. Strength pulsed though her veins with each beat of her heart. The warmth of the Kuna in her chest was more powerful and amazing than ever. She'd never realized before how it existed within her, sort of like a parasite living off its host, but as a welcome guest. Now it existed as if it had always been there, a part of her since birth, as necessary to her body for survival as her lungs, heart, and brain. The one could no longer survive without the other. Her shard pulsed and she longed to connect to it, complete the merging, but old fears had her holding back. She still wasn't sure if she could control it, despite all she'd been through. The time would come when she would have to attempt it, but right now the risk of the Fallen was too great.

She raised her hands in front of her eyes. The barbs and tube were gone, her skin perfectly clear, still slightly glowing beneath the surface. She touched her forehead, the nodes no longer there. She could feel everyone watching her, letting her acclimate to her new visage. Her gifts were now a complete part of her, she need only think the word and every sound intensified. She could hear their breathing, sense their body heat. She could hear past the room to people talking and working outside. She calmed her hearing and looked at her friends, at the love of her life.

She grinned. "Time to fight back."

CHAPTER 40

THE GATHERING

Macy rested in the newly installed swing on the front porch of Moony's, watching the sun set with Tolen by her side, her head on his shoulder, their hands clasped together on her knee.

Despite sleeping the day away after completing the Crown her body still craved rest. Her mind didn't. Her dreams had been extremely vivid while her body slept.

She stifled a yawn. Toke said that even though she'd completed the mental and emotional tasks of the Crown, and her mind and life force had been empowered and enlightened by it, making them ready to rock-and-roll, it might take her physical body a day or two to catch up. It'd been through a lot in the last week.

Her thoughts drifted to her strange dreams, dreams that when she woke they discovered weren't exactly dreams, but her subconscious mind giving her insight into what she should expect from her new body and gifted life force. In the dreams, once the Crown fully settled over her, as she fully merged into her power, her connection to Tolen and his gifts also increased. Their minds became more closely linked than ever before. He still couldn't block her if she wanted in his head, but she had total control over which thoughts she shared, and they could talk back and forth to each other in their minds. Tolen's words entered her thoughts as easily and naturally as Bastian's did.

But the core emotions that had made it so hard for him to be in her head before, she could easily shelter and protect from him, which allowed him to stay focused and in control of his own overprotective emotions. But by far the strangest, yet amazing, thing her dreams told her: her light would feed Tolen's and Tolen's light would reciprocate to feed hers, creating a constant cycle of renewal and strength.

When she'd finally woken up to late afternoon light pouring through the window and Tolen met her eyes from where he'd slept on Keelyn's bed, she knew he'd seen her dreams, that she'd subconsciously shared them with him.

Was that. . . Is this real? He'd whispered in her mind.

The familiar tremor in her life force, the tremor she'd always attributed to a connection to truth, seemed to be singing. *I think it is.*

As they'd eaten dinner and chatted with everyone, they began to feel the cycle of light engage between them and Tolen whispered to her mind that it seemed to be helping clear his *Second Sight*. He called her light the antitoxin to the mist the Fallen had somehow placed over his Second Sight. Not even they could keep her out. It gave him hope that when the time came and they had to battle the Fallen, they would be getting more than they bargained for.

As strange as it was to be in what appeared to be an entirely new body, Macy couldn't deny the idea excited her. Not necessarily fighting the Fallen, but an opportunity to use the power she could feel surging through her veins against the Dark, to swing a giant punch against the evil running rampant throughout the earth.

A group of six youth, ranging in age, walked by and nodded. Their eyes were curious, but they only stared a fraction longer than comfortable. To explain the burst of white-light that had startled everyone as it shot out every window, crack and crevice of Moony's when Macy completed the Crown, Toke had told the settlement that Light's Aid had come to join the Ninth. Since then he said they'd been walking by in small groups throughout the day, and word must have spread that her and Tolen were outside because the longer they sat here, the number of gawkers had increased.

"They think you're an angel." Tolen whispered as they passed.

She chuckled and looked down at her arm—there *was* still a tiny hint of a glow. "I guess appearances can be deceiving.

His chest bounced with a quiet laugh. "Or accurate. It depends on how you look at it." He kissed the top of her head. "That was the longest week of my life."

"Me too. Even though I was out for the majority of it." She laughed again, but it didn't feel as natural. With Transcendence over, the next phase of the plan would begin and she knew the road ahead would make the last week seem like a sunny, happy vacation.

They sat silently for a time, enjoying one another's company but she knew they both were contemplating what tomorrow would bring. While her and Tolen had slept a group of new arrivals had streamed into the settlement. A group they were thrilled to see when they all tried to squeeze into Moony's for dinner (some had to spill out onto the back porch) —Incrah and a large number of Radia Warriors, their Doogar friends Deegan and Kiad from the Binithan, the Lafar Tolen had rescued from the Shadow Realm, and his friends Sashan, Tashta, Belch and Hunsí from the Honitahai village where Tolen had Transcended.

Her dad had also contacted Toke that afternoon. His group would be returning in the morning, with the final Descendant in tow. Rune and Brina would arrive then as well, the gathering of the Chosen now complete. But while Macy was extremely excited to be reunited with family and friends, their presence forced her to accept the reality of the coming battle that much faster.

Tomorrow morning, they would select captains and go over the battle plans Tolen and all the others had devised while Macy Transcended. Tomorrow evening she would perform the Awakening. Tolen had filled her in on the basics of the plan, the full details she would learn in the meeting with the captains tomorrow. He would have taken the time to explain everything, but she'd wanted one last night just relaxing quietly by his side, content to wait to let reality fully settle in. What she did know was already enough to make her palms tingle and bring unwanted doubts and fears to her heart. In less than 24 hours their battle plans would be in motion. In just over 72 hours the assault on *To'Degani*, the final fight to save the world, would begin.

The sun dropped below the eastern barn, a rooster crowed announcing the close of day, and a tiny little red bird landed on the arm of the swing. A beautiful little thing.

LaUnahi. Macy whispered in his thoughts. *Little bird. It was a bird just like this one that Bastian got the idea for my nickname. He said she was red like fire, and tiny like me. He said that being red could sometimes put her in more danger to predators, but this didn't stop her from trusting her wings.*

I love that.

I think he was trying to tell me to trust myself, and my gifts.

And maybe a little about your destiny too. A dangerous one, but you were made for it. Given everything you'll need to succeed at it.

She pushed tighter against him as the bird took flight. Tolen kissed her cheek and they waited for the first stars to begin glittering in the night sky before they went back inside to try and sleep for one more night outside of reality.

o o o

Tolen kept his grip tight on Macy's hand as they followed their friends and the newly selected captains and lieutenants back to Moony's where the Descendants were already waiting. Their little group had managed so much in the past week, more than he could have ever imagined. He didn't doubt a miracle had taken place and that the Light was close by and guiding their every step.

He'd had to stretch the borders of Onaepha to bursting. It now covered several miles up and down both sides of the river and they were still tightly packed together. Approximately 18,000 people, Hidden-kind and Chosen Ones had taken refuge here, 15,000 of which would be joining the battle. They had high hopes that once Macy completed the Awakening they'd be able to add at least another 10,000 to the number of warriors.

With a number of 25,000 warriors in mind they'd selected five captains, including himself, and each captain had selected an additional ten lieutenants. Each captain would be over a brigade of 5,000, each of their lieutenants leading platoons of 500. Tolen had selected Incrah, Rune, Quasar, Blaze, Sienn, Max, Brina, two more Chosen ones named Rhett and Tyge, a close friend of Incrah's called Sarai, as his lieutenants.

Macy, their secret weapon, would be working within his brigade where he could protect her. But they'd all agreed she would try not to access her freaky powerful light-Kuna until absolutely necessary. Her actions on Eamun's island had told Daemon she was Light's Aid, he'd already have creatures on the lookout for her. Once she used her gift, she'd be a key target. For as long as possible she would only focus on being Tolen's right hand, using their ability to speak without speaking to utilize his Second Sight and her uncanny connection to the Light to coordinate attacks and relay information. Prophecy or no, he was going to do everything he could to ensure the time for her to be the secret weapon never came.

Tolen shifted his thoughts to the captains they'd selected. He only knew Skye, the talented Lafar who'd helped Tolen rescue her people from the Shadow Realm. The others were selected from a large group who had been willing to accept the role, and then chosen after showing their various skills and Tolen conducted a character test using his Sphere ability. They then chose three of their lieutenants now, and accepted instruction to choose their final two from the pool of humans who would arrive later.

Sashan, Tashta, Hunsí, and Toke would stay in Onaepha. The wounded would be sent here and there was no one better than Tashta to organize their care. Toke would keep them in supplies, Hunsi would maintain the role of leadership and guidance, while Sashan would use his connection to the Watchers both in the army and spread throughout the world to catch as much of the future as he could—although he said with so many factors in play, the future changed moment to moment. Even he could not see the outcome of the war. They were mostly hoping he could uncover more about the Fallen and their plans. Jonas and his village of warrior trainers and trainees were supposed to arrive any moment to help prepare the troops. Jonas had promised to bring a large group of Spheres with him to help strengthen the shield over Onaepha. Something Toke was particularly happy about since between Tolen and Macy's power, and now Sashan's arrival, the *Athstazia* seemed to be working at its max.

Everything was coming together, falling into place, and as long as Tolen could keep his mind off that single line in the prophecy, he could almost convince himself it was excitement not trepidation he felt. *Almost*.

It took a few minutes for everyone to find a seat facing the side wall where maps and Toke's diagrams hung. The Descendants all gathered in one row, except for River who'd elected to take the seat beside Brina. A smile tugged at Tolen's lips, despite the graveness of his thoughts. Max had introduced the two that morning with a plea to Brina to help River with his Dicernan Relic. From the way River watched her, it was an arrangement he liked. Brina's feelings were cautious, but still gave Tolen hope that maybe one day, when this was all over, something could blossom there.

Rune closed the door and joined Tolen and his other lieutenants in front of the rows of people. Macy took the last seat in the first row and gave him an encouraging smile. Warmth pulsed into his body and the trembling in his hands stopped.

"Thank you everyone for coming. For your willingness to move forward on such short notice. For trusting the prophecy. For trusting me." He cleared his throat, picked up the thin stick Toke used to explain his diagrams, and tapped San Francisco on the world map hanging at the center of the wall. "Darsapean is staying on *To'Degani* where Gyeesta's power strengthens him. We've all agreed that our best chance to stop them both is to storm *To'Degani*. The mist has reached as far inland as Colorado, but the land mass only touches the continent in a sort of land bridge, here." He ran the point of the stick from San Francisco to the Mexican border. "The Dark currently controls all the cities that butt up against the land bridge."

Tolen then pointed just back from the land bridge. "So, we'll set up our forces just back from the Dark controlled towns with contacts we've allied. We'll be in the mist, but if we time it just right we should be able to stay hidden long enough for a coordinated rush attack."

He gestured to the audience. "Captains, you'll each select one hundred warriors from your brigades that will be dispatched to the areas of the world with the highest concentrations of the Dark. But the majority, our greatest strength, will gather here. The hope is that once we storm *To'Degani*, their creatures will be called back in to fight, taking the strain off those other areas, and then we can destroy them all."

A young man in the back raised his hand. "What about placing some forces on the Marshall Islands, come from the ocean side of *To'Degani* as well? Entrap them."

Incrah shook his head sadly. "Each of those islands has been taken by the mist, we'll find no allies there, and Legion guards the waters. We would have no safe place to launch our forces."

Several in the crowd nodded gravely.

Tolen checked his watch. "Captains, Toke will be sending messages to the warriors here via the Comm's in each house directing them where they can find their brigade. He has a sheet here for each of you showing where you can gather and begin training. By lunch we hope to have several Radia Warrior trainers here to help you prepare your troops." He glanced at Incrah who nodded.

"Eat lunch with your brigade and get to know them. The Awakening will take place at dusk. As the humans join us, many, if not most of them, will be extremely distraught. Please be patient and kind. Help them to feel welcome here. We'll give them a day to get settled and then ask for volunteers to join us. We'll then take six days to prepare our forces. One week from today, at dawn, we march on *To'Degani*." The faces looking up at him reflected the same concerns he held. He could see in their faces that it wasn't near enough time to train an entire army, but they had no choice. But with the concern he saw something else, something that warmed his life force and increased his hope. They, like himself and Macy, and all their friends knew—the cause for which you were fighting had more power to motivate and move to action than any amount of training ever could. When you were fighting for your family, for your right to live, skill didn't matter near as much as will.

He dismissed them and they all raised their fists to their hearts before slowly filing out of Moony's, some of them whispering between one another, others deep in thought. Macy, Rune, Keelyn, Max, and Toke stayed behind to help rearrange the tables and chairs back into groups.

"So, you ready for this?" Max pushed a chair beneath the table Macy had just maneuvered into place.

Macy whispered, but it still carried to Tolen a table away, "I have to be."

Max squeezed her shoulder. "You'll do great."

Rune clapped her on the back. "We have faith in you cousin."

Are you really okay Mace? Tolen asked gently.

Just nervous for tonight.

Tolen pushed the last chair into place and crossed to her side. *How about we go somewhere private for lunch and have a picnic? Then we'll do something fun until dinner. Sound good?*

Sounds perfect.

Tolen kissed her cheek. "Hey guys, I'm going to take this little lady on a picnic. We'll be back in time for dinner."

"Have fun." Max smiled.

Tolen dropped his arm over her shoulders and with monstrous effort pushed the worry aside, determined to only focus on having a good, no drama allowed, several hours with Macy.

CHAPTER 41

THE AWAKENING

Macy sat in the bedroom she shared with Keelyn, twisting her promise bracelet round and round her wrist. The picnic with Tolen had been wonderful. He'd actually managed to find them a tiny little alcove at the base of the mountain were the sounds of battle training barely met their ears. The hike afterward had done a fairly good job at distracting her from what she was about to do, but the worry had quickly returned the moment they stepped foot back in Moony's. She'd hardly been able to swallow a bite at dinner and had finally escaped to her room—using the excuse she needed some alone time to prepare.

But how do you prepare for something no one has ever done and therefore has no advice on how to prepare? She had less than an hour until she was to perform the Awakening and she had no idea how to do it.

So much had happened in their short time here. The Shadows had been set loose again, probably to hunt for Tolen and Macy, but so far Nahmala's *Athstazia* was doing its job, with Toke's help of course. But, the moment they left its protection all bets were off. The readings Toke was getting from her life force had him warning much the same thing they'd said would happen to Tolen after he Transcended—that not even the Spheres at the Citadel could shield her power anymore. She'd always been good at shielding herself, but Toke was worried. He'd told Tolen to do what he could to help shield her using his Sphere ability and his watch when they were near each other, but part of her wanted the Dark to know what was coming for them.

The death, the carnage, the hate, the humans fighting amongst themselves while the real enemy sat back and watched. It was time to end the Dark once and for all. She was ready, but…

Bastian, I'm so scared.

I know LaUnahi, Bastian soothed, his voice pained but sympathetic. *But it is as Tolen said, you were made for this. Appeal to the Light. They will comfort you. Give you the direction you seek.*

She'd only talked to the Light a handful of times. It wasn't that she had intentionally ignored them or anything. She'd just accepted they were all knowing and would do whatever they wanted whether she talked to them or not. She'd had her moments of anger with them, frustration. But she knew now it came from not fully understanding Them. She still didn't, but it *was* clearer.

Hey up there…um…I'm sorry for not talking to you more. She dropped her head into her hands. *I guess I didn't really know what to say, or maybe just how to say it. It's easier to think things at you than outright talk to you.*

A subtle warming of her Kuna and the words began to tumble out. "I don't how to do the Awakening. And I'm—I'm terrified to accept the prophecy." She squeezed her eyes shut against the tears that tried to fall. "I don't know why you picked me to be your gift. I don't know why it would be me when there's people like Keelyn out there who are just so *good,* or Tolen who, let's just say it, totally fits the role of martyr." She pushed her fists to her closed lids. "Ugh, that makes it sound like I'd want them to die instead of me. That's not what I mean. I would take their place a million times over, anyone's place. I'd rather it be me. It's just. . .I don't *fit* the role. I'm obnoxious, stubborn, selfish."

You see with your eyes Lasan. A gentle rumble of voices filled her mind. *We see the heart. We chose you, and we do not make mistakes. Trust in that and trust in yourself. When the moment comes to Awaken the human race, you will know what to do.*

Warmth pulsed through her body, not Kuna, but the warmth she associated with Tolen, Bastian, her parents, her friends. *Love.* She was loved by the Light. The warmth in her chest increased. She loved Them too. And she *did* trust Them. She just needed to trust herself.

She laid back on her bed, allowing the feeling of love and peace to envelop her like a gentle embrace. Her eyes closed and did not open again until Tolen shook her shoulder.

"It's time Mace."

She sat up and stretched, the warmth still lingering, lifting her up, calming her fears, and deepening her resolve. She met Tolen's loving gaze and mustered the most genuine smile she could. "Let's do this."

o o o

Toke's portal wall glowed softly behind her as she stood with her fingers pressed together, letting the Kuna pass from hand to hand. The calming scent of eucalyptus and roses around her head cleared away much of her remaining self-doubt.

She could feel the love of her friends, her *family*, surrounding her fueling her courage. Only Tolen, Toke, Keelyn, Rune, Brina, her father and the rest of the Descendants would be audience to her attempt. Toke to monitor the actions of the humans through his many screens and gadgets, Tolen and her friends to lend support in any way she may need, physical, mental, or emotional, and the Descendants to sever the Pact.

She took a deep breath, focusing on her trust in the Light, knowing that They wanted this. They would guide her. They would show her how to do it.

Her shard pulsed and she followed the urging to stand in front of the line of Descendants. She paused in front of her father and words began to fill her mind just like when she'd been shouting at Rune. She knew they were not her words, but that they needed to be spoken.

"Over a thousand years ago the Pact was made. Made out of fear. Since that time the demons of the Dark have hunted our kind, tortured their dreams, their thoughts, sucked away their hope, turned them to evil. They have made many of our brothers and sisters into Darkened, the worst kind of demon—human in looks only, their life forces slaves to the Dark." Her entire body began to glow.

"The Chosen have tried to stop them. They've sacrificed and fought and died to protect our race. But the Dark has grown too powerful for the Chosen and Hidden to fight alone. The time has come to tear down the Shroud hiding the Dark and let our brothers and sisters see what has brought them so much pain and suffering. Let them choose to join us and fight back."

"Maximus Burdow," her lip twitched and he grinned. "You are the direct descendant of Thaer Candra, leader of the original nine makers of the Pact. He wielded the Claver Relic, a gift of Watcher Sight for him to lead, guard, and protect the human race. When the Pact was made and the Shroud created, the Relics were sealed away, never to be reunited until the time to sever the Pact would come. That time is now. Please present the Claver." Her father held out his Relic and she touched the silver stone with the tip of her finger. A soft glowing began at the center moving outward until it filled the entire stone and cast its white light onto his face. "Maximus, as the rightful heir of the Claver, as the descendant of Thaer Candra, do you choose, willingly, to revoke your ancestor's decision and break the Pact?"

Her father lifted his fierce gaze from the Relic to Macy's eyes. "I do."

A strange whooshing passed through the room, as if someone had opened a window, but no one had moved.

She continued down the line. Similar wording just a switch of names, places within the original nine, and roles of their Relics. As she paused at each one she began to piece together which fakes matched the real Relic and why her father had chosen them.

The old woman with the water-caller Relic, *Leenwa*, had long, wavy white hair and deep blue eyes that glittered like the ocean in sunlight.

The young girl with a huge smile on her face holding a bright yellow stone, the Lóklana—Light Relic.

A middle-aged man who's thick brown hair stirred without the aid of wind, bearing a curvy stone in the shape of a mountain scene. The Arwah, wind shifter Relic.

Honitahai, the nature speaker Relic. A vibrant green stone with veins of yellow in the hands of a teenage girl, her hair the color of teak with a lined birthmark on her upper arm.

Télora, the earth mover Relic. A deep brown stone covered with pits and scars held by a small boy, no more than eight, whispering numbers under his breath, with eyes the color of denim that stared out with gentleness. He met her eyes only long enough to utter his "I do."

Animashta, the animal listener Relic. A carved stone in the shape of a wolf. The wielder a teen boy with mahogany hair.

Kunamin, the fire wielder Relic. A bright orange stone mottled with patches of red and blue cradled by a girl with fiery hair and a sharp disposition.

And lastly River Hok'ee. Wielder of the Dicernan, the unseen Relic.

With every Relic glowing, and the willing consent of every Descendant, the wind in the room increased, surrounding Macy and the Descendants in a circle of warmth and light.

Her thoughts suddenly shifted to her race. Jealousy was what she'd once felt when she thought of other humans, at their simple lives. She'd done her duty, and loved it, but she'd missed the life she could have had. Today as she thought of them, there was no jealousy, only pity. Sorrow that the Pact had ever taken place and a strong desire to set it right.

She caught her reflection in a mirror on the wall, even her eyes were glowing yellow. A window opened in her mind, a window that showed her thousands upon thousands of humans with a gauzy white film covering their eyes.

The will of the Nine has been accepted. The Pact is broken. The voice of the Light entered her thoughts. *Awaken them.*

She imagined the warmth inside pushing outward to the people, the film over their eyes seemed to catch fire and dissolve to ash. The humans blinked, their faces quickly shifting to masks of horror. Even those who had been asleep were awake and afraid.

Comfort them, the Light directed.

And she saw herself, an angel of light standing in each of their mind's eyes, explaining to them what they were seeing, what was really happening in the world. Many grasped onto her words, believed them, some not until they noticed they were not the only ones seeing her in their minds, others not at all—others chose to follow the enticements of the Dark, these she left alone, pulled from their consciousness. To the others she sent a plea, opened an opportunity.

To all the warriors, anyone who chooses to fight, come to Onaepha and join our army that will soon take battle against the Dark.

To those who want a refuge from the storm that is to come, to protect your families and loved ones, come to Onaepha and you will be safe.

Toke's portal wall opened in a flash of white light and human after human began stumbling through. Some seeking refuge, others ready to fight.

CHAPTER 42

A LEGEND RETURNS

THE MORNING OF the battle Keelyn shook Macy awake at 4 A.M. She sat up too fast and the dark room spun. Last night the state of their nerves had kept them both awake so they'd stayed up well past midnight whispering about all the possible scenarios they would face when they walked through Tolen's portals.

They dressed quickly and silently. All their speculations and worries had already been expressed. They shared one quick hug before they hurried to the main room where Tolen and Rune waited already carrying their gear on their backs.

The week had passed in a flurry of activity. Tolen had the brains for strategy so he'd spent much of his time working out the final details with the captains and lieutenants while she spent the majority of her days helping train the troops. Toke had used his portal tricks to arm almost the entire army with Kamud's and other awesome weapons. This was especially helpful for the humans who were used to guns, which don't work on the Dark. Toke's gadgets were fairly easy to figure out and even easier to use. Macy had been surprised to find she actually had a knack for teaching, even enjoyed it, despite the scary reason she was doing it. She'd worried that once the tale of the Awakening rolled through Onaepha they'd just see her as a freaky humanoid, but after the first day training they'd treated her as one of their own.

They walked out the door of Moony's and several soldiers waved, nodded, or saluted on their way to meet up with their brigades.

So far a little over 15,000 humans had crossed through the portal. More continued to arrive, and Tolen had gotten his wish. Nearly 10,000 had dedicated themselves to the fight and had been training with their brigades. They would storm *To'Degani* almost 25,000 strong.

They all prayed it would be enough.

They paused in the middle of the street where Tolen would be opening fifty gates simultaneously which would allow each platoon to instantly arrive at their drop point. He hadn't said aloud how much this feat concerned him, but Macy could see it in his eyes each time it was mentioned. It took a tremendous amount of power to open one gate, let alone fifty, and it always created a ripple in the Balance that could be tracked. The *Athstazia* had been strong enough to shield Toke's portal and the occasional gate Tolen needed to open before, but Toke feared the surge of Tolen's power needed to open fifty gates at once would overload the *Athstazia* and reveal Onaepha to the Dark. Which meant Tolen had exactly one shot at this.

She didn't doubt his ability to do it. But he did.

She threaded her arm around his waist, their heavy packs bumping against each other, and spoke to his mind the same reassuring words he'd said to her just days ago, *You got this.*

He looked down, his worry filled eyes searching her face. *So do you.*

Despite how much he didn't like her destiny, he didn't doubt her ability to be the secret weapon everyone needed. But he knew she did.

He kissed the top of her head and their light passed between each other, lending the warmth and courage they each desperately needed.

Conversation quickly became impossible as more and more soldiers arrived, lining up in their rows, deep into the forest, waiting for the signal to march. But words weren't necessary when every face mirrored the same expression. Doubt and worry, mixed with courage and fierce determination.

Fifteen minutes later Toke arrived and handed Tolen a Comm— one of fifty he'd scrambled to build over the week. "They're all directly linked to the captains and lieutenants and to me." He tapped his temple and waited for Tolen to push his thumb to the screen so the Comm could record his bioelectricity. It beeped and Toke pointed to a small depression on one side of the silver oval. "Hold this button down and you'll be able to broadcast your message aloud to the entire settlement."

Tolen nodded, took a deep breath, and started to speak into the Comm. "To the soldiers of the Light I offer my gratitude for your willingness to fight." He paused and Macy tightened her hold on his waist. "As the Ninth Chosen, I am to lead you, but it's not me you're fighting for, and it's not for glory, or reward, it's not for land, or power. Today we go into battle to fight for those things that truly matter. We fight for our loved ones, for our wives and our husbands, for our children, for our brothers and sisters, for our friends." His eyes moved from Rune, to Keelyn, to Quasar and Blaze, Incrah, Max, Sienn, Brina and River, Kiad and Deegan and all those he could see who gathered in front of them. Their little brigade of 5,000. Macy watched several grasp each other's shoulders or give one armed hugs.

Tolen gripped the Comm so tightly Macy could feel the tension in his arms. His voice rose until it reverberated in her bones—the sure and commanding voice of the Ninth Chosen. "We fight for the right to live in a world without darkness!"

A huge cheer echoed through the crowd and from the deepest reaches of the trees, she'd be amazed if it hadn't been heard three states away.

She joined the cheer, screaming so loud her throat hurt. She jumped up and kissed Tolen's cheek, her love for him stronger than ever.

It took several minutes to settle everyone down so Tolen could have the quiet he needed to concentrate. Toke had accessed human satellites and security cameras to study the land bridge patrols and help them decide on the most strategic points for Tolen to send everyone. They'd decided to time the opening of the gates to be in between the last patrol of night and the new one at sunrise, when the creatures would be busy maneuvering the shift change. They hoped to have at least thirty minutes at their rally point to get situated, and familiarize themselves with their area before the attack began at dawn.

To keep her hands from trembling and distracting Tolen, she thought about something he'd said about the humans who'd joined them. They were in awe of the Chosen Ones, and cheered by the way the Descendants wielded their Relics, they even viewed Max as their leader, but it was her that had become their symbol of hope. Her light had touched them at the core, with her around they felt braver.

Tolen's hand flew to his forehead and he spoke into the Comm with his eyes closed. "Ten seconds." He spoke through his teeth, the veins in his temples popping.

Rune, Brina, Quasar and Blaze moved closer to Tolen's side, the lieutenants whose gates would open to the same place as hers and Tolen's—a large abandoned strip mall outside what was left of Disneyland. Her father, Incrah, Sienn, Rhett, and Tyge stayed fanned out. Their gates would be taking them to the opposite side of Anaheim in an empty apartment complex.

She watched the hands tick on Tolen's watch. The only sound to be heard were thousands of muted breaths creating an intense wind, filling the air with anticipation. The air in front of them began to shimmer and all fifty gates flashed open.

The troops knew this was the signal and instantly began to rush through as quietly as they could in all their gear. Tolen's face purpled and Macy continued to feed him light until the last soldier passed by. Rune had to almost carry Tolen through. Her feet just passed the barrier when the gate snapped shut.

She pulled Tolen down behind a pile of broken shelves and wiped the sweat off his face as everyone began pulling off their packs and strapping on their weapons. If everything went as planned with the first assault and they took the land bridge, they'd be returning here, as base camp, to resupply. "You okay?" she whispered.

He nodded, but she could sense the toll it'd taken on him. "Did everyone get through?"

"We waited until everyone passed before dragging you through." Rune squeezed Tolen's shoulder and helped him strap on his sword. "You did good captain." He winked, but Tolen still looked panicky.

"The mist is too thick here, I can't *see* them through it."

"We can't worry about that, Tolen." Quasar sat down between Blaze and River, their backs against a display of laundry detergent, eyes staring out the grimy windows at the heavy mist.

"He's right." Macy touched Tolen's clammy cheek, sending more light hoping it would help calm him and restore his energy.

Keelyn held out a canteen and a sweetened meat cake. Brina, a handful of vitamins. "We have to focus on our platoon now, trust the others to follow the plan," she said.

Tolen downed the water, swallowed the meat cake in three bitter-faced bites, the vitamins in one, then grit his teeth and nodded.

Minutes ticked by as everyone checked their armor and filled their pockets with emergency supplies. Anything to stay busy and keep their minds from traveling down scary roads as they waited for the attack to begin.

Macy finished adjusting the sheath on her back and slid her knife into the scabbard on her thigh, her thoughts on the other soldiers they couldn't see doing the same. Despite agreeing that they couldn't worry about them, she couldn't stop herself from wondering if they were all safe and undetected.

A flash of black ran by the windows.

"Raksasha." Macy placed her hand on the sword hilt between her shoulders.

"Good thing you had all the Chosen wear Camouflage." Rune's hand rested on Keelyn's shoulder as if ready to throw her behind him at a second's notice.

Macy's shard pulsed, a flicker of heat, and something she didn't recognize.

Come out, come out little Chosen. It's time to play, Sorsha's voice mocked in Macy's mind.

Her legs twitched, shoved her to a standing position. Beside her the same thing seemed to happen to Keelyn, Rune, and Brina—and to the dozen Chosen nearby. Tolen remained the only Chosen not affected.

Blaze pinched the Last in his fingers, the red shard beginning to glow soft gold. "They're using their device on the Chosen Ones. The Fallen have come."

Quasar stood up to block the doors. "What do we do? They can't take off their shards."

"Fight the connection." Tolen grabbed Macy's hand. "Fight it! I broke through it back at Baskin Robbins, it has a weakness, you've got to find it."

The Chosen pushed their way forward, more stood to block their way, and they raised their hands to use their gifts against them, their eyes horrified.

"Quasar we've got to destroy those devices!" Tolen rushed past Macy, she could feel his despair but could do nothing to help. Her body moved without her consent, drawn to the voice in her head.

The half of their platoon that wasn't Chosen, or trying to hold them back, pushed their way out the doors, determined to fight the Fallen. Macy watched them go, terrified for their lives even as her body fought to get the others out of her way.

A loud boom, the sound of shattering glass. Someone, Chosen or Fallen, Macy couldn't tell had blasted away the front doors. Screams! Some of the Chosen had knocked down their fellow soldiers and were trampling them as they ran out the opening and quickly disappeared in the mist.

Macy fought against the pull but her body didn't recognize any command from her brain. Her life force screamed, her gifts screamed, the Kuna fought to leave her chest, but her body had become a prison, shackles that bound her to the voice outside.

Tolen tugged on her arms. She could hear his voice, but it was like listening to a radio with bad signal. Rune, Keelyn, and Brina marched at her sides, their eyes mirrored masks of horror as their feet moved in unison with hers. Quasar, Blaze, and River tried to pull them back, but they were failing.

She'd reached the remains of the front doors. A line of Raksasha and Kezgani stood in the middle of the street, bloodlust in their eyes.

A sight that would normally have sent her Kuna straight to her palms, but it stayed trapped in her racing heart. Bile rose in her throat as she stepped over the glass, entered the street, and saw what waited for them deeper in the mist.

Behind the demons a strange veil of shimmering blue protected Sorsha and the Fallen, thousands of Darkened, and at least the same number of creatures that looked almost human if not for the red eyes, black pointed teeth, and sharp horns sticking out the sides of their heads—the Fallen's mutated offspring?

"Fight it Macy!" Tolen shouted in her ear still yanking on her arms.

She couldn't open her mouth to speak. *Tolen, I'm trying,* she screamed with her mind, *but I can't break the connection.*

"Try harder!" He grabbed her face, but couldn't turn it toward him. He could do nothing but march by her side his face a mask of horror.

Two Chosen walked straight to the wall of demons and the Raksahsa stabbed them through the heart.

"*Tin'ruhl!*" Tolen shouted and the ground beneath them shook, successfully knocking them all off their feet. "*Win'tashta, vin'akra!*" A crushing wave of saltwater blew toward them, wrapped around the scrambling demons, swept them away, but the Fallen and their soldiers were unaffected, safe behind their wall of blue.

The Chosen were getting to their feet, moving toward the shimmering blue, and again no one could do anything to hold them back.

Tolen threw his right hand up and called up a wall of dirt and asphalt, and with his left grabbed Macy's shoulder. Her body pushed against his hold. "No, Macy." His fingers dug into her flesh, made more painful as she pushed harder against his hold, but she couldn't stop her body. The Chosen around her were trying to climb Tolen's wall. A series of loud thuds said something beat them against the other side. Tolen's face purpled, his grip slackened, and she wrenched free.

A blue light flashed, a portal to her left opened and arms wrapped around her pinning her elbows down and rolled her onto the ground. "Fight it baby girl." Her father's voice growled in her ear as she struggled against his hold. "Come on. You're stronger than they are." He grunted when she elbowed him repeatedly in the ribs but he didn't let go. Tolen dove on top of them both and his wall crumbled to dust as his hands moved to help hold her down. They could once again see the Fallen behind their force field.

Her body thrashed harder. She wasn't strong enough, she couldn't fight what she couldn't touch. It was a part of her, to fight it would be to fight herself. That wasn't possible.

Another flash. This one white moving swiftly past the front of the shimmering force field protecting the Fallen. As it passed a bright blue line appeared in the force field, as if it had cut into it. The blue light ran past again and again, back and forth, brighter and faster, more lines appearing as it went, and the field began to crack. Macy's body squirmed while her heart fought against the pain brought on by what she was seeing.

Rune, Keelyn, Brina, dragging Quasar, Blaze, and River behind them were almost to the shimmering wall. The blue flashed in front of them a final time and like a full bottle hit by a bullet, shimmering pieces of blue shattered outward in a blast that sent the pieces skittering across the pavement where they disappeared in a blue haze.

Horror covered the faces of the Fallen for a split second when the non-Chosen fighters began rushing for them. But they waved their devices and Macy's body stiffened, her Kuna heat flooded her palms against her will, one hand pulled free of her father's hold, it turned toward Tolen's face, inches from her own. The other Chosen were doing the same, pausing only to turn their hands toward their fellow fighters.

"Destroy the devices!" someone shouted, a voice Macy thought she recognized but couldn't put a face to. And the flash of blue appeared again in between and through the Fallen, sparks flew and some of her fellow Chosen paused, shook their heads, and raised their gifts on the Fallen.

Macy's hands began to glow. *Tolen, get my dad out of the way. You too. I don't want to hurt you.*

"I won't let you go." Max cried.

"Oh yes you will." A cold voice spoke and a woman with crusty black, dead looking skin, sapphire eyes and flowing silver hair stepped forward.

"Sorsha," Rune spit through clenched teeth.

"Well done young one." Another form stepped out of the mist his bright blue eyes fixed on Rune. A man so normal looking it was almost more terrifying than seeing Sorsha without her scarf. "Thank you for bringing us Light's Aid."

The flashes of blue got brighter, closer. *Please hurry, help us!* Closer, the light came, and she saw it was from a huge shield, a shield of glowing bluish white. The shield carrier also wielded a Kumad, his powerful arm and uncanny speed cutting down the enemy with an ability she'd never seen in all her years as a Chosen. But the group of Fallen stalking toward them seemed not to care that hundreds of their fellows, Darkened, and offspring were losing their lives behind them.

"Soveryn," Max breathed near Macy's ear, despair in his tone.

"Do I know you, human?" Soveryn leaned on his sword and glared at Max.

"No, but I know you. You killed my Watcher," he growled through his teeth.

"Did I?" He flicked a spot on his arm. "Hmm."

Max released Macy and flew to his feet. Tolen tried to grab him but without her father's weight Macy's body had begun thrashing again. Max ran forward, sword raised, Macy's heart drumming behind her ribs with terror. Soveryn moved to meet Max's blade, his sword coming down in a sideways arc too fast for Max to block. Macy's life force pushed toward him, wanting to save him, but to let the Kuna free would be to send it straight through Tolen.

Another sword appeared out of the mist, blocked the blow, followed by arms, dirty wings, and scraggly gray hair.

Bastian!

"Connect to your shard *LaUnahi*. Destroy those infernal devices! Fight!"

Sweat broke out on her lip, dripped down her cheeks as she fought the force that held her bound.

You've got this Mace! Tolen pushed his light into her, fighting the wall inside her.

The force that held her bound. She'd accepted her destiny. She'd transcended. Her body and life force were no longer separate, they were one. She'd mastered the body. *Move your hand Macy.* She coaxed herself like she were a split personality. Slowly, painfully, her hand moved to her shard. The sounds of battle echoed around her, more sparks and flashes of blue. Bastian fought both Soveryn and Sorsha. A dozen Raksasha began to move toward Rune, Keelyn, and Brina. Tolen, Quasar, Blaze and River fought them back, but more were coming. More were coming and the Chosen were standing there as unmoving targets.

Her hand hesitated for only a moment before grabbing her shard. With a burst of light her hand was free. She pushed toward her shard, for the first time welcoming the connection, begging for it. The group in front of them knew she was Light's Aid, but somehow she knew the time had not yet come for her to reveal the strength of her gifts. She pulled back slightly but pushed enough until she felt the force holding her crack. Another flash of light and her body began to convulse, her power of her shard fighting against the power that held her body hostage. Tolen was knocked onto his back but he scrambled back up, grabbed her face in his hands, she felt his warmth, his love.

You've got this!

"I've…got this!" She screamed. An echoing boom, a loud crackle like lightning, and a thousand sparks lit the sky. Each device popping and smoking, the Fallen dropping them to the ground. A subtle clearing of the mist and the Chosen were free to fight once more.

She flipped to her feet and drew her sword. Tolen bumped against her back his own sword drawn as two Darkened rushed forward to engage them. Macy spun and one of their swords grazed the armor covering her ribs. She blocked three more blows and the Darkened backed up, bared their teeth and hissed. She let them come forward, feinted right, and as the two lunged she swung swiftly side to side cutting them both down.

Where was Tolen?

She looked left. Rune and Keelyn had engaged Sorsha, a stack of Darkened dead at their feet. A bunch of creatures to her left were grabbing wounds that seemed to come out of midair and she knew Brina and River were accessing their Dicernan to fight invisibly. Bastian still fought Soveryn.

To her right, Tolen battled a dozen Fallen on his own. She rushed toward him but the blue shield fighter got their first, swinging furiously and the Fallen fell. The fighter then ran back into the heart of the battle, moving lightning fast, leaving a path of destruction in his wake.

Macy caught up to Tolen and relief washed over his face. "They came up behind us. I had to turn and fight them." He panted. "I knew you could do it."

"Who *is* that?" Macy pointed to the blue shielded man.

Tolen swung his Kamud, relieving another Darkened of its head. "I think—"

Rune and Keelyn suddenly appeared at their sides. "Who is that guy?" Keelyn clutched her ribs breathing fast. "He got close enough for Sorsha to see his face and she took off."

The shielded man continued to run through the mass, a bright blue streak, until the Darkened and what was left of the Fallen began to retreat. They watched Bastian swing at Soveryn, but he noticed his retreating forces, touched something hanging around his neck and in a flash of blue disappeared.

"Tolen? Do you know him?" Macy put her hand on his elbow.

"It's Daedal Téloran. My father."

"Your dad?" Macy squinted through the mist. The last time they'd seen his father he'd been an emaciated, tortured, remnant of a man. The man walking toward them now was legend reborn.

Bastian and Daedal walked slowly toward them. Daedal pulled a shimmering silver helmet off his head. Some of the Light fighters bowed to him as he passed.

Bastian paused beside Max. They all watched Daedal move toward his son.

Macy felt Tolen's pride and sorrow when Daedal stopped in front of them, his silver brown hair barely disheveled, but black blood covered his armor, his sword, his hands, and a long smear crossed his left cheek.

"Are you alright?" He asked, his eyes roving over Tolen's face. His deep timber so unlike the weak whisper Macy remembered.

Rune cleared his throat when no one answered. "Yeah, thanks to you."

Daedal looked at Rune and his eyes widened. "*You.*"

Rune's eyes narrowed. "Me?"

"It has been nearly twelve years but I have thought of you nearly every day since that night." He gripped Rune's shoulder and recognition flared in Rune's eyes. "It pleases me to see you well. Especially after I learned it was Sorsha who came for you. I never should have left you alone. I am truly sorry."

Rune opened his mouth to respond but the other fighters were gathering around them. One of the Lafar touched Daedal's arm. "Have the Protectors returned?"

Daedal put a hand on the woman's shoulder and nodded.

"We are stationed throughout the world. I am here to help my son and you, the fighters for Light. To do what I can to bring forth the fulfillment of the prophecy." He spun in a slow circle. "I will fight with you until my last breath." He paused in front of Tolen and Macy, an arm's length away, his eyes unsure, his powerful life force like a warm fire. "We have taken the land bridge, but the Dark will regroup. We need to be ready."

Tolen stepped forward and wrapped his arms around his father. Daedal's strong arms enfolded his son and despite what had happened Macy experienced a moment's joy at the reunion Tolen had always wanted.

CHAPTER 43

THE SECOND WAVE

Tolen shoved the meat cake in his mouth too preoccupied to gag from the lack of flavor. Macy gnawed on a piece of jerky beside him. The other soldiers around them were all doing the same, filling up on water, shoving as much food and vitamins in as they could without puking.

Tolen had *seen* a flash of the Dark moving back in for another attack. They had little time to regenerate and put the next phase of their plan into action.

He'd sent the bodies of their dead to a mass gravesite in Onaepha, a number that was far higher than they wanted to think about, and the wounded to the med building where Tashta and the Spheres could patch them up. Tolen would have healed them, but he needed to keep his strength for battle and protecting Macy.

He shook his head and checked his watch. 8:16 AM. Impossible to know it was still morning as the mist covering the area blocked all light from the sun. Despite their brief win against the Dark, it still looked like dusk. Only the shapes of things could be deciphered. The only real light came from the fires still burning in the rubble and the interesting sparkles the Lóklana had somehow conjured to float above them like stars.

Daedal patted Tolen's back and his shard pulsed with joy, the same joy *he* felt despite the fear of what was to come. His father's presence had inspired hope among the fighters, deepened his own hope. It was incredible to see him whole and healthy. He'd said Tolen's mother was doing better as well. Maybe when this war ended he would get to see that for himself.

Bastian adjusted his wings, wings that didn't look as clean and healthy as they used to be, so he could replace the sheath around his waist. Tolen wondered briefly if something was happening to Bastian from being here in the earth realm with so much darkness.

Tolen glanced at Rune holding Keelyn, standing close to his father. Strange that they met while Daedal was out trying to stop Tolen's destiny. That Daedal had been the comfort Rune needed on the scariest night of his life. That his kindness still had an impact on Rune to this day. He'd shown them an old jar, long since empty, that he kept in his bag that once contained ointment that Daedal shared with Rune. He'd kept it so he would never forget the kindness of a stranger. Crazy that they would all somehow end up connected again. Maybe there really was no such thing as coincidence, as Bastian always said.

Rune fingered the knife at his belt. "Well, we've lost the element of surprise. We can't go Braveheart now. And the Dark knows Macy's an even bigger threat than they thought. First she destroyed their gate. Now she's taken out their biggest weapon against the Chosen. They're going be gunning for her." He finished with a concerned look at Macy.

The joy bubble around Tolen burst, his emotions pushed against the wall he'd been trying to maintain, and his palms began to sweat. Too much truth lay in that statement. He needed to be ready to protect the Gift at all costs, not an easy feat when hundreds battled around you and you were meant to also protect *them*. But the best way to protect them was to protect the Gift. The power of Light that walked among them.

Daedal lowered his canteen. "Which is why we'll need to tweak the plan moving forward." He shared a loaded look with Bastian and a mixture of dread and anticipation pulsed through Tolen's shard. The look on the faces of the others said they felt the same. Whatever plan these two had in mind would be a wise one, but also a dangerous one. Tolen placed one hand over his shard that had started pulsing with nervous anticipation, the other he used to grip Macy's and pull her against his side.

Bastian nodded at Daedal who met Tolen's gaze for a fraction of a second. "We will play on the arrogance of the Dark, call out their strongest fighters. Soveryn, Daemon, and Legion."

o o o

Ten minutes before Tolen would open the gate to the heart of *To'Degani* he stood beneath a broken street light, Macy tucked tight against his chest, their hearts beating in time with each other, a fierce symphony behind their ribs.

He didn't know why he'd thought the end wouldn't come until later. Why he'd thought they would be battling the Dark for years, not hours. He fought against the pain behind his eyes that forced him to see the truth. He had known. He'd just let his imagination run away with his hopes and forced his conscious to accept them instead.

He'd used the Comm to contact all the other captains and relay the new plan. No one had any arguments. It was a good plan, even if it scared him to death.

There were no surprises in the volunteers for the ploy. All of his lieutenants Rune, Incrah, Max, Quasar and Blaze, Sienn, Brina, Rhett and Tyge, plus all who remained of their brigade. Keelyn, River, Kiad and Deegan, and all the Lafar that had fought with them on Eamun's island. An army of just over 5,000 would engage the thousands guarding Darsapean and Gyeesta.

His arms flexed tighter around Macy. He could sense her fear—fear that she fought to keep in check, not wanting it to give an edge to the Dark. She was almost as scared of the prophecy as he was. But not quite.

Sacrifice could mean figuratively speaking. To that hope he'd hold.

If the plan went perfectly, the other warriors would defeat the demons here and join them at the center of *To'Degani* to finish off Gyeesta together. *If* it went perfectly.

But, in the short time Tolen had been a knowing part of the Hidden world, he'd yet to see a plan go without a hitch, and even though his sight had cleared with Macy's help, there were too many factors at work, too many decisions in play, or not yet in play, to allow him to see more than a few minutes ahead. Not to mention he needed to stay in the moment, focused on Macy's needs, and his soldiers' needs, something that was much harder to do if he was concentrating on a constantly shifting future.

As their forces lined up behind them Tolen ran his hands through Macy's ponytail. *We can do this.*

We've totally got this. Her fingers twitched against his back.

You're amazing. He kissed the top of her head.

You say that a lot. But he knew she could sense how much meant it. He felt her emotions calm the tiniest bit.

Because I don't want you to ever forget it.

"I love you, Tolen. Whatever happens, I'm really glad things came together this way with you and me." She kissed his chin.

"Me too." He swallowed. "And I love you."

"Beyond time." Macy tapped his watch and Tolen leaned down to kiss her, not caring they had an audience, letting the strength of his love flow into the kiss, holding nothing back, unafraid of losing control. All that stuff was balanced now with what really mattered—that she knew, beyond a shadow of a doubt, that he loved her and would love her for whatever was left of their lives and eternity after that.

CHAPTER 44

THE DARK ISLAND

Tʜᴇ ʟᴀsᴛ sᴘᴀʀᴋʟᴇs of Lóklana light faded and Macy moved out of Tolen's embrace, freeing her hands to unsheathe her sword.

He kissed her cheek, sending a burst of his light straight to her heart, warming her Kuna. "Ready?"

The life forces of the people she loved pulsed beside her, strong, encouraging. Bastian and her father on her left. Tolen, his father, and their friends on her right. The rest of their brigade shifted behind them, their life forces focused, strong. "Ready as ever."

"Remember how you once told me life isn't fair?" Tolen pushed a lock of hair behind her ear. "Well, I don't feel that way anymore." *Life with you is perfect.* He touched his forehead once to hers before raising his hands to open the gate that would send them all to the heart of *To'Degani*.

Macy pulled her breath in and out through her nose, letting the Kuna roll to her palms and fill her fingers with its gentle glow. Anger with the prophecy threatened to overwhelm her and she pushed against it, ignoring its implications like she had from the moment she'd heard it. She wouldn't let herself worry about things she didn't know. She thought of Tolen's speech to the troops. She would fight for her loved ones, and for the right of everyone to live in a world without the Dark. Let what may or may not happen, happen.

She closed her eyes for a brief second, sending permission to her life force to let it *finally*, fully connect to her shard. Her limbs trembled with thrill and slight overwhelm by its power as it rushed through her body like a jolt of electricity, but this time she no longer feared its power or the Fallen. Everyone needed her to be brave enough to use it. *She* needed it. She remembered how it had felt when she'd first allowed the connection to her healed shard, how she'd realized their shards loved them.

I'm sorry I stayed away so long. An answering pulse of love and sustaining light filled her heart. It had missed her. Tears pricked her eyes and she wrapped her fingers around it. *Together.*

Her enhanced eyes picked up the tiny pinpricks of blue appearing throughout the mist ahead of them—the life forces of Dark creatures gathering for battle. Then the air shimmered and opened to another space, darker, colder, and stained by the Shadows that curled and undulated through the mist. The deepest concentration swirled around a castle that mirrored the one from the Shadow Realm. She could just make out the top parapets with Dark creatures standing guard, Legion perched above them on a platform as wide as the castle roof.

Tolen led the way through the gate into the heart of *To'Degani.* The Dark had robbed LadonRyn of all its former beauty, the blueish gray light drained everything of its color. Not a single flower remained, and the trees, the once beautiful and majestic palms, were nothing but gray skeletons reaching toward a darkened sky, their bare branches swaying without a trace of wind. Phantoms had taken residence inside them, another layer of protection for the monster inside the castle.

The gate snapped closed behind them with a loud hiss. Wailing met her ears and a wave of darkness swept over their little group. Suddenly dizzy, Macy grabbed Tolen's arm. This place was so much worse than the Shadow Realm. The power here unfiltered evil. Gyeesta, the Dark, in its purest form.

"You've got to fight it, Macy." Tolen nudged her shoulder pushing some of his light into her. She could feel him holding his emotions back, his fear for her life. He couldn't fight if he let his fear take hold. She had to stay strong for him, for herself, for everyone.

A shield of light seemed to surround her like a protective bubble and warmth filled her all the way to her bones—Tolen had tapped the

Sphere button on his watch and Keelyn had reached out to touch her shoulder.

Her knees stopped shaking and she took a slow breath. *Help me resist,* she whispered to her shard and felt its pulsing reassurance. More light infused her body, clearing her thoughts.

We've got this, Tolen encouraged.

The phantoms swayed their dead branches, reaching for them as they marched toward the castle. Small annoying Kinchomen lizards ran between the branches and roots, blue tongues flicking, hissing threats in their odd language between their razor sharp teeth. Macy and Rune and dozens of other Kunamin who marched with them shot bursts of flame, taking the lizards out one by one while Tolen and his fellow Honitahai called up roots, buried deep and dormant beneath the sand, of little use to Gyeesta, that wrapped around sections of the trees squeezing until a crack opened, then Keelyn and her Lóklana friends sent a burst of light inside, killing the phantoms until every tree became nothing but statue sentinels surrounded by the smoking remains of Kinchomen.

But the castle gate did not open. Surely Darsapean was curious in his lair. With their life forces shielded, and Macy's light subdued by the strength of the Dark here, he would not sense the power that walked so boldly toward him. To him, this tiny little group of 5,000 light fighters held no real threat. Daedal had been right. Darspean's lack of immediate response proved his arrogance. Even Legion watched them, his wicked eyes piercing through the haze. He flapped his wings once, and then curled up on his platform, uninterested. Right now, neither Darsapean nor Legion feared them.

Macy's palms tingled. *Time to change their minds.*

A few hundred yards from the castle the next layer of Darsapean's protection became visible through the mist.

Row upon row of Raksasha, with yellow eyes carrying a greenish hue in the blue light, ochre poison dripping from their claws to the sand, giant Shrieg bats on their shoulders ready to take flight. Mixed within their numbers, Gungruin mimickers, Kezgani demons, Daklafar Dark elves, Kludde, and hundreds of unnamable creatures. Thousands upon thousands guarded the entrance to the castle.

Even if they defeated these, behind them lay their greatest challenges, towering in the background another row of at least one hundred DéHool wolves, ten feet tall at the shoulder, saliva dripping from their fangs, their red eyes thirsting for blood, led by hairy, ax wielding Thrundoon. If they defeated those monsters, then Daemon would come, bringing Legion with him. If by yet another miracle they killed the Master of the Demons and the Dragon of Death, Darsapean would follow, bringing his Shadows with him. And finally if they lived that long, if they could actually succeed against such odds, Gyeesta itself would come to finish them off.

A sliver of doubt fought its way into Macy's heart. Her shard pulsed with encouragement, as if mimicking Tolen's *You got this*, and a trickle of smoke curled from her palms. The smell of eucalyptus and roses mixed with cloves and earth as Tolen's Kuna flared to life beside her. The doubt burned away by the heat of determination she raised her hands, but before either of them could send even a spark, Bastian had taken flight, and Daedal had rushed through the horde in front of them, sword and armor gleaming. Bastian flew down the line too fast to follow, his machete slashing at the DéHool. Daedal was lightning again, a bright blue streak weaving in and out of the line, taking out the Thrundoon before they knew what came for them.

Blaze raised the Last, it's golden light gleaming, strengthening the Chosen's shards, brightening them, enhancing their gifts and the rest of their army plunged into the mist toward the creatures. Macy's shard glowed so bright she could see its reflection in the eyes of the first Raksasha she burned through. She left her sword on her back, relishing in the strength of her Kuna. The harder she fought, the more her skin began to glow. If Darsapean knew the true prophecy, he would now know who she was, but she couldn't pull the power back. Fully connected to her shard, her true destiny burned as truth through her veins. The Gift could no longer be subdued.

No Macy, not yet! Tolen screamed in her thoughts, his pain cut deep into her heart, but she knew the time had come. The moment for which she'd been born. Fear still threatened, but purpose and faith in the Light's plan subdued it.

I am who I am. I will not hide.

A burst of light shot from her shard and the row of Raksasha in front of her covered their eyes. Without conscious thought she charged forward, a storm of light. Her fire crackled and glowed brighter than any Kunamin around her, brighter than Tolen's, taking out dozens of demons at a time. She focused on destroying the pulsing blue she could see in her mind's eye while protecting the pale yellows of fighters for Light. Her body glowed, a bright blaze of light and righteous fury.

She skidded to a stop at a wall of Gungruin. Gungruin who now mirrored dozens of their own fighters, fighters who stood back unsure who to kill and who to protect. Tolen slid in beside her.

I can see them. She pushed the images of the blue pulses to Tolen's mind. "Leave the Mimickers to us!" She yelled to the other fighters. As they shifted around, she raised her hands at the same time as Tolen. The storm of light resumed and between them the Gungruin were almost too easy to defeat.

Bursts of fire, flaming wind, swatting branches, clangs of swords, and the twang of arrows. Macy heard it all as she ran through the throng with Tolen by her side. Together and gifts unrestrained they fought with their fellows until every Dark creature that had faced them lay dead in the sand. Nothing lay between them and the castle but piles of dead bodies. Too many of their own lay among the dead, but Macy couldn't think about them, not yet. The Dark had not taken their hearts. Their sacrifice had not been in vain.

She could feel Darsapean's rage. His arrogance replaced with fury and a trace of fear. Her lip curled. *Come and fight you cowards.* She sent the thought with all the force she could muster toward the castle.

You're going to regret that challenge Chosen One, Gift of Light, Darsapean's voice rumbled through her thoughts, his evil shook her to the core and dimmed her light a fraction.

Tolen's horrified expression met hers—he'd heard it too. Darsapean had discovered the full prophecy. He knew who she was, which meant he also knew she was the Light's secret weapon.

As soon as this thought finished a wall of black erupted from the castle gate. Winged creatures, by the hundreds, Legion leading them with Daemon on its back. Thrundoon leading even larger DéHool, and the remaining Fallen stalked forward with Darkened at their flanks, led by Soveryn and Sorsha wielding glowing swords and shields.

"Sorsha is mine!" Rune growled and sprinted forward, Keelyn close behind.

Tolen met Macy's gaze once before they plunged after. Macy drew her sword, swinging it with her right arm, throwing fireballs with her left, strength surging from her shard through her limbs—her transcended body no longer tired from the effort as it once did. Eventually she would lose steam, eventually she would have to regenerate, logic said this, but right now the battle and the power of resolve replenished her energy better than a hundred sugary suckers and hours of sleep.

Fire erupted everywhere. The smoke of creature and dead mixing with the mist affected visibility to all but her who could see the life forces. A conjured wind and the smoke cleared. Tolen's power mixed again with the other Chosen. Fierce winds, roots, water, rock, even sand blew about distracting, destroying. Swords swung and arrows flew—the Dark had met its match.

As Macy swung and blasted with Tolen at her side she caught glimpses of Bastian's wings glittering with internal light as he engaged Soveryn in a furious clash of swords, of Rune's flame and Keelyn's light as they fought Sorsha who cowered from Keelyn's light behind a smoking shield.

Macy melted the head off a Kezgani, her growing hope at their advancement pounding in time with each stomp of her feet as she danced through the puddles of black and red blood. She could feel Tolen close by her, but only caught glimpses of him through the fighting, the focus on what was in front of them.

A series of pain-filled screams had her changing course and running left where Daemon flew Legion into the fighters. With every swoop the dragon came up with a fighter in its rear foot that it quickly ripped apart with its front claws. Daemon laughed from its back as the fighters' swords were unable to penetrate Legion's hide.

Legion opened his maw and shot a burst of fire across the field of fighters, sending them ducking for cover.

Divide and conquer.

Kunamin soldiers rushed forward, pulling the fire into themselves and redirecting it at Legion, but the flames went out in a puff the second they hit his scales. Macy pushed her legs faster, arms swinging and blasting at the flashes of blue as Legion dove again. But the sand gave little purchase and her feet slipped and slid. Legion's claws were inches away from a human girl wielding a crossbow.

Macy raised her hand, but another flash of blue shot across Legion's back and it tumbled in the sky, Daemon lost his grip and fell to the sand. Legion burst back up in the air at the same moment Daemon flipped to his feet. Daedal rolled past him and retrieved the sword he'd thrown, raising it up just in time to block Daemon's blow. A gap opened in the battle as the brothers began to circle each other.

Tolen paused and she was about to call to him, but a streak of silver soared by in her periphery and she had to roll out of the way of a Thrundoon's ax. She swiped her sword across the demon's legs and he dropped to his knees. She slit his throat, jumped back to her feet as Legion prepared for another dive, and raised her palms, "*Mi'no ha!*" She twisted her fingers, until the fire ball was as large as Legion's head and sent it flying, knowing it wouldn't penetrate his skin but hoping for a distraction.

She'd aimed for his face, but she'd misjudged the creature's speed. The ball just grazed the tip of his tail. But the distraction worked. Legion screeched and flipped around. She couldn't see any burn marks but her flame *had* done something that it didn't like. Its hollow eyes locked on her face. A brief second's realization made her heart sink and then soar. Legion would go after no other target now. She scrambled to her feet, releasing fire from her hands in one long jet as she ran right to another gap in the battlefield, a place where the amount of dead hindered movement, drawing Legion with her. She leapt onto an overturned cart as Legion dove. She dropped and sliced at his hind leg, knowing it wouldn't work, but using the distraction to send fire into his face. Her Kamud somehow cut through the scales and Legion screeched in pain, swinging his head side to side, and rose back in the air. She'd opened a gash on his right flank. Its blood spattered the ground and angry red burns bloomed on its face.

Not a single sword or gift had worked against Legion. *None but hers.* A Gift of Light. Legion was a creature of total darkness and only the light given her could defeat it.

A brief moment of triumph quickly melted into terrible truth as she tried to get back to her feet and ready her sword for the next attack. In a normal battle every strike of the Kamud pulled strength from the opponent, and pushed it back to the wielder. But the last strike of Legion seemed to have done the opposite. Macy's arm had begun to shake with weakness that was moving up into her shoulder. She was the only one who could stab it, but to do so would take her strength. Another realization as Legion hovered above her, both wanting and fearing to attack. The Kuna heat had lessened, as if icy water had been thrown over the place it lived inside her. Her gifts would work against it, but to do so would also take them from her.

Her mind searched through possibilities as Legion hovered. She could throw her knife, but the eye was the only target that had any hope of causing damage and it was small, far away, and his claws would rip her in half before he was close enough to throw with accuracy. She licked her lips tasting blood and sweat, the only real option taking shape in her mind. Legion circled, readied for another dive, and a voice issued in her head. *Lasan, where the Light is, Darkness cannot be.*

She looked into the black eyes of her attacker and raised her sword, pushing as much strength as she could to her arms, rolled the last of her Kuna into her palms, forced it into the blade that burst into white-hot flame, and planted her feet.

o o o

Tolen surged forward, striking, parrying, jumping the dead, but too slow. *Too slow!* Macy had disappeared. He could feel her somewhere to his right, but he couldn't see her through the mist.

Daedal had knocked Daemon off Legion. Tolen had paused, distracted for a split second. He'd been another second away from following Macy to engage Legion when another sight had rooted his feet to the sand. His mother arrived in a pillar of silver, wielding a glowing silver sword and shield. He'd never seen her fight before. In his vision of the Radia Revolution, she'd been in the sky holding a scepter that controlled the power of the Last Shard and enhanced her Sphere ability to protect the fighters. The only mother he'd known had been weak and sickly. Areen Téloran was a warrior—there was no other word for it. She moved so fast, a halo to Daedal's lightning strikes. He'd let his parents, *his parents* battle with Daemon distract him.

But at the moment when he was sure they could win, would win, Daemon rolled back from their swords, slammed his fist into the sand and a cluster of thick black roots shot up from the ground and wrapped around his parents' arms. Daemon's sword plunged, aimed for his father's heart. Without thinking Tolen ran for their battle, *"Los'lon!"* The tip of Daemon's sword pricked his father's armor, his mother screamed and another root yanked Daemon's arm back, wrapped around his sword.

Tolen dropped to the sand, slashed at the roots holding his parents back. Daemon yanked free of the root holding him and the dance resumed, three to one.

"Tolen go!" Daedal parried a blow from Daemon's sword as Areen cut at the roots Daemon continued to shoot at them.

"You need help!" Tolen's head and heart warred against each other. He was to protect Lasan, but these were his parents, *but Macy!*

He swung in quick succession after each one of his father's swings. Daemon met them blow for blow.

A familiar scream, *"Mi'no ha!"* and pain shot up his arm, it fell limp to his side, his sword clattered to the sand, but it wasn't *his* pain.

Horror—Macy's in trouble. Reality—Daedal's sword was a beat too slow raising up, Daemon's a beat faster as it flashed toward Tolen's chest.

I've failed.

A flash of red hair, a spark of silver, a burst of blood. Daedal screamed.

Areen had thrown herself in the path of Daemon's sword. Her life to save her son.

Tolen scrambled out from under her body. Daedal dropped down beside them and pulled Daemon's sword from her body. He cradled his wife in his arms. Anger such as Tolen had never experienced consumed him, pooled in his extremities, encased his heart.

There is darkness in the Ninth. He remembered Daemon saying that night they'd fought on Eamun's island when Tolen used his Dreamer ability. His one and only Dark gift. It consumed him now. The anger, the hate, the *rage* fueled the animal inside, the side that would not be hindered by logic. That would not accept that he had not succeeded in battle with this creature in the past without help. The side that said Daemon had to die no matter the cost.

He raised his eyes to see a look of shock roll across Daemon's face and the tiniest bit of regret as he looked at Areen, the woman he'd once loved. His eyes flashed to warm brown for a split second before he shook his head, his horns glistened in the silver light from Areen's shield and the yellow returned to his gaze, the regret pushed away.

Daemon pulled a knife from his belt.

Tolen jumped to his feet. "*Tin'ruhl!*" The dark Dreamer voice issued from his mouth and the sand shoved upward launching him in the air above Daemon. He spun, swinging his sword in a swift arc as he passed over the demon's head, the Kamud cut through flesh and bone. He landed on his feet and watched with satisfaction as Daemon's head rolled off his shoulders.

"Areen, stay with me. Please." Daedal's sobs pulled the rage from Tolen's heart, slammed the Dreamer back to the corner of his mind. He dropped to his mother's side, tried not to look at the pool of blood growing under her body where she lay in his father's arms. He went to place his hands over her wound, but she grabbed them. "No, Tolen. It's too late. Go. Save Macy…" Areen's eyes closed and Daedal dropped his forehead to hers.

Heat rolled to Tolen's palms. *Macy.* With one last look at his parents, he jolted to his feet, the Dreamer pushing again for place as the rage, dread, and fear created an inferno inside his heart. He held the darkness back, focused on his shard, his connection to Macy. To her light and warmth. He swung his sword and threw fire, refusing to think of what he'd left behind, focused only on one thing, reaching Macy.

He passed battle after battle. Human against Darkened. Chosen against Fallen. Lafar against Daklafar and a dozen other arrangements. He blew past Bastian as his machete chopped off Soveryn's sword arm. He passed Sorsha standing over Rune, her sword held high, one of Keelyn's arrows in her side. Tolen's step faltered the tiniest bit, but then Keelyn was there, her face bloody, plunging Rune's sword into Sorsha's back.

Two battles won, but one more loomed, one he kept trying to ignore as it flashed across his sight, one he couldn't stop, couldn't prevent, couldn't win *for* her.

Creatures dropped as swiftly as he ran, cursing the shifting sand beneath his feet, wishing for a moment he had wings like Bastian, the one thing the Light hadn't given him. He was going to fail Them. He was going to fail Macy.

Macy's sudden despair rattled his life force. Her sorrow at the pain *he* was going to feel had him subconsciously slowing his steps as he approached a thinning of the mist, a clearing of sand covered with bodies. Pain, searing pain, shot through his chest—*not his pain*. His eyes raised to a broken cart in the center of the bodies, to Macy standing on its side, her arms raised, her flaming sword deep in Legion's belly, his front foot on her chest, her blood gushing between its claws.

Legion toppled to the side, dragging Macy with it.

Tolen raised his fist and in a gust of wind the cart flew out of the way. He leapt forward, his head and heart screaming in denial at what he saw on the other side. Tears streamed down his cheeks as he dropped to his knees to lift her body into his arms, her skin no longer glowing but bone white, and yanked Legion's claws free. *No, no, NO!* He held his shaking hand over the puncture wounds on her chest. His fingers glowed, "*Lon'adras!*" he screamed through his sobs. "*Lon'adras!*"

Her eyes opened, met his. *I love you. . .Beyond time,* she whispered in his mind.

Then her body dissolved to ash in his arms.

CHAPTER 45

FROM THE ASHES

Legion's body disappeared in a flash of black vapor, and Tolen fell forward as Macy's ashes fluttered to the sand. "Macy! Macy!" He sobbed.

His watch dinged. The sun symbol appeared and turned black like a total eclipse. The sky darkened to blackest night. Of course. Light had just died in his arms. He buried his head in his hands, oblivious to the sounds of the battle still raging around him, as the sobs overtook him. She'd sacrificed herself to destroy Legion, to save them all. A sparkle danced across his closed lids and a tiny burst of familiar warmth fought to enter his heart. He cracked his fingers. Macy's shard sat in the sand, pulsing blue, partially buried in her ashes. He picked it up, tears still streaming from his eyes, trying not to disturb her too much, and curled his fist around it.

In every vision he'd had of Macy's possible death he'd experienced pain, but it had been distant, disconnected. The real thing? There were no words to describe the agony. Everything that made him who he was, his very heart and soul had burned and died and now lay in the pile of ash at his knees.

Macy. His chest bounced with repressed sobs. He had to get back to the fight. He had to ensure her sacrifice hadn't been in vain.

…with a Gift of Light to sacrifice in death. Macy had taken out every last weapon the Dark could use against them, saved the Chosen, and destroyed Legion. They were free to fight on equal ground.

The Dark and the Light.

Truth, but he couldn't make himself stand. He couldn't leave her here, alone.

A sickly blue light pulsed from the castle casting a deathly glow on the fighters. A triumphant cackling echoed from inside, a laugh Tolen had heard before while trapped in the Shadows veil and again when Misery fell, and the sounds of battle faded as everyone, fighters for both Dark and Light, paused.

Darsapean.

Heat flared in Tolen's chest. A desire for revenge pushed against the grief, fed the Kuna inside him. The Dreamer sought again for control. He fought it back as he raised his eyes to the castle.

One powerful weapon remained under Darsapean's command.

The Shadow Wraiths.

The curling black mist surrounding the castle swirled into a funnel above the castle faster and faster, pulling the grayer less dense mist from the island into itself. Larger the tornado grew, louder the screams of the stolen souls within it.

The last time they'd faced the Shadows, Tolen had nearly died. Only Macy had been powerful enough to stop them, to send them back to their realm.

Macy. His chest seared and the Kuna within him roared.

Tolen's anger spiked as the wind increased, threatening to blow her away. Still clutching her shard in his fist he twisted the fingers of his other hand and the wind around her ceased, twisted them again and a barrier of revolving sand encircled her ashes, further protection from anything that came too near.

He suddenly became aware of people standing behind him. Max, blood trickling from his lip and down his chin, silent tears raining down his cheeks to mingle with the blood. Bastian, his lips clenched tight against the pain. Daedal, the armor on his chest still stained with the blood of Tolen's mother. Rune, tearless but agony rolling off his life force in waves. Keelyn her eyes glued to Macy's ashes, her face frozen in shock. Brina and River panting as if they'd just arrived. Incrah holding his sword aloft.

Quasar, pain in his gaze. Blaze, chest heaving, the Last still glowing gold at his throat, and Sienn with a bow in her hands and empathy in her eyes.

The draw-bridge opened, drawing all their eyes as the forces of the Dark cheered.

From the dark castle a chariot shrouded in blue flame, pulled by four winged creatures with horse heads and dragon bodies, burst forth, Darsapean at the reins. Tolen had seen this image before, in a view of the past of the last great war between Light and Dark, the Radia Revolution. No difference could be determined between the creature then to the one riding toward them now, unless, if possible, Darsapean had become even more evil.

Blue flames flickered off the small horns running down his forehead to the tip of his nose and the three long silver ones rising out of the top of his head like a crown. The shiny black scales that covered his mammoth frame undulated like a snake across his arms as he waved a long silver scepter over his head. His blood-red gaze fell on them, the pupils dancing like black flames. He opened his mouth and Tolen remembered a second too late what would happen next.

The roar that issued from Darsapean's mouth dropped all fighters for Light to their knees.

Tolen covered his ears with his fists.

Dark creatures began to rush forward, ready to strike the fighters where they sat paralyzed by Darsapean's power.

The first line of fighters went down, hewn where they knelt.

Tolen, Tolen, you have to let me go.

Macy? It couldn't be. He was imagining it.

Let me go. Her voice pushed past Darsapean's scream, past the evil that held them bound, he heard nothing but her voice.

Time slowed to a crawl while one choice fought to be made. For this frozen moment his mind was free, his limbs able to move. He looked to the sand swirling and protecting Macy's ashes, felt the heat of her shard in his palm. *I can't.*

Tolen, you must let me go. It's time to fight. It's time to end the Dark on this planet once and for all.

His body shook, the pain coming back full force, like he'd been slammed by a train going a thousand miles an hour.

Sweetheart. Areen's voice cutting through the pain. *Sweetheart you have to let her go. Let her fulfill her purpose. Let her go.*

A scream erupted from Tolen's mouth, the pain, the heat too much to bear. The Dreamer knocked again but he held it back. He lifted his hand to still the sand, to free the ashes, and thought his heart would explode. "*Pench Ni'yalo.*" The sand fell and Macy's ashes rose into the dark sky. Her shard burned his palm. He raised his fist to his lips, kissed the burning shard and set it free where it soared upward to rejoin her ashes.

∘ ∘ ∘

Well this is weird. Macy's hand flew to her mouth, only there was no mouth there. But she could definitely see. She could see Legion laying on the ground dead—which meant she'd killed him right?

Then where was she?

The cart she'd been standing on suddenly flew to the side and revealed her body there on the sand, Legion's claws buried in her chest. Tolen leapt to her side.

Holy shifters! I'm dead!

∘ ∘ ∘

Tolen's shard started to bounce on his chest, its light blinding.

Bastian's words came back to him from the day he'd first put on the shard. *One day you'll understand more of its intents and purposes.* A Chosen's shard gave them their gifts, the ability to see the Dark, but Tolen's gifts were born in him. Clarity bloomed and he ripped the cord from his neck, unwound the shard, and opened his palm. It shot to the sky straight to where Macy's ashes continued to swirl, lit eerily by the castle's blue light and her shard within. His shard met hers, and a burst of warm red filled the center of the ashes, red that turned swiftly to brightest gold.

An echoing boom.

Darsapean's roar cut off.

Time resumed.

The fighters for Light jumped to their feet to meet the blades about to cut them down. Darsapean's red gaze moved to Macy's swirling ashes and the glowing golden shard within them. For a moment a burst of hope filled Tolen's chest, but Darsapean opened his mouth again.

"I'kashti Degani!" With those words the Shadows dove toward the fighters. The screams of the souls trapped within them dropped the fighters for Light back to their knees as the Wraiths filled them with despair, fear, doubt, and they were forced to relive every painful life experience a thousand times. Macy's death replayed over and over in Tolen's mind.

A flash of light, a spark like a firecracker, the roar of a raging inferno and Macy's ashes burst into flame, a gigantic ball of fire roiling and curling in the sky.

Darsapean's eyes widened. He moved his arm and the Shadows flew straight for the fire ball at the same moment a burst of white light left it, shooting down until it covered Blaze. The Last on his chest began to glow blinding gold, he held it high, thousands of shimmering strands of gold shot out, moved through the crowd, touched the shards of every Chosen, turning them blinding white. The screams of the dead quieted. More threads to every fighter for Light. A golden thread hit Tolen's chest and the horrible replay in his mind stopped.

Fight, Tolen, Macy's voice urged.

He dragged his body to its feet, his heart had joined the ashes that once were Macy. He raised his hands and began to call his gifts—fighting to fulfill his role as the Ninth. *"Mi'no ha, vin'akra, marsha, win'tashta, tin'ruhl, los'lon, radi'non. Vast aktra!"* A thousand more voices joined his, the Chosen and Hidden calling their gifts to fight. Life to fire, wind, animal, water, earth, nature and light, fight for us!

Gales swept through the throng, water rushed in wide streams carrying Darkened and other demons off to drown, palm trees left their spaces and rushed into battle, animals of every kind rushed in to sink their teeth into the creatures, bits of light began to burst through the dark haze over the island.

Darsapean raised his scepter, out of which a cloud of darkness grew protecting him from the light. He called to the Shadows again but Macy's fire ball had engaged them, it rolled and dove through their black depths, dragging them higher and higher into the sky.

The ball of flame began to take shape. A bright light against a dark sky. Larger than Legion it grew. In its center, beautiful red and gold wings appeared, tipped with dancing flames, and a long body began to form with a blood-red shard embedded in its chest.

A phoenix! Something moved behind Tolen's ribs. The beat of a healing heart.

"*LaUnahi!*" Bastian yelled across the battlefield. "The little bird has been reborn!"

The shard in in the phoenix's chest glowed brightest gold as the body continued to form—long legs and muscled arms swathed in red-gold armor, a head of flowing blonde hair, eyes of molten flame.

People cheered, "*LaUnahi,*" but Tolen shouted, "Macy!" Kuna blew through his veins, not driven by anger or hate, or a desire for revenge, but pure unequivocal joy. Macy's fiery gaze fell on him and her beautiful voice filled his mind. *Let's do this!*

Tolen raised his hands to release his gifts, powered by love and gratitude, as Macy dove through the Shadows again and again. The darkness within them began to fall as black rain to the blue-gray sand.

Darsapean screamed and aimed his scepter toward Macy. A bolt of black lightening shot out of the tip, missing her by inches. The heat peaked in Tolen's chest and he pushed his feet into the sand, calling to every gift, running as fast as he could toward the master of the Dark.

The dragon-horses reared as a flock of hawks swarmed the chariot, and a herd of gigantic boars attacked their feet. Roots ripped and tore at the chariot's metal. Wind and water slammed over and over again into Darsapean's face. The thrashing horses broke the reins and overturned the chariot as they bolted for the castle, being pecked and chased the entire way. Darsapean jumped free of the wreckage and Tolen shot fireball after fireball at his head.

But Darsapean conjured a shield of blue ice that swallowed Tolen's flame. He raised his scepter and shot a bolt of black lightening. Tolen twisted his fingers and his own shield made of fire and light appeared just in time to stop the bolt with a sizzle that shoved him backwards several feet in the sand.

The black rain continued to fall. Tar-like, heavy, coating the sand as Tolen blocked Darsapean's blows and shot flames back.

The sand began to tremble and shift at their feet. The droplets of black took form, became men, women, and children glowing palest yellow. They looked around them, up at the phoenix, and flew to join her.

The rain changed, became clean and cool. The sky lightened to palest dusk. Darsapean paused his attack to look up. Tolen risked a glance and nearly collapsed in awe.

Macy had healed the Shadows. Their black mist had become sunset pink, they moved and twisted around Macy's winged body like a ribbon, returned once again to their true state as Wind Whisperers. The pale-yellow souls, now freed from their prison inside the Shadows, flanked Macy's sides with flaming armor covering their bodies. The soul on Macy's right seemed vaguely familiar. She had Macy's build and her smile. *Macy's mother!* A burst of light and another soul appeared at Macy's left. Areen! Five more flashes all wearing flaming armor. Dane! Keelyn's twin Connell, Mahto, Quasar's son Spark, the last one also familiar but his features were no longer melted and he had all his limbs—Nahmala?

Macy motioned to the Whisperers and an unearthly and beautiful song issued from their pink mist. This time it was the creatures of the Dark who cowered and covered their ears.

The flaming army of destroying angels converged. They shot through the battle as streaks of light, passing swiftly through the island and Tolen knew they would continue through every part of the world, destroying all that was left of the darkness.

A bolt of black shot past Tolen, grazing his arm, returning his attention to his foe. His skin began to twitch and his arm fell motionless to his side.

CHAPTER 46

LAUNAHI

Macy's wings lifted her slowly up and down, warm, amazing. She'd never felt more alive as the Whisperers curled and twisted around her and she watched her angels bear down on the servants of the Dark.

Tolen! Her healed shard warmed, and the heat in her chest rolled lava hot down her arms, just as it had the first time the Dark nearly took Tolen from her, the moment when she'd realized she loved him. But this time she had total control.

She dove. "DON'T YOU DARE!" Her shout carried over the sounds of the battle and the metal of Tolen's shield. *Whoops.*

She knocked Tolen out of the way—gently she hoped, wrapped her burning hands around Darsapean's neck, and whirled back up into the sky. He screamed as her fingers burned into his flesh, his black blood sizzling away between her molten hot fingers.

He struggled against her hold but it could have been a feisty kitten in her hands for all the power he had against her. He twisted his scepter and managed to shoot bolt after bolt upward, but the light coming from her wings swallowed each burst of black. But she could feel the black draining some of her power, dimming her light just a fraction.

A burst of Tolen's light passed into her shard brightening her wings once more, at the same moment some of her light flowed back to him, healing his arm and energizing his gifts—a circle of shared light, a burst of combined power. The Ninth and the Gift as one. "Time to die scumbag!"

She increased the heat in her fingers and squeezed Darsapean's head until he dropped the scepter to claw at her hands. Tolen's light continued to push toward her, her hands turned brightest white, Darsapean's features began to melt, their combined light more than he could resist. She pushed the warmth, the light from her fingers, urging it deeper into Darsapean's body, and an animal-like scream of pain left his mouth. "You're finished." His red eyes widened, she squeezed tighter, and the Dark King exploded in a cloud of black vapor.

She tightened her wings to her body and dove headfirst for the ground, her shard warning her what would soon follow Darsapean's defeat. She unfurled a little too late and nearly knocked over Tolen and the row of people standing with him, as she landed not-so-gracefully, covering them with a rain of sand. "Sorry." She tried to whisper but her new voice had a lot more power than she remembered.

"That's my girl," her father said with pride while shaking sand from his hair.

Tolen reached for her, but they weren't going to get time for a reunion.

The ground shook, a fierce guttural wail filled the air, and night covered the island once more. Gyeesta had come.

○ ○ ○

The Dark laid thick and heavy across the sky, a layer of evil that blocked the sun. But the darkness held no power over Tolen. It couldn't touch his heart. Against the backdrop of night Macy's flaming wings brightened the sand and her angels' fire glowed as streaks of light and flame throughout the battlefield. A sight of hope.

"For victory in the coming tide." Max whispered and grabbed Macy's glowing hand.

"Where the light is, darkness cannot be," Bastian spoke from Tolen's left.

Darkness could not defeat pure light. Tolen took Macy's other hand, feeling the love between them as a tangible thing in the warmth that surged into his heart and rolled through his body.

Macy's voice entered his thoughts. *How is it possible that we're about to face the worst enemy yet, but I'm happy?*

He squeezed her fingers, resisting the urge to wrap her in his arms and kiss her full on despite the building wall of evil bearing down on them. *I think it's like you told Rune. Love is the whole point to life, to everything. Even if we die tonight we did it for love and beside those we love.*

By the light of her glow they welcomed their friends back to their sides. Rune and Keelyn, Brina and River, Sienn, Incrah, Quasar and Blaze. Macy's angel army continued to pass through the darkness, taking out Gyeesta's remaining minions one by one.

He felt Gyeesta's rage but with Macy by his side, he knew they could defeat it. What they had feared would be their greatest challenge, their hardest battle to win, was not this one. It would not be easy, not in the slightest, but the most difficult battle had already been won. To defeat *fear*. The Dark had used its greatest weapon against them and they had risen up to face it. They had done what they knew they must no matter the cost, no matter the sacrifice. They had already proven they were more than the darkness that fought for their souls. The light would *always* defeat the darkness if they would but trust in it.

He touched his chest, where his shard once rested. He understood now. Because he'd been born with his gifts he'd only needed to be a guardian of the shard until Macy became a form that could wield the whole. He looked around at his fellow fighters without a trace of fear or doubt.

A hundred portals opened and thousands of fighters from around the world streamed in behind them all gathered together for the Final Battle. Toke must have recruited more Movan friends. The Dominants and their Protectors appeared among them, their ancient power pulsing in the darkness, hands and swords aimed toward the sky.

A fierce grin lit Tolen's face. "Time to end the Dark on this planet once and for all." He mimicked Macy's words and focused on the Chosen, all of them standing in the darkness, witness to Gyeesta's last stand, and sent a call to their minds.

We were given a gift, each of us. A power of light to defeat the darkness. To defend the defenseless, to sacrifice our own will for the will of the Light.

His hands began to glow as bright as Macy's. Another light in the dark night.

And we have done so. We have all fought bravely and now we can end this, end it once and for all. We can destroy Gyeesta, remove its threat from our world. The glow moved from his hands to his entire body.

But it won't be our shards or our gifts that do it, but the power of light inside us. It will be who we are and who we've chosen to be. It will be what we do and have done, what we will do and choose to do from now through forever. He touched Rune, Keelyn, and Brina. Instantly they began to glow. They turned to other Chosen around them, touched their hands and the glow continued, Chosen to Chosen, until all among them glowed bright and strong. The Chosen then touched the light fighters around them, sharing their light, and one by one they all began to glow. Bright as day in the darkest night.

Tolen pushed the call out farther, to every life and mind he'd been set to watch over.

We have all been chosen, every Being on this planet, human and Hidden. We've all been given gifts of light to defeat the darkness inside us and outside. We've been chosen to fight for what we believe in, for what we know to be right. For love. And family. And hope for a brighter tomorrow. Choose now to send your light out against the darkness. Choose now to follow the Light forever more.

You have been Chosen. Will you accept your destiny?

A universal and resounding, "Yes!" sounded in both his mind and out loud. A thousand flames erupted in the darkness as everyone's bodies glowed brightest white, a blinding fire that quickly spread, faster and faster, a rolling flame of healing light, a flame Tolen could see in his mind's eye lighting the whole earth.

The light around them shone, but the Dark didn't fade. The Dreamer within him quivered and Tolen suddenly understood why he'd been given a single Dark gift.

A *ninth* gift.

The Ninth Chosen, wielder of the eight Light gifts, a descendant of a Protector, a Sphere, and somewhere in his past, a Watcher. A member of the *Eché-mah Ladon,* Light Messengers of the Hidden race. Born with power and a divine birthright to be a guardian of the *Gift* and a leader of armies.

Where the Light is Darkness cannot be. But in order to defeat darkness, they needed a gift that could understand it and connect to it. As Bastian once said, only darkness can understand darkness. Macy, being a Gift of *Light,* could not hold such a power. It could not be a part of her.

The Light did create in him the ultimate protection for their gift and for the world. A powerful warrior. A captain to lead armies. A guardian, a protector, a friend. And lastly, a person of the Hidden race, strong enough to wield a gift of darkness, but good enough not to succumb to it, so he would be able to use it at the right time and in the right way.

Whole in purpose and place.

The prophecy, his role as the Ninth, finally made perfect sense. A destiny he could now hardly wait to fulfill.

For what he knew would be the last time, Tolen let his life force connect to his Dreamer ability. The roll of heady power shot through him. The rage, the greed, the selfishness, and the illogical strength coursed through his body. His mind instantly connected to the Dark. Once he'd feared this gift. He didn't anymore. He knew he was stronger than it. Light always conquers dark. As this truth pushed through him and surged into Gyeesta's mind, he felt the barrier that protected the Dark from the Light begin to crack, open a hole in its armor.

Gyeesta, Tolen's arms trembled as he spoke as a Dreamer to the mind of the Dark. Macy sent him more of her light and a fierce smile lit his face. *You are finished.*

"Now!" He raised his and Macy's entwined hands.

The Dominants unleashed their gifts at the Dark wall in the sky, Tolen and the Chosen released theirs. Protectors and fighters for light gripped arms and shoulders, sharing their strength. Macy shot burst after burst of light from her hands, great streams of white flame.

The Dark began to crack. Gyeesta screamed a shockwave of pain and horror.

The Dreamer within Tolen twisted and flailed, its power inside him slowly dying. *Macy, now!*

Macy shot up into the sky, dousing them all again with sand, her flaming wings cutting a bright streak through the sky. She raised her hands, twisted them and a burst of white light, wide as her wingspan, shot toward the Dark. She flew so fast he worried she would collide with it, but her wings carried her through the hole she'd made. A million cracks spidered across the Dark, light spilling from behind them. The influence of the Dreamer within Tolen disappeared. An explosion rocked through the air, knocking them all onto their backs, and Tolen gazed up into a perfectly clear, pale blue sky.

CHAPTER 47

COMETH THE GIFT

Tolen wondered if his heart would burst with joy as Macy landed in the clean bright sand. The shard in her chest had calmed to a sparkling red-gold and as she tucked in her wings her army fell to one knee beside her. In one swift movement, the remaining fighters for Light all did the same, Hidden, Chosen, and human united together to bow in respect for the *Gift of Light* that had saved them all. He made to kneel but Max shook his head and gestured to the people who were also saluting him. Their gratitude hit his life force, making his throat tighten.

Not a single creature of darkness remained, dead or alive. The whole earth had been cleansed by the *light* fire of its inhabitants. LadonRyn gleamed even more beautiful than its former glory. Tolen could almost feel the earth singing beneath his feet. The fighters for Light who had died were carried up by the Whisperers, what Bastian called *Layla*, and delivered beyond Light's door to dwell in peace forever.

Macy lifted her mother up by the hand as Max came running out of the crowd. He grabbed Allison up in his arms and spun her around once before they disappeared behind Macy's wings as she embraced them both. The flames on them brightened with her joy.

And then a reunion unlike any other began. The redeemed dead were greeted by the thousands of Light fighters who knew and loved them, or who just wanted to show their gratitude. Bastian went to Nahmala and the two grasped shoulders, then he went to Macy to be embraced by her whole family. Keelyn and Connell touched their foreheads together, Rune's arms around them both. Brina and her parents fell to their knees, arms wrapped over each other's shoulders. Areen and Daedal stared into each other's eyes. Mahto and Sienn ran for each other and shared a fierce embrace. Quasar and Spark sat in the sand, tears of joy in their eyes as they spoke in quiet whispers. The love emanating from the gathered burst free in a visible series of white sparks in the sky. A celebration of the world's redemption from evil.

Tolen stood back from the crowd, close enough to Macy so he could feel the heat of her wings, but far enough back to not intrude on her reunion with her family. Soon three people left the crowd and came to his side. His parents and Dane.

"Nice work my friend. Aragorn would be proud." Dane winked, raised his short arms, and Tolen dropped to a knee to embrace his best friend.

"Thank you for everything Dane."

"It was an honor *Conchla Mindra*." Dane patted Tolen's back. "An honor."

As the fireworks ended a gentle voice issued from the sky. *It is time to come home.*

The voice of the Light.

Macy's army looked skyward then back at their loved ones.

Tolen shook Dane's arm in the Hidden way, hugged his mother, and Daedal gave her one last kiss. He saw Mahto and Sienn doing the same. Quasar and Spark spoke a final promise. Macy and her mom, Keelyn and Connell, Brina and her parents, all had one last embrace. Then with a final wave, the angels became pillars of light and shot into the sky.

Bastian grasped Tolen's and Macy's hands. "It's time for me to go as well."

Macy's wings twitched as she wrapped her arms around her Watcher. "I love you Bastian. Thank you."

"I love you too LaUnahi, my little bird." His blue eyes sparkled. "I couldn't be more proud." He disappeared in a flash of light and Macy's gaze fell on Tolen. Max moved to stand beside Daedal, giving these last moments to them.

Tolen swallowed, fighting back the pain, and raised his eyes to hers. "You have to go too, don't you?" The molten fire in her eyes had left, revealing the bright emerald of the girl he loved, the girl he was still Promised to.

"I think so." Her eyes filled and she looked up at the sky.

He too looked away, fighting to hold back the tears. This was a far better a way to say goodbye than when she'd dissolved to ash in his arms. At least this time he could hold her, kiss her, but he couldn't seem to get his feet to bridge the few steps between them. He couldn't bear to think it would be their last embrace, their last kiss.

Her hands were suddenly on his chin, pulling his eyes down to hers. "I love you."

He choked back a sob. "I love you."

Beyond time, she whispered in his mind. *I'll be waiting for you behind Light's Door.*

Tears ran freely down both their faces as he answered. *And I'll be dreaming of you every day until then.*

He pulled her to him and she wrapped them both in the shelter of her wings. Fire and light. Love and oneness. He would never be complete without her.

He gripped so tight his arms started to throb. *Goodbye Macy.*
Good—

"*McLacy Allicandra Burdow, Tolen Daedal Téloran,*" The Light's voice interrupted. "*We have something to say to you both. You each chose to sacrifice your own will for the will of the Light. You set aside your fears, your doubts, your hopes, and your dreams to save this world from darkness.*" Tolen's feet started to go numb and he had to remind himself to breathe. The Light continued, "*With every sacrifice comes a reward.*"

The entire island seemed to be holding its breath.

"*McLacy, upon your Transcendence you were asked if you accepted your destiny, to which you responded yes. But another question you were not asked. At Transcendence every Chosen is asked if they want to continue the rest of their life as a Chosen One, or if they would rather return to a human life.*

"*Your human body died when Legion sank his claws into your heart. The Dark robbed you of a future as a human. But your sacrifice entitled you to a gift, a gift to be reborn as your soul form. A Kunamin Phoenix of Light. You accepted this gift and once again you used it, not for yourself, but for others, to save this world from endless night.*

"We believed at your Transcendence that you would fulfill your purpose and it is for this reason we chose not to ask you if wanted to return to a human life at your Transcendence. You were not asked then so we could save the decision for you now as a final gift for your sacrifice. But for you the question will be slightly different. As you cannot return to your human body you will have two other choices. "You can leave through Light's Door and begin eternity with us in the highest realm of the Light…" Tolen's fingers went as numb as his toes.

"Or, you can stay here in the earth realm, an immortal being with the power to shape-shift into the phoenix, a Chosen One, set to guard and watch over the earth realm until it too passes over."

Tolen's knees wobbled. He knew what he wanted, and he believed he knew what Macy would want. But what if her desires had changed in this new form?

"Step forward Keeper."

Blaze left his place beside his Lafar and human friends and walked to stand beside Tolen.

"McLacy Allicandra, you have been Chosen. Will you accept your destiny to guard the races forevermore, or do you choose to return with us beyond Light's Door?"

Blaze held out the Last where it had begun to glow brightest gold.

"Reach out and touch the Last with the tip of your finger and your desire will be granted."

Macy touched her finger to the Last shard.

A golden sphere formed around Macy, lifted her into the sky, burst into red and gold flame and began to spin round and round like a small reddish sun, moving higher and higher in the sky. Just when Tolen feared she'd decided to leave, the sphere began to slow down and shrink smaller and smaller. The spinning stopped when it reached just above their heads, the flaming sphere had begun to morph into a shimmering red and gold dress that brushed a pair of tiny sandaled feet. The sparkling blood-red shard still rested in the skin between her collar bones—now a permanent part of the body. A flowing halo of golden hair fell over her shoulders and framed the most beautiful face Tolen had ever seen, would ever see. Her eyes opened, vivid green. Her feet touched the sand and Macy ran straight to Tolen's arms. He lifted her up, spun her around, planting kisses all over her face, her tears warm on his lips.

"*Tolen.*"

He stopped spinning them around, but held Macy close to his side, dizzy from the incomprehensible joy.

"*For your sacrifice you are also entitled a gift. What would you ask of us?*"

Tolen looked at Macy. "Everything I could ever want is right here."

A rumble resembling a chuckle shook the sand beneath their feet. "*How about immortality by her side?*"

Macy nodded vigorously and Tolen chuckled through his tears. "Yes, I'd like that."

∘ ∘ ∘

THE END

EPILOGUE

One year later.

MACY RAN HER hands over the folds of the soft white dress draped across the chair. A soft ocean breeze blew in through the open window stirring the pile of curls on her head. She took a deep breath, hoping the smell of the Gardenia's and Plumeria growing outside her hut would calm the butterflies in her stomach. Her insides trembled so much she was beginning to think they were having a party in there.

Keelyn pulled the dress off the chair, helped Macy step into it, and tied the sash. "I can't believe you guys actually waited a year." She adjusted the shoulder straps then sat Macy back in front of the mirror.

Macy tried not to look at the nervous girl staring back at her, a girl whose reflection she still had a hard time getting used to with the perfect skin, wise eyes, and blood-red shard that glowed between her collar bones. "That's how long we were supposed to wait, silly. You and Rune did."

Keelyn couldn't hold back a grin. "Yeah, but you and Tolen are immortal now, so why does it matter?"

Macy chuckled. "Dad really wanted us to wait until next year when I officially turn eighteen." The past year had taken forever to go by with no battles to fight as a distraction. Living on the beautiful—and romantic—island of LadonRyn, surrounded by people being Promised and Centered left and right. "Thank goodness he gave in. Immortal or not, another year and a half would have killed me."

Keelyn laughed. "Not to mention Tolen."

Macy's cheeks warmed and she started fidgeting with the sash at her waist.

"Are you nervous?" Keelyn picked up a handful of orange and yellow flowers and started weaving them into the pile of curls on Macy's head.

The stomach butterfly dance increased. "More excited I think. I feel like I've been waiting for this moment my whole life." She watched Keelyn's reflection in the mirror. "Were you nervous when you were Centered to Rune?"

Keelyn's face turned the color of a fresh tomato but her smile stretched ear to ear. "Terrified."

"Why?" Macy sincerely wondered. Keelyn and Rune had been Centered for a week and their happiness was almost nauseating. Keelyn still couldn't contain her glow whenever Rune walked into the room. They often teased them about bringing sunglasses with them to hand out when joining anyone's company.

Keelyn fingered a couple of flowers in Macy's hair, moved a curl this way and that. "It took so long for him to admit he loved me. I kept worrying it was just a dream." Her hands dropped to her sides, her eyes moving out the window where Rune was supposedly helping Tolen get ready and her skin started to brighten.

"I know how you feel." Macy followed her gaze outside and her shard pulsed with excitement. "Maybe it is all a dream, but that doesn't mean it isn't real."

○ ○ ○

Macy paced behind the screen hiding Tolen and the wedding guests from sight. She kept sneaking glances at herself in the long mirror beside her. She still hated dresses, but she couldn't deny how excited she was to see Tolen's face when she walked out. He'd picked the dress, a favorite from the Citadel, the only variation the colorful red and gold sash around her waist, an idea from Keelyn. Brina had picked the shoes—comfortable, flat, lace up sandals. Tolen was going to wear the white button-down shirt Macy loved, also from the Citadel, with an addition of Rune's as a surprise for her. She couldn't wait to see him either.

Centering ceremonies were generally small, with only the couple's closest family present. But Macy wanted a mixture of Hidden *and* human tradition. So, they'd invited everyone, literally, who lived on the island with them, and *all* their friends. Instead of a reception, there would be a send-off, Hidden-style. A celebratory feast with dancing and then Tolen would open a gate to the island in the Carribean where he was born. There they would spend their first week as husband and wife.

She could hear the soft chatter of their friends and loved ones on the other side of the screen and imagined their faces now, certain she would be able to focus only on Tolen once she was allowed to leave the screen. She pictured Jonas, Incrah, and all the Radia Warriors sitting on a row to themselves, still somewhat imposing. Tolen's friends: Quasar, Blaze, the Lafar, Hunsí, Sienn, Belch, Tashta, Kichaya, Sashan, and even the Doogar would be sprinkled among the guests. Rune, Keelyn, Toke, Brina and River—who only had six months left before their own Centering, would be sitting on the front row so Rune could make faces at them through the whole thing. Everyone they loved would be there in person. Those who had passed would be there in spirit, she could already feel them gathering.

The screen fluttered and her dad stepped up beside her. "They're ready for you." He kissed her cheek. "You look beautiful sweetheart."

"You look nice too dad." She squinted her eyes. "Old though."

"Ha, ha."

"Just kidding." He *did* look older than she remembered, but also happier, even though loneliness still touched his gaze now and then.

He tugged on his collar, he loved dressy clothes as much as she did, and held out his elbow. "Ready?"

Macy tucked her arm around his and bit back a grin. "Are you?"

He laughed, the lines beside his green eyes crinkling. "Come on kid, before I change my mind."

The music started, the *Layla* sung softly and Max pushed the screen aside.

She'd been right to think of their friends before this moment. As soon as she caught sight of Tolen waiting for her in the center of the

Circlet, a flame patterned tie at his throat, the same love and desire pouring from his life force that poured from hers, she had eyes for no one else.

Max walked her to the Circlet and put her hand in Tolen's then moved to sit next to Daedal at their right.

Toke raised a small black book and had them place their hands upon it.

The vows they'd written were simple. A mixture of Hidden and human tradition and some additions of their own. The words didn't matter so much to them as the promises they were sealing.

They exchanged rings matching the bracelet Tolen had made, but in the place of flowers on his ring, flames.

Toke joined their hands together again then placed his hands over theirs. "I pronounce you bonded for eternity. You may kiss your bride." He stepped back and Tolen took her face in his hands, his eyes studied her for the quickest second before his lips came down on hers.

o o o

They walked hand in hand along the sand, watching the sun touch the water as the gate closed behind them. The only sounds were the island wildlife and the rush of the waves. Tiny lights flickered just off shore in the distance from their private honeymoon cottage nestled snugly in the tall palms.

Tolen walked so close his hip kept brushing her side, sending sparks through her body. "So, I was wondering…"

"Yeah?" Macy absently put a hand over her stomach. The butterflies still partied.

He pulled her to a stop just off the front porch and started swinging their arms. "Before we go in, will you do something, real quick?"

She raised her eyebrows, for a moment distracted by his eyes. One burning earth, the other icy flame. "Do what?"

Tolen bit his lip and tipped his head with a grin that made her toes start to tingle. "LaUnahi?"

"Seriously?" The intensity of his gaze moved the tingle to her fingers.

Tolen took a quick breath. "Please?"

She tried for an exasperated "*Fine,*" but the emotions she could feel spilling off him moved the tingle to her chest where it heated the Kuna and caused the shard to sparkle red-gold across his face. "I'm still not very good at it. We should probably go back down to the beach so I don't destroy the porch."

Tolen's smile could have lit the forest on fire as he led her back down to the beach and bowed out of the way.

She winked at him and closed her eyes to focus for a half a second. The joyous warmth trickled swiftly through every cell, and her body lifted into the air and erupted in flame. As living fire she spun, the heat and flame licking across her body, changing it, removing the shroud she wore to cover her true self, the gold shard gleaming in her armored chest and landed as *LaUnahi*, Phoenix of Light, in front of her husband.

You are amazing. He touched her face and she felt that something again, a burn inside that had nothing to do with Kuna and everything to do with Tolen.

You say that a lot, she thought back, and laughed at the expression of awe on his face.

"Because it's true." He pecked her lips. "You can change back now."

"I dunno, this is kinda fun." She flapped her wings and doused him with sand.

He shook the sand from his hair. "Okay." But then he cheated, he pushed *that* kiss into her thoughts. The kiss at the rest stop that had awakened something inside them both they'd had to push away—the kind of kiss they had not allowed to be repeated once in the last year so they could keep their Promises. He pushed it into her mind with every bit of intensity he could remember, and that one little thought had her spinning back to normal human form without conscious thought to do so.

Tolen wrapped his arms around her waist. She could feel his heart racing in time with hers before he lifted her up into his arms and started back to their cottage. "Our forever starts today, McLacy Allicandra Téloran."

"I like the sound of that." Her shard sparkled joyfully in her chest as he carried her over the threshold, lowered his lips to hers, and kissed her in a way that said their fairytale had just begun.

About the Author

USA Today Bestselling author K.A. Parkinson was raised in a small suburb where she spent her summers hiding under her bed with a book, a flashlight, and a bag of cookies. She began writing to give teens she mentored clean and inspiring stories that not only entertain, but teach powerful messages. She is now the author of six novels. She continually seeks through her books and public speaking to encourage both youth and adults to pursue their goals and follow their dreams.

She currently resides in Utah with her two children and a bunch of chickens.

If you would like to learn more about K.A., her books, and/or public speaking engagements, you can sign up for the K.A. Parkinson Community Newsletter at www.kaparkinson.com.

A Chosen Life, book one in The Chosen Chronicles,
is the winner of the 2017 Rone Award for Novel Excellence.

ACKNOWLEDGEMENTS

I can't believe it's finished. The Chosen Chronicles has officially come to a close.

I've now written six books, and by the grace of God, am a USA Today Bestselling author. If I could go back and tell the shy little girl reading *The Lion, the Witch, and the Wardrobe* by flashlight under her bed that one day she would be able to say that, I'm almost positive she wouldn't believe me. Then again, we have a tendency to believe things about ourselves as children that we let go of as adults. Maybe she would be the one looking at me and saying, "I believed in me, why didn't you?"

Before I begin my list of thanks, I want to take a moment to dedicate this series to the dreamer who may be hesitating to go after his or her goals. I can promise you, you're going to hit walls. You're going to find out that it wasn't what you thought it would be. You're going to regret it at times. You're going to want to give up. *Don't.* You'll never know what you can do if you don't do it. You'll never know you can fly if you don't open your wings. *Go for it.*

My biggest thanks must go to God and my family—thank you for giving me purpose and allowing me to experience true joy.

Thank you to all the students and teachers who've welcomed me into your classrooms and writers clubs for continually reminding me what I love most about writing—the readers.

Thank you to my amazing writer's group: KayLynn, Becky, Rebekah, Brittany, Marla, and Amy. Ladies, without your feedback and encouragement I'd still be sitting on the floor with my head between my knees, holding an unfinished book. Spring and KayLynn thank you for the writers retreats that removed distraction so I could hit my deadline, sort of…(sorry Kirk).

To the team at The Scene Company: Kirk, thank you for believing in me and my books. Heather, thank you for being the first one to want to give them a try (and getting Kirk to agree with you), and for your superb skills. We did it guys!

Adelaide Thorne, thank you for the endorsement. To get such a glowing review from an author I admire is beyond amazing.

Deborah Bradseth of Tugboat Design is a genius. That's it in a nutshell. I couldn't ask for a more talented cover designer, and bookmark designer, and well, everything designer. Thank you for helping me build a beautiful brand.

To my Beta Readers, thank you for your time, feedback, shares, and reviews. It helps me more than I can say and is truly appreciated. High fives guys!

And lastly, to my readers who have followed Tolen and Macy's journey to the end. Thank you for the encouragement and messages telling me I had to finish this story no matter what. All of this is for you *and* because of you.

Appendix

Terms and Titles

Light: The source of all that is good.

The Guardians: Those who oversee and guard the realm of earth. They dwell within the Citadel of Light.

Light Realm: The dimension where the highest followers of Light reside. It is divided into two separate realms within the realm, Highest and Transitory. The Highest Realm is where the embodiment of Light itself resides, along with Seraphs, Ahway, and Mee'nah (see definition below), and those devoted followers of Light who have died on earth and passed through Light's Door to dwell with The Light forevermore. Transitory is the home of the Guardians, some deceased who are working toward progression to the Highest Realm, and a number of Spheres who protect the realm. The living can dwell here for brief periods to find healing and peace, but it is not a place of permanent residence.

Spheres: Have the ability to shield the power of another's life force from affecting the Balance, therefore hiding them from the Dark. They can sense the character of a person by the way they affect the Balance. They also have the ability to realign the cells within the body to heal almost any injury.

Balance: The force that binds humans and Hidden-kind. It shifts and sways with actions of good or evil. It is how the Light knows who to select as Chosen.

Life force: The matter, or intelligence, put into the body to give it life. Created with immense energy to power and control the physical body— the driving force. It will survive even after the physical body dies.

Dark: The source of all that is evil.

Shadow Realm: The dimension where Daemon, the Demon Master, resides. Home of the Shadow Prison where the Dark tortures its enemies. This is also where creatures of darkness—demons of the blackest nightmares—are released into the human world to torment mankind.

Misery: The phantom dimension used as a prison by the Light to hold the Dark's most powerful ally, Darsapean, leader of the armies of the Dark.

Darsapean: A ruthless and horrible creature responsible for the deaths of hundreds of thousands of Hidden kind and human kind during the dark days. He was imprisoned in Misery at the end of the Radia Revolution, a war that ravaged for nearly one hundred years. He is joined by thousands of other creatures so evil the release of which would mean an end to life as we know it on earth.

Hidden: The source of all the world's myths and legends. A people who came to the earth realm long ago. Humans can see Hidden kind if they are human in appearance and these Hidden can dwell with humans if they choose, but they must keep their gifts a secret. If they have Hidden defining features, (long ears, half-human/half animal, etc.), humans cannot see them because of the Pact.

Pact: An agreement made at the end of the Radia Revolution between Hidden and humans. A *shroud* was placed within the Balance that would shield humans from creatures of the Hidden world, including the creatures of the Dark. The following human generations would have no knowledge of the truth behind the myths.

Radia: The star that once gave life to the Hidden's original world.

Radia Shard: When Radia died, shattering into pieces, and the Hidden escaped to earth, she sent her shards to the Watchers to guard them and tame them. Once the Pact was formed, and Light did not want to leave the humans defenseless, the Watchers' shards divided in half, one half was sent to a human child the Light selected through the Balance. Through the shards each child could now see the Dark and was given one elemental gift to aid them in their duty. These became known as the Chosen.

Watchers: Watchers once had the ability to sense past, present, and future as it affects the Balance. Once the Pact was made, their Radia Shards split and their gifts became centralized to their Chosen wards whom they are to train and protect. Watchers also carry out orders given them by the Guardians, and oversee and educate the realm of Earth.

Chosen: Human children selected at six years old through the Balance to protect mankind from the monsters of the Dark.

The Ninth Chosen: A child of prophecy said to once again unite humans and Hidden in a Final Battle against the Dark for the fate of Earth. This child will have all the gifts of the Hidden within his life force.

Protectors: Those deemed to be completely loyal to the Light; warriors, overseers of all distribution of power among mankind.

Seraphs: Messengers and deliverers of the Light's justice and mercy.

Reckoners and Restorers: Those who are called by Seraphs or Protectors as either builders and guardians to countries, peoples, and individuals, or deliverers of justice.

The Lost Ones: Once Chosen, they remain good, but have become disenchanted toward the ways of the Light.

The Fallen: Watchers who have turned their talents to the Dark.

The Last Shard: In a final attempt to give hope to the human race after the Pact, the Last Radia Shard was sent to Eamun Woodlore, a Watcher, and with it he received the prophecy of the Ninth Chosen. This Last Shard holds more power and light within it than any other shard on the planet. Only the Keeper it chooses can wield its full power. If the Keeper dies, the Last chooses a Seeker as the only one who can find it and deliver it to the new Keeper.

Doogar: Dwarf-like creatures who live underground. Gifted in wood and metal work.

Lafar: Elves who are on the side of Light

Movan: Creatures with the ability to sense and manipulate bioelectricity. They are responsible for all of earth's technology.

Radia Warriors: Tall, powerful warriors whose sole duty is to protect Hidden kind from the monsters of the Dark.

The Order of the Nine Realms: The system of harmony that allocates the highest followers of Light. It is divided into three categories: *The First Realm of Three* contains those creatures so close to Light that they can only visit the earth for short periods of time: Seraphs, Ahway, and Mee'nah—creatures who fulfill duties only known to the Light. *The Second Realm of Three:* Guardians, Spheres, and Protectors. *The Third Realm of Three:* Watchers, Restorers and Reckoners, and Chosen.

GIFTS OF THE LIGHT/ CHOSEN ABILITIES:

All gifts are a connection allowed by the source, a union, it is not control.

Honitahai: Nature Speakers. They have the ability to grow plant life at will, as well as communicate with nature to seek aid.

Kunamin: Fire Wielders. They can create, maneuver, throw, and snuff fire with their hands.

Télora: Earth Movers. They can ask the dirt to do their bidding, forming walls, weapons, and raise or level mountains.

Arwah: Wind Shifters. They can use the power of wind to aid them in any way.

Dicernan: Unseens. These can disguise themselves within the Balance and become invisible.

Leenwa: Water Callers. These can call to water and maneuver it to meet their needs.

Animashta: Listeners. They understand animal's thoughts and communicate with them. They can project their own thoughts and desires into the animal's minds, as if they are sharing thoughts. It enables them to work together as a flawless team—so long as the animal is listening

and willing. The animal always has a choice—it is not forced the way
the DéHool are.

Lóklana: Radiance. These can call light in darkness from within the life
that stores it.

CHARACTER INDEX:

Followers of Light:

Macy Allicandra Burdow: Chosen (human)

o Parents: Max and Allison Burdow

Tolen (Parks) Téloran: The Ninth Chosen (Hidden-kind)

o Parents: Daedal Téloran (Protector) Formerly held captive in the
Shadow Prison.

Areen Téloran (Sphere)

Forrest Bastian: Watcher. His mortal life now complete, he has joined the
Guardians. He still remains Tolen's and Macy's Watcher.

Jonas: Sphere and shield to the Unastra training camp

Quasar: Lafar

Hunsí: Chief of the Hinkta Honitahai tribe

Mahto: Honitahai

Sienn: Half Lafar, half Honitahai

Sashan: Leader of the Watchers

Belahee'chay (Belch): Honitahai

Tashta: Village Mother—one who takes in the orphaned

Tahaka: Naiad, currently teaching in Hunsí's village

Kichaya: Commune and Hinkta Tribal Elder

Blaze: Lafar

Tokharian (Toke): Movan, leader of the Lost Ones

Rune: Chosen, Kunamin

Brina: Chosen, Dicernan

Keelyn: Chosen, Lóklana

Connell: Chosen, Animashta

Nahmala: Watcher

The Dominants: Those who are most powerful in the gifts and are responsible for training the Ninth. Can only be in the earth realm for brief periods of time for their own protection.

O'shae—Arwah

Took'rah—Animashta

Kyndras—Leenwa

Dunrath—Télora

Nephen—Lóklana

Jun'tar—Kunamin

Ras'met—Honitahai

Vindi—Dicernan

SERVANTS OF THE DARK:

Most servants of the Dark cannot come out in daylight.

Darsapean—Lord of the Dark, formerly imprisoned in Misery.

Daemon—Demon Master and High Captain of the Dark, resides in the Shadow Realm. His highest goal is to give control of this world over to the Dark by freeing his master, destroying all the Chosen, and annihilating or enslaving Hidden and human kind.

Legion—Darsapean's most prized creature. A dragon formed from the souls of a thousand demons.

Shadow Wraiths—Thick, black, oily mist-like creatures who hide in storm clouds. Once they find you they use your fears to paralyze you, then you either become part of them, or they take you to the Shadow Prison.

Raksasha—Blood Trackers. Main purpose is to find and kill the Chosen. They resemble burned human skeletons, but with black fangs, over-long arms ending in long, razor-sharp, poisonous fingernails, and yellow eyes.

Night Demons—Blood drinking demons who pull themselves up from the ground to feed on the death of the battlefield. Their decaying flesh is covered with maggots and bloody scabs. They are bald, have no eyes, or legs. Night Demons are one of the most grotesque creatures born of darkness.

Divinators (crows)—Their eyes have been replaced by Oracle, or seeing stones. Whatever they see, their masters see.

Reconn—Chameleon type creatures. Not very powerful they are used mostly as scouts.

Phantoms—These mist-like creatures are placed within the dead or dying to reanimate and control them. Often placed in dead trees as spies.

Ookra—Small, with large heads, batlike ears sprouting tufts of dark hair, and overlarge hands ending in claws. Slaves to the leaders of the Dark, they dwell in the Shadow Realm.

DéHool—Giant demonic wolves with red eyes. One of their greatest purposes is to hunt and destroy Watchers.

Daklafar—Once Lafar-Light Elves, but now serve the Dark. Once beautiful, they now are dark, filthy, and deadly.

Tormentors—Tall women with gray skin, lifeless black eyes, and floor length orange hair. Their screams cause unbearable pain. The dark uses them to extract information from their prisoners.

Kreydawn—Mindless creatures controlled by Suppressors.

Suppressors—Single-eyed creatures with no mouth. They control the Kreydawn.

Thrundoon—Huge men covered with black fur. Extremely strong. Masters of the DéHool.

Sundrák—Sentry's posted outside the cells of the Shadow Prison. Bald, translucent skin, no eyes, just an overlarge nose in the center of their face set above blood-red lips. They sense body heat.

Shrieg—Gigantic, venomous, bat-like creatures, often found with Raksasha or Daklafar.

Kinchomen—Lizard like creatures, more of a nuisance than dangerous.

Gungruin—Tall gray skinned creatures that can take on the appearance of anything they touch. Water is the only thing that can melt through their disguise.

Kezgani—Once Animashta until they followed the Dark. They now can shape-shift into an animal and withstand limited sunlight. Their animal side allows them to not affect the Balance in the same way most Dark creatures do, making them harder to detect.

Kludde—Soul Trackers. Once they identify their prey they memorize their soul print, enabling them to track them outside the Balance.

BASIC HIDDEN LANGUAGE DICTIONARY:

Ladonradi—The Light

Degani—The Dark

Dembasi—Watcher

Iyahika—To Watch

Liosladon—May the Light lead and protect you wherever you may go.

Ladon—Light. Light come forth is Radi.

LaUnahi—Little Bird. Bastian's nickname for Macy.

To'—The

Y'na—I am

Hai—Here

Mindra—Chosen

To' Conchla Mindra—*The Ninth Chosen*

Vast—Fight

Pench Ni'yàlo—*Be still*

Lon'adras—*Heal*

Dón—For

Y' takra—*Take me*

Da'bay—Friend

Ke'ay—*Help*

Mea—Me

Chan'ta—Please

Mah'ne—Journey

I'kashti—*Summon*

Minradak-con-siadras—This ground is sacred and protected. The words spoken to bless the earth and make it burial ground, protecting those buried from the Night Demons.

To'conchla serith hune doocrah—The Ninth shall lead them.

Den aktra—Aid us

Den mea Tin'ruhl—Aid me Earth

Chosen Terms:

Mi'no ha—Life to fire

Vin'akra—Life to wind

Ma'sha—Hear me animal

Win'tashta—Water hear my call

Tin'ruhl—Earth hear my call

Radi'non—Light come forth

Los'lon—Nature hear me

Vel'don—Veil me within

Words said to increase the body's natural abilities. Each word when said with intent has the power to speak to the life force and ask it to enhance that body part:

Konsh'la—The ears. Makes your hearing stronger.

Inreedo—The eyes. Makes your eyesight stronger.

Mig'nata—The body. Increases strength.

Lon'adras—heal, repair, return

Places of Interest:

Poverty Island, Lake Michigan: Eamun's Island

Whisper, West Virginia: Macy's hometown

LadonRyn: An invisible Hawaiian island, also known as Nowhere

Salmon Challis National Forest, Idaho: Where Onaepha—the safe haven—is set up

9 781951 411022